**"Must I spell this out?" Francesca asked. "The child in the vision had green eyes. You have two green-eyed children."**

"No." Kat shook her head. "It can't be. It's impossible."

"Frannie," Stephen said. "You were under a lot of pressure when you experienced your . . . vision. We'd just been through a major ordeal. You were stressed out. I'm sure that what you saw was clear, but—"

"It was more than clear, Stephen. It was truth. You and Kat were destined to conceive a child of light. Asteroth knew it as well as I did. He was determined to stop you then, so it makes sense that he'd return to finish what he'd begun."

"But we have daughters!" Kat protested.

Francesca's eyebrows rose. "Your point?"

"I guess . . . I guess I always thought the child of light would be a boy. I assumed we were safe because we had no sons."

"Why Katerina, my sexist little lawyer, what an assumption."

## Also by Jill Morrow

Angel Café

# The Open Channel

Jill Morrow

PARAVIEW POCKET BOOKS
New York London Toronto Sydney

An *Original* Publication of PARAVIEW POCKET BOOKS

For information address Pocket Books, 1230 Avenue of the Americas, New York, NY 10020

ISBN: 0-7434-8627-7

First Paraview Pocket Books paperback edition April 2005

10 9 8 7 6 5 4 3 2 1



Cover design by Dave Stevenson; cover image © PictureArts; cover image © SuperStock

Manufactured in the United States of America

For information regarding special discounts for bulk purchases, please contact Simon & Schuster Special Sales at 1-800-456-6798 or business@simonandschuster.com.

*For my parents,*
*Roz and Stan Morrow.*
*You will never be so far from me that I can't carry you in my heart.*

# The Open Channel

# Prologue

## BALTIMORE

MEDITATION NO LONGER CAME EASILY. AT FIRST, FRANCESCA was distracted by her sunburned skin and aching eyes. But two weeks after the ordeal with Asteroth, her skin no longer itched, and her eyes no longer required sunglasses. Why, then, was she still unable to immerse herself in spirit as completely as before?

Her soul felt pried open. She was aware of a darkness hovering at the edge of the light, as if a door had been left ajar. Even her physical surroundings seemed overly vivid and coarsely drawn.

Today she was determined. She sat cross-legged on her living room floor, eyes closed, breathing measured.

Finally, behind her closed eyelids, she caught the beautiful image of light she'd so missed. She nearly laughed with relief.

But something was different. She was not alone.

In the center of the pulsing sunburst sat a baby. It cooed, its green eyes smiling out at her. She instantly recognized the child.

But why?

"Yes, child," she said cautiously. "I remember who you are."

A cold wind swept through the living room, rustling the leaves of the ferns on the windowsill. Francesca's eyes flew open at the sound of a deep, mocking voice.

*"And so,"* it said, *"do I!"*

# FIFTEEN YEARS LATER . . .

# 1

## BALTIMORE—SEPTEMBER

Angel Café had grown during the past fifteen years, grown to the point where even its proprietor, Stephen Carmichael, had to concentrate long and hard to recall the offbeat little eatery it had once been. The restaurant had originally inhabited one small row home in Baltimore's Federal Hill. Ten years ago, however, Stephen had bought the film-processing store next door, acquired a liquor license, and guided his eclectic coffeehouse into the world of fine dining.

Elegance had come along with expansion. Angel memorabilia still highlighted the five small dining rooms, but now it nestled amid far more opulent trappings. Rich, velvet draperies framed leaded glass windowpanes. Antiques gleamed, inviting diners to forget the hubbub of the twenty-first century for an hour or two. As always, the delicate china place settings did not match each other. Now, however, they rested on thick ecru table linens, bathed in the soft glow of ivory tapers.

"Exquisite," the critics raved. "Charming," the customers gushed. "Exhausting," Stephen would have added, had anybody asked. The restaurant was open from eleven in the morning until ten at night six days a week, but the hours he spent there had never been tamed into anything resembling a schedule.

Today was no exception. It was only mid-morning, but he'd already put in five hours. Now he stood behind the polished wood counter in the lobby, checking the day's reservations. Down the hallway behind his right shoulder, he heard the clink of silver as one of his employees ran a last-minute inspection of the restaurant's main room. A giggle floated from the tiny dining area adjacent to the lobby. Stephen pulled a wry grin. Good. Let the staff laugh. They were in for one hell of a day. Not only was the restaurant booked solid, but Cybertec, Inc. had nabbed the upstairs room for an afternoon business meeting.

His grin melted into a grimace. He'd have to put in a personal appearance for that one, do a little schmoozing.

Stephen had once loved working a crowd. He had an easy, natural smile, clear green eyes, and a gift for glib repartee. But he was fifty years old now, with a wife and two school-aged daughters. The schmoozing part of his profession seemed a whole lot more intrusive than it once had. It was such trivial nonsense. He had to admit that most aspects of the business world were.

"I'm getting old," he said out loud, carefully returning the reservation book to its proper place. Age was the only way to explain why the thrill of success no longer intoxicated him. He leaned against the counter, pushing his wire-rimmed glasses up to the top of his head so that he could massage the bridge of his nose. Glasses. Something else he couldn't get used to. Oh, well. At least he still had a full head of hair. The black was peppered with gray, but he could always palm that off as distinguished.

An insistent knock on the front window broke his reverie. Stephen glanced up, forehead furrowed. People without reservations often showed up early, angling for a good position in the line that formed around mealtimes. He usually forced a pleasant smile to his face and pointed at his watch. Today his smile was genuine. The woman on the steps was in her early forties, with thick, dark hair pulled back into a chignon. She wore a deep red business suit, cut to show off the kind of curves that could still send him into the realm of fantasy.

Her name was Katerina Piretti, and she was his wife.

Stephen hurried across the room, threw the bolt, and swung open the door.

"Hey!" he said. He bent to kiss his wife, but Kat swept past, depositing her briefcase on the floor with a loud thud before turning to face him.

"Where were you?" she demanded, one hand planted firmly on her hip.

Stephen appraised the smoldering expression on her face. "Watch the front, Laura, okay?" he called into the main dining room. He lifted Kat's briefcase and started back to his office.

"Give me that." She followed him, drawn to her briefcase like a magnet to metal.

"Jeez, what's in this thing? Bricks? No way are we staying out there, Kat. I don't believe in making my employees take sides in family disputes."

She remained quiet as the office door closed behind them. Stephen set the briefcase by the wall and sank into an armchair.

"What's the problem?" he asked.

"Where were you this morning?"

"Here, of course."

"Since when?"

He hated telling her "since when." Lately she'd been harping on his hours, angry that he got so little sleep and spent so little time at home.

He gave a weary sigh. "Since five-thirty."

Kat flushed, momentarily speechless. Apparently the hour was even earlier than she'd anticipated.

"Inventory," he added lamely. "I told you about it when I clicked off the alarm this morning."

"Was I awake?"

Of course not. At that hour, even the dog hadn't been awake. Kat had been sleeping peacefully, a soft breeze from the window stirring a few strands of her long hair. Stephen had longed to slam the alarm clock against the wall and curl back beside her. They'd made love the night before, and he knew that she was still naked beneath the wreck of bedclothes they'd left behind. How tempting to crawl back into bed, wrap himself around her small, familiar body, and start this new day in the same fashion they'd ended the old one.

But businesses didn't make it without effort and sacrifice. Now, as he sat among his fine antiques, the sounds of his bustling restaurant outside the office door, he was annoyed that his wife couldn't understand this.

"Forgive me," he said, eyebrows lowered. "I was under the impression that you appreciated my financial contribution to our lifestyle."

Her wide brown eyes nearly bored a hole through his forehead. Her lips pursed. He'd made a tactical error. Kat was a partner with the law firm of Harper, Madigan and Horn. Money was hardly the issue. They both knew that he could afford to ease his schedule. The truth was that he just couldn't make himself do it.

He surrendered. "Okay. So I came in early. What's the big deal? Where on earth did you expect me to be this morning?"

Her mouth twitched. "In the carpool line at school."

"What?"

"You heard me."

Jesus Christ. He remembered now. Today was the first day of school. He and Kat had hashed out a schedule only the other night. She'd had a circuit court hearing scheduled for early this morning, so he'd agreed to drive Julia and Claire to the private prep school they attended.

"Shit." He clapped a hand to his forehead. "Shit."

"Add one for me while you're at it."

"Come here." Through his remorse, Stephen reached out a long arm, hooked it around his wife's waist, and drew her onto his lap. Her expression softened. "I'm sorry, Kat. What happened?"

She shrugged. "What *could* happen, Stephen? I dropped my file off at the office at seven o'clock this morning. Right now some junior associate is probably melting into a puddle on the city circuit court floor. Thank God it's only a routine motions hearing. I took the girls to school."

"Did you explain to them that I wanted to be there, but that the restaurant—"

"I told them you forgot."

"Kat!"

She stared him down. "You're a grown-up, Stephen.

It's time to take responsibility for the choices you make in your life."

She was right, of course. Furthermore, she lived what she preached. Kat worked hard, but Julia and Claire always came first. Kat covered all the bases. She ran the kids to doctors' appointments, kept contact with their teachers, and knew at any given moment their clothing sizes and preferences. Stephen didn't know how she did it. He was afraid to know, because then he'd be obliged to jump in and work some of that same magic.

Kat leaned her head against his chest. She looked tired. Despite her makeup, Stephen could see the delicate purple circles beneath her eyes. She was losing weight again. He moved his hand up from her waist. No doubt about it, he could count her ribs if he wanted to.

He'd have to hire another manager and start spending more time at home. It wasn't fair that Kat had a demanding job *and* total responsibility around the house.

Maybe he could fit interviews in next week.

Kat lifted her head and met his gaze. "You'll need to pick the girls up at four o'clock," she said.

"Four? That may not work out. I've got a corporate meeting here, and it may go on—"

"You also have an eight-year-old and a thirteen-year-old."

"But—"

"Not to mention a wife who has a deposition scheduled at two. A wife who just bailed you out, I might add. Do it, Stephen."

She pulled herself up from his lap. He opened his

mouth to protest, but words failed him. She was right, and that was all there was to it.

"I'll be there," he said.

"Promise?"

"Yes."

She started toward her briefcase, then stopped. "I forgot. Aunt Frannie's back."

Stephen brightened. Francesca Piretti had practically raised Kat. Beyond that, she'd rapidly become one of his most trusted friends. He wished she didn't travel so much. There were times he felt he could use her advice, or at least her ear. But it was almost as if Francesca's home could no longer contain her. She'd traveled voraciously these past fifteen years, all through Europe, the Middle East, and much of Asia. This time she'd gone to England. Had she really been away since March?

Stephen sighed. Francesca had left the convent thirty-five years ago. Sometimes he wondered if she meant to leave them as well.

"When do we see her?" he asked.

"She wanted to come by as soon as possible, so I invited her to dinner tonight. It's strange, Stephen. She sounded . . . well, urgent."

"I'll tell the girls she's coming. They'll be thrilled."

"She wants to see them, too, but she was very definite. She needs to speak to you and me alone."

"Alone?"

"Yes, you remember that. It means 'without kids.' "

A low murmur drifted down the hallway from the lobby. Angel Café was open and ready for business. Stephen instinctively rose from his chair.

"Wait," Kat said. "Say good-bye to me before you slip back into entrepreneur mode."

He laughed. "What?"

"I hate it when you close up on me. It's as if my voice can't penetrate. The only sounds that get through are work-related: silverware, china, cash registers . . ."

"Okay, okay." He gathered her into his arms and bent to kiss her lips. Her arms tightened around his neck.

She meant more to him than Angel Café ever could. He knew that. He knew it without a doubt as he held her close and felt the beating of her heart against his chest. He knew it as he opened the office door and escorted her down the hallway to the lobby.

"Mr. Carmichael!" His hostess appeared beside him, unusually flustered. "I think a reservation fell through the cracks."

He was already poring over the reservation book when Kat slipped out the front door.

# 2

THE DINING ROOM CANDLES ILLUMINATED FRANCESCA Piretti's smooth face and made her white shoulder-length hair glow in the dreamy half-light of the room. She was sixty-five years old, but to Julia Carmichael she appeared as timeless as a finely sculpted statue.

"You won't believe how much homework we get in third grade." Claire pushed aside her half-full dinner plate and dropped her head to the table. "Three pages of spelling, Aunt Frannie. Handwriting and math, too."

From across the table, Julia watched as Francesca kissed her sister's rosy cheek. Claire looked like a cherub run amuck. She was tiny, like their mother, with tousled dark curls that never stayed in place and an endless supply of energy. Sometimes Julia wished that she, too, were the small, cuddly type. She knew better. At thirteen, she was five foot five, with long, slender legs, a straight nose, and a full lower lip that made her appear to be pouting even when she wasn't. The only physical trait she shared with Claire was her eyes. Both Carmichael girls studied the world through wide eyes the color of clear green glass.

"Genetic trickery," Francesca often said with a crooked smile. She seemed to find something intriguing about the fact that Stephen's genes had beaten out Kat's.

Well, there would be nothing intriguing about any part of this evening, that was for sure. Julia listened to the clatter of dishes in the kitchen and knew that her father would soon be out with dessert. After that, ancient history awaited her, followed by an English essay and several pages of algebra.

She let out an inadvertent groan.

Francesca smiled. "Tired, Julia?"

"Yes."

"Julia is perennially tired," Kat said from her seat at the end of the antique table. She'd rushed home from her office only fifteen minutes before Francesca's arrival, shedding her business suit through the upstairs hallway and reappearing downstairs in a sweatshirt, jeans, and tennis shoes.

"The transformation." Stephen had grinned as she'd dashed into the kitchen to help him with dinner.

"Shut up," his wife had growled, still yanking at hairpins.

Now Francesca's piercing gaze cut through the soft candlelight to land on Kat. "Julia is not the only one who's perennially tired," she said. "You look like a wraith, Katerina."

"I'm quite all right, Aunt Frannie." Kat coolly flipped a lock of long hair back over her shoulder. "Life just gets a bit hectic now and then."

"You can't afford to let it get that way."

"You're so right. I'll quit work, Stephen can close the restaurant, and we'll pull the kids out of school. We don't really need a house or food or anything."

Francesca hesitated, then shook her head. "I should have come back months ago," she said.

Stephen entered from the kitchen, interrupting as if

on cue. "Coffee, Frannie? It's good and strong, and I brought some biscotti from the restaurant to go with it."

A corner of Francesca's mouth turned up. "Very well, Stephen. Change the subject if you must. We'll get back to it later."

Julia hid a smile with her hand. Okay, so maybe it was dumb, but she loved her family intensely. Sure, there were days when she wondered what punishment she'd pull if she stuffed a sock into Claire's constantly chattering mouth. And she wasn't entirely comfortable with the fact that her mother occasionally passed for her sister. And her father, though capable of elegant sophistication, cracked the lamest jokes she'd ever heard . . . in public. But she was lucky, and she knew it. At least her parents cared, and her family was tight.

This made it even harder to understand the sense of dissatisfaction that had recently settled over her.

Get over it, she told herself crossly, glaring at the biscotti in the middle of the table.

But the little finger of discontent poked her again. The beautiful dining room, furnished with a combination of her father's expensive taste and her mother's practical eye, suddenly struck her as unbearably bourgeois. Only mediocre lives could emerge from the refined chaos of this house. She could look forward to a prep school graduation and admission to a respected college, followed by years and years of drudgery in a dull career.

Just like her parents.

She eyed them. Her father stood behind her mother, his hands resting on her shoulders. He was talking to Francesca, something about Italian roast coffee beans.

Her mother sat curled in her chair, looking as if she might fall asleep at any moment. Well, no wonder, with such scintillating conversation. Julia rolled her eyes. An existence of domestic boredom was obviously acceptable to Stephen Carmichael and Kat Piretti. She couldn't believe that, between the two of them, they couldn't pull up one adventurous bone in their bodies. But if day-in, day-out predictability was enough for them, so be it. She, for one, expected far more out of life.

The pressure of a steel gaze forced her to meet Francesca's eyes. Her great-aunt was studying her. Julia squirmed, feeling as if her thoughts had become visible to everyone in the room.

"Aunt Frannie." Claire tugged at Francesca's sleeve.

"Wait, dear." Francesca covered Claire's hand with her own. "Julia, did you want to say something?"

Yes! Julia thought. "No," she said, shrugging as she reached for the biscotti.

A weird shiver raced through her body, making even her teeth and tongue itch. Before her eyes, as if someone had laid one picture atop another, the cluttered dining room table suddenly merged with a different, unfamiliar table. There, next to Claire's milk glass, stood an unexpected metal goblet filled with deep red wine. A wooden bowl of salt sat in the middle of the table, one edge of it blending into the family's crystal saltshaker. Hastily averting her eyes, Julia saw a huge, hazy peacock, feathers translucent in the candlelight. It rested on a platter, but looked as if it might instantly rise to its feet, thoroughly alive.

She yanked back her hand.

"Julia?" Francesca peered at her.

"Whoa!" Julia blinked, and the table returned to normal. "Illusion food!"

"What?" Her sister giggled.

"Did you say 'illusion food'?" Francesca asked.

Claire wrinkled her nose. "What's that?"

"It's your mother's cooking," Stephen said. "It looks edible, but it isn't."

Julia ignored the shove her mother gave her father. Her eyes remained locked with Francesca's.

"Julia," Francesca said, "do you know what illusion food is?"

Julia searched her memory. For a brief instant, she'd not only known what it was, she'd actually longed for it. All knowledge, however, had disappeared with the image of the table. She weakly shrugged and shook her head.

Francesca's gaze remained steady. "Illusion food was very popular in the Middle Ages. It was food crafted to look like something other than it was. Golden apples made of veal, pitchers of pastry—"

Julia licked her lips. "Dead peacocks dressed to look alive?"

"Yes."

Kat jerked to her feet, palms flat on the table. "Julia, you're studying this in school, right?"

"No." Julia looked up, startled. A spot of red had appeared in each of her mother's cheeks. Her eyes glittered as if she had a fever. "It's no big deal, Mom."

But apparently it *was* a big deal, because even her father had taken a step forward. "Have you read about it, then?"

Oh, this was just great. Now they thought she was unbalanced or something. Next they'd be squeezing in visits to a psychologist. They'd do whatever it took to make sure she stayed within the boundaries of their ordinary lives.

She jumped up, slamming the back of her chair into the buffet. "Yes, that's it. I read about it. Excuse me. I have homework to do."

Claire reluctantly rose. "Me, too. Can I do my homework in your room with you? Please?"

"If you promise not to talk."

Julia avoided Francesca's eyes and hurried from the room, Claire trailing behind like a tail on a kite.

"Illusion food," Claire was saying. "I'd make stuff that looked like vegetables but was really chocolate."

Julia nodded absently. She could tell already that her sister planned to chatter away. That was okay. It would give her time to think about all the unusual images that had crossed her thoughts with increased frequency these past weeks. She'd figure them out. She just needed a little time.

And privacy. There was no way her parents would ever understand this stuff.

Julia guided Claire into the bedroom, then firmly closed the door behind them.

"You still haven't told them anything about it, have you," Francesca said flatly as the bedroom door closed overhead.

"About what?" Kat studied the tablecloth.

"Spare me, Katerina."

"It never comes up."

"What do you mean, 'It never comes up?' Don't your children ask how you two met?"

Kat squarely met her gaze. "Of course they do. And we tell them the truth, that we met at Angel Café."

Francesca's arm dropped to the table with a thud. "That's a mighty edited version of the truth."

Stephen's eyebrows lowered. "Damn it, Frannie!"

"Shhh!" Kat pointed toward the ceiling.

He sank into a chair beside his wife. "What the hell are we supposed to tell them? That we were introduced by Demon Dating Service?"

"God brought you together."

"Absolutely. But the rest of the story is—"

"The rest of the story is the truth, Stephen. You can't deny it simply because it's unpleasant."

"Unpleasant?" His mouth twitched. "Try terrifying."

Kat put a limp hand to her forehead. Her right temple was beginning to throb. She was getting entirely too many migraines these days. This confrontation was not going to help in that department.

"Okay, Aunt Frannie. So we're weenies. We don't know how to tell our daughters that, once upon a time, their parents battled evil spirits. Maybe it won't be so hard to discuss when they're older. In the meantime, it's over. What's the point in dragging it all up again?"

Francesca leaned forward, eyes flashing. "It is not over, Katerina. *That's* the point."

Kat's stomach did a double flip. She must have looked as ill as she felt, because Stephen was instantly beside her, his arm wrapped tightly around her shoulders.

"Frannie." A pleading note crept into his voice. "Don't do this to us. What we went through fifteen years ago was enough weirdness to last a lifetime."

"What you went through was a reality that few ever see. How the two of you can close the door and walk away is unfathomable."

"We had to!" Kat said fiercely. "Life goes on. We got married. We had children. Not everyone can afford to check out of physical reality. Not all of us can just take off for Europe when the edges get rough at home. Some of us have to stay behind in the trenches and muddle through daily life as best we can!"

Francesca flinched. Bull's-eye.

Stephen stood with a sigh. Without a word, he tugged open the buffet cabinet and pulled out a bottle of Frangelico. It was one of Francesca's favorite cordials, but the grim lines around her mouth did not disappear as the nut-brown liquid splashed into a glass. She accepted the drink stoically, then waited while Stephen poured for Kat and himself.

"Okay, Frannie," he said wearily, passing his wife a glass. "What is it you're dying to tell us?"

"Don't patronize me, Stephen Carmichael. I knew you at your most obnoxious, and I loved you anyway."

Kat's nervous laughter broke the tension in the room. Stephen, too, managed a small grin as Francesca raised the liqueur to her lips. She took a small sip of Frangelico, closing her eyes to savor its sweet warmth.

"This conversation is long overdue," she said, setting down the glass. "You know it is."

Kat cleared her throat. "Aunt Frannie, listen to me. You raised me, and you did a good job of it. You taught me the same values that Stephen and I have passed on to Julia and Claire. They know right from wrong. We're raising them with love, teaching them to respect others. What's wrong with that?"

Her aunt's face softened. "I raised you with what I knew. We've learned so much more since then. Oh, Katerina, I don't deny the terror of it, but can't you see that until you teach your children that spiritual evil exists, you leave them defenseless?"

"Please." Kat's voice cracked. "Can't they stay innocent just a little longer?"

Francesca leaned across the table and lowered her voice. "Asteroth is back."

The name fell like acid rain. Kat heard Stephen's sharp intake of breath and felt a fine layer of sweat bead her forehead. For years that name had haunted her thoughts and disturbed her sleep. It had taken nearly superhuman effort to safely sequester it from the normal flow of her life. Now it intruded again, catapulting her back to that horrible day fifteen years ago when she had battled Asteroth, ancient demon of darkness.

She'd known even then, as the battlefield had erupted in flames around them, that Asteroth would somehow emerge unscathed. He was not physical. Flames could never stop him. That battle, played out in an ordinary house on a sunny summer day, had been merely representative of an unseen, smoldering undercurrent that Kat knew in her heart still thrived. If she hadn't wanted to explore it then, she certainly harbored no desire to revisit it now.

Asteroth. She'd actually stood before him. She'd felt his foul breath blow across her face. She'd nearly succumbed to the empty suction of darkness that awaited those who chose to accept his favors.

"He can't be back," she whispered.

"Where is he?" Stephen asked. Kat glanced at her husband's drawn face and thought for the first time that he'd begun to look old.

"I don't know," Francesca said. "I felt him while I was in England. That's why I returned."

"England?" Stephen poured himself another drink. "I don't understand."

Francesca sighed. "I don't understand, either. I was in Lincoln, you know, visiting an old friend. I spent a good deal of time in the cathedral. It's centuries old, mind you, and it's pure heaven to meditate there. The community of saints feels so strong! Still, it was in the cathedral that I felt the truth: Asteroth has once again pierced the veil of physical reality. He is incarnate."

"But not here in Baltimore." Kat groped for clarification.

"I don't feel him here, no. But something has changed, and I don't know what it is."

"You mean a general change, right?" Stephen asked hopefully.

"No, Stephen. I mean a specific change. One that centers within your household."

Kat turned the color of alabaster. "Excuse me," she said, leaving her seat.

Stephen rose to follow as she rushed from the room, but Francesca held him back with an iron grip.

"Attack this at its root, Stephen. Standing by her once she's sick isn't half as effective as strengthening her before she reaches this point. Any fool can see that she's utterly exhausted."

"Oh, yeah?" He glared at her. "Well, your cheery news certainly isn't helping matters."

They listened in silence as the toilet flushed. Then Kat returned, white but composed.

"Let's get this over with, Aunt Frannie," she said.

Francesca nodded. "Do you remember the vision I had shortly after the battle?"

"The baby?"

"Yes. The baby whose birth Asteroth tried to prevent. The child of light, he called it." She paused. "*Your* baby, Katerina."

Stephen swallowed. "So?"

"Must I spell this out? The child in the vision had green eyes. You have two green-eyed children."

"No." Kat shook her head. "It can't be. It's impossible."

"Frannie, you were under a lot of pressure when you experienced your . . . vision. We'd just been through a major ordeal. You were stressed out. I'm sure that what you saw was clear, but—"

"It was more than clear, Stephen. It was truth. You and Kat were destined to conceive a child of light. Asteroth knew it as well as I did. He was determined to stop you then, so it makes sense that he'd return to finish what he'd begun."

"But we have daughters!" Kat protested.

Francesca's eyebrows rose. "Your point?"

"I guess . . . I guess I always thought the child of light would be a boy. I assumed we were safe because we had no sons."

"Why, Katerina, my sexist little lawyer, what an assumption."

Stephen suddenly dropped his cordial glass, not even noticing the golden stain of Frangelico seeping through the damask tablecloth. "You think that Asteroth is at the bottom of whatever happened to Julia tonight."

"I think it's possible," Francesca said. "I can't see how it could be true, though. Fifteen years ago he had a human channel. He can only operate in physical reality if a human allows him access to a physical body.

That hasn't happened here. But I feel an urgency, as if something is brewing."

Kat propped her head in her hands. Once before she'd been called to spiritual battle, and in the face of all disbelief, she'd answered the call. Why did it have to happen again?

How could anyone ask this of her twice in one lifetime?

# 3

## LINCOLN, ENGLAND, 1360

ALYS'S RED HAIR CASCADED ABOUT HER CREAMY SHOULDERS, falling in the path of Gregory's lips as they traveled down her long, smooth neck.

"Ah," he said as she shivered. "Am I the cause of this?"

"Who else would be?" She lifted his chin to peer into his eyes. They were dark brown, like burnished walnut. If she looked closely, she could catch a glimpse of her own eyes, narrow and slightly tilted, reflected within their depths.

Gregory sank into the soft goose down of the pillows. Alys's bed was small, but her linens were always clean and fragrant. They smelled faintly of lavender, as did Alys herself. There were never any fleas in her bed. He smiled. There wouldn't be. They wouldn't dare.

Alys's finger traced his lower lip. "What is the meaning of this smile?"

"I remember when I first saw you. You were running to the manor hall from the meadow. You carried an armful of daisies. Sunshine clung to your hair."

She bent to kiss him, her curtain of hair filtering the light from his view. "Such an old story, Gregory. I was twelve years old."

"The image is etched on my heart. It could have been eighteen days ago instead of eighteen years."

"Eighteen years. Truly that long?"

"Yes."

Alys reached out to smooth the dark curls from his forehead. Her fingers played briefly over the shaved tonsure at the crown of his head, then returned to lift his chin again. "We have been fortunate for a very long time, my friend."

He caught her hand and brought it to his lips. "Not fortunate. Blessed."

With a sigh, Alys rose from the bed. Gregory tucked his palms beneath his head and gave himself over to the pleasure of watching her. Her high forehead and slanted gray eyes set off hair that erupted into the colors of a summer sunset. A wiser man would perhaps heed popular warning. Even the peasants knew that red hair bespoke a petty nature clouded by a lack of passion in love. Gregory knew better, though. Alys was too practical for pettiness. And as for passion . . . She was more than a match for any man, though he was the only man who would know that.

His eyes drank in her ivory body. How lovely she was! She was thirty now, but her breasts were still as small and high as a young girl's. Her narrow waist curved into generous, white hips, and her slightly rounded stomach . . .

He swallowed hard.

"Forgive me, Alys, but I cannot look upon you without wanting you."

"Then you must close your eyes, for it is nearly time for Vespers." Her chemise fluttered down about her body.

Gregory did close his eyes. For one gracious moment he was again a young priest come calling at the manor of Lord Richard de Clairmont. He watched once more as Alys, Sir Richard's fourth and youngest daughter, skipped out of the meadow and into his soul.

He was forty now. The lines around his mouth no longer faded when his smile did, and his knees often creaked when he rose from prayer. The untried notions of his youth had come and gone as surely as had the seasons. His perceptions of the world altered with each day he had breath in his body. He was sure of only one thing in this wheel of life: Alys de Clairmont was God's most precious gift to him.

Soft fingertips brushed his forehead.

"Will you stay?" Alys's husky voice caressed him. "There is wine in the cupboard, if you like, and half a loaf of bread."

He shook his head, then opened his eyes.

She stood fully clothed before him, Alys, prioress of Saint Etheldreda, and mother to the twenty-eight nuns cloistered there.

He pulled himself from her bed and reached for his clothes. "I must go. But I will return to celebrate Mass two days hence."

She coaxed a few errant strands of hair beneath her wimple. Her forehead, suddenly vulnerable, invited kisses. Gregory regretfully harnessed the urge.

His worsted robe itched as he knotted the cord at his waist. It called him back to business.

"Alys, my love, the bishop bids me ask whether your accounts are in order."

A corner of her mouth turned down. "Of course they are."

"He has not received word from you in so long that—"

"You may tell His Excellency that the priory's farms prosper and that the churches tithe steadily. Have you more trivial nonsense for me, Father Gregory?"

He had the grace to blush as he adjusted his cowl. "I am again to remind you that boarders are no longer allowed here. His Excellency deems such contact with the world damaging to the virtue of the gentle souls gathered in this nunnery."

"When His Excellency provides the rent money our boarders bring in, I shall consider his request."

"Madame, it was more than a request."

She tipped her face up to kiss him. "Yes, I know. And if you were not so fair a messenger, I would plant a solid kick on your rump and bid you pass it to the bishop with my regards. You have dutifully delivered your message. Think no more of it."

Gregory winced. Think no more of it. He wished the bishop would choose another envoy for missives to Saint Etheldreda. He disliked any situation in which he and Alys could not be allied. Ah, well. At least the accounts and daily manipulations of the priory allowed ample opportunity for visits. For this he was grateful.

Alys walked to the narrow window of her chamber and pushed aside the white gauze scrim that blocked it. Since the tribulation of the Black Death twelve years ago, most villagers shrouded their windows with heavy black cloth. The practice surely banished illness from the hearth. Unfortunately, it banished light as well, and Alys abhorred darkness. She found even the white scrim an unwelcome barrier to the outside and endured it simply because it kept out the incessant bugs of early summer.

"They are late," she said.

Gregory drew close behind her. "Who?"

"I sent dames Joan, Catherine, and Margaret to aid the novices in haymaking. They will all be late for Vespers."

"But of course they will." It was Corpus Christi week. The air carried the scent of summer to come, beguiling the mind and teasing the senses. Dame Margaret was much older than Alys and, left alone, would have been reliable. Dame Joan, however, was only seventeen, scarcely older than the two novices in the priory's charge. And Dame Catherine was a silly young woman who would squawk like a chicken through the streets of Lincoln if someone suggested it. Gregory had no doubt they'd been seduced by the day and would not return to the priory until the sun hung low in the western sky. Furthermore, he suspected that Alys had known this long before dispatching them.

"They can be no better than what they are," she often said.

He wondered briefly what the bishop would think. Then, as a soft breeze drifted into the chamber, he no longer cared.

They quietly studied the landscape together. Alys's chamber, tucked away in a turret of the chapter house, offered a view of rippling golden wheat and green grass. The land was flat, good for raising the sheep whose wool the nuns spun into yarn. The towers of Lincoln Cathedral, some fifteen miles away, dominated the landscape. Lincoln itself sat atop a hill, at the end of a road left behind by the Romans long ago.

Alys's hand stole into his. "You're thinking of the sea

again," she said, and he smiled. His homeland was south of the Wash, where marshy patches of land poked from the sea one moment, only to entirely disappear the next. Seldom did a day pass that he did not long for the water.

He squeezed her hand. "Fortunately, I have found respite here."

The sound of horses' hooves drew their gazes to the dirt road that led through the gates and into the courtyard of Saint Etheldreda's.

"You were mistaken," Gregory said. "The sisters are back in good time."

"No. Hear the wheels? This cart is far heavier than ours. We have visitors."

His heart thudded to his toes. "Alys, please. No more boarders. The bishop—"

"The bishop needn't know."

The travelers emerged from behind a wall of wheat. Alys squinted, then took a startled step backward. Her hand flew to her throat.

Gregory stared at her. "What is it?"

Her eyes remained fixed on the travelers as they passed the small guesthouse and trotted through the priory gate. "It is a plague I do not deserve," she said, and swept from the room.

Careful not to be seen in the prioress's window, Gregory peered into the courtyard.

She was right. There, mounted on a fine chestnut horse, wheezing as though he'd run instead of ridden, sat Lord Richard de Clairmont.

"Corpus bones," Gregory muttered, quickly following Alys through the door and down the stone steps.

* * *

Her father had more wealth than taste, so it did not surprise Alys to see Sir Richard so badly attired. She planted herself before him, arms crossed against her chest as he huffed and puffed his great bulk off his horse. His scarlet tunic nearly matched the color of his jowls. His soft leather girdle, failing in its quest for a waistline, sagged beneath a straining, sweat-stained belly. Alys took a determined step backward. The half moons of sweat rimming Sir Richard's underarms indicated that he and his horse would smell alarmingly alike.

Gregory's soft footsteps halted behind her. She raised her chin and waited for her father to break the silence.

She had not seen him in five summers, but boarders and tradesmen carried news that wafted through Saint Etheldreda's gates. She therefore knew that he'd married again last autumn.

Though her mother had died years ago, each of Sir Richard's subsequent marriages had pricked Alys's heart. His second wife, Eleanor of Kent, had been a rich widow twenty-six years his senior. She'd doddered through the manor house, painfully aware that she'd been married purely for her fortune. She'd been expected to die within a year or two after the wedding, and with the help of the Black Death, she'd obliged.

Even Alys had to admit that her father had genuinely liked his third wife. Alys herself might also have learned to like Matilda had the young woman ever mastered the art of chewing with her mouth closed, or had she occasionally washed. But Matilda had lasted only a year, dying in childbed and taking Sir Richard's newborn son with her.

Now there was Elizabeth, whose fourteen-year-old body held the promise of many sons.

Alys could not understand why her father sought additional heirs. Her own mother had given him two sons and four daughters, more than enough to secure his bloodlines. But Sir Richard was wealthy enough to follow any whim he chose.

And on this point Alys could agree: Elizabeth, with her whinnying giggle and vacant stare, could only be called a whim.

She watched as he finally turned to face her. Sand-colored hair flowed from beneath an indigo cap. The cap was festooned with peacock feathers, which dipped into his eyes. A golden mantle, trimmed with ermine, flapped awkwardly as the breeze slipped beneath its hem.

Sir Richard hesitated. Then he pulled the cap off his head and swept into a deep bow.

"Madame." His tone dripped with sweetness.

Alys knew at once that he wanted a favor.

"It has been too long since last we met." He took a tentative step forward. His fingers flexed as if promising a hug, yet not sure how to deliver one.

Alys did not hold out her arms. Her gaze traveled past her father to the ox-drawn cart behind his horse. Its cargo was covered with burlap, but she could see a bedpost poking through, along with a sack that trailed meal. She recognized faithful John tending the oxen. He and her old nurse were the only members of her father's household she actually missed. Years ago, the sight of either of them would have been enough to start a stream of tears down her cheeks. Now she simply turned away.

There, sitting atop the cart, was a girl Alys had never seen before. White-blond tendrils of hair escaped from a long, straggly braid. Pale blue eyes met the prioress's scrutiny.

Vacant as a doorpost. Was this, then, the imbecilic Elizabeth? How dare her father bring that girl here!

"What is it you want, sir?" Alys demanded in a hard voice.

Sir Richard's reaching arms dropped to his sides. He wiped the sweat from his florid face with an open palm.

"This is how it's to be, then," he said irritably. "Mind you, Alys. You may be prioress here, but you still owe me the respect due a father."

"I think not," Alys said. "I am dead to the world, remember? I am unable to inherit a speck of your land. I may not even lay claim to any remembrance of my mother. You kindly pointed this out when you left me here so many years ago."

His face grew redder still, until she feared he might suffer a fit at her feet.

"You are here through your own doing, madame. If you'd followed my bidding like a good daughter—"

"The man you'd have sold me to was repulsive."

"Not a sale, Alys, a marriage. And with his lands in my possession, I could have—"

"He was a sixty-year-old monster with a taste for the lascivious."

"An apt match, daughter! An apt match!"

Alys clenched her teeth. "That would never do for me, sir. I have not the nature of your new wife, Elizabeth!"

With a growl, her father lumbered toward her. Gregory intercepted, quickly grabbing the wrist of Sir Richard's raised hand. Sir Richard took a step backward, then spat on the ground near the priest's feet.

Gregory spoke quietly. "You must curb your tongue, sir. She is not your dairymaid."

"That she isn't, Father Gregory." Sir Richard nailed him with a narrow-eyed glare. "She's your mistress. Or do you actually suppose that no one in the village knows why the priest and the prioress get along so famously?"

The color drained from Gregory's face. Alys spoke before he could say more than her father needed to know. Sir Richard was incapable of any thought beyond the base. The shot was pure conjecture, and she preferred that it stay that way.

"Who is this?" she asked abruptly, pointing toward the girl atop the cart. "Could it be the new lady of the manor? You must forgive my ignorance, my lord, but there have been so many that I simply cannot keep them all straight."

Her father looked blank. "Lady of the manor?" He followed his daughter's gaze back to the cart, then started to chuckle. "Oh, no, no, no. The lady Elizabeth is unable to travel. She is with child, daughter. With God's blessing, I shall have a new son by Michaelmas."

With his chest puffed out like that and the crepey folds of his neck, he reminded Alys of a barnyard cock. She would have liked to pray for the birth of a daughter. It would serve him right, the boastful bastard. But she couldn't in good conscience entrust another daughter to his care. She knew too well how foul a fate that was. Better Sir Richard have a sturdy, pugnacious son, the kind who would grow up quickly and seize his father's property.

"Then who is this?" she asked again, examining the girl.

Sir Richard turned to wave the girl down. "Come."

The girl stared past him as if she hadn't heard.

He raised his voice. "Isobel, come here!"

"Is she deaf?" In spite of herself, Alys stepped closer to her father.

"Deaf? No, madame, she hears well enough. Isobel!"

Alys watched as Isobel slowly slid from her perch. She moved like a cat, her lithe, fluid motions belying the emptiness of her expression. She wasn't very tall, but the ripeness of her body marked her more woman than girl.

Sir Richard waited until she'd drawn near, then closed a hand around her upper arm to pull her to his side. "Isobel, this is your aunt Alys, prioress of Saint Etheldreda."

Aunt Alys? Alys's mind traveled through the years. Of course. This would be her brother Geoffrey's daughter, the one born shortly after she'd taken her vows.

What in creation's name was she doing here?

Her eyes darted suspiciously to the bed in the cart. "What's wrong with her?" she demanded.

Sir Richard's fingers fanned innocently across his chest. "Wrong, madame?"

"You clearly plan to leave her here. What's wrong with her?"

"She has professed a deepest desire to serve God."

Alys turned to Isobel. "Have you?"

The girl stared back silently. Alys gently touched her shoulder. Isobel remained passive.

"Sir," Alys started, "I doubt that this child professes anything, let alone a vocation. Can she talk?"

Sir Richard's shoulders sagged. "No."

"Is she dim-witted?"

"How do I know, if she won't talk?"

Alys turned and strode back to Gregory. "I won't keep her."

A strangled yelp escaped from Sir Richard. He hopped behind her, all pretense of dignity gone.

"You *must* keep her, Alys! You cannot turn her away! Tell her, Father Gregory! Make her do it!"

Alys stopped so suddenly that her father nearly plowed into her. She swung around, a rosebud of scarlet dotting each pale cheek. "And what do I tell the sisters here? That we have become a refuge for the feebleminded? That they must now make room for the addled in their midst?"

"Tell them that she is deeply devoted to God!"

Both turned as one to stare at Isobel. Her gaze rested somewhere over Gregory's shoulder, focused on nothing in particular. It did not inspire thoughts of devotion.

Sir Richard grabbed his daughter's hand. "Alys, please. I have brought all you require. Here is her bed. More furniture will arrive in a day or two. She has a new habit to wear, and I have included provisions for the priory."

The prioress pointedly removed her hand from his grip. He squirmed. A new stream of sweat trickled down the side of his face. Then he squared his shoulders and set his jaw, once again a man in full control of the situation.

It was too late. Alys had noted his desperation.

"I remember my brother Geoffrey's ways," she said. "He is so very much like you, sir, able to catch the whiff of profit wherever it might lurk. Why have you not traded this girl in marriage? Surely you can gain something valuable in return."

Sir Richard averted his eyes. "None will have her."

"Why not? She's comely enough, and I would think a mute wife might be well prized in the circles you frequent. Well?"

Her father mumbled at his feet. "Things happen when she's about."

" 'Things'?" Gregory asked.

Sir Richard glared at him, but there was no way to avoid an explanation. "There are those who claim she possesses an evil eye."

"Is she a witch?" The priest's eyebrows rose.

"Oh, no. Nothing like that. Just . . . things happen."

Alys's head swiveled toward Isobel. The girl looked dirty, young, and daft, but little else appeared amiss.

Sir Richard jumped to fill the silence. "*I* think it's nothing, mind you. Pure coincidence, every incident."

"Suppose you relate the incidents and let us decide." Gregory said mildly.

Sir Richard shifted his great weight from one foot to the other. "Little things. Nonsense things. Cream curdles in a manor house where she is a guest. Crockery breaks as she passes through a scullery. Horses go lame."

Alys nearly rolled her eyes. Was this what was meant by the evil eye? Why, this was no more than mere superstition. This was simply the way people chose to explain away a mute. It was no better than the belief that hunger pangs were caused by a worm in the stomach.

Yet here stood her father, looking nervous and

frightened despite his labored attempt at nonchalance.

"You know how tongues wag . . ." His voice trailed into the air.

Alys knew all too well.

She glanced again at Isobel. The girl was examining her dirty fingernails, mouth pursed in concentration as if this were a most difficult task.

It was not the priory's responsibility to take in the shire's unwanted ones. Isobel would survive if sent home. Surely she would be clothed, fed, and given a place to sleep. Sir Richard was vain and stupid, but he wasn't barbarous.

Was he?

Alys hazarded a glance at her father. A touch of arsenic in the food had a way of making difficult situations disappear.

She shook the thought away. Isobel would be left alone, sure to inherit her fortune eventually. Then she'd be too attractive a prize to ignore. A husband could overlook the peculiarities of a rich wife.

Hadn't that been the fate of Sir Richard's second wife, Eleanor? Traded like a pig simply because she possessed a fortune and then treated with enough disdain to let her know it.

"I will give you whatever you want," her father said. "What does Saint Etheldreda need, daughter? I will send salted herring by the barrel. Chickens. Cheese."

Saint Etheldreda always needed something. Alys recognized the expression that flashed across Gregory's face. It clearly said, "No more boarders!"

"Ale?" her father added hopefully. "Do you need ale?"

Resigned, Alys once again searched out Isobel's eyes.

To her surprise, the girl smiled, a broad, white smile that made her actually seem beautiful.

And, in that smile, Alys caught a glimpse of her own dear mother.

At least the girl's teeth were good. And her body seemed healthy, despite her addled mind. Perhaps she could be taught to spin, or even to embroider altar cloths.

"Money," Sir Richard said. "On Isobel's feast day, daughter, I will make a substantial offering."

She could fight all but her own emotions. With a sigh, the prioress surrendered. "Oh, very well. She may stay."

Sir Richard's obvious relief made her long to reconsider.

"Good!" he said heartily. "Good! I will rest the night in your guesthouse, then depart in the morning. Is supper—"

The priory bell began to toll, a timely call to Vespers. Alys brushed away his tiresome voice with a wave of her hand. She turned on her heel toward the chapel, leaving her father, his entourage, Isobel, and even Gregory behind to do as they chose.

She could pray, eat her supper, even retire for the evening. She could travel the wide earth, and the problem would still be waiting whenever she chose to face it.

She'd already learned this truth: beauty and pleasure faded all too quickly, while trouble stayed forever.

# 4

ALYS LOOKED UP FROM HER ACCOUNT LEDGER AS LIGHT FOOT-steps scurried up the stairs. This would be Dame Margaret, whose tiny feet had made the journey to the prioress's chamber several times a day for the past week.

Sure enough, here came the telltale knock: three scratches that sounded as if Margaret possessed claws instead of fingers.

Alys set down her quill with a sigh. She already knew why Margaret had come.

*"Benedicite,"* she called.

Dame Margaret opened the door with a surprisingly hard shove and fairly spilled into the chamber. "It's her again, madame. I will not have it!"

*"Benedicite,"* Alys repeated evenly.

"Of course. *Benedicite.*" Margaret's watery blue eyes blinked rapidly. She had seen fifty summers now, forty-two of them at Saint Etheldreda's. She'd ushered many of her current sisters through the novitiate, so Alys had thought nothing of adding one more charge to her care.

Dame Margaret lifted her chin. "I know she is your kinswoman, madame, but—"

"What is Isobel's failing now?" It was best to avoid matters of kin. Both women knew that bloodlines had contributed to Alys's appointment as prioress, a position Margaret had long coveted and perhaps even deserved. Unfortunately, though her baker father had lived an honest, holy life, he'd acquired few tangible assets and no political connections. All the prayers in England could not have elevated Margaret to prioress.

Margaret's nose twitched. "Her failing, madame? You must see it with your own eyes. It defies description."

"Please. I am extremely busy. Father Gregory comes tomorrow to review our accounts."

Margaret lowered her brow. "You'd best hope he doesn't review our embroidery."

"Embroidery?"

"The novices have been stitching all morning. We could not tend the gardens in the rain, so we have spent our time practicing embroidery so that we may properly stitch altar cloths."

"And Isobel is dismal with the needle? Surely you can teach her how to sew."

"She embroiders exceptionally well." Margaret's tone darkened.

The prioress paused. "Is she insolent, then?"

"She does what she must."

Oh, but Alys was tired of riddles! Could no one plainly speak their mind? She was suddenly irritated by everyone she knew: her father, with his flimsy subterfuges, Gregory, with his gentle entreaties, each and every nun in her care who did the utmost best to hide behavior her prioress would not have minded anyway.

"Then what is it?" she asked, unable to mask her rising annoyance. "Will this visit be like yesterday's visit, and like the one before that? Will you tell me once again that Isobel is simple, that you cannot fathom where her mind might be? We already know this. Have you anything new to add?"

Margaret shut the chamber door and stepped quickly toward the prioress. Alys nearly recoiled when the other woman grabbed her hand, so unaccustomed was she to the touch.

"Madame, she is more than simple. There is something amiss within her that I cannot explain."

"What happened?"

Margaret licked dry lips. "I was observing the embroidery, as I always do. All young women need guidance with the needle, for boredom makes their stitches ungainly. Dame Joan still stitches with great galloping loops and hoops. No one possesses my own skill with—"

"And Isobel?"

"Isobel's work was the last I examined. She sits to herself, you know, quite alone. She seems to find the company of others burdensome."

Alys was not surprised. There were days when she herself could not abide the thought of one more chattering tidbit falling from the nuns' lips.

Margaret continued. "My heart fairly sang when I saw Isobel's cloth. The stitches! Tiny and true, as if an angel had guided her fingers. And the colors! She has a knack, madame, for placing two strands of thread so closely together that the eye is utterly beguiled. The shade seems a rich purple, but upon closer study, it is indigo and crimson stitched tightly side by side."

A vague relief filled Alys's mind. Good. Isobel had a talent, then, a gift that could occupy her days and ward off the dangers of idleness.

But Dame Margaret looked far from pleased. She

clasped her birdlike hands tightly against her breast and furrowed her brow.

"I thought to praise her," she said. "I knew such praise could lead to vanity, but the poor child has so little to commend. But when I lifted the cloth from her lap and viewed the piece as a whole, words lodged in my throat. That cloth had been empty but two hours before. Now it was covered with exquisite stitchery. Expert stitchery." She swallowed. "Upon my soul, no one can stitch with such speed. It put me in mind of witchcraft, madame."

Alys turned away in disgust. "Oh, Margaret. Not you, too."

"And the image itself!" Margaret plowed forward, clearly determined to finish what she had begun. "It is not natural. No maiden would think of such . . . such a thing."

Unlike Margaret, Alys harbored clear memory of her own young womanhood. She knew without a doubt how vivid a girl's imagination could be, how whispered tales from stable boys could muffle a mother's soft warnings. It had taken Gregory's tender patience to untangle the profane from the profound in her own heart, and not every woman was blessed with a lover such as he.

"We will rip the stitches out as quickly as possible," Margaret said.

"Yes, of course. If the design is ribald, it will be reworked. But, Margaret, I will hear no more talk of witchcraft. Isobel's swiftness with the needle is a blessing, not a curse."

Margaret stepped forward, mouth opened to speak. Then she set her lips into a thin line and unclasped her hands.

"Naturally, I chastised her," she said.

"Naturally."

"She plucked the offending cloth from my hands and dashed away. She is mooning near the priory gate. You can see her if you gaze through your window."

Alys instinctively did just that. Sure enough, Isobel stood staring through the bars of the gate, the cloth crunched in both hands. She looked like a statue set in the wrong place.

"If *I* were prioress, I would go to her at once," Margaret said beneath her breath. "We are between cloudbursts, and she knows not enough to come in from the rain."

"That will be quite enough." Alys did not turn around.

*"Benedicite."* Dame Margaret shut the door behind her and darted down the steps.

The rain had already begun when Alys reached the priory gate. Isobel remained poised at the entrance, gazing out the gateway at the rutted mud road on the other side.

If she would move even her smallest finger! Alys hated to admit that Margaret might be correct about the girl's empty head.

She reached out a hand and nudged her niece's shoulder. "Isobel."

As usual, it was like talking to the priory well. Perhaps water tumbled and bubbled beneath, but the outer brick certainly gave no sign of it. Isobel remained unmoved, staring straight ahead.

Alys crossly glanced down at her own silk-laced kirtle. She had paid a pretty pence for it, and now fat water droplets splattered its length, settling right through to her fine chainsil shift.

Perhaps Isobel was too dull-witted to seek shelter, but Alys was not. She grasped the girl's hand and firmly tugged her toward the cloister.

"Now, then," she said as they ducked beneath the roof. "What is this all about?"

Why did she continue to question this half-wit? Isobel would never answer. Her listlessness went beyond the lack of a voice. She possessed only two or three facial expressions, each a slightly different shade of dull. The smile Alys had seen that first day was but a memory now, a silly befuddlement meant to trick her heart into thinking this girl showed promise.

The rain continued to fall in a monotonous drizzle. Alys glared at it and marveled at the Creator's ability to re-create her own mood for the entire world to share.

"Very well," she said, for it did no good for both of them to remain silent. "Let me see it."

She held out a hand. Isobel's vacant gaze traveled from the open white palm to the crumpled cloth.

"Yes." Alys nodded. "That."

Well, the girl was at least obedient. Her hand moved in a smooth arc to deposit the cloth into the prioress's waiting grasp. Then she returned her eyes to the road.

Alys turned her back to her niece as she fingered the cloth. Damask. She'd have to speak with Dame Margaret. If the novices were going to practice their needlework, she preferred that they ruin cloth not quite so dear.

Without further hesitation, she flipped back a corner of the cloth.

The colors struck her with the heady richness of an autumn day. How had Isobel done this? Everywhere Alys looked, her eyes feasted on a riot of color. Each strand of thread begged to be noticed, both individually and as part of a pattern. Dame Margaret had rightfully noted the crimson and blue, but she had not prepared the prioress for the careful symmetry with which they had been stitched. The purple they made was worthy of royalty.

Alys drank in the other colors. Red and yellow thread created a gold almost sinful in its richness, while blue and yellow looped together reminded her of a green meadow.

What a gift this child had been given! What Isobel could not express in words, she'd been allowed to say with her fingers. Alys turned in openmouthed wonder to praise her niece. Isobel had once again drifted toward the gate and now stood in the drizzle, staring through the bars.

Alys clamped her mouth shut. How could such glory flow through the fingers of one so addled?

She narrowed her eyes and opened the cloth. This time she looked past the surprise of color and workmanship to see the pattern they'd created.

"Dear God!" Her cheeks burned red.

Dame Margaret had warned that the picture was vile. Alys had expected a vision of foolish lewdness. Human nature was prone to such trifling, and young people always thought themselves wise in matters they knew nothing about.

But the picture reflected nothing sensual, distorted or otherwise.

A man smiled out from the cloth. Golden hair fell past his shoulders. Eyes the color of lapis lazuli met Alys's gaze. Isobel had stitched a wide, insolent smile.

This was an imperious face, although Alys quickly decided that this thought was born of her own imagination. This was but embroidery, after all. How ridiculous to assume that Isobel's flying fingers could give a face such smugness!

An aureole of bright red and orange framed the man's head. A circlet of purple banded his forehead. Isobel had not had time to stitch a body, but the suggestion of a hand had been completed. It was clenched into a tight fist.

And caught within the strangling grip of that fist was the cross of Christ, shattered and dripping blood.

Not debauchery. Sacrilege.

Alys hastily crossed herself, then crumpled the cloth.

"Isobel!" she called sharply.

With a good deal of difficulty, the girl dragged her gaze away from the road.

Heedless of the rain, Alys strode across the courtyard to stand before her niece.

"What is this?" she asked in a fierce whisper, ball of cloth beneath Isobel's nose.

Isobel stared at the cloth, then at the prioress.

"Where did this picture come from?" Alys shook the cloth. "Did someone teach you this, or does it live within your heart and head?"

Forehead creased, Isobel reached out to take the cloth from her aunt's grasp. Alys watched her slowly unfurl it, then study it as if trying to remember.

The girl's hand softly stroked the image's hair. Then, with surprising gentleness, her finger traced the stitched lips. Her own lips curved into a nearly beatific smile.

"What *is* this?" Alys repeated, voice trailing in the wind.

Isobel grabbed her aunt's finger and tugged it toward the cloth. Alys stared at the picture, then at her niece's glowing face.

"No!" She yanked her hand away. "I will not touch it!"

The girl drew back, mouth a perfect O of surprise.

Alys wrenched the cloth from her hands. "You will tear this out, do you hear me? You will rip out every stitch, every thread! Then come to me that we may ask God's forgiveness."

Isobel's mouth pursed. Alys could nearly see the explanation bubbling within her head. There was no contrition in her niece's face, no recognition of wrong. Instead, Isobel's mouth opened as if to defend her work.

Alys quickly covered her niece's mouth with a long, cool finger. "Silence," she whispered. "If you cannot examine your heart, you must at least examine your soul!"

But what folly was this? The girl was mute. She had no voice with which to explain.

With a sudden jerk, Isobel turned back toward the priory gate.

"Come." Alys grabbed the girl's hand, but Isobel pulled it back and, face pressed between the rods of the iron gate, planted herself firmly in her spot.

Then Alys heard it: the unmistakable sound of horses' hooves galloping over the road. Even as the women listened, the gallop slowed first to a canter and then to a trot.

Isobel squirmed with excitement. Alys arched an eyebrow as the rhythm of the hooves slowed again.

Suddenly she knew. The horses were coming to the priory.

There was music now, the strumming of lutes accompanied by the steady beat of a drum. A high, clear tenor carried a melody above the instruments. The tone was pure, but the song seemed discordant, unlike any tune Alys had ever heard before.

"Mummers, Isobel," Alys said, then wondered why she'd felt the need. Her niece was perhaps daft, but she'd grown up in a manor house. She knew what this was. Corpus Christi week had drawn to a close, and the musicians and magicians who'd entertained throughout the shire were simply traveling on.

The singing stopped as the party came into view. Streamers flowed from the two carts in the procession. Strings of tiny bells draped around the horses' necks chimed gaily with each fall of a hoof. The second cart was piled high with the rickety wooden flats and props used in performances. Six men sat still as stones in the lead cart, so still that Alys could not tell which one of them had sung before.

"Here," a deep voice said as the cart drew to a stop before the gate.

Alys thought the men must be kin to each other. The youngest was perhaps fourteen, a wan youth with no front teeth and a bony red nose. The eldest could have been many times a grandfather, so weary of the world did he look. All shared the same somber expression and deep, dark eyes.

A man emerged from the center of the cart and stepped lightly to the ground.

"Here," he said, and Alys recognized his voice as the one that had spoken before. "I will stay here." He planted himself before the priory gate, arms folded across his chest.

He was younger than Alys, with long yellow hair and strong, slender limbs. His gaze, so fathomless, rested upon her with the stickiness of honey.

"Madame Prioress." He neither bowed nor kneeled before her. "May a poor traveler find respite in your guesthouse?"

How had he known her as prioress? Against her will, Alys averted her eyes. He was comely enough, but even though a sturdy iron gate separated them, the chill in his visage made rivers of ice trickle through her own veins.

Such unease did not suit her. She calmed her troubled spirit and forced herself to meet his stare.

"Do you speak for each man present?" she asked in a loud, clear voice.

A muscle twitched in his jaw. "Nay, madame. I speak only for myself. My colleagues travel on." As if to prove his words, the man turned toward the caravan. Two satchels flew from the crowded cart and landed at his feet.

"All my possessions in this world, Madame Prioress. But do not fret. I am well prepared to pay for the privilege of staying here."

Alys's eyes followed his hands to the leather purse tied securely to the sash at his waist. She noted that this was neither beggar nor laborer. No dirt lodged beneath his fingertips. His skin, smooth and white, reflected neither the tan hue nor the leathery texture brought about by hours of toiling in the sun.

She could not recall meeting him before. Why did she know his face?

He pointed an elegant finger at the cart. Without a word from anyone, the horses began to trot away.

"Wait!" Flushed, Alys pulled herself from her pondering. "We have reached no agreement. I have not consented to your stay."

The man reached for his purse. She saw a flash of gold as he emptied the contents into his hand.

He reached through the bars of the gate, turned the prioress's hands upward, and carefully delivered the gold pieces.

"Is it enough?" he asked.

Enough? Her eyes widened. It was enough to repair the priory's aged cart and even to find a decent ox to pull it. It was enough to add doves to the dovecote, to replace the cow that now served more as a pet than as a source of butter, cream, and cheese.

She looked up to find the stranger's gaze trained upon Isobel. The girl stared back at him, her face awash with joy.

The man's face cracked into an unexpected smile before he turned his gaze from Isobel and strode toward the guesthouse.

Suddenly, Alys recognized him.

Her stomach lurched as she whipped toward her niece. Isobel stood with a foolish grin on her face, the damask cloth trailing from her hand and onto the ground.

Only the eye color was different.

"Rip him out!" Alys hissed in a harsh whisper. "Rip him out of the cloth at once!"

# 5

## BALTIMORE

The warm sun bathed Julia Carmichael's face, making the day feel more like June than early October. She lay atop a grassy bank in front of the school library, half listening to her schoolmates' chatter as it swirled about her. This was her study hall period. She should have been inside the library instead of outside, busily attacking tonight's homework. She'd considered that for about a second before giving in to the irresistible call of the sweet air.

She was not the only one to succumb. Other students dotted the lawn and sidewalks, their sweatshirts and books strewn everywhere. Campus looked more like a beach than an institution of learning.

Julia reached back a lazy hand to adjust the knapsack beneath her head. That beach idea was worth keeping. On days like this she liked to pretend she was spending the summer on her own in Ocean City. She could see herself now, stretched luxuriously across a blanket against the scorching sand, the tiniest of bathing suits showing off her deep tan. Okay, so tanning wasn't good for you, but if she slathered on enough sunscreen, she could emerge a bronzed goddess by the end of one day.

A corner of her mouth turned up. At least she'd inherited her mother's olive complexion. Her father's fair Irish skin burned in less than half an hour.

Oh, brother. Did her parents have to invade even her best daydreams?

She sighed. Ever since that night she'd stupidly blurted out, "Illusion food," she'd felt herself under scrutiny. Sure, life had gone on in the usual way. There was still the typical hustle in the morning as everyone flew out the front door to various destinations. Her mom and dad continued to work hard. They were, if possible, working even longer hours than they'd worked at the beginning of the school year. Lately the family's dinners had been completely hodgepodge, ranging from chicken marsala from Angel Café to cans of condensed soup and scrambled eggs. Beneath the rhythm of family life, though, Julia could tell that something had changed.

In the weeks since that fateful supper, Julia had felt her mother's eyes following her. She would glance up at dinner to find Kat studying her. She'd catch the living room curtain falling back into place as she turned from the mailbox. Just last week, she'd lifted her head from tying a shoe to see her mother poised at the bedroom doorway as if awaiting an invitation.

"What?" Julia had asked, tossing her head.

Kat had hesitated, then forced a bright smile. "Nothing, sweetheart," she'd said before retreating down the hall.

*Nothing.* Only her mother could make that word drip with so much "something."

Maybe her mom wasn't acting any weirder than usual. Kat got into moods sometimes, and even her daughter could tell that she was working way too hard these days. A case she'd hoped would settle was heading for court. Never was she more brittle than when juggling fifteen hours a day of trial work plus all the responsibilities of home, too. Julia sighed. It wasn't unusual for her mother to go a little manic at times like this.

But her dad had no excuse. Stephen Carmichael, always so laid-back, was usually as cool as a father could ever be. He'd kept his wits during that awful hundred-degree August week when both Carmichael girls got poison ivy. He'd even managed to stay calm last year when Claire had wandered away and gotten lost at the mall. As far as Julia was concerned, her dad was the first person she'd call in an emergency.

Not lately, though. Her father wasn't around the house a lot these days, but his questions certainly were. He'd taken to calling home just as she walked through the door after school.

"How are you?" he'd ask, a tight edge to his voice crackling through the phone wires. "Anything happen today?"

Like, what was supposed to happen? He didn't seem to be looking for a schedule of tests and presentations. She always ran the parade of schoolday events past him. He'd pause at the end of it, apparently waiting for something else.

Of course, there *was* something else.

Julia flung an arm across her face. The sun, so comfortable a moment ago, had begun to bore a hole through her forehead.

She was such a phony.

At least there'd been no more unexpected images

blending in with her day-to-day scenery. That was a relief. While the mystery of the unknown still intrigued her, she certainly didn't want to "see" misplaced stuff.

She was far more comfortable with the pictures that now visited her dreams.

Bedtime was almost as good as a movie these days, although Julia had to admit that there wasn't much of a plot. Once or twice a week the same characters showed up in her dreams. Sometimes they stood in the woods, but usually they emerged from soft fog. Julia could not see their faces clearly, but their blond hair gleamed through the strange fuzziness. She didn't think it would be long before she'd see them better. Their features seemed to grow a little sharper with each visit. More important, she had the oddest feeling that these people had something to say.

She'd had repetitious dreams all through her childhood—dreams about houses, monsters, and chases. No dreams had ever carried the sense of intrigue that these did. These dreams drew her in, made her want to know more. Although she couldn't deny that they made her nervous, she couldn't wait to see what happened next.

The strident clang of a bell pierced her thoughts. Julia groaned as she pressed herself into the grass. Time to hustle to her next class.

Rush, rush, rush. She felt like a mindless ant scurrying in circles around an anthill.

She clenched her eyes shut.

It was there. That weird ringing sound that usually filled her ears before the blond people appeared. Julia stiffened. Those people were only supposed to show up in her dreams. What were they doing here, in broad daylight?

The bells rang more clearly than usual, high and sweet, with pure, open tones. Now Julia heard a man's voice as well, mellow as a woodwind as it intertwined with the bells.

She could open her eyes. She could tell the bells, the voice, and everything else to come back at night when expected.

But here came the people, imprinted against the back of her eyelids, and she found it hard to tear herself away.

It was the blond man and the girl again. This time, an iron gate separated them. The girl strained against it, arms stretched through the bars toward the man. He faced her, both feet firmly planted on the hard dirt ground. Then, with an indifferent shrug, he reached out a long finger. He aimed it toward the keyhole on the gate, stuck it in, and turned the lock. To Julia's amazement, the gate flapped wide open. The girl tumbled forward with the force of the swing and ended up crumpled at the man's feet.

Julia watched, transfixed, as the girl wrapped her hands around the man's leg. Slowly, hand span by hand span, she pulled herself up until she stood before him, arms wrapped around his waist.

The man studied her, hooking her gaze in his for a moment. Then he pulled her hands from his body and took a firm step backward.

For the first time, his face grew focused in Julia's mind's eye. He sneered . . . not at the girl before him, but at the girl relaxing on the school lawn.

Julia's eyes flew open. A clammy mist of sweat covered her forehead as she struggled to regain her bearings.

It was a dumb soap opera dredged up from the depths of an overactive imagination. She would call it *The Young and the Hopeless* or *All My Morons* and sell it to Hollywood for a fortune.

"Hey."

Her pulse pounded through her temples as she whipped toward the voice. Her friend Meredith stood above her, sweatshirt tied around her waist and knapsack dragging on the ground. She looked sloppy and real. Julia felt absurdly grateful.

"So are you coming to French, or what?" Meredith asked.

"Yes." Julia scrambled to her feet. "Yes."

"Check your locker," Meredith said. "There's a pink telephone message slip sticking out of it."

Message slip. Good. Something else real. There'd been so many of those slips in the past few weeks that Julia already knew what this one would say: "Please pick up your sister at the lower school after class—Dad" or "I may be a little late. Love, Mom."

Ordinarily Julia would roll her eyes at this imposition. It irked her that her parents could not handle their own schedules without her help. At this moment, however, the shelter of routine was downright appealing.

She swallowed hard.

Damn. She was going to have to get those blond people back into her dreams where they belonged.

Too bad she didn't know how.

# 6

THE WOMAN AT TABLE A-6 HAD LIPSTICK ON HER TEETH AND A voice that reminded Stephen of ground glass. He'd stopped by because he'd recognized her as a regular lunch customer. He'd had no intention of standing tableside for what seemed like hours, listening to her drone on and on about mushrooms. Even her dining companion, a stout man in his fifties, looked as if he longed to stuff a forkful of arugula into her mouth.

"Well," Stephen said when the woman finally paused for a breath, "since you're so fond of mushrooms, I recommend the grilled portobello sandwich. I think you'll enjoy it."

"Oh, Mr. Carmichael, I know I'd enjoy anything you'd care to serve me." She actually batted her eyelashes. Stephen thought that sort of thing had gone out with cigarette holders and white gloves. "Tell me, do you brush the mushrooms with olive oil?"

As he opened his mouth to respond, he felt the light pressure of fingertips in the crook of his arm. He looked down to his right to see his wife. Her presence was so unexpected that for one moment his mind did not register who this elegant woman in the navy blue suit was.

"Excuse us, please." Kat smiled sweetly at the diners and led her husband toward the lobby.

Stephen quickly covered her hand with his. "Is everything okay?"

"Everyone's safe, if that's what you mean." She pursed her lips. "It seems that you and I are going on a little field trip this afternoon."

"What do you mean?"

"Aunt Frannie's waiting out in her car. She's taking us to the cathedral."

He stopped short. "What for?"

Kat slammed an exasperated hand to her hip. "Why, Stephen, to pray, of course. What else?"

He was momentarily speechless. They'd reached the lobby, and his gaze swam over a crowd of people. The restaurant was running ten to fifteen minutes behind with reservations, and there were still several parties hoping for a break in the rush so that they, too, could be seated.

"I can't leave now," he said, amazed that anyone would think he could.

"Gee, what a coincidence. Neither could I." Kat pressed against him to make way for the hostess to lead a party of six into dining room C. "I'm doing my best to settle that Mowery case, and I'm sure not going to accomplish much from a pew. I need this expedition like I need head lice."

He rubbed the back of his neck. "Then why are we going?"

"Like we have a choice."

"Just say no. Postpone it. Tell Frannie we'll call her tonight."

She stared at him as though he'd spoken in tongues.

"Okay," he said. "So she doesn't take refusal well. All the same—"

"I suggest you come, Stephen." Her hand was in his, tugging him toward the door. "She says it's extremely important. She also said that if we're not out the door in five minutes, she's going to barge into the lobby and start complaining about how high your prices are."

Jesus Christ. Stephen passed his free hand across his forehead and closed his eyes. He could barely remember missing Frannie during those long months she'd spent in England. She'd been so odd lately that he was ready to personally finance a return trip.

Her weighty pronouncements about Asteroth had turned him into the kind of parent who checked on every breath his kids took. Julia had begun to throw him those pained expressions that marked him as a totally uncool father. Even Claire, usually so easygoing, had pointedly informed him that she was perfectly capable of walking across the street to her friend's house without his help.

All this, and he'd still seen nothing to indicate that Francesca's fears were on the mark.

"All right," he said, arm dropping to his side. "Let me tell Laura that I'm leaving, and we'll go. It's time to end this stupidity once and for all."

"God, Stephen, I wish we could." An errant lock of hair escaped Kat's chignon and trailed against the soft curve of her cheek. She looked so forlorn that he couldn't help brushing a quick kiss across her brow before weaving through the crowded lobby in search of his assistant manager.

Francesca ignored the car horns honking at her. She was double-parked in the middle of Light Street, but since her flashers were on, she felt little responsibility for the annoyed drivers stalled behind her. The lane of oncoming traffic cleared regularly enough. Those overwrought people could simply wait for a break and drive around her.

She leaned back against the headrest. This was why she hated to drive. Everybody on the road seemed to think that the most important goal in life was to arrive as quickly as possible at the next destination. It would do them all good to slow down a little.

Her gaze returned to the entrance of Angel Café. As if on cue, Kat peered around the heavy oak door. She made an "okay" circle with her fingers, then ducked back inside the restaurant.

Good. Francesca let out a long breath as another car sped around her with an angry squeal of wheels.

Kidnapping both Stephen and Kat had been a risky proposition, one that had demanded every ounce of starch she possessed. Even the openmouthed expression on Kat's face as her aunt barged into her office had not deterred her. In fact, the secretary's patronizing "I'm so sorry, Ms. Piretti, but the lady insisted!" had only strengthened Francesca's resolve. How could Katerina sit in the sterile trappings of that stodgy law firm while total chaos rolled and bucked beneath her feet? How could she ignore the obvious: that her reality was not "business as usual"?

The turmoil Francesca had felt since her return to Baltimore had intensified, grown nearly mocking in its ability to evade definition. Prayer and meditation were disturbed by singsong chants and taunting laughter. She tossed in her sleep, images of death and destruction branded on her mind. Although she could not pinpoint the exact source of the disturbance, neither could she deny her sense of it. She'd experienced this greasy tinge of darkness before. She recognized a challenge when it was thrown her way. She couldn't believe that Kat and Stephen did not.

The car door opened, and Stephen slid into the passenger seat beside her.

"Okay, Frannie," he said, mouth set in a tight line. "You win this one. What gives?"

She pulled the car into traffic before Kat could even slam the back door. "What can I say, Stephen? Thank you for working me into your busy schedule."

"This isn't convenient," Kat said for at least the fourth time since they'd left her office.

"Buckle your seat belt." Francesca executed a sharp right that sent her niece tumbling against her seat.

They rode in silence for a few minutes, through the congestion of cars at Harborplace and up Calvert Street. Francesca glanced at her rearview mirror in time to see Kat canvass the front entrances of both city circuit court buildings. Pavlov's little dog was programmed to feel guilt for every second spent away from the practice of law. Stephen, too, looked tense. His arms were wrapped tightly across his chest, the fingers of his right hand tapping an uneven rhythm against his left elbow.

She waited until they'd turned onto Charles Street before relenting. "I suppose you'd like an explanation."

"Damn straight," Stephen said.

"This wouldn't, by any chance, have anything to do with your belief that the forces of darkness are upon us?" The brittle edge to Kat's voice told Francesca that her niece was ready to dismiss any possibility of danger.

Stephen twisted in his seat. "Because if it does, Frannie, we need to talk. Kat and I have watched the kids like hawks this past month. There is nothing . . . I repeat, *nothing* . . . happening to them."

"Oh?" Francesca's eyebrows rose. "And how can you say that with such assurance?"

He set his jaw. "I just know."

"Just as you knew there was nothing happening fifteen years ago when you began receiving vague messages to pass on to Katerina?"

He colored. "That was different."

"Asteroth *is* incarnate. I know this. If you two aren't willing to protect yourselves and your children, at least let me try to do it for you."

"But, Aunt Frannie, what's the point in stirring all this up if it isn't necessary?"

"Humor me, Katerina."

They drove in silence past the campuses of Johns Hopkins University, Loyola College, and the College of Notre Dame. The Cathedral of Mary Our Queen rose majestically before them on the left, its white spires climbing high into the clear, blue sky.

Francesca glided into a parking spot in front of the massive building and alighted from the car. Stephen and Kat exchanged one last glance before reluctantly following her up the steps and through the heavy metal doors.

Although it was warm outside, the cavernous cathedral always felt cool and subterranean. Francesca did not come here often, but she knew exactly where she wanted to be today. She strode briskly down the left aisle, accompanied by the echoed tap of Kat's high heels as she and Stephen hurried to keep up. They passed through the blue, scarlet, and golden beams of light that filtered through the tall stained-glass windows. Statues gazed down at them in benevolent silence. Francesca sailed past, stopping before only one: Saint Michael the Archangel. He towered above them, clothed in full armor, sword upraised for battle.

"We're going to need him," Francesca murmured.

Kat laid a hand on her aunt's wrist. "Aunt Frannie, why are we here?"

"We're here because I need a clue about what's happening, Katerina. I need to return to that vision I had fifteen years ago."

Stephen's brow furrowed. "The baby?"

"Yes, the baby." With one last, lingering look at Saint Michael, Francesca turned and continued toward the back of the church.

"How do you return to a vision?" Kat asked. "Can you actually do that?"

"I don't know," Francesca admitted. "But I think I can. Meditation and prayer transcend time and space. Haven't you ever been lifted, catapulted into an entirely different realm?"

Kat turned pink. One corner of Stephen's mouth twitched, as it always did when he was trying not to find something automatically ridiculous.

"Well." Francesca's words ricocheted off the stone wall. "It's high time your spiritual nature intruded on the rest of your oh-so-busy lives. I can't imagine how you've both kept it out for so long."

Stephen's shoulders slumped, but Kat's chin jerked up. Francesca recognized the gesture from as far back as her niece's kindergarten days. Katerina was a powder keg just hoping for a match.

They rounded the rear corner of the church. To their left was the Lady Chapel, dedicated to the Virgin Mary, a blue and gold island of peace in the midst of a raging world.

"Here." Francesca entered and settled herself into a pew.

"I still don't get it." Kat frowned. "I thought you always meditated at home."

"Not this time. I won't go back to that place alone."

"Place?"

"That vision. I need to launch myself from a safe place with good, strong vibes to it. This chapel crossed my mind. I always go with my light-guided intuitions."

She'd spent years trying to dull the sharp memory of that vision. She remembered herself alone in her living room, settling into the comfortable rhythm of meditation. She remembered greeting the pulsing light that always engulfed her whenever the confines of physical reality melted away from her consciousness. She knew she could remember the vision that followed, too. Unfortunately, it had come with dark perimeters and a curious suction toward a vacuum that she never wanted to face again.

She was vulnerable. That sooty darkness had left a crack within her that she feared could be pried open once more. She still awoke gasping from unsettling dreams, unable to recall details, yet certain that a gaping chasm had once again sucked her in. She had nearly slipped fifteen years ago. There was no guarantee that she wouldn't slip again.

She couldn't risk it.

"I can't do this without at least one of you," she said. "The protection you can give me is vital."

Stephen hesitated, then slid into the pew beside her. "I'm not good at this," he said with a helpless shrug.

"It's been years since I got those weird messages, and since then . . . well, Frannie, I don't even know what I think about this spiritual stuff anymore."

She studied him, a gentle smile playing about her mouth. He'd mellowed over the years, losing a compass that had previously operated only where money and women were concerned. Katerina and the girls had played a large part in that transformation, but there was more to it than that. She would never understand why people expected "spiritual stuff" to arrive with bells and whistles. All Stephen had to do was gaze back over the course of his own life to see a trail of miracles.

"You don't have to be good at this," she said. "You just have to trust that God is good at it."

He threw a sideways glance at his wife. Kat gave a barely perceptible snort.

Stephen gingerly reached for Francesca's hand. "What do you want me to do?"

"Close your eyes and pray for clarity." She closed her own eyes, reassured by the pressure of his hand in hers. She noted that Katerina remained standing outside the pew. That didn't matter. She only needed one other.

As always, the radiant light welcomed her. For as far back as she could remember, it had always awaited her, strong and complete, glowing with a serenity and love that she'd never been able to duplicate in her physical existence. Reaching the light was never a problem; leaving it was. Never did she feel as whole as when she lost herself within this presence.

The light brightened. Stephen's prayers must have connected with her own.

Usually she would step toward the light, allow herself to become immersed within it. Now, in her mind's eye, she regretfully turned her back to it. Its warmth urged her forward.

She drew in one long, slow breath, then carefully exhaled. Another.

A tiny spark of fear flickered within her. She had to concentrate harder than usual to keep her breathing deep and even. Finally, she drifted a level deeper, as if someone had administered a touch of anesthesia.

A picture flashed across her mind. It took only an instant to recognize one of the steep, narrow streets of Lincoln. She frowned. It was Lincoln as she'd known it this summer, yet different. These streets were not paved. These windows had few glass panes.

Images flew quickly through her head, requiring her full attention. It was as though she raced through a gallery wing of paintings. Over here was the sanctuary of Saint Leo's, the neighborhood church she'd known since childhood. Next came a solemn, dark-haired girl dressed in white, rosary beads spilling through the fingers of her right hand. Francesca gasped as she recognized her own First Communion.

Next came a baby, but not the one she sought. This one rested in her mother's arms, the sleeve of her white christening gown clutched in a plump little fist. A stab of yearning pierced Francesca's heart. The baby was Katerina, but it was the mother she longed to hold. Though young and glowing in the mind's eye, Lucia had been dead for nearly forty years, now.

There was no time to think. The images piled up even faster, as if somebody had pushed a fast-forward button. Glimpses of places and times long gone raced through her in a frenzied version of *This Is Your Life*.

Then the reel of memories slowed. Francesca found herself catapulted back fifteen years, back to the time when Katerina and Stephen had first met. She saw them at Angel Café, glowering at each other across a table as they had so often done during those surreal months of Asteroth. There was Tia Melody, the psychic who'd allowed the demon access to her body and their lives. Her purple eyes glittered behind rhinestone glasses. Her platinum hair formed a fuzzy aureole about her weathered face.

Suddenly, Francesca saw the burned facade of Tia's house as the aftermath of that last horrible battle smashed through her mind.

She swallowed away a pang of nausea and murmured a quick prayer for Tia's soul.

And there, seated calmly in the center of a pink-white mist, was the baby.

The heat on Francesca's back grew more intense as she studied the child. It studied her back, green eyes wide, little fists pumping at the air.

Something deep in Francesca's heart longed to cup the tiny face in her hands. Its features seemed so familiar. Julia and Claire each possessed a pair of those wide green eyes. In fact, Francesca could assess each individual aspect of this baby's face and find its counterpart in one of her great-nieces.

Yet the child was not identical to either of them. The vision unmistakably blended both Katerina and Stephen's features, creating a baby that only they could have produced. The mind's eye, however, had blended the genes in a thoroughly original way.

What child was this?

She recoiled as an unwelcome voice shot through her head: *It is me you might ask.*

Asteroth.

A ribbon of frosty air wrapped across her forehead. Reluctantly, Francesca raised her eyes from the light of the baby and gazed toward the empty darkness lapping the edge of the mist. She recognized this odd delineation between light and dark. She'd seen it during the battle with Asteroth. It was here she'd been pried open, left vulnerable.

The darkness receded, lightening to a fuzzy gray. An odd half-light of orange flashed through it. Now Francesca could see buildings, their soft outlines solidifying before her eyes. Her ears picked up the mellow trill of a woodwind. A pungent whiff of thyme made her stifle a sneeze, then gulp for more.

A voice floated through the air, a true, clear tenor teasing the notes of the woodwind.

An expected question danced before her: *Do you want to know more?*

She swallowed and returned her gaze to the baby. The vision was fading away, taking with it the key to all danger at home.

Whether she wanted to know was irrelevant. She had to know.

"Yes," she said. "Show me."

An enclave of buildings suddenly surrounded her. She stood in the midst of a courtyard, the warm sun beating down on her bare head. An iron gate rested shut behind her. Beyond it she saw a small house, bits of straw and pebbles poking through the mortar between its stones. Its wooden door was ajar. She noted a hard-packed dirt floor strewn with rushes inside.

Francesca took a tentative step forward. A short cloister connected a small church to a solid building. Like the house outside the gate, these structures were made of gray stone. Francesca squinted as she took a closer look. Arched windows lined the wall of the church. The windows in the other building were square. Heavy wooden shutters blocked several.

She knew a convent when she saw one. She'd once lived in one, after all. That solid building with the turret would be the chapter house and refectory. She guessed the wing that extended toward the rear housed a dormitory.

Laughter from the cloister made her jump. Two figures passed between the columns, heads close in conversation. Francesca froze, vulnerable in the wide open courtyard. There was no use darting away. Any sudden movement would attract attention.

The figures stopped, then turned to peer across the courtyard. Francesca's hand fluttered to her throat as their gazes drew near. She drew herself up, steeled to speak.

Their stares plowed right through her.

They couldn't see her.

The taller woman leaned her elbows against the edge of the cloister wall. The other woman stood beside her, arms crossed against an ample stomach.

Propelled by unbearable curiosity, Francesca took a tentative step toward them.

"Mark it well," the small one said in broad, flat tones. "Isobel is gone again."

The unfamiliar accent drew Francesca even closer.

Both women were smaller than she and dressed in a style she'd encountered only in history books. White wimples veiled their heads. The older one, short and stout, wore hers so low upon her forehead that it covered part of her bushy gray brows. The younger one had pushed hers back as far as it could go, revealing a broad expanse of white forehead and the start of a blond hairline. She wore a high-necked azure gown girdled by a leather band low on her hips. She tugged at a scarlet cloak trimmed with tattered fur. Her companion wore a green gown partially covered by a deep blue tunic. A metal pomander dangled from a chain about her neck.

"She did not come to Matins this morning," the older woman said with a sniff. "If she were not kin to Madame Alys . . ."

Francesca blinked rapidly as she sorted through the clues. They spoke the language of nuns, but their clothing certainly did not identify a particular order. If anything, they seemed on their way to a costume party. And their voices! She had to concentrate very hard to understand the odd intonations. She felt as though she were somehow translating a foreign language, as if she shouldn't be able to understand them at all.

The younger woman's eyes darted from side to side, reminding Francesca of a cat who knows exactly where his prey likes best to hide.

"I know where she goes," the woman said.

"Dame Joan, I'll have no idle gossip!"

Joan sidled away, chin tilted coquettishly. "As you wish, Barbara." Francesca saw that she couldn't be older than eighteen. "If you really do not care to know—"

"No, wait." Barbara raised a pudgy hand. "Perhaps it is my duty to know her whereabouts. Then I may help guide her footsteps toward the path of God."

Dame Joan gave what Francesca could only call a smirk. "She goes with *him.*"

"Who?"

"The boarder. The one with the fine shoulders and magnificent legs."

The other woman sniffed. "I did not note them."

"Then you are dead, Barbara. That is all there is to it."

Barbara's cheeks grew rosy. Then her hand landed on Joan's arm. "How do you know this?"

Their shoulders hunched as they drew together, heads touching. Francesca took several steps forward, but their words, rising and falling in a rhythmic cadence, were lost to her.

A low hum started in her ears. Although the day was fair, a chilling vapor wrapped itself around her ankle. The image of the women fine-tuned itself. They'd seemed quite clear before, but now their contours grew even sharper. Her senses practically ached with the increased clarity. She saw that Dame Joan's fair skin was sprinkled with badly powdered freckles. She caught a whiff of vinegar from the pomander dangling down Dame Barbara's thick front.

Her head began to throb. The chill at her ankle snaked about her leg, then twisted like a belt around her waist.

The nuns had stopped talking and glared with disapproval across the courtyard. Francesca turned to follow their line of vision.

The wrought-iron gate creaked open. A girl with hair the color of moonbeams sauntered through, each curve of her ripe body visible beneath the clingy fabric of her long midnight blue dress. Her eyes brushed past the tightly drawn lips of the sisters in the cloister. Infuriated by her insolence, they turned as one and swept into the church.

The girl tossed her head and passed so close that Francesca could smell the cloying scent of rosewater clinging to her unwashed body.

But Francesca barely noticed the girl. She stared instead beyond the gate. A tall, broad-shouldered man returned her gaze. His dark eyes nearly drilled a hole through her forehead. The frigid current continued up her spine, crackled through the air and ruffled the man's long blond hair. His lips curved upward in an empty smile.

"Welcome, Francesca," he said as the girl entered the chapter house. "I've been waiting for you."

A blast of wind blew through the cathedral chapel, rustling the altar cloth and knocking a pile of prayer cards to the floor. Kat jumped. Stephen's eyes flew open as Francesca's hand slipped from his grasp.

The shrill beep of his watch alarm pierced the air. His pager whirred to life. From deep in her briefcase, Kat's cell phone rang loudly.

"My God!" Stephen leapt to his feet as Francesca's limp body slid to the ground.

# 7

THE LINES OF THE COURTYARD WAVERED AS A JAGGED CURRENT raced from Francesca's toes, through her body, and out her scalp. Crackling electricity jammed her hearing. Her hands instinctively flew to plug her ears, but the sound came from deep within and would not be blocked.

Then the noise stopped. The tingling stopped as well, leaving her limbs loose and relaxed. Lightness such as she'd never known flooded through her. She wanted to float. In fact, she was surprised to find that she wasn't floating.

She felt no connection to human form. She remembered her body, of course. One didn't inhabit a shell for so many years and then forget all about it. She simply no longer required its presence. Perhaps she might next express herself as a whiff of smoke, a vapor, a pulsing star. The freedom intoxicated her.

She frowned. Not quite all of her being stood in this convent courtyard. A particle still rested in the body of the aging twenty-first-century ex-nun. Apparently, she still had a task to complete before she could totally relinquish her physical identity.

She called her mind back to business. The vision of

the baby. The recognition of Asteroth's presence in Baltimore.

With a sigh, she allowed the physical image of Francesca to once again encase her. The body wasn't solid, but it granted her the identity she required. She examined her right hand. The gold band Francesca always wore glinted on her third finger.

Her gaze met that of the man behind the gate. His figure stood solidly before her. How odd. She knew Asteroth to be a spirit . . . a fallen angel. Now that she'd regained use of her spiritual eyes, she'd expected to see beyond his temporal form and into the deeper dimensions of his nature. But this creature before her was clearly physical. He'd left distinct footsteps in the mud of the road. Even now, his shadow darkened the ground.

His eyes widened slightly. "You have escaped the limitation of a physical body."

"Yes." Francesca tilted her head, considering. "And you have acquired it. How? Why?"

His features contorted. "It matters not. I will crush you."

To her own surprise, she realized that she was not afraid. A comfortable sense of serenity flooded her.

"You can't," she said. "You can't unless I allow it."

She thought she detected a flicker of fear across his face, but it could have been a trick of the sun as it ducked behind a cloud.

"Hear me well, Francesca. I am a far older spirit than you. You know more than you did, but not as much as you should."

"I know I walk in the light."

His knuckles whitened as he clenched his fist. "Do not cross me. All that I desire *will* come to pass. You are but an inconsequential nuisance, easily silenced."

"I will not cross you, sir," said a gentle voice from the road. "Only pray cease to prattle when there is no one near to hear it. It unnerves me."

Asteroth swung around to face a brown-robed priest.

The priest smiled. "Master Hugh, is it?" Francesca made note of Asteroth's earthbound identity.

"Yes." Hugh's eyes narrowed. "And you are Gregory."

Father Gregory nodded. Despite his good-natured tone, the stiffness of his slender form betrayed uneasiness. "You've been in residence for over a week now, Hugh. When do you resume your journey?"

Hugh spun on a soft leather heel and strode into the guesthouse.

Gregory slipped through the iron gate and walked noiselessly across the courtyard toward the chapter house, his smooth agility reminding Francesca of a cat. She watched as he disappeared through a doorway. She knew by now that she had crossed centuries as well as continents, yet Gregory possessed the sort of face that transcended eras. With those soft brown eyes, that prominent nose and chiseled chin, he could have belonged to sixteenth-century Italy, eighteenth-century France, or twenty-first-century America.

So Asteroth was here, human in medieval Lincoln. And yet she'd felt his presence in modern Baltimore.

How?

She'd begun this search in good faith. It had led her

here. She would remain safe as long as she stayed within the protection of the light. That meant accepting guidance in God's time, not her own.

Thankful for invisibility, Francesca cautiously moved toward the church. She would wait where the light felt strongest.

# 8

"THERE!" ALYS LURCHED TOWARD HER BEDROOM WINDOW, craning her neck to catch a better view. "It has drifted into the church!"

"He will not leave. Ever." Gregory folded his arms across his chest and lowered his brow.

"Did you see it? That . . . that shimmering form in the courtyard has floated like a petal into the church!"

"He will stay well into the bishop's next visit, and we shall all pay for it. Alys, why did you defy my wishes?"

The prioress passed a limp hand across her forehead. She was tired. Hours meant for sleeping were now spent tossing and turning as she worried about Isobel's disobedience and wondered whether the boarder would ever leave. She rose from her bed each morning with bones heavier than when she'd retired. And now she was starting to see images that simply weren't there.

"Alys." Gregory was beside her now. "You've not heard a word."

"Don't heckle me, Gregory. I heard you."

He sighed, then pulled her close. "Why is it I can never remain angry with you?"

"We should never put this to rights if you could."

They turned as one to stare through the window. The summer sun rested a little past peak, bathing the courtyard in strong, persistent rays. This was the time of day when Alys most missed the meadows of her girlhood. How she longed for a field of deep, fragrant grass in which to rest her weary body!

The guesthouse door slammed open. Hugh emerged, wooden recorder in hand. Alys and Gregory instinctively stepped back into the shadows of the room.

With a sly glance toward the prioress's bedroom window, Hugh lifted the recorder to his lips. Mellow tones floated on the air, teasing Alys's ears. The somber walls of her bedroom melted away. She saw herself seated in the Great Hall of a manor house as a courtly minstrel played the pipes solely to please her. An ermine-trimmed cloak sheltered her from the chill draft that passed through the brightly colored tapestries adorning the stone walls. She heard the welcome cacophony of footsteps and voices as her lord, her Gregory, strode into the hall, accompanied by his huntsmen and dogs.

"My Alys." He swept her into his arms. "Could anything on earth surpass the joy of coming home to you?"

Oh, to forget Saint Etheldreda's and capture the life she might have lived!

The unattainable images buzzed through her head like bees. She angrily batted them away.

"I do not like his playing," she said.

"I do not like anything about him." Gregory's eyes, clouded with discontent, did not leave Hugh's tall, retreating form. Alys wondered what pictures visited her beloved when the boarder piped his melodies.

But Gregory shrugged away any unhappiness. Only

a wistful sigh revealed that he, too, had been transported far beyond Saint Etheldreda's iron gates. "Where does he go?" he asked.

"I do not know. I do not care."

"You'd best care, my love, for here comes one of your own flock to follow him."

Alys stepped toward the window ledge. Indeed, Isobel crossed the courtyard, skimming across the earth on light feet. With the confidence of one who knows that nothing can stop her, she reached the gate and firmly tugged it open.

The tones of the recorder grew fainter, but still they taunted Alys's ears, inducing an exquisite melancholy that seemed nearly sacred.

How much she had sacrificed! How hard she had worked for so little, and how unappreciated were all her efforts!

"This cannot continue." The shock in Gregory's voice pulled her from her misery.

"No," she agreed, irritation rising. She started quickly toward the stairs.

Gregory turned to follow.

He was beautiful with those long, strong legs. His golden hair glinted in the sunlight. She could watch him for hours as she perched lightly on this tree stump like the butterfly he often told her she would become.

"Yes, Isobel, a butterfly," he'd say in mahogany tones. "For a butterfly transforms itself from the lowly to the sublime. You, too, shall do this. You shall burst from your cocoon in brilliant glory if you listen to me."

Words such as these often made her frown. She considered herself quite glorious already, definitely more akin to butterfly than caterpillar. But then, she never understood much of what Hugh said. Fortunately, her desire for him did not require an understanding of his whims.

Sun streamed into the forest clearing, inviting day-dreams. Isobel paid it no mind. Instead she studied Hugh through half-lidded eyes. His gestures were sharp and sure. The arrogant thrust of his chin made her stomach tumble over and over itself like currents in a stormy sea. His long, tapered fingers bespoke elegance, but she'd seen those hands crack thick branches in two. How strong he was!

She'd felt his embrace only in dreams. Countless dreams she'd had of him before coming here, enchanting dreams that studded her nights like gems on a goblet. Of course she'd recognized him when he'd finally arrived in the stark light of day. Hadn't he called her for months?

Perhaps she did have the second sight her grandfather so feared. She didn't know. She knew only that her mind possessed countless thoughts for which God had somehow forgotten to provide a voice. Her father claimed that her lack of speech came as punishment for past unknown sins. Her mother wrung her hands and proclaimed that those sins had made the daughter stupid as well as silent. Isobel herself had long ago decided that her only sin was allowing her parents sovereignty over her.

For years she had endured their cockeyed plans to marry her off to one unsavory character or another. Would it be the drooler or the pockmarked merchant, the four-month-old noble or the eighty-year-old addle-pate? No wonder she reveled in breaking pottery and striking all who vexed her! Such violent actions kept her safely unwed. But then her parents had inflicted their latest indignity: this odious idea that she spend her life locked away in a dreary priory with her haughty aunt Alys and a passel of moldy nuns. Oh, the havoc she'd intended to wreak!

She'd first dreamt of Hugh last Michaelmas, before the frosts of winter had settled in. Soon, daytime drudgery ceased to matter. After all, there was always Hugh waiting for her when she closed her eyes at night. He alone did not require spoken words to understand her heart. She'd never once doubted his existence, for how could anyone so loving be anything but real? Indeed, it was her waking hours that took on a tinge of the otherworldly.

Dream-world Hugh had even given her a sign of his presence. One night, in the midst of the dream, he'd raised her fingertips to his lips. She'd winced at the prick that stung her soft finger pads as he kissed each one in turn, but she'd awakened renewed, the ability to quickly stitch her thoughts whirring through her hands.

She shifted on the tree stump. He'd been good to her. He'd been true. Miraculously, he'd even lifted himself out of her dreams and into her waking hours. What more could she ask?

Much more, it seemed. Now that Hugh stood before her as a living, breathing man, her skin itched to feel his touch. The thought of his hand on hers sent violent shivers up her spine. How could he care so much for her, yet never ever touch her?

Hugh's shoulder muscles rippled beneath his tunic as he dropped an armload of kindling into the center of a small stone circle. Isobel sighed. There'd be another fire today, a fire in the midst of this hot, fair summer afternoon. That meant a lesson.

"Damn them all!" Hugh's voice rumbled through the clearing. "I had not planned on so little time. We must make haste. Come to me, Isobel."

She slowly rose.

He stood before her, arms outstretched. She glanced quickly at his face, avoiding his eyes. As much as she loved to watch Hugh, she could never meet his eyes. In her dreams they had been deep, clear blue. In life they resembled pits in the earth, so endlessly dark were they. She let her gaze wander. She wanted to bury her face in his hair. She'd never before met a man so clean. Hugh's hair always shone, and his clothes were never lined with rings of sweat.

"Come." His sharp voice urged her forward. She hadn't realized she'd stopped walking.

He flexed his hands. She knew from past lessons what she was to do. She stepped forward and raised her hands to mirror his. Spreading her fingers, she matched her fingertips to his, moving them close, yet not touching him.

"Yes," he said softly.

She drew in a deep breath. His musky fragrance teased her nostrils and made her head spin.

"Good girl, Isobel." His voice caressed her. "You remember this from yesterday. Can you now see the power between us?"

She dragged her gaze away from his chest and dutifully observed the space between their fingertips. He always promised that she would see magic there, but she never did. Once she thought she saw a faint pink light around her own fingertips, but it had been rapidly devoured by an odd, sooty cloud pouring forth from Hugh's hand. Surely such ugliness wasn't what he'd expected her to notice. One blink, and the vision had vanished. She'd stopped trying to see after that.

"Do you see anything?" he asked.

She shook her head.

"Empty your mind. Let me come to you. Let me fill you."

His words sent chills through her. They'd danced through this ritual before. She was to stand still and clear her head of thought. Sometimes she felt a roar of wind between her ears. Once she'd felt her knees buckle as her mind whirled around and around inside her skull. Hugh had caught her as she'd reeled backward. He'd set her back on her feet, plucking his hands from her body as quickly as he could.

She'd actually seen him smile that day.

Was that, then, what he wanted?

Usually she kept her eyes closed during their lessons. Today discontent welled within her, making it hard to stand still in her solitary darkness. Cautiously, she opened her eyes to see. Hugh's deep eyes remained closed. His hands stayed rigidly upraised.

Isobel's restless stare raked his body. His powerful arms tensed as he stretched out his hands. He'd planted his feet firmly on the ground, his legs spread wide apart. His thighs looked as hard as the rocks he'd piled about the fire.

Isobel's small, pink tongue licked her lips. Her hands trembled. He knew so very much about her. Why couldn't he sense this knot in her stomach? He had to know how desperately she longed for his touch.

Quickly, before she could change her mind, Isobel took a deep breath and pressed her hands against his.

A jolt of heat raced from Hugh's fingertips through her own. She nearly fell backward as a wave of passion slammed through her, turning her insides to molten gold. She wanted to pull him into her very being, to be swallowed whole by him. Her eyes widened and her mouth dropped open with the intensity of her own reaction.

But if she was surprised, Hugh seemed aghast. His eyes flew open as palm met palm, fingertip met fingertip.

"No." His body began to shake. "I cannot touch you like this."

But his body and his mind seemed at odds. Despite his words, his arms encircled her waist. He yanked her toward him, crushing her against his hard chest.

"I . . . won't!" The words twisted away as he bent her back and roughly kissed her lips. Isobel gasped.

"No," he muttered against her neck. "This will not happen to me. This cannot happen to me. Damn this body!"

She had lain with one other man before, a gentle young shepherd whose tentative hands and moist lips had left her more out of sorts than pleased. Hugh's hand felt like a claw on her breast, but she did not care. She pressed against him, returning his kisses with ferocity that had long desired an escape. Sweat dripped in rivulets from his brow. She eagerly licked the salt from his lips.

Her small hand snaked across his hard stomach, coming to rest on the hardness between his legs. Before she even knew quite how, they were both on the ground, rolling in the prickly grass.

"No!" Hugh groaned, but then his mouth was back atop hers. His skin felt like a smoldering fire.

Suddenly he seemed a man gone mad. His sharp teeth pierced her lower lip, then his mouth left hers to travel down her neck. The rip of fabric broke the stillness as he tore the front of her dress. Her pink nipple disappeared into his mouth. The sucking hurt, but she could have borne it. It was his heat that shocked her. The five fingers gripping her thigh scorched her skin. The hand cupping her breast to his mouth might have been a stone from the oven.

His hungry mouth returned to hers. Steamy breath flowed through her, filling her until she thought she'd burst.

An odd power flooded her, sending thoughts topsy-turvy and pushing them to the side of her head.

"Is all flesh this weak?" Hugh whispered into her ear. "Is this the price I must pay for human form?" He wedged his hand between her legs, forcing them open.

Her mind's chaos seemed related to his touch. She could feel power flow though his fingertips, through his tongue as it probed her mouth, even through his belly pressed against hers. This was almost more than she could bear.

Suddenly she knew: if he took her now, she would die.

An unfamiliar force raced through her mind and to her tongue.

"No!" she shrieked.

Hugh grew rigid above her. Her own hands flew to her mouth.

"You spoke," he said.

She nodded, mouth covered. The word had come

from her body. Somehow, though, it had not been her voice.

Hugh raised himself to his knees. "Speak, Isobel!"

Terrified, Isobel opened her mouth. No sound emerged.

"You cannot?" He looked oddly elated.

She shook her head.

A slow, crooked smile spread across his face. His odd dark eyes glowed nearly orange in the sunlight.

"We are triumphant," he said, voice low. "We will meet again soon, Isobel. This is what must be."

She recoiled. Was this, then, the reason for the endless lessons? Could the two of them create that overwhelming power again, the one that wanted to rule her thoughts?

Branches cracked in the underbrush.

"Cover yourself." With a dispassionate glance at her exposed breasts, Hugh disappeared into the forest.

Isobel quickly rose, pulling her mantle about her.

Alys stood before her, Father Gregory at her side. Their eyes darted about the clearing, but Isobel knew that their search was futile. Hugh had left her quite alone.

But not for long. She had no doubt that there would be longer lessons now. Hugh would work his magic again and again, threatening to engulf her each and every time.

She would let him. He had given her a voice.

# 9

KAT STARED WITH UNSEEING EYES OUT THE HOSPITAL WINDOW. The day, still a brilliant blue, mocked the fact that Aunt Frannie lay motionless on the room's sterile bed, attached to more medical equipment than her niece had ever known existed.

Kat bit her lower lip. Francesca would surely choose any alternative to this nightmare. How often had she heard her aunt remark that she wanted a quiet, dignified death, one marked by as little medical intervention as possible? Yet here she lay with neither a diagnosis nor a prognosis, simply a medical mystery hooked up to machinery.

One of the offending machines began to beep. Each beep correlated to a throb in Kat's aching temple.

"Jesus, Stephen, make it stop."

Her husband hoisted himself from his bedside chair, brow furrowed as he tried to locate the source of the noise.

A heavyset nurse with white hair bustled through the door. "That'll be her IV," she said in soothing tones. "It'll take me only a minute to change the bag, and then you can have your privacy again."

Kat watched as the nurse efficiently unhooked the empty bag. Privacy. Well, of course. The medical profession, thoroughly stymied by Francesca's lack of symptoms, expected her to die. Why not? All her vital signs indicated that she was asleep. There was nothing technically wrong with the woman in that bed. But there was nothing right, either. Nothing roused her. No amount of pushing, prodding, or pricking restored her to consciousness.

A muscle twitched in Stephen's jaw. "Excuse me," he said to the nurse, "but what happens next?"

The nurse untangled the IV tubing and straightened to face him. "Next?"

Stephen nodded. "Will there be more tests?"

"Oh." She ran her palms down the front of her brightly patterned smock. "Well, Mr. Carmichael, I can't say that I really know. The doctor should be in soon. You can ask him about it."

"What usually happens in these situations?" Stephen pressed.

"Every situation is different." The nurse's sympathetic smile enveloped Kat as well as Stephen. "I would assume that we'll keep searching for answers. In the meantime, we can at least keep our patient comfortable."

Kat's stomach tightened. She took a step forward, eyes trained on her aunt. "I don't see how anybody could be comfortable with all those tubes invading her body."

The nurse reached for her hand. "Don't worry. She's not in any pain."

Kat met Stephen's gaze. "I want to take her home," she said.

The nurse flushed, then tightened her grasp on Kat's fingers. "Oh, no, Ms. Piretti, I'm sure that wouldn't be wise at this point."

Kat extricated her hand from the crushing grip. "Stephen, I want to take her home."

"I'll fetch the doctor." The nurse nearly spun from the room.

Stephen studied his wife's determined face. "Are you sure?"

She drifted to his side and quietly rested her head against his chest. Together they observed her aunt. Francesca's hair fanned across the pillow, so white that it almost disappeared against the paleness of the pillowcase. Her face, smooth and unlined, was the color of alabaster. Translucent eyelids flickered now and then, and pink lips rested in a tiny half smile. She looked at least half her age.

"She isn't in this room," Kat whispered.

"Not in this room?" Stephen held her close.

Kat shook her head. "I don't know where she is. I can understand a spirit leaving a dying body, but Aunt Frannie isn't dying."

He swallowed hard. "I wish we knew that for sure."

She jerked away from him. "Show me some evidence that she is! Nobody here seems able to do that. Her body is working exactly as it should."

"She won't wake up," Stephen reminded gently.

Kat stared at the floor. "I know," she said in a low voice. "But I also know my aunt. She isn't in that body, and bringing her back has nothing to do with medical science."

He instinctively recoiled from her words, but she would not stop.

"You know what I'm saying, Stephen," she insisted.

A grimace flashed across his face. She could almost

see his mind struggle to tear away the veil of his own disbelief. She, too, longed to keep that veil intact, hung as it had hung for years as a buffer between the steady rhythm of their shared life and the harsh surreality they'd glimpsed so many years ago.

Finally, his eyes met hers. His voice sounded hollow. "You think this has something to do with Asteroth."

"I can't rule it out." The words seemed bleak, yet a curious release fluttered deep in her heart as she set them free. Some dark, festering secret had been exposed to the light.

Footsteps clattered down the hall. Claire tumbled into the room, followed by Julia and Angel Café's assistant manager, Laura.

"Mommy!" Claire catapulted into her mother's midsection.

"Thanks for bringing them, Laura." Stephen pulled a wan smile.

"No problem." Laura shifted her weight from one foot to the other. "Don't worry about the restaurant, Mr. Carmichael. We can handle it. We'll page you if there's a problem."

Stephen opened his mouth to say that he'd be back as soon as he could. Then he caught sight of Julia's face. Her lower lip trembled as she stared from her mother to Francesca. Her eyes were such a uniform green that they appeared almost opaque.

"Thank you," Stephen said instead as Laura left the room.

Claire walked toward the bed. "Aunt Frannie's in the middle of a good dream," she said, reaching out to pat Francesca's hand.

Kat and Stephen exchanged glances.

"That's a nice thought, sweetie," Kat managed to say.

"Well, it's true." Claire cocked her head. "She's smiling. See?"

"Knock it off, Claire." Julia's brows lowered.

Stephen wrapped an arm around his older daughter's shoulders. "Aunt Frannie isn't in any pain, Julia. I like Claire's idea that she might be seeing something special."

Claire nodded, mouth curved upward in a grin. She seemed quite at ease, not at all rattled by the unsettling scene unfolding around her.

Kat drew in a deep breath. "Ladies, we're taking Aunt Frannie home with us."

"Like this?" Julia's jaw dropped.

Kat squared her shoulders. "Like this."

"It won't be hard, Julie." Claire bent to pull up her drooping knee sock. "She's just sleeping. We can take turns watching her. We'll say prayers to keep her safe, of course."

Kat and Stephen stared at their younger daughter.

"Um . . . of course," Stephen said, for Claire had somehow delivered the very tone he and Kat had hoped to find.

Julia turned toward the window. Her heart thumped so loudly in her chest that she wondered why doctors did not swarm into the room to hook her up to a heart monitor.

This couldn't be happening. Aunt Frannie was always the very picture of health and energy, ready to tackle every new challenge that crossed her path. Somehow, it had never dawned on Julia that even the resilient could die. She felt foolish. *Everyone* died. Why hadn't she recognized this possibility before?

But Aunt Frannie couldn't leave her now . . . not when so many strange things were happening . . .

A scowl crossed Julia's face as she tried not to cry. She should have told Aunt Frannie about the bells and the weird people a long time ago. She suddenly knew that her great-aunt would have understood.

As if on cue, the errant bells rang through her brain again, louder than ever, clanging at a frequency that bordered on shrill. She tried to ignore them.

It was different this time. The blond people did not appear before her as they usually did. Today she felt their presence on either side of her. To her right stood the girl, hair the color of moonbeams. Julia felt the tickle of fingertips against her arm as the girl turned an odd, flat gaze in her direction. The man stood to her left. She caught a glimpse of shoulder-length blond hair as the strong aroma of musk assailed her nostrils.

The contours of the hospital room wavered. A breeze caressed her skin. Leaves rustled. The scent of wild thyme tickled her nose. She wondered how she even knew what that scent was.

In an instant, the room whirled about her. She lay in a forest clearing, pinned to the grass, the hardness of the warm earth pushing up against her shoulder blades. Intense heat scorched the front of her, pressing against her like an insistent inferno. Blinding sunlight streamed over the shoulder of the man on top of her.

The blond man. He was the one crushing her, squeezing all the breath from her lungs!

He raised his head and met her stare. She gasped

at the empty darkness of his eyes, then tried to roll from beneath him. His mouth came down hard on hers.

With all her might, Julia wrenched her head away.

"No!" she shrieked. The word echoed through the forest, reverberated against the dull beige hospital walls.

Her parents flew to her side, vivid reminders that she did not belong in the world those other people inhabited.

"Everything's okay, Julie," her father said, cradling her in his arms.

Kat reached for her daughter's hand. "I know it's a shock, honey, but we'll get through it. Aunt Frannie will have the best care we can give her."

Aunt Frannie. Julia shot a wild gaze toward Francesca. How peaceful she looked, resting against the pillows. How safe!

But there was something more here, something that Julia couldn't explain even if she tried.

She untangled herself from her parents' arms and took a few cautious steps toward her great-aunt.

Thyme. The faint scent of thyme played on the air surrounding Francesca's bed.

Julia blinked rapidly. Could nobody else in the room smell this?

Claire's small hand took possession of her own. "Everything will be fine," Claire said, green eyes round and solemn. "You know Aunt Frannie always does what's best."

Aunt Frannie.

Julia's stomach churned. She longed for a confidante, even if that confidante was only eight years old.

She opened her mouth to speak, but quickly shut it as a white-coated doctor, clip board in hand, strode into the room.

"Everything will be fine," Claire repeated as her mother short-circuited the doctor's protestations with a simple wave of her hand.

# 10

WHATEVER HER METAPHYSICAL STATE, FRANCESCA'S SENSES and perceptions had intensified. She stood motionless, overwhelmed by the ageless familiarity of the priory chapel. The fragrance of melting beeswax candles tickled her nostrils. Scores of tiny candle flames danced before her, their tricolored light illuminating the dimness of the sanctuary. Their glow softened the edges of the wooden pews until the burnished wood offered a sincere invitation to sit. Delicate feathers of smoke curled upward toward leaded-glass windows. Francesca wondered what prayers they carried with them. She had learned in her travels that people the world over harbored similar fears and hopes. She could only assume that this applied to centuries as well as locations. What mother did not agonize over the well-being of her child? What spouse did not mourn the loss of a life partner? Did anyone who ever drew breath not long for prosperity, be it through a bountiful harvest or a canny stock market investment? Francesca was certain that mankind shared fundamental prayers.

She raised her eyes to the stained-glass rose window high above the altar. She knew that its peaceful symmetry was meant to be an endless hymn of praise to the Virgin Mary. It was a mandala, a constant call to harmony in the midst of a jangled world. Light filtered through the pattern, splashing color across the stone floor. The juxtaposition of scarlet, blue, and gold nudged a memory. She studied it. Where else had she seen this pleasing pattern of color spilled across cold gray stone?

Forehead puckered in thought, Francesca drifted toward the front of the church. Her finger trailed across the gleaming back of a pew. The smooth wood caressed her fingertip with the softness of a rich velvet cape.

Much about this place felt familiar, but that did not surprise her. After all, she'd grown up in a tightly knit Italian community anchored by the Church. Indeed, she'd devoted a number of her adult years to the convent. Even now, she remained a churchaholic who dove into the atmosphere of old churches the way other people dove into books. Churches felt like homes away from home to her, places where she could always speak the language.

That was it, of course. It was not the church building itself that felt thoroughly familiar. It was the atmosphere. The texture of this place struck a chord.

She carefully lowered herself into a pew. This place felt like the modern-day Lincoln she'd visited last summer. She'd recognized that while still in the priory courtyard. There was more, though. The vibrations here resonated somewhere else as well. Where?

The thought pounded against her consciousness, striving for recognition.

Baltimore. The Cathedral of Mary Our Queen.

Her heart turned a somersault as her gaze darted back to the colorful pattern of light on the floor. It didn't matter whether she now sat in the medieval priory or the modern-day cathedral. Both places enveloped her in the same manner, shared the same vibrations. Though each occupied a different patch of time and space, they apparently shared an energy frequency.

Could this explain how she'd closed her eyes in one century and opened them in another?

Francesca drew in a slow, deep breath, grasped the pew before her, and closed her eyes. Experience had taught her that most answers were available to anyone brave enough to listen.

A low hum rushed through her ears. She recognized it as a chord, a dense structure of individual notes layered one atop another. She tentatively studied them. They seemed constructed of constant movement, though they possessed no apparent beginning or end. She suspected that if one could escape the physical boundaries of the mind, these notes—bands of energy—could be ridden like waves straight into any location whose frequency they shared.

This, then, was the ticket back to her body, the way home to Baltimore.

Her eyes flew open. Regaining her body would be like incarceration in a full-body cast. How unfair to have to settle for the limitation of physical form after tasting the freedom of existence without it!

But she had little choice here. She couldn't desert Kat, Stephen, and the children now.

She pushed away her misgivings, once again closed her eyes, and braced herself to slip into the next level of consciousness.

A glittering whirlpool of light sucked her through its vortex. Warm, fragrant air caressed her cheek. She felt herself lifted, then tumbled over and over until the light burned seamlessly and she couldn't tell whether she floated upright or upside down.

She lost all sense of time. She certainly didn't care; this delicious feeling could last forever, as far as she was concerned.

Then, with no warning, all movement stopped. Francesca went limp, as relaxed and sun-drenched as if she'd just washed up on the hot pink sands of a tropical beach. She knew that her fantastic journey was finished, that she'd landed back among the living in Baltimore.

With a small sigh of regret, she opened her eyes.

The cold stone wall of the medieval chapel met her surprised stare.

Her jaw dropped. What on earth could this mean? If she'd reached this era through an identical twenty-first-century frequency band, she should have been able to return through the same door. Why hadn't it worked?

The creak of hinges jarred her from her reverie. Voices floated through the opening church door. From instinct rather than necessity, Francesca ducked behind the pew.

A tall woman clothed in emerald green glided into the chapel. Strands of bright red hair escaped from beneath her wimple and strayed across her furrowed brow. Francesca recognized the man who followed her as Gregory, the priest she'd seen earlier. His gaze never left his companion as he tugged the chapel door shut behind him.

"It cannot go on." The woman's low, husky voice was as musical as a voice could be without actually singing.

Gregory's brows lowered as he crossed his arms against his chest. "You're right, Alys. It cannot."

"She must leave Saint Etheldreda's at once." Alys paced a few steps away, then turned in a swirl of skirts to face the priest.

"*He* must leave Saint Etheldreda's at once!" Gregory drew himself up to his full height.

Safely hidden behind the pew, Francesca took stock of the situation. Gregory's tonsure and coarse brown robe marked him as a man of the Church. Alys apparently resided at this convent—Saint Etheldreda's, was it? She spoke as if she might even have some authority here. Yet this confrontation between priest and woman felt more like a lovers' quarrel than anything else.

"Alys." Gregory's voice grew gentle. "Isobel is to be pitied. She is but a child, and a mute one at that. She has neither the wits nor the strength to protect herself from the influences of that vile boarder you've allowed into your midst."

"She is not a child!" Alys snapped. "She wouldn't even be here had my brother found a wealthy lord willing to wed her. Furthermore, I suspect she is possessed of both wits and strength in abundance. She goes her way as she sees fit, Gregory, and that will never do."

He plowed forward with the unstoppable force of a boulder shoved loose from the top of a hill. "Still, Alys, it is Hugh who must go. You know this."

Alys turned a straight back to him and strode away.

Francesca stifled a gasp. The Hugh they spoke about so freely was Asteroth.

She watched as Gregory stroked his chin with his hand. He studied Alys carefully, clearly pondering her mood and wondering what method would best douse the fire. Francesca had once read that the eyes were the windows to the soul. It had seemed a pretty sentiment at the time, but not a very realistic one. Gregory, though, proved the maxim. She could read his heart in his dark, brown eyes. Here was a man so deeply in love that he could never escape it.

He took a tentative step forward. "Alys." A twisted expression flickered across his face. He quickly mastered it. He straightened, then extended a beseeching hand. "Alys. Your boarder is comely to look upon. He surely brings you a sweet taste of the world you left behind. Can it be that you feel . . . a tenderness . . . toward him?"

She did not turn, but answered in a low, steady voice. "How very little you must think of me, and of yourself as well. Hugh distorts the air he breathes, perverts the very ground he walks upon. See? He has even caused you to doubt my love for you, a love as constant and predictable as the cycle of the seasons."

He fairly flew across the floor to gather her into his arms. Francesca obligingly averted her eyes as they kissed. She had been correct all along: people did share universal needs and yearnings, no matter what the trappings of their lives.

"He must not come between us," Gregory said quietly. "We cannot allow it."

"No." Alys leaned her head against the rough fabric of his robe.

"We can only resolve this together, my dearest heart."

"Then, Gregory, you must come to me as a man, not as a priest. You must be first my beloved, then the bishop's envoy. Can you do this?" She backed away from the circle of his arms and captured his gaze with her own. Francesca wondered how any man could escape the pull of those luminous gray eyes. Alys, more beautiful than ever in this moment of vulnerability, inspired an overwhelming desire to protect.

Gregory lifted her chin with a gentle hand. "I am yours, God help me."

"Good. Hear me well, then, for our time together surely grows short. Isobel must leave."

"But Hugh is the one who—"

She interrupted with a firm finger against his lips. "Yes, Gregory, Hugh must go as well. But Isobel is the reason he has come here. Can you not see this?"

"Why would he come for Isobel?"

Alys shivered. "I cannot say. It doesn't even seem possible, yet I think it must be so. She knows him, Gregory. She knew him before she came to Saint Etheldreda's."

He hesitated. "Perhaps they forged an alliance before she came to you. Mayhap he followed her. Surely if he compels her to his side, we may be certain it is not her conversation he craves. But if you banish Hugh and shelter Isobel, such nonsense will surely end."

Alys shook her head. "There is more to this, though I can't say what. Please, Gregory. Isobel must quit this place. The thought of her chills me."

Gregory cast a furtive glance toward the chapel door, then once again pulled Alys close. "You're trembling."

She melted into his arms. "I'm frightened," she whispered, and the startled expression on Gregory's face told Francesca that this proud woman had never before uttered those words aloud.

"You are not superstitious," he chided.

"No. And this is why you must heed me. You know as well as I that no vocation brought me to Saint Etheldreda's. I am here for my father's convenience and can lay no claim to a blameless life. Still, I believe that the Creator in great kindness walks with me and cares for me. My very prayers are infused with worry these days, Gregory. Something is amiss. I feel it in every breath I take."

Francesca did not doubt this. Asteroth was a creature of darkness who could sow only evil wherever he traveled. She remembered Isobel as the young blond she'd observed earlier. Mute or not, she'd certainly managed to communicate. The insolent tilt of the girl's head as she strode through the courtyard, the upward thrust of her breasts and the seductive sway of her hips were a sexual invitation to any man. Hugh, however, was no man. If he was drawn to this young woman, there had to be another reason. Francesca agreed more with the troubled Alys than with the gentle priest who loved her so. Something was seriously amiss. Unfortunately, she could not deny an additional truth: the danger ran deeper than Alys could ever imagine, and its root did not rest in the physical world.

Francesca rested her fingertips on the floor and flattened herself against the back of the pew as Alys and Gregory walked down the center aisle toward the back of the church. The hem of Alys's skirt brushed across the top of her right hand. The delicate scent of lavender wafted by as the two passed.

They stopped midway down the aisle.

"You must send a letter to your father, Alys," Gregory said. "Tell him to fetch Isobel, for you will keep her no longer."

"He will not come."

"But you are prioress here.

"I have been ever easy for him to ignore."

Francesca leaned out into the aisle so that she could better hear the conversation. She caught the small smile that played about Gregory's mouth as he reached for Alys's hand.

"I could write the letter for you, but I'm afraid I must break your heart and do it as the bishop's envoy."

Alys was not too distraught to recognize the irony in his words. A full smile broke across her face, making her look at least ten years younger.

"Only for the letter, Gregory," she said. "Then I must have you back."

This time, Francesca did not turn away when they kissed. She slowly stepped into the aisle, gathering every clue she could. Alys and Gregory were in the presence of a greater evil than they knew, and Isobel seemed pivotal to that danger. Francesca could no longer afford to meditate in the chapel, waiting for an illuminating stroke of inspiration to spur her onward. There was too much to learn, and God only knew how much time she had.

A sharp cry roused her from her own concerns. She quickly turned toward the priest and the prioress. Gregory leaned toward Alys, his arms the only barrier between her and the floor.

Alys stared straight ahead, eyes wide. Her right hand covered her open mouth. All color drained from her face.

"Gregory!" she gasped, pointing a shaking finger.

Confused, Gregory obediently followed her stare.

"Alys, my darling, there is nothing to see!"

Francesca pulled in a sharp breath.

The prioress's finger pointed straight at her.

"Please." Francesca extended a hand toward the prioress. "Don't be afraid."

Alys blanched the color of oyster shell. "Don't talk to me!" She ripped herself from Gregory's protective grasp and dashed from the church.

Gregory stared, desperate to see whatever Alys saw. His shoulders slumped in defeat as he turned and hurried toward the door.

# 11

SOMEBODY HADN'T SHUT THE BATHROOM FAUCET ALL THE way. Kat tugged her feather pillow over her ears in an effort to block out the steady rhythm of water smacking porcelain. It was only a drip. How could it burrow so deeply into her consciousness that it actually gained the power to keep her awake? What was this, the aural equivalent of "The Princess and the Pea"? She slammed her pillow back behind her head, then propped herself up on both elbows to take stock.

The bedroom remained shrouded in soft shadows of gray. All was still, and rightfully so. The bedside clock that Stephen insisted on setting twenty minutes fast read 2:15 A.M.

Her gaze traveled to her husband. Stephen always looked so peaceful when he slept. The lines on his forehead and around the corners of his mouth relaxed. With his thick hair brushed away from his face, he seemed innocent, even vulnerable. Kat usually envied his ability to sleep so soundly. Tonight it simply drove her crazy. She begrudged him every second of sweet rest.

She'd worked downstairs at the kitchen table until well past midnight, mapping out an opening statement that she'd probably never use. Trial was due to begin this morning, but opposing counsel had called her office at six o'clock last night, hinting that his bear of a client might settle. That raised mixed emotions. While it was always great to see a case go away, this stupid matter had consumed her life for days. It had allowed very little time for communication with anyone outside of legal circles, including her own family. There had to be some way to justify her absence when everyone needed her so. She ached to stride forcefully before a jury, translating her frustration into righteous indignation against the opposing party.

The case had also provided a welcome buffer against the reality of Aunt Frannie, who lay unmoving in the guest room down the hall. Kat swallowed hard. No, she wasn't quite ready to kiss this case good-bye.

She shivered. Winter had rolled in with a blast the day before. Earlier in the evening, the chill had invigorated her. Now the frost settled directly into her bones. She pushed her arms back under the quilt and molded her body against the warmth of Stephen's. He gave an obliging snore as he draped a dead arm across her.

This was it. If she couldn't fall asleep now, wrapped in her husband's embrace while the glow of a full moon flooded the bedroom, why, she'd never fall asleep.

She'd never fall asleep. The drip intruded again, wedging itself into her brain with the subtlety of a buzz saw.

Kat bolted upright. Stephen's arm dropped to the pillow. She glared at him, willing him to awaken and share her misery. He merely rolled over, looking even more comfortable than he had before.

She hauled herself out of bed, reached for her bathrobe, and stormed out of the room.

They had bought this house for a song over fourteen years ago, back in the days when rehabbing a handyman's special still sounded like fun. Kat remembered her brand-new wedding ring glinting in the sun as she and Stephen sanded the wide wooden planks of the gracious front porch.

"We're nuts," Stephen had said, running a hand through hair still paint-speckled from their last project. "We're busy people, Kat, way too busy for this sort of thing. Besides, we'll never need a house this big. What were we thinking?"

"We weren't," she'd replied, not adding that "not thinking" had been a vast improvement over the past year, when most of her tired thoughts had been sucked back to the surreality of their clash with Asteroth. She'd learned that nightmares could be far more real than the sunny, solid house she and Stephen had just purchased.

She'd expected that horrible day at Tia Melody's to remain seared across her mind for all eternity. Somehow, though, she'd gulped back her terror and forged ahead. She'd had to. How else did one rebuild a life after all perceptions were shattered?

It had taken some time to emerge from the shadowlands. When she finally had, she'd been only half surprised to find Stephen waiting for her. Only he could understand what she'd experienced; he'd experienced it, too. He, too, had risen from the ashes determined to re-create a viable existence. After all they'd endured together, she'd recognized him as the only man she wanted to keep forever.

Now she allowed a tiny ray of pride to penetrate her foul mood as she neared the offending drip. Despite the constant demands of dual careers and parenthood, they'd done a good job renovating both this house and their lives. She was glad that Stephen's opulent taste had prevailed over her own frugality. The rich, red oriental runner blunted the cold of the dark wood hallway floor. Antique angel sconces threw soft, benevolent light against cream-colored walls. The delicate scent of orange and clove wafted from a small mahogany table, where an antique Chinese bowl sat filled with potpourri.

They'd worked damn hard to rebuild a normal world. How dare anyone try to destroy it now?

She stepped over the sleeping dog, entered the bathroom, and savagely yanked the cold-water spigot shut. Why couldn't life be more like a faucet, releasing information a little bit at a time? Perhaps she could deal with it, then. A drip of memory here, a drop of present reality there, turn it off when you'd had enough . . . she'd figure out a solution to each little particle in turn, just as she dissected each issue in a lawsuit. Then she'd present a solid defense, calculated to decimate any force of reason thrown her way.

Except that the forces opposing her had nothing to do with reason. She'd had to admit that three days ago in Aunt Frannie's hospital room, when even her logical, compartmentalized mind could no longer block the unbelievable truth: Asteroth was back.

She wandered out the bathroom door, bending to scratch Rosie behind the ears. The chocolate lab opened one eye and halfheartedly licked her hand before once again surrendering to sleep. Dogs and men had a lot in common.

She hesitated outside the guest room door. Aunt

Frannie rested here, peaceful in the old four-poster that dominated the room. Kat still didn't understand the peace. She was not a romantic at heart and seldom picked up vibrations anywhere. This guest room, however, had suddenly become an exception. She could feel that the room had changed once Aunt Frannie entered it. Before, it had been a pretty guest room, neat and somewhat sterile in the way that seldom-used rooms are. Now a nearly tangible blanket of peace transcended the ordinary nature of the place.

If she let herself, Kat could remember other occasions permeated by this core of serenity and joy. She'd felt it in certain church sanctuaries, had been nearly overwhelmed by it during her own wedding ceremony. It had visited on and off throughout her pregnancies and immediately following the birth of each precious daughter. Its message then, as now, was that all was well.

That was the part she really didn't understand. All was *not* well. Aunt Frannie remained motionless in that bed, a small half smile on her face, a touch of rose on each pale cheek. Yet even the intrusion of medical equipment could not dim the feeling that everything was under control.

With a deep sigh, Kat pushed open the door and entered the room.

Aunt Frannie, of course, had not moved. At least she appeared comfortable. Watching her, Kat could almost forget the tubes and monitors invading her aunt's privacy. It was as if Francesca's body simply didn't follow the rules anymore. Indeed, even though Kat and Stephen had adamantly refused a feeding tube, Aunt Frannie continued to look well nourished and comfortable. Kat did not share the day nurse's amazement at this. It no longer surprised her that Francesca's condition defied medical explanation. She knew without a doubt that her aunt's state owed very little to physical reality.

She settled into the oversized armchair at the head of the bed, tucking her cold feet beneath her.

"Oh, Aunt Frannie," she said quietly. "How am I supposed to figure out what to do next?"

Francesca didn't move. Kat reached out to grasp her aunt's hand. The fingers felt warm and smooth to the touch.

"Mom?"

The unexpected voice made her jump. She turned to see Julia framed in the doorway, nightgown diaphanous in the soft hallway light.

"Julia! Are you all right?"

Her daughter shrugged. "I couldn't sleep."

"Come sit with me." Kat extended an arm. Julia hesitated briefly before skimming across the floor to wedge herself into the chair beside her mother.

Kat smoothed her daughter's hair. Her own mother had died years before she herself had reached her teens, but she'd heard more than her share of horror stories regarding adolescent independence. Thank heavens Julia still required parents.

"How is Aunt Frannie?" Julia asked.

"The same."

"Do you think she'll stay this way forever?"

"Nothing stays the same forever, honey. I just don't know what will happen next."

Julia studied Francesca. Kat watched her daughter's expression melt from fear to sadness. There was so much that needed to be said, whole portions of the past that she and Stephen had kept from their children in deference to their childhoods. But Julia, on the brink of young womanhood, was rapidly leaving her child days behind. With a twinge of guilt, Kat wondered if Francesca had been right. Perhaps she and Stephen should have long ago prepared their daughters for the fact that the world encompassed more than they could see and touch.

Julia licked dry lips. "What does the doctor say?"

Kat sighed. "He's baffled, and rightfully so."

"Rightfully so?"

"I don't believe this is a physical ailment, Julia."

Julia's eyebrows rose. Kat restrained herself from downloading every scrap of information swirling through her head. Instead she wrapped an arm around her daughter and pulled her close.

"Aunt Frannie has always been something of a mystic, honey. She . . . we . . . have a history of dealing with . . . forces of spirit. Anything can happen when you do that."

Julia looked confused. Kat didn't blame her.

"Julia, Aunt Frannie was deep in meditation when she lost consciousness. I think this is a spiritual state, not a physical one."

Julia's gaze returned to her great-aunt. "You mean, like an out-of-body experience?"

Kat hadn't thought of it quite in that light before, but now that Julia said it, it occurred to her that this was exactly what she meant. Francesca's body was here, but the essence of her spirit was definitely elsewhere.

"Yes," she said, relieved that her daughter had been

able to provide a definition for what she herself thought true.

"Where do you think she is?" Julia asked, as calmly as if she'd inquired when dinner might be served.

Kat shook her head. "I don't know. I could kick myself, too. Fact is, I've been so busy these past few weeks—"

"Months," Julia inserted flatly.

Kat ignored her. "I've been so busy that I haven't had the luxury of a decent conversation with any of you. Perhaps if I'd taken the time, I would have learned more about Aunt Frannie's focus."

They sat quietly for a moment, the stillness of the room broken only by the ticking of the clock on the dresser.

"Mom." Julia's voice sounded loud in the silence. "What did you mean about spiritual forces?"

"Aunt Frannie has always tried to view life through spiritual eyes. That means she doesn't always see the physical world as most people do."

"You said 'we.' "

"Yes." Kat looked away. "I meant your father and me."

The words carried the same impact as the childhood discovery that teachers do not live at school. Julia obviously couldn't decide whether to snicker or be appalled.

"Oh," she finally said, her tone more indulgent than anything else. Kat remembered the teenage propensity toward thinking of oneself as worldly and sophisticated as could be, while parents are unenlightened bumpkins with the life experience of lollipops. She knew at once that her daughter defined parental spiritual journeys as forays into irregularly scheduled masses, with the occasional racy trip to a Protestant church on the side. It irked her to be perceived as so one-dimensional.

She chose her words carefully. "I can't go into everything right now, but we'll need to talk about it soon. Just believe me, Julia. Aunt Frannie's viewpoint hasn't been as wrong as I wish. The reality she recognized is a lot more powerful than the physical one we handle most comfortably. Unbelievable evil exists. I should know. I battled it."

"You did?"

"I did. And I learned that evil is ingenious. It can come cloaked in extreme beauty. It can play on your fondest desires. Before you know it, you've been promised the answer to your deepest longing. Riches, romance, excitement . . . evil will sneak into your consciousness and offer whatever you want at no apparent cost."

Julia's fingers tightened around her mother's arm. Kat restrained herself from loosening the painful grip.

"Mom," Julia started in a tentative voice, "have you ever had super-realistic dreams? You know, the kind where you're not sure whether you're asleep or awake?"

"Yes. I'm not sure that everything you experience while asleep is a dream, though."

It was hard to tell in the dim light, but she thought she saw her daughter blanch.

"Um . . . what if those dreams kind of happen when you're awake?" There was a red-flag edge to Julia's voice.

Kat leaned forward, searching her daughter's face for clues. "What do you mean?"

Julia's expression clouded. She blinked rapidly, as if

a series of images were flashing before her eyes and she couldn't decide which ones were safe to share. Finally, her gaze met her mother's.

"Nothing," she said, and Kat slumped back in disappointment.

"Are you sure, honey?"

Julia rose stiffly from the chair. "I guess I should try to get some sleep. I have a French test tomorrow. Are you going to stay in here all night?"

"No. Just a few more minutes."

Julia wiped her palms against her nightgown. Kat wondered why her daughter's hands were perspiring in the first place.

"Hey," she said as Julia reached the doorway. "I love you, Julie. Will you remember that?"

Her daughter nodded, then slipped away from view.

# 12

ISOBEL LOVED THE NIGHT, WHEN FAMILIAR LANDSCAPES cloaked themselves in darkness and daylight expectations disappeared until the sun rose. Her spirit soared at night. She could roam the earth at will under benevolent darkness, with no one to appraise her actions and tell her how lacking in humility they were.

Of course, she had to admit that nobody had hounded her today, or even the afternoon before. Although the sun had shone bright and hard over Saint Etheldreda's, the rhythm of the day had been set askew. The church bells had tolled the canonical hours as usual. Meals had been placed on the table at dependable times. Aunt Alys, however, had failed to appear. Instead the bishop's envoy, that wan Father Gregory, had appeared in the refectory doorway during supper. He'd requested that the sisters pray for Madame Alys, who'd taken to her bed with a mysterious malady.

Isobel's broth-sopped bread had actually stopped halfway to her mouth as she'd noticed a look of glee flash across Dame Margaret's rheumy face.

"Oh, Father Gregory, our prayers are ever with our dearest Madame!" Dame Margaret's voice had risen with excitement. "And you may surely depend upon me to assume the prioress's duties in her absence. But whatever could be wrong?"

Father Gregory had simply nodded his acknowledgment of her words and disappeared into the shadows beyond the doorway. His exit had left the nuns free to babble. What ailed their usually hale prioress?

Isobel had blocked their chatter from her ears. She herself had been the subject of too many waggling tongues to pay much heed to what was said about others. Besides, she cared nothing about the workings of the priory. Let these silly chickens squawk amongst themselves over the handful of grain Father Gregory had tossed them. She had weightier matters to ponder.

She did not care if Aunt Alys stayed tucked away out of sight for weeks. Kin or no, she thought the prioress haughty and cold. The less seen of her, the better. What bothered her more was that Hugh, too, had rendered himself invisible.

Their last encounter had left her yearning for him, aching for the moment he would once again reach for her. She had expected that moment to come sooner rather than later. She wasn't a child. She'd recognized the power of Hugh's desire, known that he'd wanted to take her as much as she'd wanted to be taken.

It had taken a great deal of effort to banish the fear that the strength of his passion might kill her. Now the thought of her own weakness embarrassed her. That fear had most likely been born of utter innocence, for surely any woman could reclaim innocence in the face of Hugh's overpowering lust. He was far more commanding than any man she had ever known. Before the heavens, his power had even commanded her voice to obey.

She'd awaited his summons all of yesterday and most of this day as well. As the afternoon shadows lengthened, she'd slipped through Saint Etheldreda's gate to knock on the guesthouse door. Only an ashen silence had met her ears. No trace of sound echoed from within, not the supple tones of Hugh's recorder, not even the scrape of stool legs against the hard-packed dirt floor. She'd felt the emptiness sink deep through her core as all hope drained away.

But now it was night. Quiet, steady breathing filled the priory dormitory as the nuns slept the few hours between divine offices. Rising quickly, Isobel drew her mantle over her shift and padded on bare feet out the dormitory doors.

She skittered across the silent courtyard, stopping midway to glance over her shoulder. Curious. Silent eyes seemed to follow her every move, though she could see by the light of the bright moon that she stood quite alone. She shivered in the fair, mild night.

Her lips curved upward as she noticed the soft glow of candlelight in the guesthouse window. Hugh was there! Did he drown in thoughts of her? Did his arms ache to again press her tightly against his chest? She could not allow herself to even think of touching him—her legs would wobble so badly that they'd never carry her into his embrace.

Swallowing against the flutter of her stomach, Isobel raced toward the priory gate and tugged at the handle.

It held fast.

Confused, she pulled again.

It was locked.

Outraged, she stamped her foot. Who possessed the gall to imprison her? Was it Dame Margaret, pompous and vigilant in her masquerade as prioress? Isobel wrapped each small hand around an iron bar and shook with all her might. The steadfast gate did not even rattle.

Had Father Gregory trapped her in this fashion? Father Gregory, who carried on his slightly bent shoulders the bishop's belief that the nuns of Saint Etheldreda's required every ounce of aid to gain salvation?

She stared at the guesthouse. She did not even possess a voice to call her beloved to her rescue. This new wave of frustration welled unchecked within her. Like a caged animal, she pulled herself along the length of the fence until she drew even with the guesthouse window.

He was there—her beloved, her savior from this hideous, empty world. She pressed her face against the bars, longing for the magic to change her shape and slip through the barrier.

Oh, how beautiful Hugh was. He sat slumped at a small table, eyes fixed on the candle burning at the center of it. His fair hair glowed in the dim light of the room. A thin band of gold encircled his head. Isobel drank in his chiseled profile, drawing a sharp breath as her eyes rested on the mouth that yesterday had pressed so insistently against her own.

He wore a white tunic bound tightly at his narrow waist by a hunter green sash. His hose were also hunter green, and his feet were clad in soft leather. He'd draped a gray wolf skin across his shoulders, as soft and clean an animal skin as Isobel had ever seen. She longed to run her fingers through the fur almost as much as she longed to run them through Hugh's hair.

She watched him grip the metal goblet before him. The muscles in his arm bulged as he lifted it to his lips.

Isobel stared, mesmerized by the motion of his throat as he swallowed.

This time, she would not shy away. She would prove to him that she was his equal in matters of heart and body.

Once again she shivered at the feeling that a silent sentinel observed her every move. She jerked her head to the side, searching for the person she knew was not there. As expected, she saw no one.

Discomfited, she returned her attentions to Hugh. He, too, appeared restless. He had straightened, and now stared toward the guesthouse door. His eyebrows lowered; storm clouds crossed his visage. Isobel pulled her mantle more tightly about her shoulders. If he ever looked at her that way, she'd melt into the earth. She twisted to see what had peeved him so.

There was nothing to see. Could thoughts alone raise such ire?

Hugh leaned toward the door, his voice smoldering in a way she'd never heard. "You!"

But no one had entered the guesthouse.

He rose so suddenly that the stool he sat upon toppled to the ground. His muscled arm swept the goblet from the table, splattering the white wall with droplets of deep red wine.

"Do not provoke me, Francesca. I will crush you!"

Isobel stared as he strode toward the window—her window. Quickly, before she could change her mind, she scooped up a handful of pebbles and threw them at the opening. Hugh leapt backward as they pelted his chest.

"Who does this?" he thundered, and Isobel recoiled at the scowl of rage that crossed his face. They were but tiny pebbles. How sharply could they sting? Hugh looked as if each had drawn a rivulet of blood.

She regained her courage and tossed another handful, taking care to hit the side of the house this time.

Hugh leaned out the window, a growl forming deep in his throat. "Who passes here?"

Isobel extended an arm through the fence bars and flexed her fingers. It took but a second for him to see her in the light of the moon. What was that look upon his face? His anger ebbed, but she could not say he seemed happy to see her. Surprised, perhaps. She had undoubtedly startled all humors from him.

His voice fell leaden in the night air. "You come to me as well?"

As well?

"What do you want?" he demanded.

Was the man daft? Had he no fire in his soul? She did not need a voice to answer his question. She pointed a steady finger in his direction.

He threw a glance over his shoulder, where something held his attention for a minute. "You know so very little, Francesca," she thought she heard him say. "It will lead to your destruction." Then he vanished from the window. She heard the guesthouse door close, and presently he stood before her.

"You should be in bed, Isobel," he said flatly.

She stared up at him. She had never before seen him in the darkness, and she liked it. His eyes did not look so odd in this light. She could take in his features without getting lost in the vastness of his stare. She reached both arms toward him, but he stood just beyond her reach.

"Go to bed," he said, but she shook her head.

His voice rose with exasperation. "There can be no lesson tonight. The time is not right. I will come to you when the time is right."

He seemed distracted, irritated and out of sorts. It was as if whatever ailed the priory ailed her beloved as well. Isobel flattened her body against the bars. This time her fingertips grazed his hard stomach.

He jumped back as if burned. "No, Isobel."

Behind him, the guesthouse door swung open, then slammed shut. Isobel's startled gaze swiveled there. Did she have a rival? Had Hugh taken refuge in the arms of another woman? She stared as hard as she could, yet saw no one. Her questioning gaze turned back to Hugh. He, too, had turned toward the guesthouse. He took a step backward toward the fence.

Isobel reached out and grabbed his hand.

A delicious wave of passion swept over her as her skin touched his. Anxious for more, she tugged him toward her, clinging to his arm with the tenacity of a barnacle.

"No!" Hugh's eyes widened.

But there it was. She had caught him again. Even as his words spoke of resistance, his arm reached through the bars of the fence to pull her close. His breath came in ragged spurts. His hand guided the back of her head until her face pressed against the fence as his mouth searched for hers.

His kisses ignited a white-hot flame within her, but the iron bars hurt as they pressed against her cheekbones. Her hands instinctively flew to his shoulders. She tried to shove him away. Did he truly mean to tug her through the bars?

He drew away from her as if drugged. His eyes glittered in the moonlight as his head lolled backward.

"Is this what you want, then?" His hand tightened against her skull. "Is this the force that parts humans from reason, reduces them to nothing better than howling dogs? Will you so eagerly lose your self for a moment of groveling ecstasy?"

He dropped his hand from her head. She relaxed as he lifted a finger to gently trace the curve of her lower lip. Then his guttural cry cracked the air as he clenched an iron baluster and pulled. The rod peeled away like a wildflower plucked from the damp summer earth.

"Come to me, then!" The bar thudded to the ground. "Come to me, Isobel. Show me what it is to be human!"

His fingers dug into her upper arm. With a mighty yank, he dragged her through the gap in the balustrade. She flew like a rag doll, landing hard against his solid chest. He caught her in his arms just before her rattled balance sent her tumbling to the ground.

Her heart pounded as she stared at his face, searching for the smallest glimpse of romantic ardor. Instead he looked like a starving man ready to dismember the roast pheasant set before him.

"I . . . will . . . harness . . . this . . . force!" His chest heaved between each word.

She began to tremble. She did not understand him. She would never understand him. Worse, she would never understand why she wanted him so, why she yearned so desperately for his touch right up until the very moment he obliged her with it. Once again, her passion melted into terror in the face of this man's hot, musky desire. The woman in her gave way to a girl who longed for the safety of her narrow convent bed.

Hugh fell upon her, knocking them both against the ground with the force of his need.

From the grassy knoll some yards away, Francesca tried to make sense of the scene erupting before her eyes. The girl, only moments ago an open invitation, stared at the man atop her with the wide gaze of the frightened teenager she was. How fortunate that the child saw only the physical, for Francesca could see that there was literally far more than met the eye. The energy of the spirit Asteroth interposed itself against the man called Hugh. A dull red aura emanated from the man's skin. Claws shared space with fingernails. Flames practically leapt from Hugh's empty eyes. A purely corporeal Francesca would have shrunk in horror, but now such a spectacle made sense to her, freed as she was from physical limitations.

Could Asteroth not see this truth?

"You can't take this girl," she called to him.

Hugh's head turned her way. "Leave me!"

Francesca shook her head, trying to make him understand. "Don't you see? Has physical form dimmed your knowledge? You'll kill her. Your energy will be more than she can bear. Perhaps that doesn't matter to you."

He stared at Isobel. The girl had grown rigid beneath him, her skin translucent in the moon's rays. Francesca watched carefully. No love or tenderness crossed Hugh's features, but that did not surprise her. What could evil know of love? Still, something else was at work here. One of Hugh's eyebrows lifted; Asteroth weighed the odds. No doubt about it, this young woman had value to him. For some reason, he needed her.

"I can master humans," he said, hands shaking like an addict in withdrawal. "Surely I can master their hungers as well. It is my right to taste what they taste."

Francesca took a step backward as he once again fell upon Isobel. He was a creature gone mad. His mouth assaulted hers as his frantic hand clawed at her breast. He rocked against her with such intensity that Francesca wondered why the ground did not shake.

Asteroth, great lord of darkness, had overlooked the fact that acquiring a physical body meant taking on physical weakness as well. Had he never once considered that his own will might be undermined by the distortion of human sensuality? Had he really considered this physical form immune from the evil perversions he himself had visited upon mankind throughout the ages? Indeed, Francesca wondered how long the body he occupied could contain such combustible energy. Already the angry red aura blotted portions of the man's pale skin from view. This host body, strained by limitless desire, would never survive the intensity of demonic sexual release.

Good! Asteroth's evil could spread only with the help of human hosts. Perhaps his scheme to reach into the twenty-first century for Kat and Stephen would die along with this body.

But he would kill Isobel in the process. Francesca could not fathom his plan for the girl, but no life was worthless enough to waste in human sacrifice.

A cry of pain jerked her full attention back. Isobel

held a hank of blond hair in her hand. Hugh, purple with rage, stared at her in disbelief. Francesca read hatred in the curl of his lip, in the tightly pulsating muscle of his neck. Still, as long as Isobel's body touched his own, he seemed helpless against the overwhelming tide of his own desire. He reached for the girl's shift, shoving it up until it bunched around her shoulders.

"You will kill her," Francesca repeated evenly.

"Men do not die from this." His hand kneaded Isobel's white body. His head dropped to her breast. Francesca averted her eyes from his long red tongue.

"You are no man," she said.

He lifted his head but did not turn her way. "I am greater than men," he said, wedging Isobel's legs open with his knee. "I will not be denied their pleasures!"

"No." She shook her head. "You are not greater than men. You are neither man nor spirit at this moment, Asteroth of the Crescent Horn. You will succeed only in destroying both the body you have stolen and the body that you need."

His gaze swung her way. His grip loosened on the girl beneath him.

Isobel took immediate advantage of his distraction. With a burst of strength, she rammed her knee into his solar plexus, then shoved him aside. He crumpled to the earth as she scrambled to her feet. Her shift floated back into place as she stared at him, her face a mixture of anger and regret. Francesca watched her slip through the broken fence and flee into the priory courtyard.

Hugh lay curled on the ground. There was nothing in the least otherworldly about the way he gasped for breath. The vivid red aura had vanished. Only a pale, deceptively human form met Francesca's eyes.

He stared up at her with reproachful blue eyes. She gasped, startled by the presence of pigment where none had existed before. But even as she watched, the blue of those eyes quickly reverted to black.

"I can never again touch her," he said, voice as empty as his eyes.

Francesca shook her head. "No. You are helpless where she is concerned. You can't control the lust she inspires within you."

He weakly beat the earth with a half-closed fist. "But I am Asteroth of the Crescent Horn!"

He looked like a man, but Francesca knew better. He sounded like a beaten child, but there was nothing childlike in his twisted soul.

Unless . . .

Was anyone beyond redemption?

A ripple of cold raced through her. Without a word, she turned and fled for the safety of the chapel.

# 13

STEPHEN PEERED INTO THE LARGE POT SIMMERING ON ONE OF Angel Café's front burners. The savory aroma of beef stew teased his nostrils. He closed his eyes. A small smile twitched at the corner of his mouth. He seldom had the opportunity to cook in the restaurant these days, but some deep-seated need had compelled him into the kitchen that morning to whip up a lunch special. Outside, snow flurries scattered through the air, lightly covering the grassy strips beside the sidewalk. Inside, steam from the stew pot laced the kitchen windows and filled the room with memories of home-cooked meals.

Stephen's black eyebrows drew together in a frown as he reached for a ladle. What the hell was he doing? Angel Café had not gained its prestigious reputation by serving rib-sticking, down-home food. He preferred guests to leave the restaurant with images of romance floating through their heads, not with thoughts of loyal dogs and dumplings. His first chance in eons to cook for the restaurant, and the best he could deliver was a dish worthy of his great-aunt Martha's farmhouse kitchen.

He dropped the ladle into its ceramic holder. Gravy splattered the counter.

"Yum!" Rachel, the waitress he'd hired just two

weeks earlier, closed her eyes and drew in a deep breath. "That smells terrific, Mr. Carmichael."

"Needs something," he mumbled, trying to think of an herb that might lift this dish from the humdrum ordinary and transform it into something more acceptably avant-garde. Basil, maybe? A pinch of marjoram?

"Oh, no!" Rachel's blue eyes flew open. "Don't change a thing. It's perfect. It reminds me of winter days in my grandmother's house."

Wonderful. But then, what had he expected from Rachel, who was as pert and blond and freckled as a *Brady Bunch* kid? Stephen winced. Rachel was just another indication of how far down the food chain he'd slipped. She was competent and pleasant, but he'd always hired his waitstaff with half an eye toward what they could add to the ambience of the dining room. He'd usually gone for the exotic, the esoteric, the downright ethereal. Slam a cowboy hat on Rachel's head, and she'd look right at home chirping, "Want fries with that?"

"Glad you like it," he managed to say, reaching for a towel to wipe his hands.

"Oh, I don't think there's anything about this restaurant I *don't* like," Rachel said cheerfully. "My folks used to take me here when I was a kid, back before you expanded."

"Really?" He tried to remember exactly how old Rachel was. He assumed she was of drinking age, or he wouldn't have hired her.

"Oh, yeah." She grinned. "I was about seven when you opened up. So you see, Mr. Carmichael, I've been a fan for quite some time."

Seven. Younger than Julia. Younger even than Claire. Stephen suddenly felt irreparably old.

"Well," he said, afraid that if he said anything more, it would brand him a geezer conjuring up memories of the good old days. He smiled, grateful that the straight white teeth in his mouth were still his own, and ducked out the kitchen door.

He slumped against the dining room wall. Was he losing his touch, becoming an anachronism in his own time? He surveyed the room with a weary sigh, almost expecting to see plush, dusty furniture draped with ancient doilies. No, everything looked as it should. Prisms dangled in each window, sending delicate filaments of light dancing off the creamy walls. The mismatched china looked artlessly elegant. The collection of angel memorabilia he'd long ago dispersed throughout the restaurant assured him that his vision, both commercial and artistic, remained intact.

But he felt so old, so utterly out of it.

Of course he did. His life consisted of work, worrying about his children, work, longing for his wife, work, worrying about Francesca, and more work. He was as used up as a dried winter leaf.

He stared at the ceiling. If he was going to have a midlife crisis, couldn't he at least have a less stereotypical one?

"Hey."

The voice jarred his reverie. He looked across the room to see Kat at the dining room entrance.

"Hey, Stephen," she said. "You look farther down than the dumps actually go."

Thank God she was alive, one vibrant particle in a world he felt atrophying about him. For some reason she wasn't dressed in her professional uniform of suit and heels. Instead, she wore jeans and boots. He caught a glimpse of a soft red sweater peeking out beneath the collar of her navy winter coat. Her hair, freed from its businesslike chignon, trailed down her back and to her waist. She looked so very much like the young woman he'd married fifteen years ago that he had to smile.

"Um . . . well, Kat, it seems I wandered into the kitchen this morning to create a lunch masterpiece and . . . uh . . . came up with a yummy batch of homey beef stew."

Her eyes widened. "Oh, Stephen," she breathed, and he could tell that she wanted to laugh. He didn't blame her; he wanted to laugh, too.

"It's over," he said sheepishly. "That debonair man-about-town who originally caught your eye is gone. Just make sure you lay out my slippers and pull my rocker extra close to the fire tonight."

"I hated that debonair guy," Kat said. "I like the good-hearted family guy who came after him."

They smiled across the room at each other. God, he missed her. Somehow, between crazy work schedules and Frannie's illness, they seldom managed to be in the same place at the same time. Even the nighttime had suffered. In the past, no matter how busy and fractured the day had been, Stephen could always count on a few hours snuggled against his wife in the safe harbor of their bed. Now Kat rose in the middle of each night to sit with Aunt Frannie. He wondered what thoughts taunted her there. He kept meaning to ask, but she always crept back to bed just after his alarm went off at 4:00 A.M., and she was asleep by the time he emerged from the shower.

"Long time, no see," he said, wondering how the

most important part of his life had become the part to which he paid the least attention.

She nodded her acknowledgment, then held out a hand. "Come."

He weaved through the tables to reach her side. Her hand, when he grasped it, was warm and confiding. He brushed a kiss against her lips, then took a step backward to appraise her.

"Vacation day?"

"First of many." She squeezed his hand. "I've taken a leave of absence, Stephen."

A leave of absence? Kat? This was the woman who'd returned like clockwork after each maternity leave, who allowed accrued vacation days to slip through her fingers like fistfuls of worthless sand. As far as he knew, Kat hadn't taken a leave of absence since . . .

. . . Asteroth.

He tugged at the hand still in his possession. She followed him into the lobby and down the small hallway that led to his office. He propelled her into the wing-backed chair near his desk and squatted at her feet.

"What's up?" he asked.

"Lots." Kat squared her shoulders. He recognized that steely air of determination, although he had to admit that it had been years since he'd seen it. "Julia's English teacher called this morning. She wanted to know if anything's wrong at home."

He looked puzzled. "Wrong?"

"Yes. I mentioned Aunt Frannie, of course. Mrs. Giles sounded instantly relieved that there might be an explanation."

"An explanation for what?"

Kat's gaze captured his. "She wanted to know if we'd noticed any unusual behavior from Julia at home."

Stephen broke their stare. He knew the answer to that one. Neither of them had been home long enough this past week to notice much of anything. There'd been time for the cursory "How was your day?" and "Do you have homework?" but that was about it.

"Damn," he said.

"You bet."

He slowly stood. "So what's happening at school? Julia's a terrific student."

"That's why Mrs. Giles called. She said that Julia's been distracted. Sometimes she'll sit in class with her eyes wide open, yet she seems to be in a dream world. This morning the bell rang at the end of class, and everybody left the room except Julia. She stayed in her chair, staring straight ahead. Mrs. Giles had to shake her a few times to snap her out of it."

For a moment, the only sound in the office was the loud ticking of the antique desk clock.

Kat's tight voice broke the silence. "I won't have it."

Stephen began to pace. "Of course not. We'll talk to Julia tonight, remind her that school is the most important—"

"That's not what I mean."

He turned to stare at her. Her back was rigid. Her hands clenched the chair arms so tightly that each knuckle blanched white.

"Put on your armor, Stephen," she said in a low voice. "This is war."

His heart thudded to his toes. She had not spoken like that in years, not since the battle with Asteroth.

Once, donning spiritual armor had made perfect sense. With the passage of time, however, the whole idea of unseen warfare had dimmed into memory alongside myth and fairy tales.

Kat's voice cut like a knife. "Do you hear me? This is war. I will not allow Asteroth to destroy our children."

Stephen opened his mouth to protest, but the words would not come. He wanted to shout that this situation defied logic and therefore could not exist. Unfortunately, he knew better. Logical or not, he'd lived through it once. Besides, he recognized a profound change in his wife. He suddenly recalled the self-righteous young woman she'd been, ready and willing to barrel forward in pursuit of justice.

His warrior had returned.

"It was different last time, Kat. We had help."

"Then what do you suggest, Stephen? That we roll over and play dead?"

"But Frannie isn't here! I don't see how we can do this without her. Last time we had—"

"—your messages," she finished with the precision of the litigator she was.

He unconsciously massaged the back of his neck. He still didn't know why he'd been the one to receive the spiritual guidance they'd needed last time. It seemed a lifetime away.

"That may never happen again," he said with a sigh.

"Maybe not. But we've got to try."

"We can't do this without Frannie."

Kat pulled herself forward in the chair. "Listen to me. My aunt is a wonderful woman, but she is not magic. She never was. She was born in an ordinary fashion, just like you and me. She lived a normal childhood. She made decisions, lived a life. What she *did* have—does have—is faith: faith in the light, faith that good can prevail over evil. We can do this, Stephen, or God wouldn't have called us to it."

Francesca had used those same words fifteen years ago.

A wave of inevitability washed over him. "You haven't talked this way in a long time."

Her fierce expression cracked for an instant. The catch in her voice went straight to his heart. "Asteroth can't have my baby," she said.

Baby.

The idea caught him off guard. His legs could no longer support him. Shocked, Stephen sank to the top of his desk.

"Kat. You don't think that Julia is the baby Frannie saw in that vision, do you?"

The misery in her eyes told him that the possibility had crossed her mind. "I don't know, Stephen. There's so much I don't know. Please, say you'll help me."

He studied her. He seldom took the time to really look at his wife these days. He knew her face as well as he knew his own, but at that moment, staring into her chocolate-colored eyes, he remembered that his connection to this woman ran far deeper than the marriage license tucked away in their safety deposit box. They'd been brought together against impossible odds, kept together despite their own attempts to escape each other. Against his will, he'd been inordinately blessed.

Help her? As if he could do otherwise. He and Kat were meant to be partners forever. Ultimately, every other distraction could go to hell.

He reached for his phone and buzzed his hostess. "Could you send Laura back, please?"

One of Kat's eyebrows raised.

"Laura can run this place on her own until Nick comes in tonight," he told her.

His wife looked as if the moon had tumbled from the sky. "You're leaving work in the middle of the day?"

He ignored her surprise. "Where do we start?"

"I'm not sure. I guess we should go back to the cathedral."

"Fine." Stephen looked up as a knock sounded on the door. "That's Laura."

"I'll meet you in the lobby." Kat rose from her chair.

Stephen swallowed hard, summoning the guts it would take to relinquish control.

# 14

The most wonderful images drifted across Kat's resting mind: pink-streaked skies and soothing ocean waves, endless blocks of time with no obligations jammed into their corners. She smiled in the rosy land of half-awake, then burrowed farther beneath the soft down of her comforter. How glorious this was. How sweet.

How utterly unnatural.

With a gasp, she bolted upright in her bed. Outside, the sky was indeed streaked with the muted pink of the setting winter sun. The bedroom clock read 5:30—P.M. This was not a moment for peaceful reverie, that was for sure.

What on earth did she think she was doing, napping the afternoon away? She never pulled this irresponsible stuff!

A deep flush overtook her as she recalled exactly how this debauchery had come about. She tugged the comforter up to her chin, trying to ignore all sensations of pleasure as the silky duvet caressed her skin.

A slight indentation remained on Stephen's side of the bed. He'd left a note there: "Gone to pick up the kids—back soon—thanks for a great time."

She crumpled the incriminating paper into a little ball and flopped back against the pillows. She'd married a loon. Oh, well, at least that loon had remembered Julia's afternoon soccer game and Claire's play date. How awful it would have been had *both* parents sunk so far into depravity that neither could spare a thought for the children.

There was no time to marvel at the fact that Stephen had actually remembered the kids' schedules without prodding. The least a reasonable wife and mother could do was have dinner ready for her loved ones when they limped tired and hungry into the house. Pushing through clinging tendrils of sleep, Kat jumped from her bed and dashed across the cold floor in search of clothes.

A fine couple of warriors she and Stephen had turned out to be. So she'd taken a leave of absence from her precious career and he'd somehow torn himself away from the restaurant. That wouldn't do them a hell of a lot of good if they couldn't stay out of bed.

She punched her arms through her sweater sleeves. Battling Asteroth the first time around had been simpler. She and Stephen had disliked each other so intensely that they'd funneled all their energy into the fight at hand.

She tugged a brush through her hair, then leaned forward to study herself in the dressing-table mirror. Wide eyes stared back, luminous enough to make her forget the delicate crow's-feet forming at their corners. Pink cheeks replaced her usual fluorescent-light pallor. She looked great. And what, pray tell, was the message here? That a little sexual satisfaction might go a long way toward curing all her ills? Wouldn't Stephen love that one!

She shook her head, hard. When had this cynical, sarcastic voice taken control of her mind and tongue?

Fact was, this stolen afternoon with her husband had been absolutely wonderful. She just wasn't quite sure how it had happened.

With a sigh, Kat wandered into the hallway, down the stairs, and toward the kitchen.

She and Stephen had left Angel Café that morning with the vigor of seasoned warriors. They'd fought this surreal battle once. They would fight it again and emerge victorious. Stephen had swung their white Volvo into the cathedral's parking lot with the masterful command of a hero who'd never tasted failure.

"What's your plan?" he'd asked as they'd stepped from the car.

Every ounce of bravado had drained from Kat's body as she gazed up at the cathedral's majestic spires. Plan? She was still awaiting confirmation that God was indeed on their side. Wasn't there supposed to be a sign of some sort? A dove, or maybe a rainbow? Even the fluffy white snow flurries of morning had tapered off, leaving only a dull gray sky that occasionally spit forth a flake or two. The oppressive grayness felt like a cloak descending over her head, muffling every thought.

"You're not getting any messages?" she'd asked, struggling to keep desperation from her voice.

"No." Stephen turned up the collar of his coat.

A miserable, damp cold had seeped through Kat's bones as she reached for his hand. Together they'd approached the massive iron doors.

The cathedral had felt more welcoming with Aunt Frannie as their guide. Francesca was someone who spoke the language of this place fluently, who understood the nuances of this lush land. Kat stared up at stained glass, statues, and wall plaques as she and

Stephen drifted back to the Lady Chapel. These details had struck her as interesting pieces of art the last time around. Now the saints seemed accusing, as if they knew darn well that she had no idea who most of them were. She gulped and turned away from the reproving visage of Saint Vincent de Paul. Suddenly it seemed vital that she recollect exactly how he'd spent his sojourn on earth.

Aunt Frannie would know.

She drew closer to Stephen. "This is downright spooky."

"Don't think that way," he said. "It's okay. This is our territory. We belong here."

Kat swallowed hard before entering the Lady Chapel. Was there any place else on earth this quiet? The silence practically boomed. She quickly settled herself into the pew that Aunt Frannie had chosen on their last visit.

"What happened that day, Stephen? You were the one who prayed with Aunt Frannie."

Still standing in the aisle, Stephen hesitated. "I don't know what Frannie did. I only held her hand."

"And?"

He groaned. "Jeez, Kat, you know how it is. Frannie talks about the light and feeling the peace of God, but I have no clue how any of that stuff is supposed to happen. I just closed my eyes and asked God to protect us and keep us safe."

"And?"

"And as a monument to my great effectiveness, Frannie slipped unconscious to the floor. Still think we can do this on our own?"

Her eyes narrowed as they met his. "Got a better

idea?" She slid down the pew and patted the empty space next to her. Stephen sank down beside her.

"Aunt Frannie would tell us to assume that your prayer was heard," she said. "Therefore, we *were* safe. Aunt Frannie *is* safe. We've just got to believe that. Do whatever you did before. I'll ask for help."

"Ask for guidance. And request some discernment while you're at it."

"Discernment?"

"That's what it's called, right? That ability to know whether the instructions you get are actually from God? After all, if you just plug in a TV, who knows what kind of programming will come through?"

She leaned back in the pew, surprised. Stephen's parents had been intellectuals who'd managed to turn every miracle or mystery into a rational event. How on earth had he remembered discernment?

"Okay." She reached for his hand. "I'll do that. Ready?"

"Go." He squeezed her fingers and closed his eyes.

Kat never knew what exactly her aunt saw when she sank deep into prayer and meditation. Anyone could tell by the serene smile on Francesca's face that she always reached a place far away from the maddening chaos of daily life. Kat had often longed to learn the secret of that peace. It seemed impossible. She herself had apparently been born with a Greek chorus instead of a mind. It chattered constantly and never lacked for comments or questions. Even now, as she closed her eyes in the stillness of the Lady Chapel, she could feel words pushing at the soundproof walls she tried so hard to erect around her thoughts.

There was nothing beyond blackness behind her closed lids. Okay. So she and Stephen were willing to do whatever mission was set before them. The only catch was that first they had to figure out what that mission might be.

A steady commentary of gibberish again strained to overrun her mental gates and interrupt her concentration. She gritted her teeth and blocked it out.

Perhaps desperation was not the right mindset for prayer. Still, what else could be expected when spiritual warfare was involved? Warriors could hardly remain passive while the need for protection and guidance clawed at their very core.

The reminder that this was war made her remember her armor. She hadn't looked at it in ages, but its image sprang readily to mind.

She could barely contain her derision. She looked like a too-old actress playing Joan of Arc.

A horde of words piled in after that unfortunate thought. Kat quickly shuttered her mind.

The armor still fit, although it looked far worse than the last time she'd seen it. The silver breastplate had a dent in it. The chain-mail skirt hung in tatters on the left side, as if somebody had repeatedly slashed it with a sword. The once shiny helmet appeared tarnished. At least the sword still gleamed. The amethysts embedded in its hilt glittered in a beam of light whose source she couldn't trace.

Aunt Frannie had sworn by that armor. She'd quoted Ephesians throughout Kat's childhood: "Put God's armor on so as to be able to resist the devil's tactics. For it is not against human enemies that we have to struggle, but against the Sovereignties and the Powers who originate the darkness in this world, the spiritual army of evil in the heavens."

Had Aunt Frannie been wearing her armor when she'd dropped to the floor a week and a half ago?

Kat balled her right hand into a fist and tried to concentrate.

*Please, God, help us!*

Nothing. Only silence.

At least she felt warm and comfortable. Even her feet, so icy only minutes before, felt as if they'd just been propped before a toasty fireplace blaze.

A tingle ran down her left arm and through the hand that rested in Stephen's. His heartbeat pulsed against her skin wherever his hand touched hers. For some reason, those strong fingers entwined within hers seemed the most important part of the room.

She opened her eyes halfway and stole a sideways glance. Stephen's eyes remained closed. She'd forgotten how handsome he was. His nose was fine and straight, his chin still strong. They framed a firm, sensuous mouth that she idly thought she'd ignored for too many days.

Ridiculous! They had work to do.

She jammed her eyes shut.

But not only did the compelling warmth remain, much of it seemed to emanate from her husband. Her thigh touched his as she shifted position on the hard wooden pew. She lingered there, enjoying the solid feel of his body against hers. A small sigh escaped as she allowed herself to melt into his side. Contentment spilled into her.

Stephen's arm enfolded her. She opened her eyes and turned to see him studying her, green eyes quizzical.

Suddenly, more than anything in the world, she

wanted to be a part of him, tucked into his heart and totally inseparable from him.

His fingers traced the curve of her cheek. "Where are your walls?" he whispered.

"Walls?"

"You always keep one or two up, even with me. Where are they?"

She shrugged helplessly as he bent to kiss her. The blue and gold of the chapel swirled about her in an appealing mosaic. She pulled him toward her as if she could never let go.

"Hmm." Stephen gently disengaged her arms from around his neck. "Come home with me, Kat."

Home? Weren't they supposed to be praying? Conquering evil?

But she couldn't protest as he led her from the pew and down the cathedral aisles. She stayed silent during the drive home, barely noticing when Stephen parked the car on the street in front of their house instead of maneuvering it down the narrow backyard alley and into the garage. Before she could even justify it, she'd found herself in bed with her husband, spending the loveliest afternoon she could remember for quite some time.

Now Kat switched on the kitchen light and sighed. Reprobates. That's what they were. How many clues and opportunities had passed them by this afternoon? Such lapses of responsibility never happened when Aunt Frannie was in charge.

Outside, the orange of sunset had given way to dusky blue. The day's clouds had disappeared, and stars began to twinkle in the deepening sky. Kat leaned against the kitchen doorjamb, staring out the French windows, past the garden, and into the night beyond.

She had prayed for answers. Answers hadn't come. Now what?

The automatic garage door whirred open. With a guilty jump, Kat dashed into the kitchen, flung open a cabinet door, and grabbed her largest pot. She'd filled it halfway with water by the time the mudroom door slammed. She pasted a smile on her face and stood in the middle of the kitchen with a jar of generic tomato sauce in one hand and a bottle of red wine in the other. Okay, so it wasn't dinner. It was at least a promise that dinner might appear.

"Mommy!" Claire flew into the room. "You and Daddy are both home at the same time!"

Kat winced. Did her daughter have to make that sound like such a rare occurrence? She bent to drop a kiss on the top of Claire's curly head. Small arms encircled her waist.

Stephen entered the kitchen with what could only be called a smirk on his face. His satisfaction was so obvious that Kat was glad Julia, right behind him, could see only the back of his head.

"What's for dinner?" Julia headed for the kitchen table, depositing her books with a loud slam.

"Julie, how long have you known your mother?" Stephen leaned over Claire's head to plant a long, hard kiss on his wife's mouth. Kat's cheeks grew warm. "Spaghetti," he said as they parted. "Your mother's all-purpose meal."

"You knew I wasn't a cook when you married me." Kat's hands flew to smooth her clothes. His look made her feel downright undressed.

"I didn't think your cooking skills would matter,"

Stephen said in a low voice. "As usual, I was right. Oh, by the way, Julia's team won their soccer game."

"Oh? Oh! Congratulations, sweetie!"

Julia sank into a chair without even a nod of acknowledgment.

Stephen set a shopping bag onto the counter. "Here." He plucked the jar of tomato sauce from Kat's hand and replaced it with a tub of fresh pesto. "Humor me."

This day had been too bizarre for words: hours of uninterrupted time with her husband, a decent home-cooked meal that they would all eat together—a curious peace threatened to invade the kitchen. All was right with the world.

"Get a corkscrew and pour the wine," Stephen instructed as he pulled salad greens, a package of fresh linguine, and a baguette from his shopping bag.

Kat surrendered and opened the silverware drawer. Claire had joined Julia at the kitchen table. Both girls pored over their assignment notebooks.

"Homework?" Kat asked.

Julia rolled her eyes. "Always."

Kat studied her older daughter as Julia reached for a pen. Mrs. Giles's bright blue English Lit book sat on top of the middle-school book pile, a vivid reminder that all was *not* right with the world, no matter how promising the moment had seemed.

There was no point in prolonging the inevitable. Kat pushed the end of the corkscrew into the cork with more force than necessary and squared her shoulders. "Julia, Mrs. Giles called today."

Stephen cocked an eyebrow, but continued to tear lettuce in a steady rhythm. Claire turned the page of her library book. Julia groaned, but her eyes remained glued to her assignment pad.

"What happened?" Stephen asked their daughter, and Kat was grateful for the reinforcement.

A nearly unreadable expression flashed across Julia's face—a thought pondered and discarded. She raised a blank mask to her parents.

"Nothing happened, Dad. Today's class was mega-dull. I dozed off, that's all. Maybe I need more sleep."

Kat stood on tiptoe to fetch the wineglasses. "Mrs. Giles said that your eyes were wide open."

Julia squirmed. "So school's taught me to sleep with my eyes open. It's a gift."

"Julie." Stephen turned to face her. "Sweetheart, this isn't an inquisition. We're on your side. What's going on?"

Julia bit her lip as she stared from her father to her mother. The depth of her pause confirmed Kat's fears that this was no adolescent malaise, no juvenile case of school-itis that could be brushed away with a sarcastic wave of the hand. Whatever was going on, it was a very real chunk of Julia's existence. Stephen's taut expression indicated that he had reached the same conclusion.

Claire's bright giggle broke the silence. "Why don't you just tell them, Julie?" she asked.

Julia shifted uneasily, then sent her sister a sideways glance. "Tell them what?"

"You know. Where you go."

Her eyes widened with surprise. "I don't go anywhere, Claire."

Claire giggled again. "Sure you do. You go to that place where Aunt Frannie is, that place with all the funny ladies in long dresses and the worried man with the hole in his hair. You know, Julie."

Julia stared at her parents, face red. "I don't know what she's talking about."

Kat flattened both hands against the countertop. The room had begun to whirl. "Julia, do you . . . see other places?"

"Not like that!" Julia jerked herself from her chair. "Nothing like that! I don't know what Claire's talking about!"

"We need to talk." Stephen took a step toward his daughter, but she was too fast. She was out of the kitchen by the time he rounded the counter, the only reminder of her past presence the sound of footsteps clattering up the stairs.

Both Kat and Stephen stared in disbelief at their younger daughter.

Claire shrugged her shoulders. "I don't understand her either," she said.

# 15

Julia reserved door slams for those occasions when she felt it necessary to make a point. This was not one of those times. It was enough to clatter up the stairs, leaving her parents openmouthed and clueless in the kitchen below. She raced into her bedroom without even a backward glance. Then, breathing hard, she closed the door with a quiet, controlled click.

How could she have thought for even a moment that Mrs. Giles wouldn't tell her parents about that morning's disaster? Talk about wishful thinking! Right. You're a teacher, and one of your best students blinks out in class, sitting glued to her chair like a first-class jerk while everyone else streams out of the room at the happy sound of the dismissal bell. Sure, a teacher was really going to ignore that one, especially after it took eons to snap the kid back to earth.

Julia leaned her forehead against the cool wood of her door and tried to steady her breathing. Her heart beat so hard against her chest that it actually hurt.

Of course Mrs. Giles had called her parents. And, just the dumb luck, they'd rearranged their overbooked lives to talk it all out with their wayward kid.

A tiny thought fluttered to the edge of her consciousness. Maybe this was a good thing. Maybe it was time to turn to her mom and dad.

No, no, no! She smacked her fist against the door. They'd think she was nuts, and she was definitely *not* nuts. She was riding a creative wave, listening to muses she'd never even known could inhabit her thoughts. Someday she'd turn all these odd ideas into a great story. Who knew? They could be her ticket to fame and fortune.

The growl of her stomach reminded her that more than creativity was at stake here. With a sigh, Julia turned to survey her room. Damn. She hadn't thought this out very well. She'd left everything—her homework, her notebooks, any hope of food—down at the kitchen table. This was not cool.

Obviously, her parents did not plan to charge up here after her. Maybe they'd grill Claire first. Yes, that was it. Her mother the litigator was probably midway through her direct examination, leaving her father to take detailed notes and come up with a cross-exam.

Actually, she kind of wished she could join them just to hear Claire's story. What in the world had her sister been babbling about? Aunt Frannie, hidden away in some secret place that she herself was supposed to know about? Either Claire's imagination was running rampant, or there was far too much sugar in that child's diet.

Her thoughts skipped away from her sister. She felt curiously restless, unsure of her next step.

She'd take a shower. That would do it. Her parents wouldn't dare barge through the bathroom door to interrogate her. A shower would give the situation in the kitchen time to settle before she had to run down and fetch her homework.

Julia groaned, then flopped down against the soft

pillows of her bed. Her head had begun to ache again, that same dull ache she'd experienced this morning in English class. It had felt like no other headache on earth. It had been more contained than most, centered on a spot in the middle of her forehead, as if someone had pointed their finger, aimed, and pushed against her skull with all their might.

Great. Eyestrain. On top of everything else, she probably needed glasses.

The pain had caught her by surprise in Mrs. Giles's class. She'd almost welcomed the familiar tinkling of bells that followed it, as it had provided distraction from what promised to be an awful headache.

Mrs. Giles had been wrapped up in her lecture, so a visit from the blond people had seemed no big deal. Julia hadn't seen them for a while—not since that strange event in Aunt Frannie's hospital room where it had felt for one brief moment as if she could be sucked right into their soap opera.

Perhaps she hadn't noticed the people for a while because she'd felt so unsettled, so totally out of sync with her day-to-day routine. Nothing ran smoothly. Nothing made sense. Why, she'd gone to open a can of soup the other day and spent minutes staring at the can opener in her hand, trying to remember what it was and how it was used. And that wasn't half as unnerving as two days ago, when she'd totally forgotten Claire's name.

She was way too young for Alzheimer's.

So the arrival of the bells in the midst of a boring lecture about *The Awakening* had brought not only respite from dullness, but also a comfortable reminder that her brain could still imagine as usual. She'd come to think of the blond people as story characters. She'd wondered what had passed in their saga since the last time she'd seen them.

A soft breeze had caressed her cheek, a breeze that could not have blown through a closed classroom window. She sat on something hard, although she knew it was not the chair attached to her schoolroom desk.

But, most amazing of all, she'd been suddenly buried in a sea of emotion. Disbelief drenched her, followed quickly by an intractable anger that made her clench her fists.

She couldn't go back to him. She *wouldn't* go back to him! She would ignore his entreaties and snub the gifts he would surely bring to entice her back to those little lessons that so obsessed him. Oh, he'd be back. But this time, she'd resist.

As quickly as it had come, the anger was replaced by a sharp pang of despair.

How could he treat her thus, as if she had no heart, no soul? Had no one counseled him in matters of love? Had his past ladies not taught him that passion need be tempered by pretty words and trinkets?

Hope dawned brightly, pushing despair back into a corner.

But of course! There had been no other ladies! At first thought, that seemed hard to believe. He was so handsome, so glorious to behold. He was neither noble nor courtly, however. Perhaps no woman of position had stooped to forge an alliance with him.

The hope brightened like a candle in the darkness. Indeed, perhaps he himself had discouraged amorous liaisons. Perhaps he'd awaited his twin soul, the one woman in eternity who could complete his heart and take her place as his true consort. Now, having found her, he'd grown so full of longing and passion that he could hardly be expected to take time for niceties.

She could advise him—if she consented to ever see him again.

"Julia!"

And Julia had found herself staring at her own reflection in Mrs. Giles's glasses, half wondering who "he" was, but mostly embarrassed by the fact that she and her teacher faced each other in an empty classroom.

Julia tugged her pillow over her head. And she'd actually thought that Mrs. Giles wouldn't call her parents? She was almost as stupid as that girl who so desperately wanted the guy who treated her like dirt!

That girl? What girl? Was *she* the girl?

Too many thoughts. No wonder her head ached.

She dragged herself to the window. She'd been born here, knew every house, tree, and bush on the street outside. Even blanketed with a thin layer of snow, the scene remained achingly the same. This comforted her. She wanted to immerse herself in the familiarity. For one crazy moment, she longed to be simply Julia Catherine Carmichael, a nice girl with a nice family living in a nice neighborhood. She wanted no more, no less.

She wanted her parents.

Maybe it was time to tell them everything.

If only this headache would go away!

She sat on the edge of her bed, waiting for a break in the pain.

* * *

Kat and Stephen stared at each other. Then, as one, they approached the kitchen table, seating themselves on either side of their younger daughter.

"Claire." Kat placed a tentative hand on the little girl's shoulder. "What were you talking about a moment ago?"

Claire stared at her with round green eyes. Her curls, never neat at best, looked as though she'd spent the day in a wind tunnel. "You mean about where Julie goes?"

"Yes."

"Oh." Claire bounced the eraser end of her pencil on the table. "I don't know where it is, exactly. I was hoping Julie would tell us so that I could find out."

Stephen reached out a hand and stilled the tapping pencil. "I'm not sure Julia knows," he said.

"Oh, she has to," Claire said. "I mean, she's there a lot. You'd think she'd know where she was."

"How about you tell us what you know." Kat pulled her chair closer to her daughter.

"Well . . ." Claire stared at the ceiling. "I can't tell you very much. Wherever it is, there are a lot of ladies in long dresses. There's one in charge, too, a very beautiful lady with red hair. At least, I think it's red. I only see the parts that poke out from under her veil. Anyway, she's friends with this man who has a lot of dark, curly hair—except on the top of his head. He has a little bald spot there."

"I see." Kat took Claire's hand, examining each little finger in turn. "How do you know this, sweetie?"

Claire shrugged. "I just do."

"Do you dream about it at night?"

"No."

"Daydream it?"

"No. Is dinner almost ready? I'm hungry."

Stephen instinctively glanced at the pot on the stove. Steam poured from the top. "Soon, Claire. You said Aunt Frannie was in this place."

"Well, yeah. She is." She said it as if it were the most obvious thing in the world, hardly noticing how pale the information made her mother and how strained it made her father.

"What is she doing there?" Stephen pressed.

"I don't know. I don't see her. I just know she's there."

"*How* do you know?"

Claire looked exasperated now, as if she'd drawn the short straw and landed a set of dunces for parents. "I just know," she said.

Kat could not repress her frustration. "Claire, baby, what else do you 'just know'?"

Her daughter cocked her head, as if listening. "Nothing, really. Except that I think Julie's getting ready to go back to that place again."

"How do you—" Stephen started, but Kat was already out of the kitchen and halfway to the stairs.

# 16

THE CHAPEL DOOR BANGED AGAINST THE WALL. HEART POUNDING, Francesca quickly ducked behind a pew. An embarrassed flush swept from her neck to her hairline. She'd stayed in this chapel for hours after leaving Asteroth, long enough to marvel that the nuns of the priory could glance right through her with total disregard. She'd knelt beside them in prayer, despite the fact that all the prayer in the world seemed unable to obliterate the nauseating memory of Asteroth, not quite human, not quite spirit, crumpled in the dirt at her feet.

Still, even that grainy horror could not change the fact that she remained invisible. There was no reason to crouch in hiding like a criminal.

Cautiously, she allowed herself to peer over the top of the pew. A loud gasp pierced the stillness; she recognized it as her own. For there, just over the threshold, stood the one person at Saint Etheldreda's who seemed able to see her.

The prioress raised her chin and stepped into the room. Wild russet curls tumbled past her shoulders, framing her pale face in a burst of riotous color. Delicate lilac shadows underlined the icy gray of her eyes. A splash of tiny freckles emphasized her ivory skin.

"Are you here, then?" Her husky voice ricocheted

off the stone walls. Francesca drew in a deep, quiet breath.

"I know you are." Alys slammed the chapel door. A burst of air swirled beneath her white linen shift, lifting it to reveal a pair of slender, bare feet. Though the shift was sleeveless, the prioress did not seem chilled. She raised her arms in a gesture of supplication. Her skin glowed like mother-of-pearl in the waning moonlight.

"Show yourself," she whispered. Her arms dropped to her sides as she advanced to the first row of pews. "If you have any mercy within you, spirit, you will show yourself. Whatever can you want of me?" She paused for a moment, considering. "Or perhaps it is not me you want at all."

The creak of door hinges tore Francesca's stare from the prioress's eerie beauty. A hooded figure slipped into the room, closing the door with a click.

Alys turned. Gregory slid the hood from his head. Deep lines etched his forehead and mouth where none had existed before. He reached toward Alys but did not touch her. Francesca could hardly blame him. In the odd half-light of the approaching dawn, Alys seemed made of the most fragile porcelain, ready to break at a moment's notice.

"Sweet Alys." The priest's voice cracked. "You must return to bed."

The prioress studied him. "Do you think me mad?" she asked.

He turned a shade paler but did not avert his gaze.

She grasped his hand. With force that banished any thought of fragility, she raised their entwined fingers to his lips. "Feel my touch, Gregory. Look into my eyes.

You know my heart. Perhaps you even know my soul. Look closely and tell me if you think me mad."

Gregory's troubled gaze rested on their clasped hands. His dark eyes met hers. She held the gaze.

The priest raised his free hand and gently traced the curve of the prioress's cheek. His fingers trailed through her tousled hair and down the soft skin of her inner arm. He cradled her hand in his own, then drew her into his arms.

"You are not mad," he whispered across the top of her head. "I should know if you were. Lord help us, Alys, you are not mad. But what, then, has come upon us?"

"I don't know." The brittle edge left Alys's voice. It was as though she'd found a well of strength in her lover's confirmation of her sanity. "I know only this, Gregory: I have not been God's holiest child, but I have believed and I have trusted. Whatever happens here is in God's hands."

Gregory hesitated. "You do not think this is retribution for our sins?"

Her icy eyes switched instantly to fire. "Sins?"

"Alys, you cannot deny that we have vowed lives of chastity, yet. . . ."

"I think I hear the bishop's voice, although it is his envoy I look upon. No, Gregory. My love for you is the truest part of my life. Would God grant me such a gift and then punish me because I rejoice in it?"

A small smile crossed his face, but Alys did not see it. She had turned back to face the empty chapel.

"Spirit!" she called in ringing tones. "I am neither bad enough nor good enough to merit your attention, so you must simply tell me what you want. Show yourself!"

Francesca stared at the tableau before her. She did not know the prioress, yet she recognized the determined set of her mouth. Gregory, too, had squared his shoulders in anticipation of a revelation he might never see.

She could not frighten these people any more than she already had. Besides, there could be great benefits to making herself known. Asteroth had wedged himself into this era, his spiritual nature undetected in human form. She could not begin to fathom his plan without additional clues. Perhaps Alys, so foreign yet so familiar at the same time, could supply the information so desperately needed.

Slowly, Francesca rose from behind the pew.

Alys's eyes followed her. The prioress stood firm this time, not even shrinking back against the man beside her.

"So," she said quietly. "You are not a creation of my fevered mind."

"No." Francesca dared not move.

"Do you see her, Gregory?"

Gregory squinted as he studied the empty air. "No."

"Then let me tell you what I see." Alys stepped forward. Francesca required every ounce of strength to keep from recoiling. "I do not see this figure clearly, you must understand. She is but an outline, and I can see through her to the wall beyond. But I see a woman of some years, with white hair and foreign clothing."

Francesca stole a glance at her down vest, sweater, and jeans. She had quite forgotten that she wore clothes of the twenty-first century.

But the prioress moved even closer, the reluctant

priest in tow. Now they stood only a few feet away, close enough that Francesca could once again detect the slight scent of lavender that seemed to follow Alys wherever she went.

"The curious part, Gregory, is that she seems quite filled with light." The prioress folded her arms across her chest. "Are you of God, then, spirit?"

Francesca began nodding before the words could even leave her lips. "I am," she said.

"She is." Alys translated for Gregory.

Unsettling as her presence must seem to the prioress, Francesca could only imagine how awful it was for the priest. He was expected to believe in the existence of a woman he could neither see nor touch. Strangely, he remained unfazed. The lines of his forehead had softened. One eyebrow raised, the facial equivalent of a question mark. Apparently, belief in the unseen did not bother him nearly as much as the fear that his beloved's mind had wandered away.

"Her voice is quite clear," Alys said. "I am surprised you can't hear it. Spirit, say more."

"I am not a spirit," Francesca said. "At least, I don't think I am."

Gregory started. "I heard the faintest of chimes. Did she speak?"

Alys nodded and plowed forward. "What are you, then?"

For one of the few times in her life, Francesca felt at a loss for words. "I don't know, exactly. But, please, I think I am here to help, somehow. Evil is here."

"Yes," Alys said. "This I know. Does the evil rest upon Isobel?"

"The young girl? The one who wanders your grounds at night?"

Alys's eyes widened, but she did not lose her composure. "Yes," she said.

Francesca thought for a moment. Something about Isobel certainly held Asteroth fast, like a magnet. "I think it does involve her, although I had not considered that fully. I speak of the one you call Hugh."

Alys blanched. Her hand fluttered to her stomach.

The chapel bells began to toll their deep call to Divine Office. Gregory shook his head as if roused from a dream.

"Lauds, Alys. The nuns will arrive in a matter of minutes."

Her hand gripped his sleeve. "She has news of Hugh, and perhaps of Isobel. I cannot leave now, Gregory."

"You must." He rested an insistent hand on the small of her back. "You are sane, Alys. I have no good reason to believe this, but my faith in God and in you will suffice for now. Still, you cannot be found here dressed as you are, rambling about a being that you alone can see."

Neither woman could refute his logic.

"Go," Francesca urged. "We can't help each other if you are locked away as a madwoman."

Alys allowed Gregory to guide her toward the sacristy door, away from the path the nuns would walk. "Come with me," she called to Francesca.

Francesca's head whirled. Her feet felt leaden. A slight metallic taste filled her mouth at the thought of leaving this haven. "I can't," she said. "I must stay here until I regain enough strength to face . . . what I must."

"We will come to you," Gregory said over his shoulder as he swept Alys from view.

Francesca realized that his faith was perhaps the strongest of the three of them: he saw nothing, yet was willing to believe.

# 17

From the depths of her priory bed, Isobel heard Saint Etheldreda's bells summon her to Lauds. Hours before, she'd actually arrived in the chapel early for Matins, still cold and shaking from her encounter with Hugh. She'd clutched her cloak tightly about her body throughout the psalms and canticles, hoping that nobody would notice she wore only a thin night shift beneath it. She needn't have worried. Most of the nuns disliked her, but they were too drugged with sleep to pay her much mind at that early hour. How fortunate. It would have required far less than Dame Margaret's gimlet stare to see that her shivering was born of more than the chill of the night air.

She did not begin to feel safe again until after tumbling, exhausted, into her narrow bed. There, amid the snores and deep, regular breathing of the nuns, fear had ebbed away, and Isobel could allow herself to review what had happened near the priory gate such a short time ago.

Hugh. Her face flamed scarlet. She could almost feel his rough hand on her breasts, the hard press of his lips against hers. She'd burrowed beneath her coverlet in the hope that curling out of sight might vanquish the memory. Dear Lord, however had he dared? How could he treat her as he might a scullery maid or serving wench? She was not royalty, but she was highborn. Such liberties should bring stripes from her father's whip upon his back.

Shame flooded her, although several seconds passed before she recognized it as such. She did not shame easily, but it seemed suddenly as if all the world were privy to her earlier nakedness and to the sin of her own desire. Hugh had not hunted her. She'd been the one to slip away to his side. She'd enticed him, offered herself up like a succulent strawberry ripe for the picking. Whatever had she expected?

She tore the coverlet from her eyes. This was no fault of hers. She could never have known that Hugh would claw at her like a wild beast!

She couldn't go back to him. She *wouldn't* go back to him. She would ignore his entreaties and snub the gifts he'd surely bring to entice her back to those little lessons that so obsessed him. Oh, he'd be back. But this time, she'd resist.

Resist. Once more, persistent shame intruded. Merciful Mother Mary help her, his touch inflamed her at the same time it repelled her. How was she to quell the blaze without him?

Oh, but how could he treat her thus, as if she had no heart, no soul? Had no one counseled him in matters of love? Had his past ladies not taught him that passion need be tempered by pretty words and trinkets?

Isobel's brow furrowed. Surely he did not whisper sweet words of love into another's small, willing ear. She could not abide the thought that his lips might kiss anyone's other than her own.

Her stomach tumbled.

But, of course! There had been no other ladies!

The hope brightened like a candle in the darkness.

Perhaps Hugh had awaited his twin soul, the one woman in eternity who could complete his heart and take her place as his true consort. Now, having found her, he'd grown so full of longing and passion that he could hardly be expected to take time for niceties.

She could advise him—if she consented to ever see him again.

Gradually, Isobel's ragged breathing had subsided into sleep. Behind her closed eyelids, sharp images of deep chasms and unforgiving fires melted into landscapes of green and yellow meadows and wave upon wave of soothing azure sea. She sighed as golden sun caressed her body.

The bells tolled for Lauds. All about her, the nuns tossed in their beds, grasping for the last threads of sleep before rising. But Isobel's eyes remained closed as she observed the meadow spread before her. The beauty of the scene paled beside the beauty of Hugh, who stood facing her.

"Isobel." His hair glowed nearly white in the sun. His eyes were the deep lapis lazuli she remembered from long-ago dreams. He stood only yards away. She longed to run to him, to fling herself into his embrace. His arms had not opened to receive her, however, and she found herself unable to move.

"You must forgive me," Hugh said, and she wondered if it was not blasphemous for a god to beg forgiveness from his acolyte. "I frightened you tonight. It should not be that way."

Isobel's eyes widened. He had more than frightened her. He had dishonored her, treated her with the highest disdain. She raised her foot, ready to slam it to the ground to show her displeasure. Then she caught his eyes, that beautiful blue so rarely seen these days. Heaven help her, she could happily lose herself in such eyes, melting against his body with a willingness that would allow him any liberty he chose.

She gently returned her foot to earth.

"It cannot be thus." Hugh's voice stroked her. "We have come too far, Isobel. To abandon our mission now would be purest folly. We must return to our lessons."

Once again, raw displeasure flooded her. This was hardly a question of missions and lessons. This was about the love that bonded them together throughout all ages. He should speak about the relentless longing for her that gnawed away at his heart. He should reveal bold plans to abduct her, to carry her away from this horrible place. She dreamed of them sharing their years in a small cottage by a distant sea, but Hugh apparently did not share her vision.

"Look at me, Isobel," he said. She jumped. She had not realized that she'd allowed her gaze to wander. "Understand me well. We cannot touch each other again. Ever."

Her mouth formed an O of surprise. Had he lost his wits?

His fists were clenched. A vein in his neck throbbed as he swallowed hard, then gritted his teeth. Isobel's indignation faded as truth dawned.

How stupid he was. Perhaps he was wise in the ways of his silly lessons. Mayhap those lessons even meant something to his sense of reason. But here, gazing upon him, she saw that this man she so desired possessed very little knowledge of his own nature. His passion for her ran through his very core. He could loudly proclaim his intent, but he could never deny her.

"Is this clear, Isobel?" he asked, and she caught the strain in his voice.

A slow smile spilled from her lips. Behold the mighty teacher. Let him believe himself master of the world, a powerful creator in command of all around him. She knew better. He was a man like any other, a slave to his own lust. She would have him as she pleased or become his downfall.

"You!" Hugh's shocked voice interrupted her victory.

She swept the triumph from her face; he need not know that she had gained the upper hand. But when she turned her full attention to him, she saw that he'd forgotten she even stood there. His eyes were riveted to another.

A girl stood several yards away, an awkward third point to the triangle they'd suddenly become. A breeze rustled her long, dark hair. Her almond-shaped green eyes darted from earth to sky. She swept a hand across her face as if trying to rouse herself from a dream. The hand dropped to her side. Every ounce of color drained from her cheeks.

"Can it be?" Hugh's words, low and sinuous, hung on the air between them. "Have we truly come this far?"

Isobel's heart thudded against her chest. She'd never before heard that caressing note in his voice.

"This is what I've wanted," he said softly, unmindful of her dismay. "Perhaps it is nearly time." He stepped toward the girl. She crouched, ready to spring away at a moment's notice.

Was this girl the reason for his distraction? Isobel

sucked in a sharp breath, then jerked up her chin. A pretty girl, perhaps. A wanton one, clearly, with her long exposed legs and full red lips. She was younger than Isobel in years, and she did not possess the soft, pliant curves that men so desired. Isobel thrust her breasts forward and allowed her cloak to part, a reminder to Hugh of the pleasures she could offer. He did not notice. His eyes glittered. She did not know when they had returned to that dark emptiness she so abhorred.

"Do you see her, Isobel?" he asked.

Her lip curled in disgust.

Hugh noted the sneer. His brow lowered as he straightened to his full height. He strode toward her, each step a muffled warning.

"No, Isobel." His hand shot out as if to strike her. He yanked it back just before his skin could touch hers. His physical restraint apparently reminded him to harness his tongue as well. "You don't understand. This creature is the next step in our path together."

Confusion mixed with anger as Isobel observed the girl. She stood frozen before them, her lips moving silently, words indecipherable. She no longer appeared as solid as she had only moments ago. Her outline remained firmly etched, but Isobel could peer straight through her to traces of blue sky and green tufts of grass. Impossible, but the girl was fading away!

Hugh noticed as well.

"No!" He stretched an entreating hand toward the ghostly figure. "Isobel! She must not leave us. Not yet!"

Isobel's hand itched to slap him. As if she had any sway over this temptress. Why, if she could, she'd vanquish the trollop from the face of the earth.

But Hugh obviously expected otherwise.

"Bring her to me, Isobel. Do it now, before it is too late!"

Fury rose like bile in her throat. Was he daft? If he wanted the poppet's favors, he could very well entice her on his own. She herself would never bring another to his side.

"Do you defy me?" He loomed large before her. His hot breath misted her face. "Isobel, I am your master. You must obey me."

No master he until wedding vows were exchanged. She folded her arms across her chest and pointed her nose in the air.

"Ah." Hugh staggered backward. "Jealousy."

Her steady gaze swung toward him. The word hung heavy on the air between them, a lofted rock just waiting to fall. Her stare sharpened, piercing an imaginary hole through his forehead. She dared him to speak of the girl again. She would pummel him into the earth.

"Jealousy," Hugh repeated, rolling the word across his tongue. He looked bewildered, as if the idea had ambushed him. "A mere human vice, yet powerful enough to destroy my greatest plans."

Isobel gasped. He had never before spoken of plans. Why mention them if they did not include her?

Hugh's eyes flickered rapidly across her face. He seemed to read her thoughts.

"*Our* plans," he said, each word sharp and clear.

Her fingers fluttered to her throat.

He stepped forward, just close enough that she could see the puff of his breath on the chilled air. "She is but an envoy, Isobel. You must understand that our plans cannot be successful without her."

Oh, a curse upon her body! It seemed to have overcome her reason despite her deepest intentions to remain calm and detached. An excited flush flooded her cheeks. Her mouth turned upward in a hopeful half smile.

"Yes, Isobel, be glad." He spoke quickly now, his stare divided between her and the other girl. Isobel hazarded a quick glance at her rival. She only hoped that the girl had heard Hugh clearly: he held no tenderness for anyone other than herself.

"As if there could be another besides you." His tone was perhaps colder than she might have liked, but his words were the very ones she wanted to hear.

She turned in triumph to face the girl, who looked a little more solid than before. Isobel assumed that her own anger had distorted her earlier vision, causing her to see blurriness where none had actually existed.

The girl struggled to speak. This time, Isobel heard her words.

"Who are you people?" she asked in a high, faint voice. "Where are we? Why can I see you?"

Isobel took comfort in the fact that the words made no sense. Surely Hugh could never be enamored of one so addled. She had little time to savor this, however. Hugh's voice, tight and insistent, demanded her attention.

"Touch her, Isobel," he commanded. "Touch her now."

She could not fathom how this poor girl might further her dreams of keeping Hugh forever. On the other hand, she rarely understood anything about this man who so entranced her. But he was her teacher. She would willingly remain his pupil for as long as his lessons promised to blossom into romance.

She stared at the figure quaking before them. The girl stared back, green eyes round with fear.

"Touch her!" Hugh hissed.

Isobel moved slowly toward the girl, extending her arm as she glided across the green grass. Her fingers, long and milk white, reached for the other girl's hand.

"No," the girl whispered, although neither of them seemed to know why.

"You must befriend each other," Hugh said. "Isobel, this is Julia Carmichael."

Julia hugged her arms against her chest. Isobel brushed her fingers lightly against the girl's arm, then forcibly grasped her wrist.

"Yes!" Hugh's voice echoed through her head as the green of the meadow whirled round and round.

She was Isobel, and she was not Isobel. She knew Hugh, and she did not know Hugh. She remembered the rushes strewn across her father's manor-house floor, yet she also recalled a big white house in a city she had never before seen. She was the only child of Geoffrey de Clairmont, but she thought that she might have a sister named Claire, a little sister with a whirlwind of curls and eyes as clear and green as her own.

Ideas bubbled to her mouth as a river of warmth raced up her arm and through her limbs. Words were rough and hard to form. She did not even understand the ones that struggled through her lips.

"Mom! Dad!" Isobel cried.

"Hold her!" Hugh shouted. "Do not let her slip away!"

As if she would ever let Julia slip away! This girl was her voice, her one chance to possess the gift of speech. Isobel tightened her grasp, but it made little difference.

She opened her mouth to beg the girl to stay. It was too late. The voice she'd just used had already left her. Only her own thoughts swirled through her mind, the same thoughts she had possessed all her life.

Julia was leaving them.

Isobel stared at the girl in disbelief, then started as she realized that Julia no longer stood alone. A woman floated beside her, a rather small woman with long dark hair and brown eyes.

Hugh's voice might have come from the bottom of the deepest well.

"My dearest, dearest Katerina," he said, and Isobel felt her own blood freeze within her veins. "You cannot alter your daughter's destiny."

The woman narrowed her eyes and raised her chin. Then she plucked Isobel's hand from Julia's wrist. The two faded away, leaving Isobel to stare openmouthed at the spot they had just occupied.

What bewitchment was this? She swung about to question Hugh, but he, too, had vanished, leaving her quite alone.

Claws landed on her shoulder, digging into her skin as they rolled her back and forth.

"Wake up, wake up!" a voice cackled in her ear. "Wake up, dullard, or you will miss Lauds!"

Isobel's eyes flew open. Dame Margaret stood above her, a watery blue glare fixed upon her face.

"Out of bed," she said, and Isobel saw at once that it was not piety that fueled the mistress of novices, but rather the strong belief that another should not stay abed while she herself trudged through the cold, damp night to the chapel.

Isobel swung her legs over the side of the bed. The

ploy worked. Satisfied that her charge was awake, Dame Margaret moved away. Isobel waited until her ramrod-straight back passed from view before dropping her head into her hands.

Had it been but a dream? She didn't think so. It had felt real—far more real than the stark emptiness of the priory dormitory, even.

Who, then, was Julia?

Hugh knew.

She must find a way to ask him.

# 18

Once upstairs, Kat had required no spiritual revelation to propel her to her daughter's side. Julia lay face up on the bed, eyes opened wide, mouth moving as though words longed to escape.

"Julia!" Kat rushed across the room, but Julia did not acknowledge her.

Kat leapt into bed and curled herself around her daughter's rigid body. One hand cupped Julia's shiny head; the other wrapped itself around her waist to pull her close. Kat shut her eyes as she struggled to tame her own wild breathing.

"She's a child of light," she muttered through clenched teeth. "And this demon is darker than anything I can face alone. Please, God, tell me what to do!"

A crushing blast of wind pinned her against the bed. The room whirled. For one crazy moment, she expected to see Margaret Hamilton fiercely peddling a bicycle in a cyclone outside the bedroom window. But when she finally raised the courage to open her eyes, there was neither a bedroom nor a window. Instead, she stood beside Julia in the midst of a fragrant meadow, staring into the oval face of an unfamiliar girl with platinum hair.

Worst of all, beyond the girl stood Asteroth.

Kat's stomach clenched as she met his gaze. She had never before seen him this clearly, not even during their fiery encounter so many years ago. Then she'd caught only jagged glimpses of him as he'd fought to materialize into physical form. She remembered that he required a human host to thrust himself into the world. He'd obviously found one here; the man before her was decidedly solid.

She wondered where "here" was. No building identified the landscape. The blond girl wore something resembling a nightgown and smelled as though she could use a bath. Asteroth's impeccable clothing appeared medieval. Kat forced herself to study him. He stood strong and tall, his face nearly beatific despite the smirk gracing those chiseled features. The eyes, as always, gave him away. Their empty blackness matched the suctionlike chasm she felt spreading beneath his feet. He was like a black hole, ready to suck in any energy he could find.

"Observe me well, Katerina." His mouth never moved, but she heard the words as clearly as if they'd been spoken directly into her ear. "Observe me and tremble."

She needed no invitation to do that. He'd nearly killed her last time.

"No saintly Aunt Francesca stands beside you." His unspoken sentence ricocheted through her brain. "No dim-witted husband can yank you away from me now. What a pity you cannot find your colleagues, for you are nothing without them."

He was probably correct. Her faith was like an underused muscle: present, but too weak to be of much service. She was every bit as tired and inexperienced as she'd been that hot summer day fifteen years ago when Francesca had somehow summoned angels of light to their side. Her heart sank as a wrenching fatigue encased her.

She couldn't do this. Why had she ever thought she could?

A slow smile spread across Asteroth's stolen face. This time, he spoke out loud.

"My dearest, dearest Katerina. You cannot alter your daughter's destiny."

Her chin jolted upward. He'd gone too far.

Maternal desperation transcended time, space, and dimension. With strength she hadn't known she possessed, Kat leaned forward and ripped the blond girl's fingers from Julia's wrist. Her eyes hardened to steel as she caught the girl's startled expression. The blond was but a pawn, malleable and weak in Asteroth's expert hands. Let her do as she pleased. Her own daughter's soul was not for sale.

Another blast of wind forced her eyes closed. When she reopened them, she and Julia once again rested upon Julia's bed, clinging to each other as if only the tiniest lifeboat rested between them and a raging, tumultuous sea. Stephen stood above them, breathing hard after his dash up the stairs. Kat followed his stare to Julia's wrist, where the outline of fingers reddened the skin like an angry tattoo.

"I saw him." Kat's words, unbelievably calm, struck Stephen as anticlimactic.

He didn't need to ask whom. One look at his wife's flushed face and blazing eyes confirmed what he already knew. "Where is he?"

"I don't know. He's in physical form, though. Julia was with him."

Stunned, he sank down onto the bed and groped for her hand. "Are you all right?"

"Later, Stephen." She squeezed his fingers, and he felt his heart regain its normal rhythm.

Together they studied their daughter, whose eyelids fluttered as though she struggled against a heavy tide of sleep. Stephen wrapped an arm around her shoulders and eased her to a sitting position.

Kat caught his gaze. "There's no time to handle this gently," she said.

He nodded, then gave Julia a small shake. "Wake up, sweetheart."

Julia's head lolled back as she fought to focus her eyes.

Kat cupped her daughter's chin in her hand, staring into her face as if she could awaken her by sheer force of will. "Rise and shine, Sleeping Beauty. It's time to talk."

Julia blinked as her eyes met her mother's. A high-pitched shriek caught in her throat. She flung her arms around Kat's neck. "It was you! You're the one who came for me!" Tears started down her cheeks.

Kat hugged her, then carefully disengaged the clinging arms from around her neck. "It's okay, Julie. You're safe for now. But this isn't a secret anymore. It's not a game. Do you understand?"

Julia gulped for air. "Mom, it was never this bad! I swear!"

"But it will probably get worse," Stephen said. "You've got to let us help."

There was no time for well-crafted adolescent apathy. Julia was far too upset to twist her emotions into anything resembling coolness. Stephen easily read the thoughts that flashed across her face. First came the confusion of a child who simply could not comprehend the situation engulfing her. Fear followed as Julia tried desperately to link the past hour's events to something even remotely routine. Finally, Stephen saw realization in his daughter's eyes and knew that she would never again enjoy the peace of innocence.

"Oh, Julie," he sighed. "I'm so sorry."

Julia gulped. "Mom, this is what you meant that night in Aunt Frannie's room, isn't it. Remember? You told me that you and Dad had once fought against evil."

"Does it finally feel evil to you?" Kat usually masked her emotions well, but this time her relief was nearly tangible.

"I don't know." Julia hung her head. "Part of it feels exciting. The other part . . . I don't know, Mom. It felt like I had no control over anything that happened to me."

Stephen and Kat exchanged a glance.

"What *did* happen to you?" Stephen asked.

"I don't know," Julia said again.

"You've got to know." Kat's voice was sharp. "You've got to tell us everything."

Stephen watched his daughter study the carpet as if the pattern held all the secrets of the world. Was she weighing the odds, trying to decipher the benefits of letting her parents share the most compelling secret she'd ever kept? The silence seemed to stretch interminably, but the clock on the desk indicated that only a minute or two had passed. Kat remained still, expression unreadable to a casual observer. Stephen, however, was far more than a casual observer. He recognized the rigid set of her shoulders, the tightness around her mouth. She would accept nothing less than total compliance.

Julia spoke so quietly that her parents had to lean in close to hear her.

"Those people—that man and the girl you saw, Mom—have been . . . visiting me . . . for weeks and weeks. First they were part of my dreams, the kind of dreams you don't want to wake up from. Then they started showing up even when I was awake."

"Showing up?" Stephen prodded.

She nodded. "I'd close my eyes, and there they were. I told myself that it was exciting, that I could open my eyes and get rid of them whenever I wanted to. Then it got to the point where I didn't only see them, I felt them. And this time . . ." She looked away.

"Don't stop now," Kat said. "You're on a roll."

Julia's brow furrowed as if she couldn't quite believe her own words. "This time it felt as if I actually became the girl. I knew things that only she could know. I wanted desperately to get out of her head, but I couldn't. Then you came, Mom, and I felt myself yanked back into my own body."

Stephen heard Kat's sharp intake of breath. They'd gone a lot closer to the edge than they'd thought. Julia had almost slipped from their fingers, lost in a space they'd yet to even identify.

He felt a tug on his sleeve. Julia stared up at him with wet eyes.

"Dad. Am I crazy?"

"No. Of course not."

"Unfortunately," Kat said, "we understand all too well that this sort of thing can happen." Her brisk, businesslike tone left little room for tears. Julia straightened and dabbed her eyes with the edge of her sweatshirt.

"Julia," Kat continued, "you said you knew for a moment what the other girl knew. Do you remember any of it?"

"I'm not sure."

"Think. Where were you?"

"It's like a dream . . ."

"Where were you?" Kat made no effort to hide her urgency.

"England," Julia said, surprised. "Lincoln, England."

Lincoln. That sounded familiar. Stephen's eyebrows rose as he remembered why. "That's where Frannie went on her last trip. Didn't she say that she felt Asteroth there?"

"Who's Asteroth?" Julia asked, but Kat ignored the question and plowed ahead.

"Where in Lincoln?" she demanded.

"Um . . . a priory. I guess that's sort of like a convent, right? It's called Saint Etheldreda's. Isobel hates it."

"Isobel?"

"That's the girl's name. Isobel. She has fifteen summers."

Kat frowned a little as she processed the archaic age reference. "What year does Isobel live in, Julia?"

Julia turned pink. "This can't be right, Mom. I must be making this up somehow. I keep thinking that the year is 1360."

Stephen's stomach turned. "He's there, then," he whispered. "In the flesh. Made physical in fourteenth-century England."

"But how?" Kat stared into space, apparently searching for a more effective line of questioning. "Julia. Tell me about the man you saw with Isobel."

Julia fidgeted as she turned an even deeper shade of

pink. "Mom, maybe I'm just coming down with something. This stuff can't mean anything. It's like astrology. Right?"

"Spill it, Julia."

Julia threw her father a beseeching look.

Sometimes Kat's tenacity drove Stephen nuts. He himself had been fairly hard-nosed when younger, willing to drive any point home if it could benefit him in some way. Age had mellowed him, however. It seemed to him now that not every situation came equipped with an answer and that some circumstances even required a bit of slack. Here they sat, drilling their daughter over admittedly upsetting events. Part of him longed to commiserate with Julia, to wrap her in his arms and carry her as far away from Baltimore as possible. He knew in his heart, though, that there was no running from Asteroth.

He would not get the "favorite parent" award tonight.

"Answer your mother," he said.

Defeated, Julia returned her gaze to the floor. "His name is Hugh."

"Hugh?" Kat pulled back, momentarily derailed by an unexpected response.

"Isobel's in love with him," Julia added faintly.

Even Stephen could tell that there was much more to the story. "And . . .?"

Julia squirmed. "You know, Dad. She's hot for him."

Stephen recoiled a bit, not sure that he wanted to know exactly what that phrase meant to his thirteen-year-old daughter.

Fortunately, Kat did not share his squeamishness. "How does Hugh feel about Isobel?" she asked.

Julia's shoulders slumped as she averted her eyes.

"Isobel thinks he likes her because he's all over her every chance he gets."

Stephen swallowed, then managed to meet his wife's gaze. She, too, understood that most of the story rested in what Julia did *not* say. Obviously, Isobel's sexual experiences had gone far beyond Julia's readiness to absorb them.

A revolting thought crossed Stephen's mind. "Kat. Is Hugh—"

She nodded.

"Then—"

"—there's more to it than we know," Kat finished for him. "And I don't think we have much time."

Stephen flopped back onto the bed. "We need Frannie," he said, staring at the ceiling. "We need her more than we've ever needed anyone in our lives."

Julia's head shot up. "She's there."

Stephen raised himself up on his elbows. "Where?"

"I think she's at Saint Etheldreda's. Isobel heard Hugh say something to someone named Francesca, but she didn't see anyone."

"How did Aunt Frannie get there?" Kat asked.

"I don't know." Julia licked her lips.

"What we really need to know is how to get her back," Stephen said glumly.

"I don't know that, either," Julia said. "What is going on? I don't understand any of this."

Footsteps clattered up the stairs, shattering the surrounding silence.

"Claire!" Kat jumped up. "I can't believe I forgot about her."

Sure enough, Claire's tousled head peeked around the doorframe.

"Are we ever going to eat?" she asked. "I'm hungry. Isn't the pasta ready yet?"

Stephen made himself sit up. "I'm sorry, honey. I forgot about the pasta. I'll be down in a few minutes to throw it into the pot."

Claire's lower lip protruded. "Everybody always forgets about me," she said. "I'm starving, here."

"Give me a break." Julia scowled. "Sometimes there are more important things to do than eat."

Claire could never stay angry for long. She galloped over to her sister, wedging herself between Julia and Kat as if that space were her reserved seat.

"Did you go back to that place, Julie?" she asked, face aglow. "Did I miss us talking about it?"

Julia's fingers worked through a lock of hair. "It's nothing, Claire, okay?"

"No, wait." Kat raised a hand. "We're a team. Besides, I'm starting to think that the two of you hold different pieces to this puzzle. Claire, this place where Aunt Frannie is . . . what if I told you that it was England?"

Claire's face brightened. "Cool! I thought it felt different."

Stephen reached out and drew her between his knees. "Not just England, Claire, but England over six hundred years ago."

His daughter processed the information for a moment, then grinned. "Double cool," she said.

"You are so bogus!" Julia exploded. "As if you know anything about this stuff!"

Once again, Kat interceded with a firm hand on Julia's shoulder. She stood and turned to face her younger daughter.

"Here's what I'm wondering, Claire," she said,

shrugging her shoulders as she fought for nonchalance. "I'm wondering how Aunt Frannie got there."

Claire cocked her head and studied the ceiling. "That's an easy one, Mommy."

Kat blinked. "It is?"

"Sure." Claire rose from the bed, tugging at Stephen's hand in an effort to make him follow. "She took a bridge. Come on, Daddy. My stomach's growling."

"A bridge?" Kat repeated, confused.

Stephen allowed his eight-year-old to pull him toward the door. Claire's thoughts had obviously flitted to other topics. She was chattering about some sort of math homework that she wanted him to see. He glanced at Julia, who still looked pale and shaken. Kat had moved to her side. She gripped Julia's hand tightly, her mind clearly straining to fit this latest clue into the story.

A bridge.

Stephen tried to catch his wife's attention as Claire led him through the bedroom door. Somewhere deep inside his being, Claire's words made perfect sense.

If he only knew why.

# 19

Isobel plunged her needle into the white cloth stretched taut across her embroidery hoop. If she tried very hard, she could almost block Dame Margaret's nasal drone from her ears. A warm breeze floated through the window, urging her to fling her sewing to the ground and run outside. Adventure seemed possible today, for she'd encountered Hugh twice that morning. Twice! And, as if that wasn't portentous enough, he'd actually seemed pleased to see her. A delightful shiver enveloped her, lifting her spirits from the damp priory chamber where she and the two other novices stitched away under Margaret's gimlet glare.

The first encounter with Hugh had come about quite innocently. He had been sitting outside the guesthouse when the novices dragged out the priory bedclothes for airing. He'd been whittling, his long fingers nimble as they turned the small piece of wood over and over in his hand. She'd smiled. He'd smiled back, an unusually wide grin that had made her heart sing. She'd sent a sidelong sneer toward Elinor and Anne beside her. Surely they'd noticed the exchange. Ever obedient, they'd turned their eyes to the sheets as if sheets were all they needed for eternal happiness.

Then, as if that one chance meeting had not been enough to rekindle all hope, Isobel had seen Hugh again on her way to the chapel for Divine Office. Of course, she shouldn't have noticed him at all. Her eyes should have been fixed on the ground before her, a fact she remembered when Dame Margaret dug a bony elbow into her ribs. Still, all the jabs in the world could not deny his presence. He'd peered through the fence balustrade as if just waiting for her. She'd managed to send him a radiant smile before Dame Margaret hustled her away.

A day had passed since the odd intrusion of the dark-haired girl. Isobel was inclined to believe that she'd conjured that meeting in the half-awake hour before dawn. It made no sense within the waking world. Besides, here were shared glances with Hugh, glances that seemed bursting with hope that had not existed in the meadow of her dream.

Her embroidery needle stopped. A sigh escaped as the heady scent of wild roses wafted past her nostrils. Oh, to be away from this stone-cold place, gathering up wildflowers to bring home to her beloved!

"Well, then." Dame Margaret's voice cut through her reverie. "Have we nothing left to stitch today, Isobel?"

Isobel narrowed her eyes. How stupid her father had been to ever believe she possessed mystical powers. Had she possessed any magic at all, Dame Margaret would now lie in a crumpled heap at her feet.

She shifted in her chair, pointedly ignoring Margaret's gaze. The other novices stitched away, reddened cheeks the only sign that they dreaded a battle. Elinor's neck remained rigid as she bent diligently over her needlework. Nervous and stringy, she was a terrible seamstress. She was, however, so docile and obedient that nobody in the priory seemed to care. It was always, "Why can't every novice be like dear Elinor?" Anne was a different story. It pleased Isobel to know that, in due time, Anne would brew her own amount of difficulty. She was pretty and round, with the desire to believe every word she was told. Girls such as Anne had served Isobel's family for years. The combination of ripe body and slow mind always led to babies. Had Isobel a voice, she might have pointed this out to her aunt Alys long ago.

Of course, Dame Margaret had made it clear that the time to tell Madame Alys anything at all had passed. Margaret's step had grown quick and determined since the day Alys had taken to her bed. The mistress of novices was everywhere now, poking her beaky nose into every nook of the priory, from kitchen to chapel. She'd even taken to carrying about Alys's large ring of keys, a sure sign that she'd elected herself acting prioress of Saint Etheldreda.

Isobel wrinkled her nose. The sheer gall of that withered hen ever supposing that she could replace Madame Alys!

The girl straightened with surprise. When had she become loyal to her aunt? Perhaps blood ties were stronger than she'd thought.

"Return to your needlework, Isobel," Dame Margaret said sharply.

If that was the only way to gain silence, then Isobel would do it. But, oh, the boredom of it all. She gazed down at the crumpled cloth in her hand. Her fingers felt blunt and clumsy these days. No color-drenched pictures came to life beneath them. She'd always been an adequate needlewoman, but she sorely missed the effortless inspiration she'd possessed for too short a time.

Dame Margaret snorted. "Much will change now that I am in command."

Isobel's head shot up. She willed one of the girls beside her to ask exactly who had placed this worm in command, but although Elinor's cheeks grew even redder, neither of the novices bothered to look up from her work. They were no better than the great fat cows of the Lowlands, who thought of nothing beyond their next cud.

Margaret met Isobel's narrow-eyed challenge. "Yes, Isobel. I have placed myself in authority. Someone must act. Alys spends her days abed, and Father Gregory is too concerned with her illness to recognize that someone must set things to right here." Although the day was warm, she drew her cloak tightly about her thin body. "This is long overdue. I can finally return Saint Etheldreda to God's fold."

Isobel knew that it would be in her best interests to feign agreement, but she could not. Her gaze hardened into a glare. Her mouth pursed in disgust.

Dame Margaret sniffed. "You have reason to fear me."

Isobel flinched, furious that her anger might have been misinterpreted as fear.

Dame Margaret's voice rose. "You and I both know that you have no vocation. You are with us because you were born to wealth and because you are kin to Alys. But no doubt about it, you are foul to your core, a rotten apple set to spoil the whole barrel. You have perhaps clouded your aunt's vision, but I am made of stronger fabric. You will not run amok in our priory, making sport with our boarders and mockery of our vows. We need boarders, God help us. Poverty cannot be choosy. But you, my dear, are expendable. You can rot in the cellar if that is what becomes necessary to cleanse this priory of your sin."

Isobel's needle shook with the trembling of her hand. She aimed its point at Margaret's midsection, ready to express her rage with action since words could not come.

Incredibly enough, words *did* come.

"Gracious," someone said in cool, measured tones. "Dame Margaret, such bile cannot possibly benefit the balance of your humours."

Margaret's gasp hung on the air. The novices looked up. Madame Alys stood in the doorway, a stately vision in emerald green velvet. The paleness of her skin only emphasized her glittering gray eyes. Elinor and Anne straightened as one on their hard wooden stools. Dame Margaret blinked rapidly. Isobel watched her neck quiver with each gulp.

Alys reached out her hand. Each long, elegant finger seemed sculpted in marble as she turned her palm upward.

"My keys, Margaret." Her voice might have been made of marble as well.

Margaret rose stiffly to her feet. "You are well, then," she said flatly, reaching for the key ring at her waist.

"Yes." Alys allowed a monstrous gap of silence to fill each corner as Margaret fumbled for the keys. Isobel saw no reason to conceal the smirk that tugged at her own mouth. She let it blossom.

The jangle of many tiny bells from outside mingled

with the clang of metal on metal as Margaret dropped the key ring into the prioress's waiting palm.

Alys closed her fingers over the keys. "I thank you, Dame Margaret, for assuming responsibility above and beyond the call of duty while I lay indisposed. Might I trouble you to continue your service? Those bells will be peddler Kate on her monthly call. Would you be so kind as to offer her some ale?"

"Yes, madame." Margaret's words, muttered through clenched teeth, were barely audible. She held her head high as she walked toward the door.

Alys's penetrating stare landed on her niece. In spite of herself, Isobel's smirk flew from her face. She squirmed.

"Oh, and Margaret," Alys began, "do allow Elinor and Anne to help you. They may return to their needlework later."

Wordlessly, the two little novices bobbed quick curtsies and scurried from the room behind the mistress of novices.

Alys's relentless stare remained unmoved. It took every ounce of Isobel's strength to keep her own eyes raised. She examined each feature of her aunt's face: the broad forehead, straight nose, full mouth. She noted the brilliant strands of red straying from beneath the soft green wimple. Alys, she saw, was quite beautiful, a wild bird of rare plumage forced into unnatural captivity.

In the end, there was no way to avoid the demanding gray eyes. Alys's gaze called her to account, demanded responsibility where Isobel usually felt none was warranted.

Alys stepped toward her, circling her seat as though cornering prey.

"And what, my little poppet, would you do with him if I let you?" Her voice was cool and melodious. Isobel wondered if she herself might have possessed such a voice had one been granted her.

Alys continued. "Would you sneak to his side under cover of night? Oh! I had quite forgotten. You already do."

Isobel's chin jerked higher.

"No, no, let me see." Alys stopped to consider, one finger pressed lightly against her cheek. "You are young. Your thoughts most likely stray toward romance. Perhaps you would run away with him. Do you fancy a cottage by the sea? Do you dream of hours in his arms?"

Isobel felt her face grow hot.

"Ah." Alys stooped until they were eye level with each other. "Never think yourself a mystery. You cannot speak, but your intentions are more than clear." She rose and turned away. "Very well, then. It is to be little Isobel borne away in Hugh's strong arms."

Isobel rose to her feet, hands clenched into hard fists. Her aunt swept around in a swirl of skirts.

"Sit, Isobel," she said, and the rock-solid core in her voice made Isobel obey.

Alys gave a curt nod. "Listen well, for we shall not have this conversation again. If Hugh loved you, I'd be inclined to let you slip away. I could easily avert my gaze while he carried you into the night. I suspect that our hearts are similar, for you are my kinswoman, and I recognize a fire in you that I think I once possessed myself. I know the emptiness of reaching for the man who should be ever by your side, all the while knowing that the love you share can never be acknowledged."

Isobel's jaw dropped. Madame Alys? In love? The room began to spin as she realized that her aunt's beloved could only be Father Gregory. Why, he was old, hardly an object worthy of desire. And Aunt Alys had been a nun for many years now. She couldn't possibly understand what it meant to burn with the flaming desire of true love.

As if she'd read the thoughts, Alys's stern expression broke into an unexpected smile. But what was this? There was something else in her aunt's visage, and Isobel recoiled as she recognized what it was. Pity!

Alys crossed to Isobel's side and gathered her into a hug. Surprised, Isobel rested against her for an unguarded moment.

"He doesn't love you, my poppet," Alys said gently. "He could never fulfill your romantic dreams. There is no good in him. Can you not see this?"

They stood frozen for a moment, Alys's fingers playing through her niece's hair. A portion of Isobel's heart longed for this tenderness to last forever. How foreign it was, yet how very nice. But the dreadful words would not leave her mind: *He doesn't love you.*

As if Madame Alys knew anything of love.

Isobel mustered her strength and shoved her aunt away.

Alys staggered backward a few feet. To Isobel's dismay, she did not fall. Neither did she stumble, although a slight tremor betrayed her body as weaker than her resolve.

The prioress drew herself up to her full height. "I am sending him away," she said, as if the past few minutes had never happened. "I came to tell you this. I will speak with him this afternoon."

She might as well have punched her niece in the midsection. Isobel's face twisted in anguish as her hands began to shake.

"As you lack a voice, I will speak for you," Alys continued in a dull, flat tone. "You hate me. You wish I were dead. You will, in fact, kill me."

Isobel's nostrils flared. She drew back her right hand. Alys's eyes followed the fist as it flew toward her in a hard, jerking arc. With a sigh, she caught her niece's wrist inches before the fist could smash into her nose.

A chilling scream from the courtyard interrupted them.

"Mercy on my soul! Mercy on my soul!" a woman shrieked over and over again.

Alys dropped Isobel's wrist and rushed toward the corridor. Isobel flew after her, down the narrow stone staircase and into the priory courtyard.

Outside, Dame Margaret and her novices stood like statues on the hard dirt ground. Chickens squawked across the courtyard, stirring up little puffs of dust as they flapped their wings. The women paid them no mind. Their stares were riveted instead just outside the closed priory gate.

The peddler, Kate, had sunk to her knees in the dust. Each hand gripped an iron bar. Her large body trembled as she tugged at the bars with all her might.

"Save me!" She swung her head toward the prioress. Wispy white hair flew from its bindings to form a thin halo about her skull. "Madame Alys! Please let me in! Save me!"

"But of course." If Alys was startled by this odd turn of events, she did not show it. Her expression remained placid as she reached for her key and hurried toward the gate.

Isobel's brow furrowed. Save the woman from what? Dame Margaret was impossible, but only to those forced under her tutelage. Elinor and Anne clutched each other, ready to topple over from the excitement of this unusual day. Clearly, neither ninny posed a threat.

What, then?

Her eyes scanned the dirt road beyond the gate and came to rest on Hugh. He stood rigid in the middle of the road, yards away from the entrance of the guest-house. His dark eyes narrowed into slits as his gaze met hers.

"Merciful Mother of God." Kate collapsed onto the earth as the gate swung open. Then, with speed that belied her size, she lifted herself and plunged into Alys's arms. "Close the gate, madame. Lock it tight!"

Alys ignored her. "Elinor, fetch a stool for Mistress Kate. Anne, a tankard of ale. Dame Margaret . . ." She hesitated only briefly. "You will find Father Gregory in the chapel. Kindly bid him come at once."

The women scattered.

Isobel cocked her head. She grudgingly admired her aunt's calm in the face of such turmoil. Despite refuge within the priory walls, Kate's shudders remained so violent that Isobel wondered how anyone could continue to hold her with such a tight, steady grip.

Hugh remained planted in the road, his very presence a silent dare to anyone who might reproach him.

Alys watched as the stool appeared. She eased Kate's bulk onto it, then rescued the tankard of ale from Anne's shaking hand. She dismissed both novices with a nod of her head, and they gratefully scampered away. Only Isobel remained, her skirts billowing in a brisk wind that seemed born of nothing.

"Drink." Alys handed Kate the ale, then waited while she rapidly swallowed.

"Now, then," Alys said as Kate's trembling subsided. "Whatever is wrong?"

The woman glanced toward Hugh. Another tremor raced through her as she quickly turned away.

"It's him," she said in a strained voice. "Have I gone daft? It's him!"

Alys's left eyebrow rose slightly. Then she caught sight of Father Gregory hurrying toward her and once again pulled her face into an emotionless mask.

"Father Gregory," she called, "Mistress Kate is in need of our aid."

Isobel's sharp eye had long ago noted that the priest did not easily conceal his thoughts. She saw at once that he'd arrived with the fear that Alys might be in danger. She watched the cloud of concern lift from his shoulders. He seemed suddenly able.

"What ails you?" he asked Kate kindly.

Kate pointed a shaky finger toward Hugh, who stiffened.

"It's him," she repeated, although the ale seemed to have calmed her earlier fear. "Do not think me mad, Father, but . . . I know him."

Dame Margaret moved close enough to hear every word. The prioress and the priest exchanged a look. Then Father Gregory turned toward the mistress of novices.

"Thank you, Dame Margaret." His soothing voice left no space for refusal. Disappointment washed across

Margaret's sharp features. She glared at Isobel, awaiting her dismissal as well. It never came.

"Thank you," Father Gregory repeated. Dame Margaret sniffed loudly and left.

Isobel noted the tableau before her. Kate sat on the stool, eagerly gulping the last dregs of ale from the large tankard. Alys stood behind her, a steadying hand resting on her shoulder. Father Gregory stood before her, awaiting more information.

Isobel might have wanted to hear the information too, but something more intriguing crossed her thoughts: to her right, the priory gate gaped open. Hugh still stood on the other side.

"You know him," Father Gregory reminded the peddler. "Who is he?"

Kate placed the empty tankard on the ground. Her blue eyes grew wide. "He is Robin the Thatcher."

The priest looked puzzled. "He does not go by this name, here. Are you quite sure?"

Her head bobbed vigorously. "Helped bring him into this world, I did. I was a midwife's apprentice in those days, and I remember my babies."

Isobel doubted seriously that this fool could remember anything, especially with more than a pint of ale sent quickly down her gullet. As far as she was concerned, Kate had nothing of interest to say. The girl edged toward the gate until she could no longer hear the old hen's mindless prattle.

Alys made a brief note of her niece's whereabouts, then absently patted the peddler's shoulder. "Why does he frighten you so?" she asked.

Kate dissolved into tears. "I helped bury him, too, just days before the feast of Corpus Christi!"

The prioress's fingers dug into the peddler's shoulders so hard that Kate jumped. "You . . . buried . . . him?"

"Are you sure of this?" Father Gregory swayed slightly.

"I never forget my babies," Kate repeated. "The plague took him, he who was to wed the miller's daughter but a fortnight from now. The village still speaks of the loss."

"You are perhaps mistaken." Alys sounded hollow.

Kate lowered her voice. "Forgive me, madame, but look closely at him. That lovely hair, bright as the sun. Those strong arms. The length of his leg. There was no mistaking him in life, just as there is no mistaking him in death."

Father Gregory helped the peddler to her feet. "Here is what I think," he said gently. "I think, my dear Mistress Kate, that you have walked long and far today in the bright sun. The young man's loss weighs heavy on your heart, for you are a woman of great compassion. Your eyes play games with your sorrow."

"Do you think so?" She brightened, eager to believe anything. "I am not bewitched, then?"

"No," Gregory said. "You are simply tired. I will take you to our Dame Catherine, who will see to it that you rest before walking again in the heat. Will you come with me?"

"I will! Oh, I will!" Relief flooded her every word.

"And you, Madame Alys, you must await me here. We have priory matters to discuss."

Alys gave a prim nod.

"Of course," she said.

She watched them walk across the courtyard, Kate's

unsteady bulk occasionally bumping against Gregory. His walk was measured, so steady that she knew he had to focus very hard to keep it that way. Surely the thoughts swirling in his head must mirror her own.

There was truth here, a truth that she might not have seen had she refused to believe the events of the past few days. Perhaps Francesca would know what this meant.

Unfortunately, that meeting would have to wait. There were other matters that also required attention. Alys caught her breath and turned to face her niece.

"What say you of this, Isobel?" she asked.

But Isobel was not there. Hugh, too, had vanished. All that remained was the gaping priory gate.

# 20

FRANCESCA PACED THE CHAPEL AISLE, TOO AGITATED TO SETTLE into a pew or even to stop walking. Fear twisted her stomach. Strange. Fear was an emotion more related to the physical than the spiritual. She had relished her invisibility, assumed that she'd shaken herself free of all physical ties that could weigh her down. But even in this odd, unexplainable existence, she could not escape the fear that Asteroth ignited within her. Why couldn't her emotions have altered along with her physical form?

She had no answers: only a pile of questions that grew larger by the minute.

She felt safer inside the chapel than she did outside. She liked it here, as she'd liked the inside of every church she'd entered since earliest childhood. Gothic or modern, big or small, she always felt comfortably warm inside a church.

It occurred to her that churches had been used as sanctuary during the Middle Ages. Anyone could escape pursuit simply by crossing the threshold of a church and slamming the door firmly behind. Nobody could harm you once you'd placed yourself under the Church's protection. To challenge that protection would be to challenge God.

A sense of relief engulfed her. Surely, what applied

in physical form applied even more now that she was further immersed in spirit. She could stay safe here. Asteroth could never penetrate sacred ground. She could remain within this cocoon, praising God's light throughout eternity, untouchable.

The idea soothed her enough that she could stop pacing. Unfortunately, respite was brief. A nagging thought instantly intruded, barely allowing time to catch a breath.

Even as a child, Francesca had had no trouble pinpointing the major drawback of sanctuary. Nobody could come in and hurt you, but neither could you come out. Medieval sanctuary had seldom provided a gateway to contemplation and prayer. It had served mostly as an escape, a place to wait it out until danger cooled outside the church door.

The thought felt sticky and unpleasant. She unconsciously flexed her fingers. It wasn't in her nature to run away.

Or was it? Her memory flickered back to that September dinner with Katerina and Stephen. Katerina's voice had remained level, but sparks had fairly shot from her eyes. What was it she'd said? What accusation had she hurled?

As if she even had to ask herself. The words were branded on her heart. She could still feel Katerina's veiled anger as she said them: "Not all of us can afford to check out of physical reality. Some of us have to stay behind in the trenches and muddle through daily life as best we can!"

Francesca winced. Her niece had always been a good shot.

Living in the spirit should have afforded more serenity than this. She'd always believed that at home, too. Each meditation session, each prayerful retreat abroad, had brought about a measure of calm, even a sense of relief. And yet there'd always been an undercurrent of discontent lurking beneath the placid surface of peace. Her sense of oneness with God and the light, so simple, clean, and well constructed, still came attached to the feeling that something more was expected of her. Now the truth hit in a painful starburst of color. Her understanding of peace had always been flawed, tilted slightly off center. Peace had never promised isolation from conflict. Despite her introspection and her studies, despite her many retreats, she had somehow missed a crucial piece to the puzzle of daily life. She'd been invited to a fine banquet and had done little more than observe it, allowing herself only an occasional whiff of its tantalizing aroma.

Frustrated, she raised her eyes to the stained-glass rose window. The vibrant colors leaned into each other, melting until their pattern shifted into a new configuration. It took only a second to remember where she'd seen this configuration before. This was the pattern of the cathedral window she'd last noticed before closing her eyes in Baltimore and breaking the binds of time.

The chapel no longer felt as cozy and comforting as it had only moments ago. Francesca's gaze strayed from the window to the stone walls, and then on to the hard wooden pews. But instead of pews, she saw an image of Katerina and Stephen. They sat on the overstuffed loveseat in the family room of their house. A fire blazed in the fireplace. Francesca could hear the crackle of burning bark, could even smell the curling tendrils of smoke as they snaked up the chimney. Outside, freezing rain pelted against the windowpane. She raised an open palm to her cheek to ward off the pounding needles of ice.

Katerina rested snug in the crook of Stephen's arm, her head against his chest. Her long hair spilled over her shoulder and down to her waist. Although she was covered by an afghan, Francesca noticed that her feet were tucked beneath her. Her toes were probably curled as well, the way they always were when she fought a headache. Francesca saw the circles under her niece's eyes and the transparent whiteness of her skin.

Stephen's fingers played absently through his wife's hair. He seemed distracted as he stared into the leaping flames of the fireplace. Francesca sank into a pew, trying to decipher what she saw. She knew Stephen well, sometimes even better than he knew himself. Like her, he was trying to decode a puzzle. She suspected that she knew all too well which puzzle that was.

Julia and Claire sat on the rug near their parents' feet, intent on a game of Tri-Ominos. How familiar they looked, yet how different at the same time. Julia was nearly a young woman now. Her face held none of the baby roundness it had once possessed. Claire, an impossible cherub, looked more like child Katerina than Francesca had ever noticed before.

Her heart began to beat against her chest, a steady, rhythmic call that spread quickly to her temples. She longed to plunge into the vision, to take the chaos that roiled through her loved ones' minds and set their world right. She wanted to join in the fray of their daily battles, to plow her way through chaos instead of analyzing it from a distance. Her arms ached to gather Katerina close and guide her to a place of serenity amidst the children, the career, the monolithic busyness that engulfed every second of her day.

"I should be with them," she whispered to no one, and the revelation so startled her that she half rose from her pew. How had she ever thought that the only way to live a spirit-filled life was to isolate herself from physical conflict? And to think that she'd chastised Kat and Stephen for avoiding spiritual responsibility! Why, her avoidance skills were every bit as honed as those of her niece and nephew. She'd seen the face of evil, had even battled it, and still did her best to ignore its subtle impact on daily routine.

She heard her own sharp intake of breath as she straightened. She reached toward the vision, for Katerina on the couch.

The image vanished, leaving only the cold wooden pews behind.

"No!" Francesca's voice trailed off in the shadows.

She was so mired in dismay that she didn't hear the chapel door swing open. She started as Alys appeared before her, Gregory by her side. The priest's focus rested somewhere to the left of where Francesca actually sat, but the prioress's direct gaze made it obvious that she saw Francesca even more clearly than before.

Words spilled from Alys's mouth. "When last we spoke, you said you had news of Hugh. Tell me."

Francesca quieted her breathing. Alys's eyes glittered; each cheek burned red, as if she had a high fever.

"Are you well enough for this discussion?" Francesca asked. Anything she said could only plunge the prioress more deeply into illness.

"I have no choice," Alys replied in clipped tones. "I must hear what you know."

"There may not be much time," Gregory said. "Something has happened."

Francesca remembered that he couldn't hear her. In fragile health or not, Alys would need to serve as their go-between.

But there was nothing fragile about the Alys who stood before her, mouth pursed and hands on hips.

"Who is he?" the prioress asked through clenched teeth.

Francesca raised a hand to her forehead. "He is Asteroth of the Crescent Horn," she said, surprised by the steadiness of her own voice.

"Asteroth of the Crescent Horn," Alys repeated slowly, and Francesca recognized that the repetition was for Gregory's benefit.

"A demon of darkness," Francesca added. "He is evil, madame, more evil than you can fathom."

All color drained from Alys's face as she stepped toward Francesca. She reached out to grasp the other woman by the shoulders, then changed her mind. Her arms dropped to her sides.

"How comes he here?" she asked.

Francesca sighed. "I have encountered him before, I'm afraid, so much of what I say is born of experience. He cannot enter our world without the aid of another. He requires a human body to inhabit."

"He requires a human body to inhabit." Alys's voice sounded as if drawn from the depths of a well.

Gregory's hands began to quiver, but his voice remained steady. "Madame, the man called Hugh is not man at all, then. The body was left through death, and evil now inhabits it."

"Are you sure?" Francesca asked.

"Yes," Gregory and Alys both answered at the same time. They turned to stare at each other.

"You heard her voice!" Alys's eyes widened with astonishment.

"Yes." Gregory looked stunned. "I heard her."

"Can you see her?"

"No, praise our merciful Lord. I am not yet prepared for such visions."

Francesca began to pace. Alys's eyes followed her progression from pew to altar and back to pew again.

"Forgive me," Francesca said. "This shocks me as much as it does you. I had known that Asteroth could inhabit physical bodies through the acquiescence of the living. I didn't know that he could pillage the dead. This makes him more powerful than I thought."

"Do not think it." Gregory folded his arms across his chest. "One can never guess the choices of the dying. Who knows what the demon promised the wretched man on his deathbed in order to gain his corpse?"

"May God have mercy on his soul," said Alys, but the sentiment was perfunctory. Her comprehension raced ahead with speed that surprised even Francesca. "Then Hugh—Asteroth, as you call him—has found a body and is here incarnate. Why?"

"I don't know," Francesca said. "I think it involves my niece and her family, but they live in a time and place far removed from this one. I can't imagine the connection. But, Madame Prioress, we both know that Hugh has an interest in your niece. Could she perhaps hold a key?"

Alys flinched. "She is no longer here."

Gregory turned to her in surprise, and Francesca saw that he had not yet heard this news.

"Where is she?" he asked.

"She has run away . . . with Hugh."

The silence spoke more loudly than words.

"I see," Francesca finally said.

Gregory gripped Alys's hand. "We must find her. She cannot remain in the hands of a madman." He flushed at his own understatement. "A demon, Alys."

Alys stiffened. "She joined him willingly," she replied in clipped tones. "I am inclined to let her suffer the consequences of her folly."

"She cannot know what he is!"

"Does that really matter, Gregory? She is a foolish young woman who mistakes lust for love and cares not who the object of her passion might be."

Gregory squeezed her hand hard enough to bring a gasp to her lips. Reluctantly, she raised her eyes to his.

"We cannot abandon her to his foul nature," he said quietly. "You know I speak truth, Alys. You know it deep in your heart."

Jumbled thoughts raced through Francesca's mind. Perhaps lust had indeed motivated Isobel, enticed her to see only what she wanted to see. She was certainly not the only woman on earth to follow her passions instead of her common sense. Asteroth, though, was a different matter entirely. He had cloaked himself in the identity of a man, but he was no man. Of course, Francesca had witnessed enough to see that lust was a powerful force over which he had little control. It was as if he'd received his stolen body without thorough instructions for its proper use. Still, she doubted that sexual desire fueled his need for Isobel. There was something else at play here, a puzzle piece floating just beyond her reach.

"Madame." Gregory had turned toward her. "You say that your family is in danger."

"Yes," Francesca said. "Asteroth means to destroy my niece and nephew, along with their children. They have two daughters. One is only eight, the other one nearly Isobel's age." She stopped short, dumbstruck by her own words.

Yes. Julia and Isobel were nearly the same age. A memory seared her brain: Julia's fleeting knowledge of the medieval banquet table . . . her odd recognition of illusion food. . . .

None of those recollections had belonged to her. For one brief moment, Julia's thoughts had merged with those of someone else.

"My God," Francesca breathed.

"What is it?" Alys asked.

"I must return to my own time immediately."

Somehow, Isobel and Julia had connected as one. Perhaps their merger had lasted only a second. Maybe it could last longer. What if it already had?

"How do you return to your own time?" Gregory asked.

"I don't know." Her glance traveled past him. Asteroth needed a physical body. For some reason, an appropriate one had not presented itself in twenty-first-century Baltimore. Or perhaps such a plan was no longer available to him. Kat and Stephen had grown lax in their recognition of the spiritual, but they would surely rear up fighting should an obvious danger to their children arise.

Isobel and Julia could become one. And Asteroth—

Asteroth needed prolonged access to Isobel's mind and soul. Was it possible that he could then cross through Isobel and into Julia?

"Isobel is the conduit," Francesca said, mostly to herself.

Her gaze returned to the priest. He stared directly at her, awaiting her next words.

"Gregory." Her heart thudded against her chest. "You can see me."

He started; the realization had apparently not yet registered in his mind. "I see a shadow where you stand. You are becoming clearer to me, madame, there is little doubt of that."

Panic rose in her throat. "Is this because your spiritual eyes are focusing, or because I am becoming a permanent part of your time?"

Neither Alys nor Gregory answered her. She hadn't really expected them to know.

"I must get back," she repeated, more convinced than ever. "I must warn my family." She hurried toward the chapel door.

"What of Isobel?" Alys asked.

"Find her!" Francesca shot back over her shoulder. "Keep her away from Hugh."

"Wait!" Gregory's voice echoed against the stone walls. "You must tell us, madame—has the demon any powers?"

Francesca stopped at the doorway, considering. "He has no more power than you allow him. But be careful. He works through your mind and senses. He can easily addle your thoughts, make you believe that lies are truth. Your faith in the light must stay strong."

"Go with God," Gregory said, but Francesca had already crossed the threshold, racing toward the priory courtyard as if she actually knew what to do next.

# 21

"AH, ISOBEL." HUGH'S VOICE FLOATED BACK TO ISOBEL AS SHE struggled to keep up with his long strides. "You heard me call to you even though I never spoke a word. Perhaps my hope in you is not misplaced."

Of course his hope was not misplaced, though Isobel could not convince him of this unless he slowed his steps. She drew in a ragged breath and increased her own speed to a trot.

Hugh's pace did not flag. "You knew to pass through the gate and follow me," he said with smug satisfaction. "Perhaps you cannot speak, but there is nothing amiss with your ability to understand. Believe me, my dear, the gift of comprehension is of far greater value to me than the gift of idle chatter."

She finally pulled alongside him, gasping for breath as she did so. Must he travel so quickly? Perhaps he feared that Aunt Alys and Father Gregory would dispatch the priory wagon behind them. He needn't worry. The wagon, pulled as it was by two ancient oxen, was no match in speed for anyone with two strong legs. Besides, if he so feared capture and retribution, why not travel hidden through the woods instead of on this dusty, open road?

She sent him a sidelong glance. He was lost in his own thoughts. They obviously pleased him well. A broad smile tugged at the corners of his mouth. His shoulders were straight and square, his back erect. He looked as if he'd stumbled upon a secret cache of riches.

Well, he might be pleased, but she could not continue. She plucked at his sleeve, demanding his attention. His face contorted into a glare as he yanked his arm away.

If she could have made a sound, she would have screamed. Perhaps the look on her face reflected this, for Hugh halted in the middle of the road. Grateful, she stopped beside him, hand fanned across her chest to calm the pounding of her heart.

"I see," Hugh said. Once again, Isobel felt as if she was a creature he had never before encountered and couldn't quite understand. "You're tired, of course. I forget that your vigor can never match mine."

She wanted to pass him a saucy smile, one that promised great future vigor in certain endeavors, but she was indeed tired. It had all been too much—a daring escape right under her aunt's upturned nose, a romantic dash down the road with the one who robbed her of breath even under ordinary circumstances, the delightful possibility that their shared future might begin right at this very moment. Such headiness required a pause. She managed a wobbly smile, then glanced about for a comfortable place to sit. There wasn't one. She limped over to the side of the road and slumped against a broad tree.

"We mustn't linger," Hugh said.

She nodded her agreement. Slow oxen or no, somebody from Saint Etheldreda would surely come searching soon.

"Come," Hugh continued, a statue firmly set in the middle of the road. "Something has changed. I can sense a hole in the fabric. It's not a split, mind you. Only a hole, and one that perhaps can be circumvented or even mended. Francesca knows something, Isobel."

Francesca? But he'd called the dark-haired girl Julia! How many rivals existed for this man's heart? Isobel placed a hand on her waist, willing him to turn and face her displeasure. He stared instead into the woods, distracted by a sea of thoughts.

"She fights alongside the angels of light," he said, his face a blank mask. "And she loves Julia as if the girl mattered. Beware love when it opposes you, Isobel. It appears trivial and useless, but hardens into brilliance before your eyes. It is like the diamond, a beautiful bauble that hides its power. It can cut through the most tightly constructed ties."

Isobel nodded slowly. She didn't understand his words, but she certainly understood love. She'd never before heard him discuss matters of the heart. This was an improvement over his usual conversation.

"Time grows short." He remained unimpressed by her admiration. "I can easily overcome Francesca while she stands alone. It is simple enough to pry one soul from its moorings. The skirmish becomes more difficult if Katerina joins the fray. Her strength is greater than she knows. I rely upon her ignorance. Once she comprehends her true nature, reaching Julia will become more difficult."

Julia again! Would that cursed girl never leave them be?

Hugh stroked his chin. "This doorway will close soon. I feel it. We must make haste."

Isobel's brow furrowed as Hugh finally turned to face her. She turned both palms upward and allowed her shoulders to rise and fall with the wave of her questions. Who was Katerina? Francesca? Why did the hateful Julia still intrude into so many moments? Even more important, what influence did any of these people have over her own hopes and dreams?

His brow wrinkled in reflection of her own. Ordinarily, his gaze upon her encouraged preening. Once again, though, came the curious feeling that she had somehow become an object of study. The coy toss of her head would not come. She squirmed and stared at her shoes.

"You wish to know who these people are," he said flatly. "You will not understand. They are evil and embittered women set out to destroy me. I must therefore destroy them first."

Isobel's hands flew to cover her ears even as she leaned forward to hear more.

Hugh's eyes narrowed. "Francesca is an old warrior. We have met before. We are perhaps destined to meet again. Left to my own devices, I would drive her mad, leave her to the end of her days chasing her vile philosophies as a dog chases after its tail. She is a protector rather than a weapon, and I deem her ridiculous. No, she may continue her wretched life as she sees fit. It is Katerina I must silence."

Isobel carefully arranged her face into an expression of rapt interest. It was not easy in the stream of such gibberish.

"Katerina must be destroyed." Hugh's voice grew icy cold. "She is not yet aware of the power she wields, of the influence she has on the child of light."

His words made no sense. Not only that, he'd made no mention of her true rival in this drama. What were his plans for Julia? Isobel settled all her weight onto one foot and raised an inquiring eyebrow. Hugh seemed to read her face as if it was a finely scripted page.

"No, Isobel," he said. "No harm must come to Julia. We need her."

They needed her for what? Unless the girl was to join them as a maidservant, Isobel could see no earthly purpose for her. And even then, she herself was not so stupid as to keep a maidservant her husband clearly desired.

Husband. Her gaze slid toward Hugh. There were so many questions she needed to ask, so many answers she hoped he could provide. She assumed that they would marry and live together in a cozy little cottage somewhere. Was this his plan as well?

His laughter jarred her from her thoughts. She had never before heard him laugh. It sounded more like barking.

"Isobel, why do I try to enlighten you? Very well, then. Perhaps, if you are a very good girl, there will be a cottage. But you must listen carefully to whatever I say. Your obedience is vital."

A thrill raced up her spine. Finally, words quite close to what she'd hoped to hear. She nodded her agreement, but stopped short of melting into unbridled enthusiasm. She, too, had demands. She took a determined step forward until she stood within an inch of him. She read the struggle on his face as a whiff of her rosewater-scented skin enticed him closer. The man wanted her. Let him speak in lofty terms of theories she couldn't care less about. She knew human nature, and this man desired her more than he cared to admit. She saw it in the clench of his jaw, felt it in the warm heat of his quick breathing.

He would kiss her now, sealing their future with a lover's token she could remember as they hurried on their way.

But he did not kiss her. Instead, he stepped backward until both feet were planted firmly on the road.

"We must go, Isobel," he said in calm, practical tones. "There is much to do and little time to squander in hiding from the Church. Come along."

She stared in dismay at his retreating back. He was an impossible riddle, an aggravating mystery perhaps not worth the effort it would take to solve. Still, he was also right. She had no desire to live the rest of her days locked away in the musty rooms of Saint Etheldreda's.

With a final gulp, she raced to Hugh's side.

# 22

"DUCK, DADDY!" CLAIRE'S BRIGHT VOICE SHOT SPLINTERS OF color through the damp, gray November morning.

Stephen looked up from his perch on the back porch step to see a snowball plop about two feet away from the toe of his right boot. Claire wasn't much of a pitcher under ordinary circumstances, and last night's snow hadn't done her any favors. Dense and wet, it had fallen in patchy clumps, leaving random heaps of white interspersed with grass throughout the backyard. It was hardly good packing snow. He opened his mouth to tell his daughter this, then quickly closed it again. Claire wouldn't care. Besides, she'd exhaust the small supply of snow soon enough and would then require entertainment. Might as well make the most of every available distraction.

"Try again," he said, confident that there was no danger of annihilation. "No, don't move closer to me. Throw it from where you are and see if you can break your own record."

Claire obligingly knelt to gather more snow. Stephen studied the smooth curve of her cheek. She looked so very much like pictures of Kat at that age—small and wiry, with eyes almost too large for her elfin face. Of course, her eyes were green rather than brown. Other than that little detail, however, Stephen often felt as though he'd taken a quick jog through time, landing years ago in Little Italy, the Baltimore neighborhood in which his wife had grown up.

The time-travel thought made him wince. That had once been the playful stuff of science fiction. Now, with Francesca supposedly stuck in fourteenth-century England, he had no desire to joke about a reality he couldn't even begin to understand.

He turned halfheartedly toward the tangle of Christmas lights strewn across the wooden floorboards of the porch. Christmas was a little over a month away. They would celebrate Thanksgiving next week, although only Claire appeared to feel the least bit festive. He knew it was premature to begin the yearly struggle with the Christmas lights. Still, it only made sense to use his time at home productively.

A misshapen snowball landed in a flowerbed about a foot and a half away.

"Darn!" Claire stamped a booted foot. "I thought I had you with that one."

A smile tugged the corner of his mouth. Claire was optimism personified. "Try again," he said, reaching into the heart of the tangled wires and bulbs. Next year, he'd wrap these things neatly before placing them into assigned boxes and pushing them out of sight in the garage.

His left foot began to tap an even rhythm on the step. He felt edgy hanging out at home on a Saturday morning, as if he were a tool left in the least useful place. He'd meant to pull back on his work hours after that glorious afternoon with Kat. He'd cherished their time together, actually longed for more of it. Still, he found it difficult to justify his existence while sitting at home. It hadn't taken long to drift back into the habit of spending every day at Angel Café.

Kat had awakened with a blistering migraine. Even Stephen, a master of the art of denial, could not pretend that this day would be business as usual. Julia had an indoor hockey practice scheduled, and Claire required attention. Kat herself had looked as white as bone china, a fact that only accentuated the dark circles beneath her eyes. Down in the kitchen at seven in the morning, Stephen had winced each time he'd heard her footsteps race across the hall to the upstairs bathroom. Poor Kat. Only a pure cad would leave her alone when she felt this foul.

He frowned as his fingers traced the string of lights in a desperate search for the end. Kat usually kept migraine medication in the house. Even she had seemed surprised to find the prescription bottle empty. Oh, well. She'd been under the weather for the past few days, feeling tired and slightly sick no matter what the hour. Who could blame her for misplacing her usual efficiency?

Asteroth's return had certainly done nothing to enhance their lives. If he and Kat had felt stressed and tired before, they were doubly so, now. The only difference these days was that they spent a little more time together as they tried to figure out what to do.

"Daddy?" Claire broke into his reverie. "There isn't any good snow left over here. Can I move next to the swing set?"

The swing set was even farther away from the porch than where Claire stood now. With any luck, her next move would carry her all the way over to the garage.

"Sure, sweetheart. Knock yourself out."

Once again, a grin escaped him. His baby might look like her mother, but her personality was all her own. Her goofy good nature warmed his heart. Her constant energy made him proud even as it exhausted him.

At least Julia had looked relaxed when her ride showed up that morning. She'd dashed out in a flurry of shin guards and hockey equipment, a positive testament to glowing good health and girls' athletic programs. Stephen wished that Kat could have seen that. It might have eased her worries to know that just sharing the burden with her parents had produced something of a liberation in their elder daughter. In fact, were it not for the fact that Francesca still lay motionless in the upstairs bedroom, it would have been tempting to believe that this latest chapter of spiritual weirdness had come to a close. He longed to relegate all that fevered talk of a "child of light" to idiotic comic-book fare.

Claire hopped around the swing set on one foot before settling onto a swing. "Aren't you going to the restaurant today?"

"I'm not sure yet." He half hoped to poke into Angel Café later that afternoon.

"Don't," Claire said. "I like it when you're home with us."

He smiled. "I know. I like being home with you, too. But the restaurant needs me."

"Why?" Claire's eyes widened over the reddened tip of her nose. "Everything runs okay when you're not there every minute."

He wanted to refute it, but he couldn't. It was exactly as it should be: years of good management practices had left Angel Café able to function without his constant presence. He'd already called down there three times that morning. Each time he'd been assured that everything was running smoothly. Why was it so hard to admit that his own sound business sense had earned him some well-deserved time away from work?

"Besides, Mommy needs you, too," Claire said, and Stephen nailed her with a searching look. She had an uncanny way of stating what he already knew and didn't feel like acknowledging. Perhaps she was more like her mother than he cared to admit.

"I know that, Claire," he said. There was nothing else to say. The out-of-the-mouth-of-babes concept was highly overrated.

He heard the screen door creak open behind him. Kat, looking lost with the huge quilt from their bed wrapped around her, padded out onto the porch in her bedroom slippers.

"Hey." Stephen reached out a hand. "You shouldn't be out here like that. You'll get sick."

She drew in a ragged breath and sank down beside him. "No, it's okay. I need a change of scenery."

He wrapped an arm around her. Her head instinctively dropped against his chest.

"How's the headache?" he asked.

"Better. I think the worst has passed. I just feel so weak. I feel like a hollow little shell with nothing left inside."

"Well, no wonder." Never mind the migraine. The way the past weeks had gone, it was a miracle they hadn't just bolted the doors, pulled down the shades, and taken to cowering in the basement.

Kat seemed to read his thoughts.

"I don't suppose you managed to figure out our next step while I was upstairs languishing in bed."

"I can't even figure out the Christmas lights."

"I haven't been much help. I'm sorry, Stephen. I've just been feeling so punk."

He gave her shoulder an absent-minded squeeze. "That's understandable. Just get well."

Kat stared thoughtfully across the yard. Claire had given up on the melting snow piles near the swing and had moved toward the back fence. "You didn't need me the last time we battled Asteroth. You got marching orders on your own. You heard the next step even when the rest of us were clueless."

"That was fifteen years ago."

"I know. But I can't help wondering how you did it. What was different?"

He couldn't help the bitter edge that crept into his laugh. "You know, Kat, I've been trying to decipher that one. The only difference I can come up with is that I didn't believe in any of this stuff then. Now I do."

"That doesn't make sense."

"Since when has any of this made sense?" He sighed. "I keep trying to cram this information into some sort of order. If I could only see some logic to it, maybe I could get back whatever sixth sense I used before."

Kat's brow furrowed as she tried to digest his words. He saw that any additional information would catapult her right back into the realm of headache pain. Now wasn't the time to try to unravel this riddle.

"Look at Claire," he said, searching for a diversion. Their daughter had found an untouched pile of snow and now dug into it with renewed vigor. "The kid never gives up. She couldn't hit me with a snowball when she stood six feet away. What makes her think she'll do it from all the way over by the fence?"

Kat smiled in spite of herself as Claire's little red mittens formed a new snowball. "She doesn't have a handle on logical cause and effect yet. That's what I like about kids. In their world, everything is still possible."

Her words hung on the air, then sunk in. They turned to stare at each other.

"We're looking for a logical solution," Stephen said.

"We don't believe for a minute that we can fight this," Kat said at the same time. She turned toward Claire again, then hastily shoved Stephen aside. A snowball whizzed past his right ear, landing in a white heap in the middle of the Christmas lights.

"Good throw, Claire!" Stephen sounded more amazed than was probably good for the kid's ego.

Claire swaggered toward them, a wide grin on her face. "You didn't think I could do it."

Stephen laughed, trying to salvage his credibility. "See what practice can do?"

Claire melted into her mother's outstretched arms. "I knew I could do it."

Kat took off her daughter's wet mittens and tucked the cold fingers beneath a fold of the quilt. "I see," she said.

Claire sighed. "No, you don't. You only think you do."

The moment was distinctly odd and made no sense. Stephen bit back the irritable words that rose to his tongue. Their daughter's precocious little voice made her sound like a rude fortune cookie, like a TV drama idea of wisdom, like . . .

. . . the child of light.

He stared into Claire's green eyes. All this time he and Kat had assumed that Julia was the child in need of protection. Could Claire be Asteroth's target, the child so dreaded and feared?

He placed a gentle hand on her knee. "Claire. Do you know how we can get Aunt Frannie back?"

She seemed to consider the question as Kat gently stroked her hair. "I've been thinking about that, Daddy. I'm not really sure, but I have some ideas."

A pink flush flooded Kat's cheeks as she, too, began to connect these new pieces of the puzzle. "Sweetheart, remember that night when you mentioned that Aunt Frannie took a bridge to get where she is now?"

Claire nodded.

"What bridge?" Kat asked. "Where?"

"I don't know what bridge," Claire said slowly. "I can't figure it out. I know that she has to come back home the same way she got to where she is."

Stephen glanced at Kat, puzzled. "But we lost her at the cathedral, and Mom and I already went back there."

"You didn't lose her," Claire said. "She chose to go. And just going back to the last place she was isn't enough, I don't think. Something must have been different the second time you were there."

"Well, of course it was," Kat said. "Aunt Frannie wasn't with us."

Stephen felt a curious sensation at the back of his neck, almost a prickle. "Kat, she wasn't with us on either end of the bridge. She didn't know we were trying to bring her back. That one change would have entirely altered the energy flow at the cathedral."

Kat put a weary hand to her forehead. "Forgive me, Stephen. I'm just not at my best. You need to be extremely precise."

He straightened as the idea crystallized in his mind. He couldn't tell whether it was his own idea or one born elsewhere. At the moment, he didn't care. It seemed the first warm ray of light he'd felt in days.

"Listen, Kat. What if the bridge we're talking about isn't a physical one?"

"Well, it couldn't be, could it?" she said, obviously annoyed. "Nobody could build a bridge to the fourteenth century."

"What if the bridge is built by some sort of energy flow? By frequency coordinates in time and space? What if it's created by things unseen?"

Kat groaned as intangibility threatened to overrun her mind.

Claire's mouth dropped open. "That's good, Daddy."

Stephen threw her a double-take, but his own train of thought drew him away from her unusual words and back to the concepts rapidly flowing through his mind.

"That still makes it all nearly impossible," he continued, almost to himself. "If we have to duplicate the same frequencies to bring Francesca back, that means we need to pray at the cathedral at the same time we did when she left us."

"It was two-fifteen in the afternoon," Kat said, surprising him with her recollection.

"How do you know?"

She reddened. "I looked at my watch to see exactly how much time I was wasting."

"Okay, then we know the time. We know where we sat in the Lady Chapel. You and I can always go back, Kat, but I'm not sure it will work if Francesca isn't in on it."

Kat's eyebrows flew upward. "What do you suggest we do, Stephen? Send her a postcard? This is nuts. It can't be right."

"Send Julia to get Aunt Frannie," Claire said.

Her parents stared at her. She shrugged.

"Well, she's already been there, hasn't she? She can go back and tell Aunt Frannie to get to the right spot at the right time."

"But Asteroth . . ." Kat's voice twisted onto the breeze.

In front of the house, a car door slammed. "Thanks for the ride," they heard Julia call.

"This can't be right," Kat tried again, but her voice sounded unconvincing.

The front door slammed. "Hello!" Julia called through the house. "Anyone home?"

Stephen cleared his throat, but Claire answered first.

"We're on the back porch, Julie. And wait till you hear what's happening next!"

# 23

THE PACKED DIRT OF THE PRIORY COURTYARD FELT HARDER than before against the soles of Francesca's feet. Her body lurched sluggishly toward the main gate. It was as if she'd plunged into a familiar river, only to discover the downward pull of an unexpected new current. Had she really grown so quickly accustomed to weightlessness that even the slightest reminder of physical form produced a metaphysical version of the bends?

Footsteps sounded from the cloister. Dame Margaret scurried across the stone walk, skirts billowing behind her like dark sails. Elinor, much younger and fleet of foot, followed close on her heels.

"Dame Margaret!" Elinor gasped. "Dame Margaret, forgive me this impudence, but I must speak with you at once."

Margaret stopped. Elinor, caught off guard, plowed into her.

"You must speak quickly, then." Margaret managed to stay upright. For all her stringiness, she seemed constructed of iron. She reached up a hand to smooth her wimple. "I must find Madame Alys at once. There is a catastrophe in the making."

Elinor flushed. "Then it is good I speak with you. I have news of Madame Alys."

Margaret's face softened as she studied the girl

before her. Francesca saw at once that the mistress of novices had a soft spot for this particular charge. She wondered briefly if Margaret thought of Elinor as the daughter she'd never had. Then she noticed the self-righteous squaring of the older woman's shoulders, the smug set of her mouth. Dame Margaret obviously saw Elinor as an appendage, a copy of herself who, with proper guidance, might rise to the heights that she herself had been denied.

Margaret lowered her voice. "Speak, then, for Isobel has run away. I must alert Madame at once. There is little time to lose."

Relief flashed across Elinor's plain face. "Oh, then that explains—"

"Explains what?"

The novice swallowed hard. "I saw Madame Alys and Father Gregory leave. They took neither oxen nor wagon and carried nothing. Madame has been so ill of late, and we have relied so on kind Father Gregory to help us through this difficult time, that I . . . I feared my own thoughts, Dame Margaret. Naturally, I sought your wise counsel."

"Naturally."

Francesca took a step closer as Elinor continued. Dame Margaret was certainly right about one thing: the nun and the girl were alike enough to relish the thought of Alys's downfall. Elinor lowered demure eyes, but her artless voice came straight from the serpent in the Garden of Eden.

"Dear Dame Margaret, you have provided an answer to soothe my worries. They have most surely gone in pursuit of Isobel. Are you sure that she has left us?"

"I watched her go."

"You didn't try to stop her?"

Margaret's mouth formed a thin, hard line. "You heard Madame Alys as we stood in the courtyard with Mistress Kate. We wanted to help; she bade us leave. I only honored her request. Besides, I was quite far away by the time Isobel left. I watched from the convent window as she slid through the gate with that viper, Hugh."

A small sigh escaped Elinor's parted lips. It was the only indication that she, too, might have enjoyed that opportunity. Margaret's razor-sharp glare chased away any remnant of yearning. Elinor hastily pulled her face into a more appropriate mask of obedience.

"Perhaps, then, all will end well," she said. "Father Gregory and Madame Alys will have her home by nightfall. And you, Dame Margaret, shall see to it that all is in order here at the priory until they return."

Francesca recognized Margaret's reaction as a good old twenty-first-century smirk. The nun sniffed as she tossed her head and started to walk down the cloister. Francesca was shaking her own head when Margaret's gaze brushed across her and stopped.

"Oh, my dear Lord." Margaret staggered backward.

Elinor rushed to her side, arms open to catch her in case she fell. "What has happened? Are you ill? Perhaps the excitement of this day—"

"No." Margaret brushed a bony hand across her eyes, then stared toward Francesca again. She blinked. "I thought I saw a woman: here, yet not here. But the vision is gone now. It was merely a trick of the light. Come, Elinor. There is much to be done. There is always much to be done."

Francesca remained frozen in her spot as the two skimmed across the stones of the cloister and disappeared from her view.

There was no longer any doubt about it. She was growing solid. Curious, she raised her hand to the sun. Not that long ago she'd actually seen light pulsing through each vein, invigorating each molecule and filling her with an otherworldly tingle of energy. Now she saw the raised veins and knobby joints of a woman in her sixties.

She had little time to lose.

She hurried toward the priory gate. Before, she'd noticed only the light and beauty of her unfamiliar surroundings. How fresh the unpolluted air had felt against her skin, how delicate the church spire had seemed against the backdrop of high, blue sky! Now she noticed more worldly details. An occasional whiff of sewage attacked her nostrils, while the yellow of Dame Margaret's remaining teeth was apparent even from yards away.

Living exclusively in spirit was one thing. Being trapped in an alternate physical reality would be intolerable. She could never survive here, stuck forever in medieval England. Never mind the daily inconveniences, the struggle against ailments whose cures remained centuries away. She needed Kat, Stephen, and their girls as much as she needed to breathe.

She stopped at the main gate. Minutes ago it had seemed the most logical destination. Now that she'd arrived, she had no idea what to do next.

"Very well," she said out loud. It helped to hear the sound of her own voice. It sounded calm and capable in the still of the summer air.

Every sinew in her body wanted to go home, but a crystal-clear truth cut straight through the longing. Even if she figured out how to get back to Baltimore, danger remained unchecked. Asteroth, who could bend centuries as well as physical form, would wait at every door. It wouldn't matter if the door were made of fourteenth-century wood or modern steel. Vile evil would lurk beyond it, crouched and ready to destroy.

"Very well," Francesca said again, settling back against the gate. She'd faced this demon before. One could even say she'd won that battle—or, rather, that God had won it through her. Her faith in the light had stayed strong, and the answers had been there that blistering day fifteen years ago. Of course solutions would await her now. She only needed to ask, then listen. The worst action she could take would be to disbelieve that.

She closed her eyes and drew in a long, deep breath. She slowly exhaled. The iron bars of the gate felt hard against her spine. The priory seemed to recede into haze as she found a comfortable, steady rhythm on which to focus.

"I'm ready," she said. "Tell me what to do. Give me the strength to do it."

The bars against her back grew warm. She thought she felt a soft kiss upon her forehead, but to ponder it would draw her out of this protected moment.

A clear little voice rang through her head, despite the fact that she'd assumed herself quite alone.

"I can help you," it said. "I am of the light. You and I fight together."

Francesca raised an eyebrow but kept her eyes

closed, unwilling to break communion with this unknown personality.

"Who are you?" she asked.

A little laugh scattered raindrops of light before her eyes. "Does it matter? Isn't it enough to know that I am born of the light and will return to the light? Besides, my dearest Francesca, your heart and soul know me so very well. Only your mind requires an introduction."

Francesca recognized some truth in this. She paused a second to concentrate on the sound of her own measured breathing. She'd almost allowed physical reality far more credibility than it deserved.

"So much better." The voice felt golden with approval. "Try to remember, Francesca. You've never fought alone. You had help last time. You always have help."

"God helped me last time," Francesca said.

"Obviously. That's a given. And if I recall, our Creator used that standard practice of letting the light flow through other people. After all, Francesca, you certainly didn't arrive at this priory on your own."

Of course she hadn't. Her mind quickly reviewed her last image of the twenty-first century. The cathedral. Kat staring down at her shoes, her watch, barely containing her annoyance. Stephen seated beside her, actually trying to pray.

Stephen.

Fifteen years ago, Stephen had been the viaduct, the channel for information despite his own reluctance.

"Yes," said the voice, and Francesca sensed a smile behind the words. Whoever this was, he or she was propelled by joy. She didn't quite understand that. Didn't this being realize the great danger they faced?

Earth to Stephen, she thought, dragging her focus back to the matter at hand. She subdued a chuckle. She was not a particularly amusing person, so this small attempt at humor startled her. Something about her companion seemed to inspire mirth.

Not earth to Stephen. It was far more than that. Dancing, light-filled energy surrounded her. She pictured it as a long, glowing stream connecting her to her nephew. The light danced before her, dazzling in its intensity.

"Let your words flow through it," the helpful voice suggested.

"Come in, Stephen," Francesca whispered, but the words no longer seemed funny. "Apparently, this is meant to be a collaborative effort. Please, open Stephen's heart to this."

It felt good to pray. Perhaps she'd allowed fear more access than she'd originally supposed.

"Open Stephen and bless this channel," she continued.

The response seemed to come from far away, like the whistle of a train rounding the bend of a miles-off mountain. Francesca's eyes flew open at the unexpected message: *Julia is coming.*

Julia?

"There." The original voice, more childish than before, sounded almost smug. "See? There is the next step."

"But Julia can't come here!" Her great-niece knew so little about matters of spirit. She was totally unprepared. Bringing her here was like sending a firefighter into the heart of a fire with no protective gear.

The presence she'd felt so strongly was already fading away.

"Wait." Francesca spoke out loud. "Don't leave me. I need more information."

A smattering of laughter answered her plea. "Oh, Francesca, I couldn't leave you if I tried."

Realization struck her full force.

"I know who you are!" she cried. "You're the child of light!"

But even the laughter had vanished, leaving only sparkling shadows behind.

Francesca returned her concentration to the ribbon of light that connected her to Stephen. She could almost envision him now, a definitely masculine form encased in shining armor.

"Julia is coming," he said again. "Take care of her, Frannie."

He raised the sword he held in his left hand and vanished, leaving Francesca alone by the priory gate.

Not really alone. She remembered her own spiritual armor and wondered briefly how she could have forgotten it. She quickly drew it on: truth buckled around the waist, integrity as a breastplate, salvation as a helmet, the shield of faith to keep away the burning arrows of evil. The sword in her hand glowed white. Spiritual battle required spiritual weaponry.

Enough whining and worrying. She was ready.

Kat awoke to find moonlight flooding her bedroom and her husband staring down at her, head propped on one hand.

"What?" She bolted upright, just missing his head with her own.

"I have a message for you," Stephen said, running his free hand through her sleek hair.

She blinked, wondering if she had fully awakened. She hadn't heard these words from her husband in fifteen years. Even then he'd swatted them away like uninvited flies at a picnic. The man before her seemed downright serene, an adjective she'd never been able to apply to him.

"Stephen. Are you okay?"

He leaned over and kissed her gently on the lips. "Put on your armor, Katerina."

She drew back with a gasp. Only Aunt Frannie called her Katerina. "What are you talking about?"

"Those are the words I heard, and I'm sticking to them. Something is about to begin, Kat. We can't afford fear or doubt right now. Put on your armor and stay close. Okay?"

Kat sank back into the comforting warmth of her bed. Even Stephen's newfound air of confidence would not calm the sickness she felt churning in the pit of her stomach.

# 24

KAT FORCED HERSELF TO STAY IN BED UNTIL SIX-THIRTY THE next morning. By then it was obvious that she'd never fall back to sleep. She was entirely too restless. Her down quilt, usually so snug and comfortable, seemed filled with pebbles instead of feathers. Even the pillows beneath her head felt hard.

With a groan, she sat and swung her legs over the side of the bed. She stepped carefully onto the cold wood floor, cringing in anticipation of her body's daily mutiny. Headaches and stomachaches had become as predictable a part of her morning as daylight. Hmmm. Not bad. Her toes uncurled a bit. She actually felt okay . . . maybe even good.

A strong arm landed around her waist.

"Come back," Stephen said, dragging her into the depths of their bed.

Kat took in his rumpled hair and crooked grin. He looked positively boyish. Still, she placed a firm hand on each of his shoulders and pushed.

"You're cute, Stephen Carmichael, but I'm getting up anyway."

"Why?" His grip tightened. "Something I said?"

"You look too relaxed for a man in the midst of a supernatural disaster. It's disturbing. Besides, I need coffee."

His eyebrows rose. "Coffee? I haven't heard you even breathe that word these past few days."

"I know. I think I'm finally starting to feel better."

"And not a minute too soon. I need you."

Kat kissed him on his stubbly cheek. "You don't need me. Not really. You did okay yesterday filling Julia in on the weird pieces of our past."

Stephen flopped back against his pillows, arm flung across his eyes. "Oh, yes, I was wonderful. I especially liked the part where our daughter stared at me like I was nuts and said that she didn't want to talk about it anymore."

"Well, what did you expect?" Kat hoisted herself from the bed and padded across the floor to fetch her bathrobe. "Adolescence is hard enough without hearing scary stories about how your parents once battled evil spirits—including the one currently out to get you."

"Ouch." Stephen remained motionless. "I don't know, Kat. It's starting to look as if Frannie was right."

Kat slid her feet into her slippers. "About what?"

"We never gave our kids any spiritual weapons, did we?"

She leaned against the closet door to study him. She'd been willing to chalk up their middle-of-the-night conversation as a dream born of stress, but there was something different about her husband this morning, something she couldn't quite identify. For Stephen to even speak in terms of spirit struck her as odd, almost as if he'd opened his mouth and spouted Hindustani.

"What's happened to you while I've been under the weather?" she asked, eyes narrowed.

He turned to face her, forehead puckered in thought. "I'm not sure. Why?"

She opened her mouth to answer, then closed it again. There was no way to describe how she felt without sounding stupid. Her husband had somehow acquired a new facet, an overlay of assured strength that had not been with him last night. How to explain that to a man who had done little more that morning than simply wake up?

She pushed her hair behind her ears and aimed for flippancy. "I don't know what's different. I guess you're just not the man I married."

"Hmm." He looked thoughtful. "Maybe I *am* the man you married. Maybe that distracted other guy was the intruder."

Kat shuddered. "Too deep, too early. I need caffeine. Are you coming, or will I have to grind the coffee beans myself?"

"I'm coming. We need to talk."

*We need to talk.* Was there anyone on earth who welcomed that phrase? It always sounded ominous, no matter what the intention. Stephen seemed to realize that as he yanked on his sweats and combed his fingers through his hair.

"It's not as if everything is business as usual around here," he offered as an explanation. "We need to discuss the next step."

She gave a curt nod. "I leave that to you, sir. After your three-in-the-morning revelation about my armor, I assume you have a pipeline of sorts attached to a spiritual advice line."

He frowned. "Don't go cynical on me, Kat. Now isn't

the time. And the armor message wasn't anything you didn't already know."

"That's just it, Stephen. Sure, I knew it. I just can't pull it up when I need it. This stuff sticks with you. It takes a while for anything esoteric to penetrate your credibility, but once it does, you seem to have no trouble using it. Why can't I do that? Why can't I stop doubting it all? Why don't I believe like you believe?"

He stared at her, genuinely surprised. "But you *do* believe. You're a fighter, Kat. You always have been."

"Maybe. I believe in God, of course. And I recognize that what's happening to us has nothing to do with the tangible world everybody else sees. But apparently I'm too cynical to get directions. I never know what to do."

"You do know what to do," he insisted. "It's just that you're a lawyer. You question everything."

"And you're a businessman," she shot back. "You focus on the bottom line. Why you, Stephen?"

He shook his head. She read the slight hurt in his eyes. "I don't know," he said.

"Well, I don't know, either." She wished she could make her tone less clipped. "None of this makes sense. I need it to make sense, or I can't fix it. How can anyone . . . or anything . . . expect me to fight effectively without facts?"

"There aren't any," he started, but she turned and left the room before he could add anything else. He winced at the ramrod set of her back, then followed her.

He caught her at the foot of the stairs, spinning her to face him with a deft tug on her bathrobe cord.

"Hey," he said. "Kat. We're in this together. It's going

to take both of us to bring Frannie back and to keep our girls safe."

She sighed, then allowed herself to slump into him. "I know, Stephen. I'm sorry. It's just very hard when I have no clue about what comes next. It's like traveling through a dense fog. I know that something horrible and unavoidable is out there, but I can't see well enough to know exactly what it is, let alone handle it."

"Well." He managed a twisted smile. "I guess we'll figure it out when we ram into it."

A rustle from the family room caught their attention.

"We are not alone," Stephen commented. "It's ridiculously early. Which kid, do you think?"

"Oh, Julia. Hands down. Claire couldn't be that quiet if she tried. I'll go to her. You start the coffee."

"Sure thing." He headed down the hall to the kitchen entrance. The kitchen and the family room actually formed a large ell, but it seemed somehow prudent to let Kat start this conversation alone.

Julia sat in front of the fireplace, crumpling newspaper to place beneath the logs she'd laid on the grate. She looked up as her mother entered the room.

"Hi, Mom. Do you mind if I make a fire?"

"Looks like you already did." Kat walked over to the loveseat beneath the window and sank into the soft cushions.

For once Julia did not roll her eyes at her mother's comment. She looked pale. The circles beneath her eyes told all about the kind of night she'd had.

"Julia, sweetie, how long have you been awake?"

"Um . . . off and on all night, I guess. I only came downstairs about fifteen minutes ago. May I light the fire?"

"Sure." Kat reached for the afghan at the end of the loveseat. The whir of the coffee grinder filled the room as she pulled the warm blanket up around her knees.

Julia's head turned instinctively toward the kitchen.

"Dad's awake, too," Kat said. She thought that Julia brightened a bit, but it was hard to tell. She watched as her daughter struck a match and lit the corner of the newspaper. Julia built good fires. The flame spread quickly, catching the dried kindling and sending eager tongues flickering upward.

"I'm sorry you had a rough night," Kat said. "I can certainly understand why."

"Yeah." Julia licked her lips, then cast a quick glance toward the kitchen. "Is Dad on his way to the restaurant?"

"No. Actually, I think he's going to put up the coffee and then come in to enjoy your fire."

"Oh. Okay." Once again, the odd expression crossed Julia's face. Kat couldn't tell whether her daughter wanted Stephen to join them or whether the idea upset her.

She didn't have long to ponder it. Stephen joined them, stopping to plant a kiss on Julia's head before sliding next to his wife on the loveseat.

"Good morning, sweetheart," he said.

Kat observed Julia closely. The girl stared at her father, swallowed hard, and then locked her gaze onto the dancing fingers of flame. Even Stephen, normally so obtuse, picked up the sudden change in the air.

"What is it?" he asked flatly. "No more secrets, Julia."

"You'll probably think I'm crazy, Dad."

"With a past like mine? I doubt it. I *do* know that time's running short."

Julia turned beseeching eyes his way. "I had a dream last night."

Kat immediately tensed. What if it hadn't been a dream at all? What if Julia had once again been transported into Asteroth's orbit? A sense of urgency raced through her as she leaned forward to speak. The warning press of Stephen's hand on her knee stopped her. She glanced at him. He remained relaxed, long legs stretched across the coffee table, arm resting against the back of the couch.

"Oh?" he said, tone casual. "Scary or helpful?"

"I'm not sure. Weird." She tucked her knees up beneath her chin and wrapped her arms around her legs.

"Mom and I are pretty good at interpreting this stuff," Stephen said. "Go ahead."

"Okay. I guess I'd been asleep for a while, because I knew that the moon was high and that everything was very still. I saw the man and the girl again."

"That would be Asteroth and Isobel." Stephen was so calm that Kat had to wonder how he did it.

"I wasn't too afraid," Julia continued. "They were far away. It was as if I was watching them through the trees of a forest. They didn't even know I was there."

"Where were they?" Kat asked, unable to wait quietly on the sidelines.

"They were in a clearing, I think. They had lit a fire, although I could see that the man was sweating. He said something . . . that they were to find stones. Smooth, white stones. He'd brought a branch of rosemary and stuck it into the ground near the fire, like a little tree. Then he told Isobel that it was nearly time."

Julia paused. The information seemed so empty, so lacking in anything of importance. Kat wanted to urge her daughter forward, to press her to remember any small detail that might explain their next step. But once again, Stephen's fingers pressed into her knee. She recognized the warning for patience. Julia glanced up at her parents. Apparently satisfied that they were still listening, she went on. "So they started searching for stones. It was so dumb. The man kept closing his eyes, reaching out his hand over leaves and parts of the ground as if he was trying to feel where stones might be hiding. It was like a creepy horror flick."

Kat had to bite her tongue to keep from blurting out that Julia was more correct than she knew.

"What happened then?" Stephen asked.

"Well, the girl started walking toward my hiding place. I didn't want her to find me, so I turned and ran away through the woods. Then it was like I wasn't running anymore. I was floating, then flying, and I . . . I saw Aunt Frannie."

"Where was she?"

"She was standing by a fence, near a gate. And, Dad, she was . . . glowing. I know this sounds totally stupid, but it looked like she was wearing light."

"It's not stupid, Julie. That's her armor. Remember? We talked about spiritual armor yesterday. We all have it. Frannie's armor doesn't look like what we think of as armor. It's like dots of light all over her body."

"That's it, Dad. That's exactly it."

Kat's brow furrowed as she tried to process the information flowing between them. Julia had actually straightened, as if she understood exactly what Stephen was talking about. The look on her face could only be called relief.

"Then I'm not crazy," she said.

Stephen frowned. "Of course not."

"Because, Dad, a voice in the dream told me that you would know what was going on."

Stephen drew back. "It did?"

She nodded vigorously. "Then Aunt Frannie said something. She said—"

" '—put on your armor, Katerina,' " Stephen finished. "Yes, Julia, I dreamed that part, too."

Kat's mouth dropped as she took in first her husband, then her daughter. It was bad enough that apparently everyone else in the room could sense the unseeable. It was worse that, even when they shared their insights, she had no idea what was going on.

"That's all fine and dandy," she said, "but what does it mean?"

Stephen, who never blushed, burned a bright red. "Julie, did you happen to get the next part?"

Julia hesitated. "I thought I made that part up."

"Well, I guess you didn't," Kat snapped. "Is there a secret password involved here, or can any mere mortal play?"

Julia gazed into the fire. Stephen took Kat's hand in his own.

"Okay," he said. "After Frannie said to put on your armor, a new voice came onto the scene."

"Whose?"

Stephen shrugged. "I don't know. I can't even tell you if it was male or female. I think it was a child, but I'm not sure about that, either."

Kat made a sour face. "And I don't suppose this voice told you which lottery numbers to play?"

"No," Stephen said. "Actually, the voice said that you were to go with Julia to fetch Frannie."

All the color drained from Kat's face. "How am I supposed to do that? I'm the least spiritually attuned of all of us, apparently."

"You did it before, Mom." Julia placed her hand on Kat's unoccupied knee. "You saved me. Remember?"

Kat ran a finger across the arm of the couch, avoiding eye contact as if it were an art. "I thought that to bring Frannie back, we needed the same configuration we had when she traveled to the Middle Ages in the first place. That means I need to be at the cathedral with you, Stephen."

Stephen threw Julia a glance.

"I heard it, too," she said. "About Claire."

Kat's stomach thudded. "What about Claire?"

"She can take your place at the cathedral," Stephen said. "Apparently, the two of you share a frequency. I don't know. I don't get it, either. I just know that that's what I heard."

"Me, too," Julia added.

Kat closed her eyes and rested her head against the back of the couch. Of course, she'd rather be with Julia than send her daughter into the unknown alone. But why did this have to happen when she was just recovering from a migraine? She felt so weak, so out of it. Never mind that she got no spiritual marching orders even when she was in tiptop shape. In this draggy state, she was sure to miss even concrete, everyday orders as well.

"I don't suppose you could go instead?" she asked Stephen, already knowing the answer.

"No, Kat. I wish I could, but I'm supposed to stay at home base."

"Tell her the last part, Dad," Julia said, and Kat's eyes flew open at the realization that there was more information to absorb.

"Kat." Stephen's arm wrapped around her shoulder, a sure sign that he meant to comfort her. "We *must* move fast. The voice said that time is running out."

"Fast?"

"Today."

She could see Stephen's lips move, even hear sound coming out of them. She recognized concern in his face. Still, whatever he was saying seemed elongated and thick, as if the sound waves traveled through salt water.

"Mom?" Julia's worried voice floated past her ears.

Stephen gave her knee a reassuring pat, then stood. "Don't worry, Julie. Mom's okay. She just needs some coffee."

Her own voice sounded far, far away. "I am not okay, Stephen."

"Yes, you are." He disappeared from her view. "You have to be."

She heard the clink of mugs, the opening and closing of the refrigerator door. The fire crackled in the fireplace, sending warmth into the room. A small thump sounded above her head: Claire, awake and ready for action. How could the rhythm of the house continue in such a normal fashion when the very fabric of her existence threatened to rip apart?

"Here." Stephen thrust a mug into her hand. Her fingers instinctively curled around the handle. "Drink it," he ordered, and as if a doctor had prescribed it, she did.

Claire's footsteps scurried above them. She was in the hallway now, pattering toward the stairs. Suddenly, the footsteps stopped.

"Whoa," they heard her say. She sounded as if she'd just seen an exotic flower in an unexpected place. "What's *this* all about?"

They all knew that she stood before the door to Francesca's room.

"I don't want to know," Kat said, but Stephen tugged her to her feet all the same.

"Hey! Mom! Dad!" Claire called as the three of them reached the landing.

"We're here," Stephen said.

"Look!" Claire pointed into the bedroom.

Aunt Frannie lay in the bed, still as ever, position unchanged. Something was different, though. It took Kat only a second to figure out what exactly had changed.

"Oh, no," she breathed.

"I can see through her!" Julia gasped.

It was true. Although still solid, Francesca appeared lighter in density. As she stared at her aunt's pale face, Kat could make out the rumpled pillowcase beneath her head. The maroon duvet darkened Frannie's pale fingers, making them rosy.

"Okay," Stephen said. "What more do I need to say?"

Kat shook her head in disbelief. "Nothing. We'll go to the cathedral as soon as the last mass ends."

# 25

A LONG RIBBON OF CARS WRAPPED THROUGH THE CATHEDRAL parking lot, disappearing behind the huge building. Stephen noted that the gray stone of the cathedral nearly blended with the color of the dull winter sky. He slowed the car to a stop as the traffic light at the entrance of the parking lot turned red.

"Looks like church is over," Claire said from behind him. Her foot once again kicked the back of the driver's seat as she twisted to watch cars stream past.

Stephen propped his elbow against the window and leaned his head on his hand. "Good thing Claire's seat-belted," he said. "Otherwise she'd probably bounce herself right out of the car."

Kat didn't react to his lame attempt at humor. She sat curled sideways in the front passenger seat, eyes locked firmly on the cathedral's spires.

"Did your inner voices warn you that we'd be sitting in traffic?" she asked.

"No."

"What good are they, then?"

He wanted to drill her with a glare, but held back. Kat always resorted to sarcasm when she felt afraid, and he certainly couldn't blame her for feeling that way now. He patted her knee, then turned his attention back to the red light.

He actually welcomed this delay. He had no idea what to do next. He'd almost accepted the fact that he'd get occasional pushes in the right direction. What bothered him was that he never got complete marching orders. How helpful was that?

He glanced in the rearview mirror. Claire still bounced around like a rubber ball on speed. Julia, like her mother, stared at the cathedral. Her eyes, wider than usual in a masklike face, glittered green. He could only imagine the thoughts running through her head.

Other kids went to camp. She was going to the Middle Ages.

The light turned green. Panic seemed not only appropriate, but downright required. Somehow, though, Stephen couldn't muster the desired hysteria. He sighed as he pushed the gearshift into first. Great. No clear marching orders, *and* no inclination to share his wife's justified fear. He could just imagine how this would enhance his marriage.

It didn't matter that both Kat and Julia had lapsed into morbid silence. Claire chattered enough for everyone.

"Hey, look! A parking place right at the front door! We're so lucky! Have I ever been here, Dad? Mom? I think I have, but I don't remember."

"You've been here," her father said. "It's been a long time, though." He furrowed his brow, trying to remember when his younger daughter had last been inside this local landmark.

"I think you were two," Kat told Claire. "Aunt Frannie took you and Julia to a weekday mass."

"I was here?" Julia looked blank.

Kat nodded.

Stephen pulled open the heavy doors at the top of the steps and they entered the silent building.

Julia wrinkled her nose. "Are you sure I've been here?"

"Yes." Kat reached for her hand. "You probably don't remember much of it."

"I don't remember any of it," Julia said as they stepped into the sanctuary.

As usual, Stephen felt awed by the intimidating heights of the cathedral. The severe angles of the architecture demanded a life account from him. He hugged Claire close. Cavernous places like this could give any kid the creeps.

Claire slipped from his grasp and started down the left aisle as if she knew exactly where she was going.

"I remember this place," she said, passing through the flickering reflections of stained glass on the stone floor.

Stephen and Kat exchanged glances, then hurried to catch up with their younger daughter.

"Wait for us." Stephen reached her first, tugging the hood of her jacket to slow her down.

"Oh, I know where I'm going," Claire said. "We're going to the Mary chapel, right? The little place in the back of the church? I just want to visit Saint Michael on the way."

"Saint Michael?" Stephen blinked.

"You remember, Stephen," Kat said, catching up to them. "The relief sculpture on the wall."

Sure enough, Claire picked up speed, her boots slapping against the stone floor. A woman in a center pew looked up and frowned, fingers entangled in her rosary beads. Claire didn't notice. Kat mouthed the word "Sorry" as they flew past.

Julia had reached her sister first. She stood staring openmouthed beside Claire at the life-size Saint Michael mounted on the wall. Tinged with gold, he resembled a medieval knight with wings. There was no denying his power. It was evident in every tensed muscle, in the unheard battle cry falling from his lips.

"Wow," Julia finally said. Kat and Stephen stopped behind her.

"Isn't he neat?" Claire's grin grew wide. "He's a warrior, Julie. See his sword?"

Older-sister pride intruded. "Yes, Claire, I know who Saint Michael the Archangel is. He's on our side."

Claire nodded her agreement. "I wouldn't want to fight against him, I can tell you that."

"He's a reminder to put on your armor," Stephen said.

"Everything's a reminder to you that we should put on our armor," Kat said, but there was softness in her voice, a crack in the brittle wall she'd so expertly erected.

Stephen wrapped an arm around her shoulders. She looked pale again. Her bones reminded him more of a fragile bird than a full-grown woman. He peered into her face. She required more care and protection than she'd ever realize or admit. She'd always come packaged with more than her share of bravado, and he'd always let her take charge of the lion's share she was so sure she could handle. She was one of the most capable people he knew. Still, would it be so awful to occasionally save her from herself? There was no reason he couldn't hang around more, help out more. There was no reason she had to look so wan and thin.

He shook his head as if to clear away the thoughts. Now was not the time to stew over this stuff.

Claire had stood still quite long enough.

"Come on," she said, marching toward the back of the cathedral.

They passed a few stragglers, several tourists with cameras in hand. Fortunately, everyone was headed in the opposite direction. Stephen had never stopped to consider what they'd do in case of a crowd.

Julia shivered.

"Are you all right?" Kat asked.

"I feel weird. It's like somebody's trying to get in."

Stephen stopped. "What do you mean?"

Julia wrapped her arms across her chest. "It's hard to describe. I can hear people calling my name. I keep growing cold, then hot, then cold again. Somebody wants me, but I'm afraid to answer."

"Is your armor on?"

"I think so, Dad. I don't know."

"It's on," Claire said impatiently. "She keeps forgetting to lift her shield, though. Anybody want to know what my armor looks like?"

They stared at her, but she remained unruffled.

"It's not like Julie's," she continued blithely. "Julie's is silver, but mine is gold colored. Not real gold, because gold is a soft metal—not good for battle. But gold colored so that when the sun glints off it, my enemies are temporarily blinded. Want to hear more?"

"I don't think I can handle more," Kat whispered to Stephen. He squeezed her shoulder, never taking his eyes from Claire.

"What else?" he asked.

But she skipped down the aisle to the back of the church and turned right, out of view.

"That child grows odder every day," Kat said in a low voice. "What about it, Stephen? Do you think she's the—"

"She's always been odd," Julia interrupted as she followed her sister.

"Stephen, wait." Kat's small hand slid into his. He turned to her, surprised by the grave tone in her voice.

"I don't understand how any of this works," she said, face turned up to his. "But I want you to know that, whatever happens, I love you very much."

The enormity of her words slugged him with full force. He grabbed her other hand. "Kat. We've got years and years left to say that to each other."

Her attempted smile fizzled. "I hope so. I want that, Stephen, but we can't be sure of it, can we?"

He gathered her into his arms, then bent to kiss her lips. She was right. He'd always assumed that they'd emerge victorious at the end of this episode, just as they had the last time. But where was the proof of that? None of his "messages" guaranteed a positive outcome. Good people died fighting evil. They always had, they always would.

He drew in a deep breath of her soft, fragrant hair, imprinting the moment onto his memory.

"I'll do everything in my power to keep you safe, Katerina Piretti," he whispered into her ear. "You can count on me."

She wrapped her arms around his neck. "I do, Stephen."

"Hey." Claire stood at the end of the aisle, hands

planted firmly on her hips. "Break it up. You're in church. Besides, we have a lot to do."

The Lady Chapel was empty when they entered its serene hush.

"How did Julia know where to sit?" Kat asked, for their daughter had planted herself in the exact same pew that her parents and Francesca had occupied during their last visit.

Stephen shook his head. Wordlessly, he and Kat each took one of Claire's hands.

"Do we sit in any particular order?" Kat sank down beside Julia.

Stephen watched as Claire stepped over her mother and sister to deposit herself at the end of their row. She seemed to have a seating plan in mind, even if he didn't. He knew only that he wanted to stay close to his wife for as long as possible.

"What next?" Kat asked. "Are there magic words or something? How do we start?"

Stephen threw a glance at Julia, then turned to study her more closely. Her eyes were closed. Her lips moved wordlessly.

A momentary stab of panic rose inside him. "What's happening, Julie?" He leaned across Kat to tap the girl's knee.

Julia's voice sounded breathy and far away. "They're calling me. And I hear bells. Really, I think I have to go now."

Kat clutched her hand. "No, Julia. Wait!"

A half smile flickered across Julia's face.

"Who's calling you?" Kat demanded.

"I don't know, Mom, but I do need to go."

"Kat." Stephen turned her face toward his. "We're out of time. Don't let her go without you."

"How did this happen so fast?" Kat's voice rose. "What do I do, Stephen? How do I get there?"

"Close your eyes," he ordered, following his own command. "Hold on to Julia in your mind and concentrate on the light!"

"Julie, don't forget your sword," Claire said in a clear voice. "And for heaven's sake, use that shield. That's what it's there for."

Kat's breathing came in hard little gasps. Stephen couldn't take the time to open his own eyes and check on her. A sudden urgency overwhelmed him, pushing him along like a gust of wind shoving a kite.

"Believe it, Mommy," he heard Claire say. "You *are* going with Julia. You'll be there."

The intoxicating aroma of roses filled the chapel. Stephen thought he heard the flapping of wings. A high-pitched, bell-like tone, delicate as spun glass, hung on his consciousness. Light seemed to pour through each chapel window, so bright that he could sense it even through his closed eyelids. The warmth of the dazzling rays caressed his skin like velvet.

Claire giggled. "That's nice," he heard her say, but there was no time to ponder it. All of his energy concentrated into one powerful beam of light. It wrapped itself around and through Kat and Julia, illuminating them from the inside out, making their skin glow translucent pink.

"Protect them," he whispered fiercely, and the light grew even stronger, pumping through Kat and Julia as if calling their names.

Kat slumped against his shoulder. His eyes flew open in time to see Julia's head drop onto her chest.

"Oh, my God!" He hugged Kat close. He'd forgotten about this part.

Claire's round eyes turned his way. "They look like they're sleeping."

If his heart pounded any harder, he would faint, too.

"Don't worry, Daddy," Claire said. "At least we know where they are."

That thought only sent new spasms of fear coursing through his gut. "Do you think they made it?"

Claire's nod was so assured that Stephen didn't even question why he now took comfort in the words of an eight-year-old.

He eased Kat into a more comfortable position against his chest.

"Claire, can Julie rest with her head on your lap?"

"Sure. But it will look silly if anyone sees us."

Other people. That possibility existed, too. Still, if they were supposed to bring Frannie back in the same fashion as she'd left before, they'd need to stay where they were. He wondered how time worked in this situation. Did twenty-first-century hours correspond with medieval ones?

"Do you hear anything?" Claire asked.

Stephen glanced at his watch. One-thirty. Francesca had melted into time at 2:15. Somehow, he knew that the door, which had cracked open then, would once again open for them at 2:15 this afternoon—if each and every necessary element were exactly in place.

"I'm not getting anything definite, sweetie."

Her eyebrows, little twin question marks, remained raised. He wished he had all the answers.

"We'll sit here a few minutes," he managed, and Claire seemed content enough with that response.

Stephen closed his eyes again, hoping for crystal-clear directions concerning what to do next.

"Pray for protection and clarity," he heard, and for one crazy moment, it seemed as if the words had come from Claire. When he checked, however, she sat still beside him, absently playing with Julia's hair.

There was nothing to do but wait.

# 26

"How remarkably mundane," Kat murmured to herself as a wall of heat enveloped her. Now, why had she said that? There was certainly nothing ordinary about the fountains of light soaring about her like an amusement park exhibit gone berserk. And the roar of wind in her ears! Really, what more had she expected from the special effects department?

She heard Julia's gasp from somewhere on her right and reached for her daughter's hand.

"Still with me, Julie?"

"Yes." Her voice sounded far, far away. "Mom, how can you stay this calm?"

Good question. Kat wondered about that herself. Maybe it was because dealing with this stuff fifteen years ago had already scared her for life. Or perhaps this whole stream of events seemed too fantastic to believe, much less take seriously. Whatever the reason, Kat fought hard to banish lines like "Beam me up, Scottie" from her brain.

Suddenly, the light and noise stopped. Kat and Julia stood alone in a wood, surrounded by slender, straight trees. Soft green moss cushioned their feet. Leaves rustled overhead. Kat thought that they must have landed, but she hadn't felt a touchdown.

"Whoa." Julia glanced up. Kat instinctively did the

same. She had never before seen such a pure, clear blue sky. The sun glowed off-center like a halogen lightbulb.

"Mom," Julia whispered. "Are we really in medieval England?"

Kat stared at her daughter. "I assumed you'd know."

Julia's eyes widened. "Me? Why?"

A sickening realization began to stir. "Julia. You were the one who had the dream. Remember? The one you shared with Dad. You and Dad are the ones who know what to do. I'm just along for the ride, to help out."

Julia slowly shook her head. "I don't think so, Mom."

"Oh, Julie, that's the way it has to be!"

"I don't think so," Julia said again. Her voice quavered. "I don't know anything. I'm not even sure where we are."

"But you said that you were called!" Kat's voice spiraled upward in the still woods. "You said you had to go!"

Julia squirmed. "I was. I did. But I don't hear anything now. I'm sorry."

Oh, dear God. First no Aunt Frannie. Then, just as it seemed that Stephen and Julia might actually crack the code to this mess, even that security blanket got yanked away.

Kat turned from her daughter and leaned her forehead against the rough bark of a tree. How could this be?

"But Julie, I don't hear anything, either. I never hear anything. You know that."

Her daughter simply stood there, waiting.

So this would be like everyday life, motherhood bolstered to the nth degree. Even in this surreal world of the supernatural, she'd need to run interference, to guide and lead where no reasonable human being would ever want to go.

There was no way out.

Kat pulled in a ragged breath. "Okay, then. Let's try to figure out where we are. Does anything look familiar to you?"

"I'm not sure. A little. It reminds me of that last dream I had, the one where I ran away from Isobel. Remember? Isobel and Hugh were searching for white stones."

Yes, she remembered. Kat again squinted up at the sky. The sun had inched a little closer to the horizon. It was afternoon. She wasn't sure if that was important, but it seemed like a fact she might want to know.

Maybe they should just start walking. But where? They could start off in one direction and end up someplace totally ridiculous, totally off point. Should they just stay where they were, then? Was there an important reason they'd appeared in this particular spot?

Who knew?

She slammed her open palm against the tree. How was she supposed to know what to do?

"Mom." Julia touched her arm. "What's next?"

"I don't know, Julia."

Julia looked as if she might cry. "Try to hear. There has to be a reason you were the one sent here."

Oh, there was a reason, all right. The reason was that this was a terrible mistake, some colossal miswiring of whatever the real message was supposed to be. Kat turned to face her daughter.

"Mom." Julia licked her lips. "No offense, but how did you get through this fifteen years ago?"

Another good question. The kid was full of them. Kat slumped against the tree and furrowed her brow.

"Dad knew what to do last time," she said.

"But you both said that he didn't really believe in anything spiritual, then."

"That's true. He didn't even believe his own messages half the time. He got them in spite of himself." There was no denying that Stephen had been a cantankerous disaster when they'd first met. Driven by success alone, he'd seemed an unlikely candidate for any sort of enlightenment. And yet words of truth had flowed through him all the same. "Aunt Frannie helped too, sweetie. Her faith has always been so strong. Sometimes I think that she believed enough to get all of us through."

Julia shook her head. "It's probably more than that. The three of you were a team. You're all a real-life example of that line in the Bible—you know, 'Where two or more are gathered, there am I.' "

Kat raised her eyebrows hopefully. "Are you hearing this now?"

"No. I just pay more attention in Sunday School than you and Dad think."

Kat rolled the phrase across her own tongue. "Where two or more are gathered . . ."

"Then God is there, too," Julia reminded. "Couldn't that be what happened fifteen years ago?"

"Well, sure, Julie. I always assumed that."

"And, Mom, couldn't that happen now? I mean, there are two of us here, and Dad and Claire are praying for us back at the cathedral . . . lighting us. Isn't that what Aunt Frannie calls it sometimes?"

Kat opened her mouth to reply, but Julia never paused long enough to let her squeeze in a word.

"You said that Aunt Frannie had all the faith back then, and that Dad let the light work through him even though he thought the whole situation was nuts. But what did you do?"

Kat stiffened. "Nothing would have happened without me. I asked the questions that set off the whole chain of events, questions that deserved answers. A great injustice had been done to somebody I cared about. I needed to fix that." She paused. Her tenacity had forced Stephen to stay the course. Even though they'd disliked each other, she'd been impossible to ignore. She'd pulled him back to the task again and again no matter how hard he'd tried to escape.

"I guess I've always been . . . um . . . determined," she said lamely.

Julia's green eyes nailed her. "Don't you think a little determination could help us out now?"

Kat groaned. Who wanted to hear one of their own lectures thrown back at them?

"Besides," Julia's voice dropped, "what if determination turns out to be some kind of gift, just like Aunt Frannie's gift of faith?"

"Okay, okay." Kat stepped away from the tree. "I'll do the best I can."

Fifteen years ago, she'd needed answers badly enough to push forward into a void. Even though she hadn't understood their mission, even though she'd found every explanation unbelievable, she'd longed for justice to prevail. Her willingness to forge ahead in the name of truth had been enough to let the light work through her.

She cocked her head to one side, clearing her heart for directions. Anything would help. An internal sentence. A word. Something.

Nothing came.

She straightened up and took a deep breath. They'd have to take some sort of action. Nothing was worse than stagnation.

"Let's walk in this direction," she said, trying to keep her voice even.

They started toward the sun, which had already dropped a bit more in the sky. Kat strained to hear at least a confirmation that they were on the right path. No voice helped her, no words materialized in her brain.

The route before them felt sterile, like a field left fallow for too many years. Kat stopped. "I've changed my mind. Let's go the other way."

"Did you hear something?" Julia's face brightened.

"No. I didn't hear anything. This way just doesn't feel . . . fruitful. I have to go with my intuition. It's all I've got."

Julia looked as if she wanted to argue. Then she swallowed back her doubts and fell into step beside her mother. The sun warmed their backs as they weaved through the sparse, quiet trees.

Perhaps traditional metal armor felt slow and cumbersome. Spiritual armor was quite the opposite. Francesca's armor energized her with each pulsing point of light. Her sword burned brightly in her hand as she strode away from the priory. She moved on autopilot now, her will surrendered and wrapped into a loving energy far greater than anything she could intellectually fathom.

*Move. Walk in this direction, down this road.*

It never occurred to her to disobey. She saw only her own fragile form on this worn dirt road, but it felt as if she walked at the head of a brilliant battalion of light.

She wanted to ask where she was going, what came next. She knew better. Answers never arrived before their proper moment. They remained contained, revealed only when fully ready. Patience, always hard to achieve, was more important than she'd ever cared to admit.

She raised her shield as an unexpected wind stirred up a cyclone of dust on the road.

One answer was already clear, crystal hard within her core: her search right now was not for Isobel, or even for Asteroth. She needed to find Julia, and there wasn't much time left.

# 27

A WISP OF SMOKE CURLED FROM THE THICK BUNDLE OF ROSEmary branches that Hugh had stuck upright into the earth. From her seated position at the edge of the stone circle, Isobel's gaze followed it upward. There wasn't much to see. The smoke vanished from view a short way from its origin, leaving behind a perfume so pungent that it almost brought tears to her eyes. Perhaps if she didn't sit so close to the flame . . . she began to back away from the stones that surrounded the rosemary.

"No, Isobel." Hugh crouched across from her. He'd made the circle of white stones so small that his knees nearly brushed against hers. "Stay close to the fire. Inhale this incense. Breathe deeply. You breathe the wisdom of eternity."

Isobel's nose wrinkled as she swallowed back a sneeze. She usually liked the smell of rosemary, but even though only the tip of one branch now burned, this scent was overpowering. What would happen when the flame traveled downward, engulfing the entire rosemary bouquet? Then the twigs and branches Hugh had arranged at the base of the herb would also ignite, sending smoke of their own to mingle with the rosemary needles he'd sprinkled on top of them.

Hugh drew in a deep, long breath. His dark eyes glittered. Isobel strained to see if their strange glow reflected the flame. There was no time to tell. Hugh closed his eyes and quickly passed his right palm through the tip of the flame.

"Let it be," he murmured. "It must be." His lips parted in silent words that Isobel could not understand.

"It will be done," Hugh said, again passing his palm through the fire. "I command it; it will be done." This time the fire seemed to answer, leaping higher and blazing with an odd green center. Isobel stared. She'd never before seen such a flame.

The rosemary burned brightly now, almost cheerily. The needles crackled with intense heat, but the wood had not yet ignited. Smoke drifted higher into the air, funneling into a fragrant column as it rose. Despite this, Isobel noticed that her eyes no longer stung.

"That's right, my dear," Hugh said. "Draw in a deeper breath. Let it fill you."

The smoke even smelled different. Had Hugh dropped incense onto the pyre? Isobel couldn't be sure, but the perfume seemed less invasive, more inviting. She slowly inhaled. The tendrils of smoke tickled her nostrils, but did not irritate her. The fire itself grew playful as its flame licked the wood. New colors danced upward: green, lavender, and deep blue vanished into curling plumes several feet above Isobel's head.

She'd never before smelled such an enticing aroma. It made her think of faraway places she'd never seen, of fragrant spices from the East and rich, royal fabrics soft to her touch.

Hugh's mouth twisted into a knowing smile. "Ah, the pleasure of the senses," he said. "Can you not smell the wonders? Touch them? I bring you these gifts. You have been deprived for too long, shut up in the austerity of a Church that is afraid of joy. Drink this in, Isobel, for you deserve such splendor."

As if she needed urging. The lovely aroma had become impossible to resist. Isobel closed her eyes as her breathing grew deep and regular.

"How did you know to find them here?" Gregory asked Alys.

"This is where we found them last time." Her fingertips pressed into his arm as she peeked through the trees to the clearing beyond. He covered her hand with his own.

Isobel and Hugh sat across from each other, a small fire blazing between them.

"An evening meal, perhaps." Alys glanced about the fire for signs of small game or fowl.

"I think not." Gregory could not keep the troubled note from his voice. An unusual foreboding swelled within his chest. He hoped that Alys would be spared this sense of panic. "Mark the fire, Alys. Have you ever seen one quite like it?"

She studied the flame, which leapt and flickered before their eyes in colors nature had never intended. The wood beneath it did not burn. The fire seemed fueled by another source, although there was none to be seen.

Alys turned toward him, her raised eyebrows an answer to his question. Of course she'd never seen a fire such as this before. And, like him, she never wanted to see another one.

He peered through the trees. "What ails Isobel?"

Alys returned her gaze to the clearing. Isobel sat with her eyes closed, body swaying slightly as if to music no one else could hear. Together they watched as the girl's hands rose slowly from her lap, palms upward.

"She does not seem ill," Alys said. "She appears happy."

Gregory's voice was flat. "She appears bewitched," he said, and Alys winced as the words, undeniable, hung between them.

"Lovely, Isobel," they heard Hugh say. His voice was soft as finest velvet. He never took his eyes from Isobel's face as his right hand reached into the leather sack by his side. He withdrew his recorder and, with a smooth, arcing motion, raised it to his lips.

Gregory flinched as the first notes slid onto the air. He was musical, and the tones jarred his ears. They were mellow enough, well played and smooth, but somehow discordant, as if someone had decided to join songs that had no relationship to each other. The rhythm of the composition, however, perfectly matched Isobel's sway. Her eyes remained closed as the smile on her face broadened. Obviously, the music did not jangle her senses as it did his. Perhaps the girl's melodic sense was as lacking as her voice.

Alys stepped forward. "We must stop this at once."

Gregory pulled her back to his side. "No, Alys, not yet."

She turned to him, surprised. He wished he had a logical explanation for his instincts.

"It may be only my fear that speaks," he admitted slowly, "but we know so little of this . . . man. They surely plan to stay here for the night. Perhaps if we watch a bit longer, we'll gain more knowledge to use against him."

"But Francesca said—"

"Francesca said to keep him from Isobel. If it appears we must act, we will."

He knew her so well that he could almost hear the thoughts galloping through her head. Oh, how she wanted this episode in their lives to end! But they had no weapons, no way to overpower this evil they knew so little about. In the end she would agree with him: finding Isobel had only been part of the task. Now they needed a way to ease her from this monster's side.

"Think quickly," Alys said as they both sank to the ground to watch and wait.

Kat caught herself before she could trip over yet another tree root. A string of curses raced through her brain as she struggled to regain her balance. Damn this. This was not her century, not her milieu, not even her terrain. Maybe she'd have a fighting chance if they could just navigate across nice, safe pavement. It was bad enough she had to operate on intuitions she wasn't even sure she possessed. Did she have to suddenly turn into Nature Girl, too?

"Are you with me, Julia?" she called, partly to disguise her own exasperation.

Her daughter did not answer. Kat paused, listening for Julia's footsteps. There weren't any.

She swallowed back the fear that leapt to her throat. There wasn't time for anything as trite as fear.

"Julia?" She turned to retrace her steps. Julia was nowhere in sight, but Kat thought she caught a glimpse of orange sweatshirt through the trees. A sigh of relief escaped as she picked up speed. There were no orange sweatshirts in medieval England. This could only be an import.

Julia leaned against a tree, eyes closed and smile wide. Her upturned palms were raised to her waist.

"Come on, kiddo." Kat grabbed one of her hands. "We've got to move it."

Julia snatched her hand away. The smile never left her face as she crossed both arms against her chest in a gleeful hug.

Kat took a step closer.

"Julia?"

No response.

Kat's eyes narrowed. "Isobel?" she asked, hardly believing this new conclusion.

A sparkling cadence of giggles erupted from Julia's mouth. Julia never giggled. Kat blanched, but continued.

"Isobel, what are you doing?"

"He loves me, I think." It was Julia's voice, but certainly not her words. "And, oh, I feel wonderful now! The perfume is so nice, and his music is just for me. I think he will make love to me soon, for why else would he strive to intoxicate me so?"

"Where are you?" Kat asked sharply.

"Where we always go, of course. There is a clearing in the woods where we hide away for all our lessons."

Kat shifted into court mode, pulling herself up to her full height and summoning every ounce of authority she possessed.

"Isobel, I need Julia. Where is she?"

"Julia?" She sounded sad. "Must that girl always intrude? Yes, you're right. She's here, too. I was too happy to notice. She is in my way. Am I always to be tripping over her? Well, she can't have my Hugh, my precious, darling Hugh."

Kat raised a hand to her chest, hoping to calm the violent beating of her heart. "You are so right, Isobel. He is yours. Bring Julia to me."

A pout crossed Julia's features. "I want to, but Hugh might be angry if I part with his sweet Julia."

Kat thought fast. "How fortunate, then, that women are wiser than men. You, Isobel, recognize the problem. Even if you hold Hugh's heart, Julia will remain a temptation. Men are so weak. As much as Hugh loves you, he will want her, too."

"Yes . . ." The voice trailed into the distance.

"Men have no control over their desires," Kat continued. "I agree that you should keep him for yourself. He is rightfully yours. I'll even help you. Bring Julia to me. I'll take care of her."

The girl's face brightened. "You will? You can do that?"

"Of course."

"Wait, then. I'll get her. I'll . . ."

Julia slumped to the ground. Kat broke her fall as best she could, then dropped to her knees beside her.

"Julia, wake up."

Her daughter's eyes fluttered open. "Mom? Mom! I know where they are! I think . . . I think I was there . . . oh, my God, I was there, wasn't I? It happened again, it . . ."

Kat scrambled to her feet, dragging her daughter up with her. "Don't crack on me, Julia. There isn't time."

The commanding tone of voice did its job. Julia blinked back her tears before they could fall.

Kat shivered as the full impact of what had just happened hit her. She wiped a hand across her brow, brushing away the terrifying thoughts along with an errant lock of hair.

"Okay, Julia. Do you know how to get us to Isobel?"

Her daughter nodded. "I think so," she said in a small voice.

"Let's go, then. And let's fill your brain with some heavy-duty light, all right? Don't leave any room for this girl to wedge herself into your mind."

Julia's nod was starting to look automatic. Kat took in the blank expression on her daughter's face and reached for her hand.

"Don't let go of me," Kat said. "Lead on."

Numbly, Julia stumbled forward through the woods.

# 28

Francesca could see the warrior she truly was, bright and burning as she strode through the forest underbrush. In her mind's eye she glowed with the intensity of five hundred candles, fueled by a source that seemed both internal and external all at once. Her sword pulsed with energy, sending a vibrant charge of strength up her arm and through her body. It invigorated her, chased any lingering particles of doubt from her heart.

She sensed her colleagues; even with spiritual eyes she could not quite visualize them. They surrounded her as pulsating columns of brightness tinged with the most beautiful colors. She understood their language. Pink, violet, gold, blue, green—each color spoke of a love so much deeper than words could convey, each a facet of ultimate light. Francesca didn't need to see these companions to know that she was at one with them.

How wonderful to be so filled with joy! She longed to immerse herself entirely in spirit, to become an integral part of these dancing patterns. She felt energized when among them, guided by undeniable directives of truth. There were no lingering questions about what should happen next. She knew deep in her soul that what her companions told her was true: she had nearly reached a destination. Another page of her journey was about to unfold.

Unfortunately, that meant she now needed to rejoin her physical surroundings. With deep reluctance, Francesca pulled her self back into the forest. The density of the air hit her like a slug to the stomach. She slumped against a tree, gasping for breath.

"Did I really have to leave you so soon?" she panted, reaching out a hand for the columns of light she no longer saw.

She sensed rather than heard the gentle, loving laughter. She had not lost them at all. They remained deep within her heart, ever at her call.

Her eyes rested on her hand. Solid and heavy, it no longer seemed connected to her. The joints creaked as she tried to close her fingers into a fist. Though her spirit had soared with joy and strength, her physical body felt more and more mired in mud. At home, she'd prided herself on her jogging and weightlifting regimen. Here she felt at least a hundred years old, anchored to a crumbling body that could surely not hold out much longer.

"I want to fly again," she murmured.

*You will,* a now-familiar chorus reminded her.

"But I can't do this." She no longer needed to gulp for air, but her breathing felt labored and difficult, as if she had to try too hard for something that should have been instinctual.

*You must do this.*

Love rested about her like a warm, safe cloak. She pulled in a deep breath and straightened to her full height, standing tall in the waning sunlight. A soft kiss brushed her brow.

"You know, of course, that you'll have to help me discern what to do next," Francesca said.

A breeze ruffled her hair. She recognized it as the gentle laughter of her companions.

*Just ask,* they said.

But there was no need to ask. She heard the rustle of leaves from somewhere on her right. A branch snapped loudly, followed by the unmistakable sound of her niece swearing.

"Katerina!" she whispered, and the joy that raced through her almost made her forget her physical limitations. "Katerina!" she called out loud, not caring if anyone heard.

There was a pause, then a tremulous, "Aunt Frannie? Where are you?"

"Keep walking and talking so that I can hear if you're getting closer."

"Oh, my God, am I glad to hear your voice! Maybe now I can make some sense of this awful nightmare!"

"Keep walking," Francesca said, brow furrowed. Stephen had said that Julia was coming. She certainly hadn't expected Katerina. Then again, those crashes through the woods sounded louder than one tiny woman could make. Katerina wasn't alone.

Kat's voice grew louder. "I knew I couldn't possibly be expected to figure this out by myself. Honestly, Aunt Frannie, you know I can't do any of this spiritual stuff."

Francesca sighed. Katerina still needed a stronger faith. Each of them had a specific part to play in this battle. Ready or not, Katerina would have to fight.

Kat stumbled through the underbrush, arm wrapped tightly around Julia's waist. A warm flush flooded Francesca's face. Every muscle ached to hold

Katerina in the same way, to gather her up and assure her that all would be well. The look on her niece's face as their eyes met chased the urge away.

"My God," Kat said simply. Her eyes grew even wider than usual, her cheeks pale.

"I look different," Francesca said.

"Yes."

"Tell me, Katerina. There are no mirrors here."

Kat swallowed. "I don't know that a mirror could pick it up anyway, Aunt Frannie. A mirror would show how snow white your hair has become, how . . . colorless . . . your skin is. But there's something else. You're . . . somehow fragile, somehow not quite of the physical world."

They stared at each other, an unwanted realization growing tangible between them.

"Good, Katerina," Francesca finally said. She fought to keep her voice steady. "You're beginning to use the spiritual eyes I never thought you'd open."

"Aunt Frannie." Kat's voice spiraled upward. "You're never coming back with me, are you? You're—"

Francesca held up a hand. "Don't let panic in, Katerina. There's no place for it in this moment. Neither you nor I know what lies ahead. This moment is quite enough to handle on its own." She turned toward Julia, who stood silent beside her mother, face a blank.

"Where's Julia?" Francesca asked sharply.

Kat snapped around, the danger of the immediate situation pulling her back from her fears. "Not again. I keep losing her. Julia!" She gently tapped her daughter's cheek.

Julia smiled, but her eyes remained vacant, fixed on

an image nowhere to be found in this part of the forest.

Kat's grip tightened about her daughter's shoulders. "Isobel," she said, staring into the girl's eyes. "Are you back with us?"

Francesca's eyebrows rose, but she remained silent.

"Talk to me, Isobel," Kat said. "You have a voice, now. Use it."

Isobel giggled, the peals of laughter falling like flower petals all around them. "I *do* have a voice. And we are in accord; I should use it. I have been so long deprived of it."

"Yes," Kat said. "Where is Julia?"

"Here." Isobel sounded vague.

"Here?"

"With me. With Hugh. But I have her tucked away. My time with Hugh is mine alone."

Kat stepped backward and studied the girl before her. Francesca held her breath, waiting. Katerina, for all her apparent lack of faith, seemed to have established some sort of rapport with this girl.

"Isobel, have you talked to Hugh about Julia?"

The girl's lower lip protruded. "I can't talk to Hugh. Not yet."

"Why not?"

"I don't know. I keep trying, but the words won't come through my mouth. I still have no voice. Perhaps I have Julia in the wrong place."

Francesca's chin rose. This meant that Isobel and Julia had yet to completely merge. Isobel could speak through Julia, but had not yet the power to use the girl's voice through her own body. There was still time, but not much. She could not fathom what might happen should the two become completely one.

Perhaps the same thought had occurred to Kat as well. She quickly wiped a troubled look from her face and continued her conversation in a measured, reasonable voice.

"I don't think you should tell Hugh about Julia anyway," she said. "You know his feelings toward her. We've spoken of this before, Isobel. The farther away from Hugh you keep Julia, the better off you will be."

A new expression crossed the girl's face, something that could only be described as a sneer. "I'm not sure I believe you anymore," Isobel said.

Kat took an inadvertent step backward. "It worked last time, didn't it?"

Isobel pulled Julia's hand from Kat's grip. This was not a good sign. It could only mean that she'd established control over Julia's body as well as her voice.

"Here is what happened when last we spoke," Isobel said. "You told me that you would take care of Julia, that you would keep her far away from my Hugh."

"And I did," Kat said.

"But he speaks of her still, urges me to keep her near. She must never be with my Hugh. She cannot. I have decided that only her voice will stay with me. Her body will stay with you. Her spirit and soul will go . . . I do not know, but neither do I care. My Hugh will work his magic for me alone, to provide me with the voice I should have."

"Let me speak to Julia," Kat said sharply.

Once again, gales of laughter echoed through the woods. This time they dripped down like acid rain.

Francesca stood solid as a statue. "Isobel," she said.

The girl's head turned toward her. A small gasp escaped her lips as her hands flew to shield her eyes. "It's you!" she whimpered. "Put down your sword!"

"I want Julia," Francesca said in measured tones. "I want her now."

"I hate you," Isobel snarled. "And you shall not win. I give her back now, but my Hugh shall prevail. And you will pay for your arrogance in ways you cannot imagine."

Kat was already behind her daughter when the girl slumped forward. "This can't go on," she said, staggering slightly beneath Julia's weight.

Francesca watched as Julia's head rolled backward. Her eyes opened. They took a second to focus.

"Aunt Frannie!" she gasped, then pushed away from her mother to fling herself into Francesca's arms. Francesca hugged her tight. "Maybe everything will be all right now!"

Francesca's eyes met Kat's over the top of the girl's head. Apparently, Julia detected none of the changes in her great-aunt that Kat had sensed. Was Kat's spiritual radar finally awakening?

"Julia, sweetheart." Francesca held the girl close. "Take us to them."

Julia nodded slowly. "I will," she said. "I know exactly where they are."

# 29

STEPHEN CAREFULLY SHIFTED POSITION IN HIS PEW, EYES GLUED to the muted light of the Lady Chapel's stained-glass windows. Time had not passed this slowly since the Chemistry 101 class he'd endured in undergrad. He nestled Kat's limp body more comfortably in the crook of his arm, then stole a surreptitious peek at his wristwatch. Had they really been sitting here for a mere fifteen minutes?

He glanced toward Claire. His younger daughter sat with her head tilted to one side, legs swinging idly beneath the hard wooden bench of the pew. At least she seemed on her best behavior. That was a switch. She usually didn't make it much past the opening hymn of the mass before major squirming took over.

He brushed her cheek with his fingers. "Thank you for being so good, sweetie," he whispered.

Claire turned round eyes toward him. "Did you just feel that, Daddy?"

He shook his head, puzzled. "Feel what?"

"That."

Okay, so she was wonderful. She was smart, too. But he had to remember that she was still only eight years old and that these maddening conversations would occur no matter how dire the circumstances.

"Tell me," he said, resigning himself to patience.

Claire's head cocked in the other direction. "Um . . . it's hard to explain. It just got . . . stronger . . . in here."

Stronger. There wasn't a chance in hell that he'd ever decipher that one.

"Okay, Claire, give me a second to think this one through." He closed his eyes and tried to quiet the loud beating of his heart. What was he supposed to know?

An image flooded his mind. Kat, Julia, and Francesca appeared ever so briefly, but the intensity of the vision nearly threw him backward.

His eyes flew open. Stronger. No wonder.

"Did you feel it?" Claire asked.

"Yes. I think your mother and Julia have found Aunt Frannie." He stared down at the top of Kat's head. For all her doubts, she seemed on the right track.

Claire rested a fingertip against her lips, considering. "That could be," she said. "All of them together would be a lot stronger than just one of them."

Footsteps sounded in the corridor, the loud click-click of high heels accompanied by the muffled plod of sensible rubber soles.

"Uh-oh." Claire instinctively swooped down to cover Julia's body with her own. "What if those people come in here?"

Stephen felt the color drain from his face. "Let's hope they don't. Sit up straight, Claire. Pretend you're praying."

"I *am* praying."

"Even better." He closed his own eyes and tried to steady his breathing. What was it they'd learned in Lamaze class? Breathe. Focus. Concentrate. Those lessons had happened too many years ago to be helpful now. His mind had become overly cluttered since then, filled with day-to-day data that proved totally useless in this situation. He would no longer recognize serenity if it walked up and slapped him in the face.

The idea that serenity might turn violent made him choke back nervous laughter.

"Stop it, Daddy," Claire hissed.

But he couldn't stop. His shoulders shook as he covered his face with his available hand.

Claire scooted along the pew, reaching an arm across her mother's slumped form to squeeze her father's shoulders.

The footsteps stopped in front of the Lady Chapel entrance.

"Oh, my," said an embarrassed voice.

"Calm down, Daddy," Claire said, just a touch too loudly. "It will be okay. Let's pray."

Stephen heard muffled whispers behind him as the footsteps scuttled away.

He removed his hand from his eyes to meet his daughter's accusing gaze.

"You're good," he said, admiration real.

"Snap out of it, Daddy." Claire glowered as she returned to her place on the pew. "We have a lot to do."

How right she was. Stephen sighed, then shifted Kat so that he could study her face. Her eyelashes formed perfect crescents against each cheek. A deep longing rose within him. He wanted desperately to hear her voice, to talk to her, to argue with her. He bit back the longing before it could evolve into a loud, echoing howl.

He leaned forward to kiss his wife's lifeless lips.

"Protect her, please," he murmured, and for a moment, the stained-glass windows appeared to glow.

* * *

Isobel's face tipped upward as if to better drink in the heady aroma of the purple smoke spiraling through the air. Alys wrinkled her nose. She could catch only a whiff of the pungent odor, but she did not like it at all. The rosemary had become merely an undertone, ceding way to a heavier, more potent perfume. The new scent smelled vaguely of musk, although Alys detected a rancid edge to it, like spoiled meat. Her eyes watered as a brisk wind blew more her way. She buried her face in Gregory's chest and choked back a cough.

His arms encircled her. "I, too, find it foul," he said. "I cannot fathom how Isobel endures it."

"She more than endures it. She savors it." Alys returned her gaze to the fire. Isobel sat straight-backed, eyes closed, smile wide across her face. She lifted her upturned palms until they were even with her shoulders.

Hugh studied the girl seated before him. Then, without missing a single note of his discordant tune, he slowly rose, uncoiling himself like a snake from the ground. Although his penetrating stare was for Isobel alone, Alys shrank even further into Gregory.

"Do you see his face?" she whispered.

Gregory nodded, jaw tight.

There were no words for the wooden blank of Hugh's expression, for the gaping, dark emptiness of his eyes. Alys shuddered. Perhaps his form was comely, his features handsome. Still, he brought to mind only images of death, a mocking sneer against all life itself.

Gregory's lips brushed against her ear as he bent close to whisper. "I want to tear the instrument from his mouth. I've heard enough of that infernal noise."

"He cannot possibly play much longer," Alys said. "What can he accomplish if his mouth and hands are so employed?"

"Look." Gregory's hands tightened on her shoulders.

The fire's curling tendrils of smoke drifted upward through the air in sharpened forms, now. At first Alys did not believe her eyes, certain that such images could not be traced in smoke and were simply creations of her tired thoughts. But she could no longer deny what she saw. Plumes of smoke twisted into faces, bloated gargoyle faces with wide-open mouths and bulging eyes. The faces floated upward, yet failed to fade away into the air. They gathered high above the fire, forming rows and rows like a diabolical choir.

"Do you see them?" Alys clutched Gregory's sleeve.

"I do," he said.

"Are they real, do you think?"

"Do you mean are they beings, creatures that live and breathe? I don't know, Alys."

The disembodied heads continued to gather, most writhing and drooling, some convulsed with wild laughter. All eyes rested on Hugh as the heads floated upward.

Hugh took the recorder from his lips. The smoke became merely smoke again, its brown, ashy plumes stretching toward the darkening sky.

"Ah, Isobel," Hugh said. "I know you feel happy, now, quite rested. Is this so?"

Isobel's eyes remained closed. Her smile, if possible, grew even wider. A contented sigh escaped as she nodded her answer to his question.

Hugh's voice coated the clearing like warm honey. "You will experience even greater joy," he said. "I promise you this. You need only listen to me, do my bidding in all things. Rise, Isobel."

Isobel slowly rose to her feet. Her back arched as she stretched, thrusting her breasts forward. She ran both hands up her body with such languorous pleasure that Gregory averted his eyes.

Hugh's chuckle was so low that the priest and the prioress had to strain to hear it.

"Really, Isobel," Hugh said. "You are so very transparent, so easily understood. Your mind rests on one thing only. You are uncomplicated, as easy to lure as a hungry, stupid carp."

Isobel's mouth formed a troubled pout. Her eyebrows drew together at the center of her forehead.

"Ah." Hugh's eyes narrowed. "You are perhaps not as . . . rested . . . as I would have you. Breathe, Isobel. Breathe deeply."

Isobel took a step toward him.

"Mind the fire, Isobel." Hugh's voice rose. "There is no need to move. Stay where you are."

Her eyes opened, glazed and unseeing. With a seductive sway of her hips, she swaggered around the edge of the fire until she stood before him.

Hugh's breathing came in sharp little gasps as he stared into her face. Her lips parted, urging him forward.

"No, Isobel," he said. "We will not . . . cannot . . . touch each other. You know this. I have told you this."

Yet despite his words, his hand began a slow arc toward her waist. Perspiration beaded his forehead as she took another step toward him.

"No!" he protested, stare riveted to the curve where her neck and shoulders met.

Alys and Gregory jumped as footsteps sounded

behind them, then dropped to the ground in an attempt to hide. Francesca appeared before them, two strangers by her side.

Alys pulled herself to a sitting position, eyes riveted to the labored rise and fall of Francesca's chest.

"Are you ill?" she asked, grasping Francesca's wrist. "Your breath comes so hard!"

Francesca pulled in another breath. "I am as well as I can be," she said. "Time is too short for explanations. My niece, Katerina; her daughter, Julia. Alys, prioress of Saint Etheldreda's, and Father Gregory. Can you all see each other?"

"I see through them," Alys said slowly. Gregory nodded his agreement.

Francesca nodded. "It's enough. Katerina?"

Kat swallowed hard. "I see them every bit as clearly as I see you and Julia. Aunt Frannie, what—"

Francesca cut her off with a wave of a hand. "My God," she said. "Hugh looks as if he could devour Isobel whole."

"Yet he will not touch her," Gregory said, bewildered. "He says he cannot."

"He's right about that," Francesca said. "He has no control over the lust that is part of this physical body. Touching Isobel could destroy them both."

There was no time for further questioning. All five of them stared at the scene unfolding before them.

"I have a feeling I should cover my daughter's eyes," Kat said as Hugh's hand hovered over Isobel's bodice.

"Watch Julia closely," Francesca said. "There is no way to tell when Isobel will invade her again."

Sweat dripped steadily from Hugh's brow as he leaned forward. His lips twitched.

The recorder slipped from his grip and dropped to the ground with a thud. His head snapped toward the sound, breaking his trance. He dropped to his knees and cradled the instrument in his arms.

"No, Isobel!" he shouted. Then, noting the clench of her fists and the confused expression on her face, he muted his tone.

"Sweet Isobel," he said. "Breathe deeply."

He quickly stood, circling the fire until it once again separated them.

"Listen, Isobel," he said. "This tune is yours and yours alone." He raised the recorder to his lips, returning to his strident song.

Isobel's eyes closed. Her fists slowly uncurled, palms again upturned and open. She, too, began to sway to the call of the recorder.

"Julia," whispered Kat, "are you okay?"

"Yes," Julia said weakly. "But it's getting harder to stay, Mom. They want me so bad. They're pulling and pulling."

"What do we do?" Kat asked, holding Julia close.

Francesca thought for a moment before dropping her head into her hands. "I don't know."

# 30

CLAIRE'S SHARP GASP SHOOK STEPHEN FROM HIS FOG. HE untangled his fingers from Kat's hair and straightened on the bench of his pew.

"What's up, sweetheart?" he asked.

Claire's eyes had grown so wide that the white completely surrounded the green irises.

"Look!" she whispered, pointing at Julia.

Stephen couldn't prevent his own gasp. Julia remained stretched across the pew, her head cradled in her sister's lap. But something was wrong. Her body appeared translucent. Stephen squinted, trying to focus his vision. This was, however, no trick of the eye. He really could see the burnished wood of the bench through Julia's jeans.

"It's like what happened to Aunt Frannie," Claire said in hushed tones.

"What does it mean?" Stephen's gaze remained glued to his elder daughter.

"I don't know," Claire said, "but, look, Daddy. It's getting worse."

Stephen stared as the grain of the wood beneath Julia grew clearer.

"She's leaving us!" Claire's voice ended in a squeal.

"Shhh." Stephen reached across Kat's slumped body and wrapped an arm around Claire's shoulders. "Don't panic, honey, please. I don't know what's going on, but we've got to believe that we'll understand it soon enough."

They watched together as Julia's form grew emptier. In seconds, only the shell of an outline remained, a delicate tracing of hair and limbs. Then, with a faint shimmer and a sound like a gentle sigh, Julia vanished.

A tremendous shiver raced through Claire's little body. "Oh, Daddy!" she gulped, running a palm across the place on her lap where her sister's head had just rested.

Stephen squeezed her shoulder, fighting back his own fear. If he gave in to it now, all would be lost. He cast a quick glance at Kat. Her head still rested against his chest. She looked as if she'd simply settled in for an inconvenient afternoon nap. He carefully removed his arm from Claire's shoulder and rested a hand on Kat's wrist. She still felt warm and solid to his touch.

"Do you think Aunt Frannie is gone from the bedroom, too?" Claire asked.

He swallowed. "I don't know. Claire, remember, Julia is with Mom, and probably with Aunt Frannie, too. They'll do everything they can to keep her safe and bring her back to us. Okay?"

Claire nodded, apparently eager to grasp any straw of hope he could extend. "Okay," she said, scrambling across both her parents to settle by his available side. "I guess all we can do is keep praying. Right, Daddy?"

Stephen nodded absently, brushing away the growing suspicion that something else would soon be expected of him.

Kat wondered how anyone as loose-limbed and relaxed as Isobel could even manage to stand. The girl reminded her of a college student who'd had too much to drink. She stood slightly slumped to one side, palms still turned upward but wrists limp, eyes closed, a goofy smile slapped across her face.

Kat stole a glance at her companions. It was hard not to stare at the priest and the prioress curled together against the trunk of a tree. She couldn't quite digest the fact that these were medieval people. For the most part, they seemed quite usual, even ordinary, as if she'd met them before. Alys was a little taller than she, but with a pallor probably born of malnutrition. Gregory, while more than half a head taller, would have been considered small in any modern population. Kat suspected that he was younger than Stephen, but he moved more slowly, like a man well up in years. With a start, she realized that Gregory was probably in the winter of his life.

"Julia." Francesca's whisper made Kat turn her head. "Julia, are you with us?"

Julia, resting against Francesca's side, met her great-aunt's questioning glance. "Yes, Aunt Frannie. I've done what you told me to do. I've built a wall of prayer."

Wall of prayer. Kat turned her attention back to the clearing, but not before catching Gregory's nod of agreement. How wonderful that everybody else knew just what to do. She had not been assigned to prayer duty, which was just as well. She still couldn't even get through a meditation session without streams of extant comments flooding her brain. Let everyone else work on their prayer wall. She'd monitor the action unfolding before the fire.

Hugh removed the recorder from his lips. "Isobel,"

he said, his voice throaty, "are you quite ready to be mine?"

A chill raced up Kat's spine as she watched Isobel's measured nod.

Hugh set the recorder on the ground. Then he slowly circled the fire until he stood directly before Isobel. Her eyes remained closed, but she seemed well aware of his presence.

He walked until he stood behind her. She did not turn to face him. A distance of perhaps eight to ten inches separated them.

Without a word, Hugh raised his arms from his side, extending them as if he were a large bird in flight. Isobel did the same, matching the rhythm of his movements as perfectly as if she could see them.

Hugh lowered his arms. Isobel followed suit.

Now it was Hugh's turn to smile, a slow, grim upturn of the mouth that made Kat feel as though she'd just walked into a freezer.

"Look," she whispered, nudging Francesca.

Francesca's eyes remained closed. Her mouth moved in prayer. She raised a finger to her lips, and Kat got the message loud and clear: "Don't interrupt me now."

A quick glance at Alys and Gregory showed that they, too, were unreachable. Their eyes were also closed. A hot flush flooded the white of Alys's cheeks. Gregory's head bowed over his clasped hands.

Julia's breathing came even and deep. She appeared, in fact, stronger than Kat had seen her in weeks. Her hand rested in Francesca's, a reminder that she did not face this bizarre interlude alone.

Hugh circled Isobel three times, yet seemed to pay her no mind. His demeanor changed with each rotation. He walked the first circle with the cockiness of a young suitor well aware of his own success in the realm of seduction. Then his shoulders straightened, his chin raised. He widened his next lap around Isobel, pacing the ground like a wild animal cornering his prey.

The third circle brought forth a conquering warrior. His stride slowed, became even more assured and proud than before. Isobel was no longer a conquest, no longer his prey. She had become his not only to control but to consume. He stopped before her, triumph chiseled in his face, eyes glittering with unearthly light.

"Now, Isobel," he said in tones of gravel, "do you choose to belong to me completely?"

The girl before him nodded slowly, as if intoxicated.

Hugh pulled himself to his full height. Kat almost sensed the malevolent spirit within struggling to gain a stature greater than the flimsy shell a human body could offer.

"Do you choose to swear fealty to me?" His voice dropped even lower in tone.

The girl squirmed. Her fingers traced down her own curves, then reached toward him.

He stepped backward. "Fealty, Isobel!"

She nodded so hard that Kat half expected to hear her teeth clatter.

Hugh moved closer, leaning in until Isobel could feel his breath against her ear. Each word fell separately, seductively, in the air. "Isobel, do you choose to pledge me your soul?"

A groan escaped Isobel, a guttural sound made by vocal cords long unused. Kat stifled a gasp, then turned to stare at Julia. Francesca, too, had opened her eyes to check her great-niece.

"Julia," Francesca whispered. "Are you all right?"

Julia's hand clutched her throat as her eyes flew open. "Yes," she said. "But I wasn't here a second ago!"

"Where were you?" Francesca's calm helped steady Kat.

Julia stared at Isobel. "There. With her." Her face reddened. "I'm sorry, Aunt Frannie. I got distracted. I started thinking about other things."

"Close your eyes," Francesca said shortly. "Pray the Rosary. Any prayer, Julia, any form of light. Don't let anything else in, no matter how small it seems."

Isobel's groan did not pass unnoticed. Hugh cast her a quick look.

"Talk to me, Isobel," he said, and even Kat took refuge in the Our Father. The words rose before her mind in gleaming springs of light. Beyond them rested a persistent darkness just longing to poke holes in that wall of light and gain entrance.

Hugh straightened. "You are more than ready," he said half to himself, "yet something blocks us. Open yourself to me, Isobel."

He stood before her now, a commanding snarl pasted across his face as he looked down at the girl. He extended his arms. She did the same. He flexed his fingers. She followed suit.

"I am ready to flow into you, Isobel," he said softly, "but I will not do it until you flow into *her*. You must flow into Julia, Isobel. You must become one with the girl before I possess you. Do it, Isobel. Do it now!"

Kat frantically reached for her daughter's hand. Francesca, too, tightened her grip. Several feet away, Alys's mouth began to move in silent petition.

A lump of panic wedged in Kat's throat. That didn't

surprise her; panic seemed perfectly natural under the circumstances. What did surprise her was the sudden realization that panic itself was a distraction, simply a clever way to pierce her concentration at a crucial moment.

Julia whimpered.

"Stay with us," Francesca urged. "Think of light, Julia, the brightest light you can."

"They want me," Julia whispered. "They're . . . they're pulling . . ."

"Well, they can't have you," Francesca said briskly. "Concentrate, Julia!"

Hugh's head whipped around toward their spot in the woods. His eyes narrowed as his chin jutted into the air. He raised his left hand, an accusing finger pointing directly at their hiding place.

"Something blocks us," he said. "Something I know well."

Kat sent Francesca a quick glance. Of course Asteroth would sense her aunt's presence. Their horrible battle remained seared in her own mind; how could Asteroth possibly forget his own defeat?

But Hugh's cold, empty eyes did not focus on Francesca.

"Katerina," he said. "You are here."

Kat staggered backward in shock. She barely felt Francesca's arm encircle her waist.

"Pay no attention, Julia," Francesca said levelly. "Don't stop what you're doing."

Hugh stepped toward them. "You know I must win our ultimate battle," he said, and Kat shuddered at the wheedling tone in his voice. He stood still for a moment, turning his eyes to study Isobel. "Is it not enough, Katerina, that you have forced me to deal with such stupidity? Save your friends. Make this easier. We both know that I will destroy the child of light."

"Child of light?" Alys whispered. "Is Julia—"

"Shhh!" Francesca silenced her with a finger against her lips.

Kat's face clouded as she laid her palm against her wildly beating heart. "It's me he wants," she said, amazed. "God help me, Aunt Frannie."

"No." Francesca's grip tightened around Kat's waist. "You can't listen to him. You can't listen to a word he says. Don't trust him."

"Yes, Katerina, it is you I want." Hugh answered as if he stood in their midst. They could not say whether or not he'd actually heard them.

"He wants the child of light," Francesca whispered fiercely. "Not you, Katerina!"

Kat looked bewildered. "Is Julia the child?"

Her aunt closed her eyes. Kat could almost feel her frantic search for answers.

Francesca's shoulders slumped. "I don't know," she finally said.

Hugh straightened. His entire body turned toward them. It seemed to Kat that he grew darker by the minute, a roiling thundercloud longing to explode.

"You may take your choice, Katerina," he said. "I shall come for Julia. I can still use her as planned. Or I shall come for you. You, too, will do nicely, and I shall enjoy destroying those who assist you: that pitiful priest and sniveling prioress, the sanctimonious and holy Francesca . . . and, of course, our fragile Julia. I shall break her like a sparrow, perhaps saving her voice for this stupid little acolyte who could never do it justice. Or, Katerina, you can come to me of your own will, and we can settle this matter between ourselves."

Every ounce of blood drained to Kat's feet. She reached for Julia, hugging her so close that, for a moment, she felt as if she and her daughter had become one.

"He can't have my baby," she said in a low voice. "I'm going out there."

"You can't go!" Francesca said. "You aren't strong enough!"

"Then think of something fast." With one deft movement, Kat slipped from her aunt's grasp and stumbled into the clearing toward Hugh.

# 31

HUGH APPEARED TALLER AS KAT DREW CLOSER, NOT QUITE OF either the medieval or the modern world. His smirk grew more pronounced. He reminded her of some overconfident lounge lizard, the kind of man already convinced that the woman he'd hit on all night would go home with him. A random thought, but surprisingly bracing. It felt good to find a solid analogy, one rooted in a physical reality that she could potentially control. Kat grabbed the lifeline, slowing her steps as her rational mind took over.

Perhaps Asteroth was some unfathomable demon, a spirit of darkness that she still wasn't sure she could ever comprehend. Hugh, however, was at least partly human. What had Aunt Frannie said about his impulses toward Isobel? Kat's mind felt too cluttered to remember. Still, Hugh was apparently given to some of the foibles and weaknesses found in other men. Even lounge lizards could be temporarily side-tracked by a well-aimed drink in the face. Asteroth was not automatically invincible. She would buy time and hope that Aunt Frannie could come up with a plan to derail him.

She pulled in a deep breath and stopped approximately three yards away from Hugh.

"Ah, Katerina." He bowed, a full, sweeping bow

even more mocking than his honey-dipped words. "How nice of you to come. But we are old friends, my dear. There is no reason to keep your distance. Come closer."

Kat turned pointedly toward Isobel. The girl stood slumped like a marionette waiting for the puppeteer to tweak her strings and bring her back to life. Her vacant gaze and mindless half smile were almost more chilling than Hugh's icy stare.

"What's this about?" Kat asked, gesturing toward the girl. "What have you done to her?"

Hugh cocked his head. "I have done nothing more than she herself has chosen. You heard her, Katerina—or, rather, you saw her nod her assent. She came to me of her own free will. She chose to be mine."

"Under false pretenses, of course. She thought you'd be her lover."

He chuckled. "Always the lawyer, eh, Katerina? I often wish you'd pledge yourself to me. Not only would it end this ugly business, but you are so damnably amusing when you wish to be. But alas, I don't suppose you'll reconsider becoming one of my own?"

Her jaw clenched as she fought back a swell of nausea. "No, Asteroth . . . if I may call you that."

He took a step forward, eyes glittering. "You may call me what you wish."

Her mind raced. What now? How on earth was she supposed to prolong this encounter?

Gregory tapped Francesca's forearm, his face ashen. Francesca unconsciously wrapped her fingers around his wrist, her eyes never leaving Julia's face. The girl sat with her own eyes closed, mouthing a decade of the Rosary.

Gregory plucked at her grip. "Someone must help your Katerina," he said quietly.

"Yes," Francesca said. "I just don't know how, yet."

"There are four of us. Surely we can overpower this—this madman."

"No, Gregory, we can't." She shook her head, mouth drawn in a grim, straight line. "He can summon his legions in a blink. He does not fight alone. He never has."

"But neither do we."

She knew that probably better than any of them. Hadn't she called on the angels of light in the past, only to be surrounded by more love and strength than she'd ever thought possible? It was one of the most joyful revelations she'd experienced. Still, she couldn't deny yet another of the lessons she'd learned along her life's path: in perfect prayer and meditation, God's time operated unto itself, without much regard for her own sense of immediacy. Light worked within the moment, and at this particular moment, she felt no push to summon the angels, her companions on this spiritual journey. Apparently an important piece of this mysterious puzzle had yet to fit. She only wished she knew what it was.

Gregory seemed to interpret her long silence as fear, for he patted her hand in the same way she herself had once comforted the elderly.

"God is with us," he said.

"I know, Gregory."

From her seat on the ground, Julia gave a little gasp. Francesca dropped to her side. "What is it?"

Julia's eyes remained closed. "A tug," she whimpered. "I feel a tug."

"Concentrate," Francesca ordered. She turned to Gregory, who looked as though he wanted to say more. "What?" she asked. "Just say it."

He opened his mouth, then shut it again. His shoulders slumped. "It is only that my hand did not pass through yours. It is not that my ability to see you has grown. You are changing, Francesca. Can it be you are becoming one of us in this time?"

She couldn't ponder this, now. If she gave it any attention at all, she would be overwhelmed by how tired and heavy she felt, how utterly devoid of energy and strength. Better to dwell as much in the spirit as possible, gaining all available energy from that source.

"Go back to Alys, Gregory," she said as gently as she could. "Prayer is your natural language; pray for discernment. We must know not only what to do next, but when to do it."

An image danced across her mind, brief but definite. Her eyebrows rose. She was well beyond the point of questioning these pushes.

"And, Gregory, pray for Stephen."

His trust in her—or his faith in God—was greater than she'd thought. He returned to Alys's side without even asking who Stephen was.

Francesca placed a gentle hand on Julia's shoulder, bowed her head, and waited.

It took every ounce of Kat's will to keep from retreating as Hugh stepped forward. She raised her chin and stood her ground, studying him with a coolness she couldn't believe she still possessed. The body he'd chosen for this outing was not unlike his own physical manifestation sixteen years ago. She winced as she remembered that day, then pulled herself back to the current moment. Remembering their last encounter could only dredge up all the fear she now fought to submerge. She refused to acknowledge his supernatural side. He stood perhaps two yards away now, a tall man for the Middle Ages, with white-blond shoulder-length hair and broad shoulders. If she avoided those awful, empty eyes, she could almost pretend that he was simply an odious human being.

Good grief, she dealt with those all the time.

"I believe you wanted to see me," she said. "You called this meeting, Asteroth. I didn't. What do you want?"

He folded his arms across his chest. "A valid point, Katerina. All these years, and you still have no understanding of why I hunt you."

She cleared her throat. "Something about a child of light, I believe."

"Yes. Of course, we both know that this is the reason I've pursued you for so long."

"But why?"

"In one way, Katerina, it is refreshing that you have no knowledge of the role you play. In another way, it is utterly infuriating, totally inconceivable that a responsibility of such reverberation is entrusted to one so obtuse. I will never understand how the Other operates."

Her forehead furrowed. "The Other?"

He spat on the ground as if to rid his mouth of some

vile taste. "Call the Power what you will," he said. "Katerina, I tried to stop you from finding your soul's mate, your destiny."

"Do you mean Stephen?"

Again, his face contorted with distaste. "The Other puts such store in the heart's longing of his children. I could not prevent you and Stephen from reaching each other, from creating the child of light. But, Katerina, there is no reason—corporeal or otherwise—that I must stand by and watch the mission come to fruition."

"I'm still confused," she said, shaking her head. "I don't know who the child of light is."

That brought him up short. He searched her face in an apparent attempt to decipher the depth of her truthfulness. Kat felt her cheeks grow hot under his scrutiny. This reminded her of those old movies where the hero sat under a bald lightbulb, surrounded by bad guys determined to make him talk. Hugh's stare raked her face. Then the smirk returned, even more gloating than before.

"Asteroth," she said, just to break the dreadful silence, "why do you need Julia? I don't understand. Why must Isobel . . . invade her?"

He shrugged. "Julia is a doorway."

"A doorway? To what?"

"Isobel and Julia share—how shall I say this in a way you will understand?—certain energies."

"Frequencies," Kat supplied.

"Yes." He refocused his gaze on her, as if her grasp of this information made him reconsider his original assessment of her knowledge. "Their frequencies harmonize, regardless of the centuries between them. Once Isobel learned to direct her energies toward Julia, it was easy for her to flow into her, even to pull your daughter into her own mind and body. She and Julia can become one in either physical shell. For my purposes, however, Isobel will inhabit your daughter's body."

A sick revulsion again threatened to overtake Kat. She pressed a hand against her stomach, hoping to quell the chaos inside. "Why does that matter?"

He spread his palms open before him. "Really, Katerina, you could solve this puzzle on your own. You're intelligent enough, unlike that woeful little poppet slouching by the fire. Isobel refuses me nothing. I can easily enter her consciousness, her mind, her corporeal form at will. When she becomes one with Julia, I will overtake them both. Julia belongs to the twenty-first century, so I will come home with you, my dear, human in your time."

The logical side of Kat's mind considered asking if there wasn't an easier way. The rest of her couldn't bear to know. He'd already told her more than she wanted to hear, yet he continued.

"You might remember from our last encounter, Katerina, that I am most . . . effective . . . when a willing human allows me access to a body."

She nodded numbly.

"Well, then." He took another step forward. "This could be perfection. Imagine. I will acquire physical form in your very home, through your very own flesh and blood." A broad smile showed all his teeth.

This time, Kat could not hold back her reaction.

"Excuse me," she said, stepping toward a small cluster of foliage.

Hugh waited while she vomited, the benign expression of a genial host pasted across his face.

She remained bent double even when the violent spasms of nausea ceased. She suddenly couldn't bear to turn and face this grinning monster, this creature who made no sense in her world, yet sought to destroy it. More than anything, she wanted to wake up in her own bed with Stephen warm beside her, ready to comfort her as she struggled to escape this bad dream.

She caught a glimpse of gold from the wedding band on her left hand. Stephen. He'd known how to send her here. His dream had directed her back in time in the first place. They had always been stronger together than apart. Why should now be any different?

"Katerina," Hugh said, his voice grating like sandpaper against her ears. "You must allow me access to the child of light."

She closed her eyes as she straightened up. She saw herself fully clad in her spiritual armor, Stephen close by her side. His armor gleamed so brightly that it nearly blinded her. Somehow, the image strengthened her. She watched as her husband tightened his left hand around his sword. Slowly, he raised it from his side, lifting it high in challenge.

"Ouch," Claire said. "Daddy, stop squeezing my hand so hard."

Stephen opened his eyes and gazed down at his left hand. Claire's fingertips did look particularly red.

"Sorry," he murmured. Perhaps he'd drifted off. For a second there, he'd felt the heft of a sword in his grip, sensed Katerina standing by his side. But, no, he still sat in his pew in the cathedral, waiting for who knew what.

Claire squirmed beside him. "Daddy, what time is it?"

He looked at his watch. "One-fifty-five."

"Didn't you say that something important would happen at two-fifteen? Isn't that when you said Aunt Frannie could come back?"

He straightened. Yes. He remembered. Frannie had disappeared into the Middle Ages at 2:15. The time and space coordinates necessary to bring her back would intersect at that point . . .

. . . if nothing stood in the way.

A tingle tickled his hands. Fine bands of light seemed to flow from his fingertips, leading to definite destinations. Where? He quickly closed his eyes. It didn't take long to feel the jolt of connection. Francesca appeared on his left, head bowed in prayer. Kat appeared on his right, but she did not look his way. She instead looked straight ahead at a cloud of darkness he could not understand.

He wanted to understand it. He *had* to understand it.

"Show me," he said through clenched teeth.

The cloud churned, its edges black with soot. A vague shape formed in the center, undefined by anything beyond its outline. Then, from the midst of this mountain of smog, the figure of a man emerged.

"Asteroth," Stephen breathed, and as if called, the man turned to face him.

Kat tried to follow the direction of Hugh's stare, but it made no sense. He glared due west, where the sun edged closer to the horizon. She could see nothing there except a thicket of narrow-trunked trees. Surely that alone could not capture his interest so completely.

His sneer turned into a snarl. The fingers of his right hand curled into a fist, which slammed into his open palm.

"I will wait no longer, Katerina," he hissed, piercing her with his full attention. "Our score is an old one. Now is the time to settle it once and for all."

# 32

"CLAIRE!" STEPHEN'S EYES FLEW OPEN. "YOUR MOTHER—"

"I know, Daddy." Claire looked up, a worried frown creasing her forehead. "She's so warm!"

It took Stephen a minute to realize that they were not talking about the same thing. He noticed that Claire held one of Kat's hands in her own.

"What do you mean?" he asked.

"Feel her head."

He didn't have to. Droplets of sweat beaded Kat's brow. Her cheeks were flushed and her breathing ragged.

"I don't understand," he started, but one look at Claire's frightened face indicated that she didn't, either.

He had to reach Kat somehow, or at least learn more about the situation. He glanced at Claire, the child who'd provided so much information when he'd least expected it. He didn't know how she'd known any of it. At this point, he didn't care.

"Claire," he said, grabbing his daughter's hand, "are you the child of light?"

She stared back at him with wide, round eyes. He read confusion there. Her lower lip began to tremble. It didn't take a genius to recognize that the tremble preceded the perfectly natural tears of any ordinary little girl.

"Never mind," he said hastily. "Forget it. But, Claire, I'm going to ask you to do something very important, and very difficult. Will you try?"

She nodded, then tried to smile. Her attempt at bravery tugged at his core. If she could do it, then so could he.

"Claire, it's vital that I get in touch with your mother." Thank God Claire asked no questions. He continued quickly, before he could stop to analyze how dumb his own words sounded. "I want you to close your eyes and turn your mind into a blank movie screen. I need you to concentrate. We have to find a way to . . . to . . ."

To what?

"I know, Daddy," Claire said calmly. "You have to know what's going on back in medieval times so that you can help. We need to bring everyone back."

Not everyone. Stephen shivered at the memory of Asteroth's cold, calculating stare, the seething hatred in his face as he'd raised his chin in challenge.

No, there was no way they wanted to bring everyone back.

He closed his eyes, squeezed Claire's hand, and encouraged his mind to go blank.

"Call them," Claire said. "They'll come."

"Call who?"

"The angels of light. They'll help, but you've got to ask them."

He could not help staring at her. She never opened her eyes, but squirmed beneath his gaze.

"Stop looking at me," she said. "You're the one who has to call them, Daddy. I'm not kidding."

His mouth felt dry. "Okay," he said, running his

tongue across his top teeth. "Okay. Um . . . We need you, angels. Help us. Please."

"In the name of God and light," Claire added, the serenity in her voice making him once again turn her way.

He wasn't sure what he'd expected. Pyrotechnics? Thunder? Nothing changed. Claire sat beside him, eyes closed, thoughts a mystery. Her hand rested in his. Kat's body remained solid on the pew, her face glistening with perspiration. The lighting in the Lady Chapel did not change.

He checked his watch. Two o'clock.

So much for the angels of light. Apparently they required a more coherent invitation, one he felt totally unqualified to issue.

"They'll come, Daddy," Claire said. "You asked."

Francesca felt a subtle shift in the energy surrounding them. She tilted Julia's chin so that she could study her face. Julia's green eyes fluttered open, greeting her great-aunt's silent inquiry with confusion.

"How are you, Julia?" Francesca asked.

Julia swallowed. "Scared."

"That makes sense. But you're completely with us, right?"

"Yes, Aunt Frannie."

"Good. Whatever you're doing is right, then. Stay with it."

Gregory and Alys rose to their feet. Francesca beckoned them over.

"What now?" Alys asked in a low voice.

"I'm not sure, yet," Francesca said. "But something is different, and we'd best be prepared for anything."

Alys swayed slightly, but her determination did not waver. "As you wish," she said.

"You and I have a score to settle?" Kat nearly spat the words. "It is of your own making. How do you choose to proceed?"

He strode toward her. It didn't take long; he'd been altogether too close to begin with. Now he stood before her, so close that she could catch the heady scent of musk steaming from his skin, could see the rise and fall of his chest beneath the sienna tunic he wore.

His hands shot out, landing hard on her shoulders. Kat shut her eyes, half expecting to explode in a cloud of smoke. Nothing happened save the unpleasant sensation of fingers digging into her skin. She opened her eyes in time to catch the surprised expression on Hugh's face. He, too, had expected something more.

"You . . . remain," he said.

"Well, of course." She thought quickly, trying to process the information unfolding before her.

She didn't need to bother. Hugh, perhaps unaware that he spoke out loud, answered some of her questions.

"My power . . . ," he started, lifting one hand from Kat's shoulder. He curled and uncurled his fingers, staring at them as if they belonged to another species. "Is it so curtailed by human form? Am I so very limited by this physical body?"

"Welcome to humanity," Kat said beneath her breath. She stepped away from his grip, poised to run.

"Oh, no, Katerina. I wouldn't think of it." He pulled her back with one mighty tug. "I am not without strength or resources. I can still summon my minions.

They remain unhampered by physical form. I can even relinquish this body I use. But you are easily broken, even if I must tend to it as a man."

"Except for what?" Kat demanded. "What can't you do if you lose human form? And how could I grant you access to the child of light if I lie dead at your feet?"

His eyes bulged as he glared at her. Perhaps the human mind that came with Hugh's body moved faster than Asteroth could piece together the ideas. Maybe he hadn't mastered the use of a human brain any more completely than he'd mastered use of the body.

She could think and analyze, but she wasn't sure she had enough knowledge. She knew that Asteroth could only enter the minds and bodies of those who allowed it. Well, that ruled her out. There was no way she'd ever be part of his fold. She was a child of the light, even if she didn't always understand exactly what that meant. Without her, though, Asteroth seemed to believe that he'd have no way to reach the child of light . . . whoever that child was.

Too many pieces missing. Too many . . .

"Isobel!" Hugh barked, facing the slumped form of the girl by the fire.

Isobel straightened. Her gaze swung across the landscape, coming to rest on his face. She smiled, a slow, dumb grin that made Kat avert her own eyes.

Hugh's grip on Kat's wrist tightened. He yanked her across his chest, pinning her against his body with an arm around her neck.

Isobel's eyes narrowed.

"No, Isobel," he said. "She is no rival to you. How could she be?"

The girl relaxed. Hugh continued.

"She is, however, in your way. While she exists, we can never be together."

Isobel raised her hands, fingers bent like claws.

"No," Hugh said. "Perhaps, if you do my bidding, I will let you destroy this one later. But for now, my sweet, I need you to do what we have practiced for so long. I need you to flow into Julia. Do it, Isobel. Do it now."

Ever obedient, Isobel closed her eyes and concentrated.

Julia began to whimper.

Francesca looked up, surprised by a new idea that had just entered her consciousness. "Why, it's Katerina!" she said. "Katerina is her children's protection! She guards the child of light!"

"Well, of course," Alys said. "She is the child's mother, is she not? There is no stronger bond of love and protection for any child."

She spoke as if this was common knowledge, as if everybody knew it. Perhaps it was one of those practical, obvious facts that Francesca had overlooked in her quest for the mystical.

"Think on it later," Gregory said. "This child needs us now." He sank to his knees beside Julia, whose whimper had turned into a low moan.

"Now, Isobel," Hugh said. "Flow into the girl now."

Isobel's arms rose slowly from her sides until they were parallel to the ground. She looked like a large bird about to take flight.

"Now, Isobel," Hugh repeated. "Enter her. You will talk, my dear. Her voice is yours for the taking, but you must inhabit her first."

Isobel rose on her tiptoes, face lifted to the sky.

"Now!" Hugh shouted.

She stood poised for a moment, pulling in large gulps of air. Then she collapsed in a heap onto the ground, head covered by her arms.

"She cannot do it," Hugh said, more to himself than for anyone else's ears. "Something blocks her. The girl is protected in some way, or stronger in her own concentration than I thought possible."

His arm tightened around Kat's neck. Her hands flew up to it, tugging it away as she gasped for air.

He spun her to face him. "Call your daughter, Katerina. Call her here now."

"No."

He lifted her until they were eye to eye. Her feet dangled above the ground. "Then I will call her. And I guarantee that she will come."

"Put her down," a cool voice said from the clearing.

Hugh released his hold on Kat, who dropped to the ground, landing on her feet.

Francesca stood at the edge of the clearing, Julia by her side.

# 33

Stephen checked his watch for the third time in a minute. Five after two. Dear God. Now what? Kat remained slumped against his chest, her face still glistening with sweat like a child awakened from a nightmare. Except, of course, that she wasn't awake. Stephen batted away the thought that she might never wake up again. He quickly kissed her lips, wishing he could breathe his own life's breath into her unconscious form.

To his left, Claire sat still, head bowed. Claire never sat still. Suspicious, he squeezed her hand. She opened one eye, gave him a little smile, and then closed the eye again.

Good. For a moment he'd worried that she, too, was lost to him, just like Kat and Julia.

A jagged edge of fear ripped through him. He couldn't bear to sit still any longer. He untangled himself from Claire and carefully eased Kat's head down to their daughter's lap.

"Daddy, where are you going?" Claire looked up as he staggered to his feet.

"I don't know." Stephen stumbled toward the altar of the lady chapel. "Claire, I don't know what to do next. I'm all out of ideas."

"Daddy—" she started, but her words were cut short by the sound of approaching footsteps.

Stephen whipped around. His eyes locked with Claire's. Her arm wrapped protectively around her mother's shoulders.

These footsteps were loud and purposeful, not the steps of a meandering visitor or an awestruck tourist. This person had a destination in mind, and Stephen had an awful suspicion that he knew exactly what that destination was.

"Somebody's coming here, to the Lady Chapel," he whispered.

Claire raised a finger to her lips. Stephen suspected that he should somehow get to her side and arrange himself in a prayerful attitude. Instead he stood frozen before the altar like a prowler caught in a flashlight beam.

The footsteps stopped. An old man stood at the entrance of the Lady Chapel, his stooped shoulders belying the determination in his walk. His hair was thick and white, brushed straight back from his brow and nearly touching his shoulders. His face, relatively unlined, was clean-shaven, dominated by deep brown eyes. He wore a charcoal-colored overcoat. Black tasseled loafers showed beneath the hem of his dark slacks. He nodded his greeting, then stepped into the chapel.

"Well, then," he said, shifting from one foot to the other. He looked from Stephen to Claire. "Good afternoon."

Apparently the back of the pew blocked Kat's body from view. Stephen nearly sank to his knees with relief.

"Good afternoon," he replied, working hard to ensure that his voice did not crack.

And now the man would leave.

But he didn't. Neither did he sit to pray, meditate, ruminate, or whatever else he had arrived to do. He remained standing in the aisle, eyebrows raised in quizzical concern.

Stephen at least had enough presence of mind to recognize that shouting would only increase his problems. Instead, he flashed what he hoped was a gracious smile and turned to face the altar. Perhaps if the man thought that he and Claire needed this time alone, he'd take the hint and leave.

The man didn't move. He remained rooted to his spot, absorbing the situation. "Are you all right?" he finally asked.

"Yes," Stephen nearly barked, not even bothering to face him.

"What about her?" the man continued. "Does she need help?"

With a sinking heart, Stephen realized that the man meant Kat. He reluctantly turned, well aware that anything he said by way of explanation would sound like a feeble excuse.

"She's fine," he said. "Really. She's just resting."

The man ignored him, moving toward Kat and Claire as if Stephen hadn't spoken at all. For the first time, Stephen noticed that he carried a black bag.

"Hey," he started, hurrying toward the pew and his wife, "she's fine. There's no need to—"

The man brushed him away, a worried look on his face. "Why, this woman's out cold."

Stephen wiped his face with his hand, catching sight

of his watch just before the hand dropped back to his side. Eight after two. He had to get this guy out of here, fast.

He drew himself up to his full height and mustered all the authority he possessed. "You know, sir, we really do appreciate your concern, but my wife is perfectly fine. She's asleep, if you must know. She works hard all week, and although my daughter and I felt the need for prayer . . ."

His voice trailed. He might as well have spoken to the wind. The man wasn't paying attention. Instead he smiled at Claire, who, with a total disregard for the gravity of the situation, smiled back. It was one of her melt-you-to-the-core smiles that no one could resist, almost an invitation. The stranger accepted it and perched on Kat's free side, reaching for her wrist as he settled in to stay.

"Pulse is good," he said. "I don't like the looks of this perspiration, though."

"It's hot in here. That's why she's sweating." Stephen thought the words ridiculous even as they left his mouth.

"Nonsense, my boy." The man didn't even look at him. "Ladies don't sweat; they glow. And this young lady is well beyond her dew point." He rested a gentle hand against Kat's forehead. "No fever. No chills. Good. Then I'm here in time."

Time! Stephen groaned. He tried to catch Claire's eye, but she was staring at this stranger as if he'd brought her presents and candy.

"Sir," Stephen started, "I appreciate your concern, I really do, but my daughter and I would prefer to be alone now."

The man fixed him with a pointed gaze. "Suppose you stop talking long enough to look at the altar, young man?"

Stephen's anger rose, hot, white, and mixed with a panic he didn't know how to control. He opened his mouth to reply, but the man had reached into his bag, dismissing him completely.

He watched as the stranger took a cloth and patted Kat's brow. "Are you a doctor?"

"No." The man softly stroked Kat's wrist. "Look at the altar."

This was insane. Stephen planted both feet firmly on the floor, set his jaw, and refused to move.

Claire sighed. Then she shifted her mother so that she could slip from the pew and hurry to her father's side.

"Just try, Daddy," she said, tugging on his hands until he had no choice but to turn and face the Lady Chapel altar.

He blinked. There seemed to be motion against the white altar cloth, almost as if the altar moonlighted as a movie screen. He squinted, then leaned in for a closer look. The motion took shape, transforming from random movement into people before his startled eyes.

More than just people: as he stared, he saw Kat, Francesca, and Julia standing in a grassy clearing. A girl he did not know pulled herself from the ground, dusting off her dress with a shaky hand.

And, only feet away from Kat, stood Asteroth. The hatred on his face burned so pure and tangible that it cut through centuries, hurling itself into the Lady Chapel of the modern cathedral.

# 34

Asteroth rubbed his hands together in anticipation. Francesca tightened her grip on Julia's shoulders, pulling the girl to her with such ferocity that Julia squealed.

Francesca winced. The journey from trees to clearing had exhausted her. Each step had felt like trudging through thigh-deep water. This last vigorous tug had sapped even more of her precious energy. Her fingers loosened on Julia's shoulder as she leaned against the girl for support.

Kat spun to face them, eyes wide with fear and confusion.

"Aunt Frannie. Run away. Take Julia with you."

Francesca slowly shook her head. As if she could ever allow her niece to become an unnecessary human sacrifice. Not only did her love for Katerina run far deeper than that, her vision was clearer. Truth glowed more brightly by the minute. Katerina was courageous, had even grown stronger in spirit than Francesca had originally supposed. But her niece still did not see through spiritual eyes. Didn't she realize that sacrificing herself would only further Asteroth's aims?

With effort, Francesca raised her right hand. "Katerina," she said evenly, beckoning her niece to her side.

Kat hesitated for only a second, but it was long

enough for Asteroth to reclaim her. His arm snaked around her waist, trapping her against his body.

"Francesca," he said, "do you never grow tired of rescuing everyone you know? Truly, is their existence all that crucial if they cannot maneuver through this reality on their own? You have paid too great a price for their incompetence. Look at you: broken and weary, barely able to stand. What is to become of you? And what is to become of those who never learned to fight for themselves?"

She didn't answer. There was nothing to say.

Asteroth raised an eyebrow. "Do you fight alone?"

"Never."

He surveyed the landscape. "I see no one—physical or otherwise. Have you been abandoned to fend for yourself? Has your most beloved Almighty left you to your own devices?"

"Surely not."

"Then summon your army, Francesca. They arrived at your beck and call when last we fought, did they not? They were legion, as I recall, angelic warriors with spears of fire and light." His voice fell hard and flat about her ears. "Where are they now?"

She knew where they were. She could feel them within her, almost as if they had become one with her. Her body had perhaps grown weak, but the energy increasing within her burned brightly. The warmth and love of her companions raced through every corner of her being. And yet this wasn't their situation to enter. She didn't know why. Her brain wanted to demand a miracle, to scream that she needed help now. Her heart, however, rested in the assurance that all would pass as it should.

She felt a gentle kiss on her brow, a mark of love from one unseen. Asteroth's head jerked up, and she saw that he'd noticed, although his physical eyes could not entirely interpret which being of light had blessed her so.

"No warriors here," he murmured, mostly to himself.

"How hard," Francesca heard herself say, "to be in essence a far-reaching spirit, encased in a slow, physical shell. There is so much you yearn to do, yet can't. Sometimes a body just gets in the way."

He glared. "It does not weaken me," he said. "It will not defeat me."

She tilted her head, a waste of energy that turned her next breath into a tight little gasp. "I wasn't speaking of you," she said.

A vein in his forehead twitched as he studied her, his gaze sweeping from her head to her toes in a slow, methodical way. She thought she saw the dawning of understanding in his face, but she could not be sure exactly what he understood.

He turned abruptly. "Isobel!"

The girl looked up, dazed.

"Go to Julia. Stand before her."

Kat lunged forward as Isobel stumbled, dreamlike, to face Julia. Asteroth tightened his hold, pinning Kat's arms to her side with one deft movement.

"Really, Katerina," he said. "You are hardly a challenge, tiny as you are. Isobel, you know what you must do."

Isobel nodded, eyes fixed upon the girl before her. Julia's face blanched white.

"Julia!" Kat cried, but her voice was obliterated by Hugh's loud, raucous laughter.

Julia averted her eyes from Isobel's vacant blue stare. Isobel, following orders long drummed into her head, cupped the other girl's chin in her hand and forced her to meet her gaze.

"Aunt Frannie!" Kat's high-pitched wail pierced the stillness.

Francesca tried to hold Julia close. It was too hard. Her hands slipped from the girl's shoulders, and her arms fell to her sides. Her legs melted beneath her as she sank to the ground.

Curious. As her body weakened, her spirit grew stronger. A wave of light rippled through her, illuminating the clearing. She actually saw her companions beside her, although she could never describe them in physical words. They seemed to be verbs rather than nouns, but only adjectives could provide a pale representation of their essence. They surrounded her in a cloud of light. How could she feel such joy in the midst of such a horrible scene?

"We're with you," one said. "Soon you'll be strong enough to fight."

"Yes," Francesca said, knowing that they were right.

Stephen's jaw dropped with horror as Francesca fell to the ground. He spun to face the stranger in the pew.

"Who are you?" he demanded, voice hoarse. "And what is this? Is it real?"

The man met his panic with a shrug. "You asked for help. In fact, you called for it. Here I am."

"I called for the angels of light."

"Yes. Your point?"

Stephen stared at the man, unsure of which question to ask first. Scratch that. There wasn't time to order his questions.

"What is this?" He gestured wildly toward the altar. "Is it happening now?"

The man considered. "It occurs parallel to this moment, yes. Time is different there, of course, but these events are happening now."

"Well, what can I do?" Stephen demanded. "How do I stop it?"

"Keep watching," the man said. "Keep an open heart."

An open heart? Stephen ran a frantic hand through his hair. "I need more information. Look, you apparently know more about this than I do. I'm begging you. Tell me what to do!"

"You'll figure it out," the man said. "Turn around and watch."

He had no choice but to comply.

"Flow into Julia, Isobel," Asteroth said, voice low. "Victory will be sweet, my dear. Her voice will come with her body. You will talk, Isobel. Imagine!"

Francesca watched as Kat opened her mouth to shriek. Asteroth's hand covered it with one smooth motion, locked firmly in place despite Kat's frantic bites.

Isobel held Julia's gaze. Julia swayed slightly, a slender reed blown by a brisk wind. Indeed, a wind had cropped up from nowhere, rippling across the grass and mingling strands of Isobel's platinum hair with Julia's brown locks.

Isobel placed her hands firmly on Julia's shoulders.

"Yes, Isobel," Asteroth said. "Yes."

The wind swirled about the girls, creating a column around them made visible by the leaves and small twigs caught in the updraft. Isobel's dress wrapped around her legs. Julia's hair lifted from her neck and back like a dark brown halo surrounding her head.

"You are almost there, Isobel!" Asteroth's shout echoed against the forest trees. "Flow into Julia *now*! Become one!"

With a bloodcurdling shriek, Julia crumpled to the ground. Isobel staggered backward.

"No!" Kat took advantage of Asteroth's distraction to ram her elbow into his solar plexus. His grip loosened. She dashed to her daughter's side.

"Julia!" Kat dropped to her knees beside the girl. "Aunt Frannie, please, help me!"

Francesca reached out and weakly squeezed her niece's hand. It took too much effort to form her lips around words that would only be perceived as useless.

Kat shook away the comforting hand and pulled Julia onto her lap. The girl lay there, lifeless. Kat cradled the still body against her own, face chalky white. Francesca recognized the rage burning in her niece's eyes. From earliest childhood, Kat's reaction to tragedy had been anger first, sorrow second.

"What have you done to my daughter?" she demanded in a low, thick voice.

Francesca plucked at her sleeve. "Not anger," she managed to say.

Kat tried to shake her away, but Francesca gathered all the energy she could and tugged.

"Katerina, look at me."

Kat pulled her gaze from Asteroth and stared at her aunt.

"Aunt Frannie. My God, you're . . ."

Francesca could only imagine how wan and broken she looked. She was deteriorating rapidly, and there was little time to explain.

"Katerina. Not anger. This . . . isn't over. Light, Katerina."

Confused, Kat returned her stare to Asteroth. He did not meet it. He did not even acknowledge her escape. Instead, he watched as Isobel dragged herself from the ground, brushing off her hands as she rose.

"Isobel," he said, uncertainty tinging his words, "you did not do my bidding."

Kat and Francesca exchanged glances.

Asteroth stepped toward the girl. "I told you to flow into Julia—to become one with her within her body. I meant for you to leave your own physical shell behind."

Isobel studied him. A corner of her mouth turned up. Perhaps she meant to smile, but it looked more like a smirk.

"Isobel, we must correct this. My lessons were clear, my sweet. I told you that our aims could only be met if you flowed into the girl, not the other way around."

Isobel raised her hand to her throat. Her fingers wrapped around her neck, gently massaging her ivory skin.

Asteroth's eyebrows lowered. "Isobel? Are you indeed with us?"

She laughed, a sparkling cadence that ran up and down the scale. "Indeed," she said, voice husky.

Kat leaned across her daughter's body. "Where is Julia?" she demanded, voice shaking.

Isobel did not turn from Asteroth. "She is tucked away safely within me," she said. "It is the least I can do for the girl who gave me voice. Poor thing will not be able to share my pleasures, but I know not what else to do with her."

Asteroth flushed. "You must enter Julia's body at once, Isobel."

Again the chilling laughter. "Why?" Isobel asked, and even Asteroth looked surprised.

"My, my," Kat said from between clenched teeth. "Another miscalculation, Asteroth. You're slipping. Did you neglect to factor in the free-will wild card? Humans come with the gift of choice. Clearly, you are not as knowledgeable about human nature as you should be."

If Isobel noticed the use of a different name for her beloved, she gave no sign of it. She sidled toward him, intent clearly etched in every sinuous motion. Asteroth backed away as she approached, hands raised in an instinctive gesture of self-defense.

"I do not want that other body." Isobel stopped before him. "This is the body that makes you burn, is it not? This is the body I choose."

Francesca felt the light enveloping her grow brighter, and not only visually. Increased energy raced through her, although her tired body impeded its flow. A high, crisp hum filled her head, a physical translation of eternal praise. Did Asteroth sense the change? Spirit that he was, he should have. But at the moment, he seemed trapped by Hugh's limited senses, flummoxed by his current situation.

"I . . . I cannot touch you, Isobel," he said.

"Ah, but you want to. Look!" The very tilt of her

head mocked him. She ran her hands up her body, stopping at the laces of her bodice. "I have waited long for this moment, Hugh. Did you think me stupid because I could not speak? Did you think I could not sense the passion within you? I know you better than you know yourself! Very well. You have given me a voice. In return I will give you what I know you want, even though you seem bent on denying yourself the pleasures of the flesh."

She stood only inches from him now. He pulled in a sharp breath, but did not back away. He seemed under a spell, hypnotized by the girl's small, quick fingers as they unlaced her bodice.

"What is this, Aunt Frannie?" Kat whispered.

Francesca placed a finger to her lips, unable to speak. It was the man Hugh's weakness, that's what it was. She only wondered how much of that Asteroth understood.

Isobel's bodice dropped to the ground.

"How odd," she said. "It is only a voice, yet it gives one such power."

She stood before him in her shift. It outlined her full breasts and the lush curve of her hips. She cupped her breasts in her hands and stepped toward him. He immediately stepped backward, part of a strangely choreographed dance.

"Do not anger me," Isobel said. "I have waited too long. Kiss me."

Beads of sweat gathered on Asteroth's brow. His eyes darted from Isobel to Francesca, then back to Isobel.

"We have work to do, Isobel," he said in a strangled voice.

"Perhaps we shall do it," Isobel said. "But first we shall do this." She placed her palms flat against his chest.

Asteroth cuffed her on the ear. She fell to her knees, astonished, then quickly scrambled to her feet.

"Leave me be!" he spat. "I will not touch you!"

"Of course you will," said a new voice.

Stunned, Francesca and Kat watched as Father Gregory shoved Asteroth toward Isobel. Her arms opened to receive him, then locked to hold him close.

Gregory rushed to Francesca, Alys close behind.

"How did—" Francesca started.

"I was told," Gregory said. "The words broke through my prayer. But what have I done?"

"Give it to God, Gregory," Alys said. "The question is what must we do next?" Her fingers fluttered in Julia's direction. "How do we—"

Kat cut her off. "We never know what to do until the last minute."

Had Francesca any energy left, she might have debated that. For the first time in her life, it seemed she knew exactly what lay ahead, and exactly what she had to do to get there. She again squeezed her niece's hand, drinking her in as if to imprint her beautiful face on both heart and memory.

"Katerina," she managed to say, "stay in the light. God's blessing on you, my love."

Kat's eyes widened with fear. "Aunt Frannie!"

But Francesca simply closed her eyes and let the light wash through her.

"Aunt Frannie!" Kat's shriek should have pulled Asteroth's attention their way, but he remained locked in Isobel's embrace, his gaze glued to hers.

"No, Katerina." Gregory's hand, surprisingly strong, rested on her shoulder. "You cannot grieve now. There isn't time."

"Grieve?" Kat's heart flew to her throat. "But Aunt Frannie isn't . . . she can't be . . ."

Gregory gently turned her head toward Isobel and Asteroth as Alys straightened Francesca's fallen body and crossed her lifeless arms against her chest.

# 35

Kat forced her shattered mind to focus. Shaken, she leaned against Gregory, grateful for the physical support. She would not allow herself to analyze the facts before her. The senses played tricks during spiritual battle. One could never draw conclusions before the fight was over.

Isobel stared up into Hugh's face as if she'd just snared a rare creature and expected an ample reward. Her pink tongue darted out to lick her upper lip.

"Dear Hugh," she said. "How I've longed to speak your name. Do you hear how my voice caresses it? I cannot believe you would deny me. Is it really so difficult to love me?"

Hugh's anguished groan rent the air. His mouth closed hard atop Isobel's, interrupting the girl's flow of words. Isobel, startled by the intensity of the kiss, unclasped her hands from around his back. They flailed to her sides as if she'd lost her footing. Then she regained her equilibrium and once again pulled him close.

Hugh lifted his lips from hers. His breath came in short, harsh gasps.

A smug smile flickered across Isobel's face. "I knew you wanted this," she said.

"You have brought ruin upon yourself." His voice dropped so low that Kat could barely hear it.

Isobel chuckled. "That happened long ago," she said as he buried his lips in the hollow of her throat. "Ah! Do not devour me all at once! We have eternity for this."

Her head turned, and for the first time, she remembered that she and Hugh were not alone. Her brow furrowed with confusion as she tried to fathom why she had not noticed all these people before.

"Hugh. Why did you not say that others were with us? Now I understand your reluctance."

He did not answer. His mouth traveled hungrily down her neck to the swell of her breasts. One hand pinned her tightly against his body while the other wrapped itself in her hair. He yanked her head back with a mighty tug.

Isobel gasped. Apparently, this was not the scene of tender passion she'd imagined for so long.

"Hugh!" She struggled to free her hands.

"Is this what you've wanted so badly?" he asked. "Is this why you have pursued me, ultimately denied my will?" A loud rip resounded through the clearing as he tore the neck of her shift and forced it down past her shoulders, exposing her round breasts. "And what have you won, Isobel? Nothing for me, for you have ruined my plan, left me to my own devices. Is this how you show your love for me?"

Isobel tried to raise her arms, but they were trapped against her sides by her ruined shift and afforded little protection.

"I am lost," Hugh murmured. "But not for long. It is you, Isobel, who will pay."

Gregory turned his head as Hugh's mouth dropped to Isobel's nipple, sucking so hard that the girl emitted a little scream. Alys half rose, but Kat motioned her back.

"You can't go to her," she said, not even questioning how she knew this. "He'll destroy you."

"She's my flesh and blood. Surely I must—"

Hugh knocked Isobel to the ground. There were red marks on the girl's shoulders, the indentations made by his fingers before his offending hand had moved elsewhere. He gripped her buttocks as if she were a heavy piece of meat to be carried to the kitchen from the smokehouse. His other hand locked both her wrists above her head. He lifted his mouth from her breast and nipped her earlobe with his teeth, then silenced her yelp with a rough thrust of his tongue into her mouth.

"You can't go to her," Kat repeated. "Oh, my God, Alys, I'm so sorry, but the time to save her has passed. Look closely. Do you see?"

Hugh's skin, usually so fair, had changed. Patches of it glowed red as burning coals. One such patch smoldered on his back, through his tunic. Another spot had appeared on his wrist, and still another formed on his thigh. A tiny patch had begun to burn on his cheek.

"What is this?" Alys's hands flew to her own cheeks.

"I'm not sure," Kat said slowly. "Aunt Frannie would know."

The thought of Aunt Frannie nearly sidetracked her into a whirlpool of emotion. No. She couldn't give in, not now, not with so much at stake. Aunt Frannie had every right to expect more from her. In fact, Kat knew what her aunt would say. Francesca's voice echoed through her head even as her brain formed the words: *Listen, Katerina. Trust. The answers are there. Accept them.*

"I think I know what's happening," Kat said. Half of

her wanted to apologize for presuming she had any answers to offer. The other half plowed recklessly ahead. "Hugh's lust has overwhelmed him. Combined with Asteroth's energy—power—it's too great for any human shell to contain."

"But the fires on his skin! What do they mean?" Alys passed a shaky hand across her eyes.

Kat swallowed hard. "Hugh will be destroyed," she said.

"Then the demon will be destroyed along with him," Gregory said.

Kat shook her head. "No. Just the human body will burn. The spirit can escape. I've . . . I've seen it happen before."

"And Isobel?" Alys asked.

Kat did not meet her gaze. "Isobel can't survive," she said. "She is one with her body, and she has given her soul to Asteroth."

A bright red spot appeared on each of the prioress's cheeks.

"There was nothing you could do," Kat said fiercely. "There was nothing either of you could do. She wanted Hugh more than she wanted anything else. In the end, the choice belongs to each of us alone."

Gregory gazed at Alys, leaning toward her as if to gather her in his arms and tuck her away from the ugly recriminations surely swirling through her mind. Alys waved him away, then nodded toward Kat.

The priest's grip tightened on Kat's shoulder. "What of your daughter?" he asked.

Kat stared down at Julia, whose head still rested in her lap. She swiped at her eyes before any tears could fall. "I don't know yet," she said.

"Katerina, you said that the spirit residing within Hugh would survive."

"Yes. Asteroth. I assume Aunt Frannie told you all about him. He is an ancient spirit. He has more trouble moving within a body than he does out of one. His essence will easily escape that burning shell."

"Isobel said that she'd kept Julia's spirit separate within her," Gregory continued. He leaned forward and passed a tentative finger beneath Julia's mouth and nose. "She breathes, Katerina. Her body lives. She has a body to house her spirit. Perhaps she can return to us."

Kat's head jerked up. "How?"

"I don't know. We must ask."

Kat gripped the priest's sleeve. "Pray. Pray for my daughter."

"Of course," Alys said. "But you are the girl's greatest protection."

"I am?"

The prioress nodded. "You are her mother. So much more than flesh and blood binds you. Does not your century recognize the strength in such bonds?"

Kat closed her eyes. She longed to process all this new information now, to roll it over and over through her brain to see if it made sense. As if any of this made sense! When would she learn that the rational part of her brain, so prized in her career and day-to-day routine, was not particularly helpful in this realm?

"I'll ask for help," she said. "I'll beg for it."

Isobel's scream sliced through the air. Hugh lay atop her. He'd forced her legs open with his knee, but her screams came more from his appearance than his actions. The gaping burn on his cheek had grown, spreading to cover half his face. More patches had erupted across his body. The stench of burning flesh filled the air as tiny flames sparked from each patch. Hugh burned, but Isobel remained unscathed by the flame.

"I can't watch this any longer," Alys whispered.

"You shouldn't," Gregory told her. "None of us should. Turn away, Alys."

He finally left Kat and hurried to Alys's side. He wrapped the prioress in his arms, cradling her head against his chest as if she were a small child. Kat gasped as a pink-white light enveloped them. The strength of their love, she realized, was every bit as powerful as the hideous flames of evil that now engulfed Hugh and Isobel. She reached a tentative hand toward the priest and the prioress until her fingertips brushed the edges of the light. A jolt of energy raced through her. It was as though she'd found a blazing fireplace after hours of wandering through the freezing outdoors.

Surprised, Kat plunged her hand deeper into the aura.

"Yes," she heard Aunt Frannie say. "Yes, Katerina. You need only ask for this, and it is yours."

Kat turned to stare at her aunt. Francesca's body lay lifeless on the ground.

"It is a battle," Kat heard, "but you do not fight alone. You never have, Katerina. And you certainly don't fight unarmed."

Alys and Gregory did not lift their eyes to the horror unfolding before them, but Kat, strengthened, raised her chin and turned to face the enemy.

Hugh's body, nearly obscured by flames, raised itself

above Isobel. Only his eyes remained clearly defined, their vacant glow reflecting the flames that leapt from Hugh's flesh. Isobel, mercifully, had lost consciousness.

"You . . . are . . . mine." The voice that rang through the clearing had never belonged to Hugh. No man could possess such deep, thundering tones.

What was left of Hugh's body rammed forward with a mighty thrust. Kat rose slowly as Isobel's body ignited, bursting into fire beneath Hugh's writhing form. The flames leapt higher and higher, sending spirals of smoke into the darkening sky.

Kat checked her armor. Helmet, breastplate, shield, sword—all was in place. She straightened to her full height.

"Julia," she called across the clearing. "Come out. You are here; let me see you."

At first, only the crackling of flames met her ears. Then a rumble began, so low in frequency that it nearly shook the ground upon which she stood. Kat became vaguely aware that Alys and Gregory now flanked her on either side. They'd brought their powerful aura with them, although she was not certain that either of them even knew it existed.

The rumbling increased. A tiny fireball of gleaming light shot from the heart of the flame. It danced, agitated, darting about like a firefly trapped in a jar. It was followed by a translucent black shape no bigger than a fist, discernable from the fire's smoke only by its thick, greasy texture.

"Julia." Kat's voice stayed steady. "Come back to us."

The rumbling grew even louder, echoing like thunder through Kat's ears. The flames diminished as, from the depths of the blazing pyre, a rolling mountain of dark vapor began to emerge. It roiled and seethed as it grew larger, towering above them.

"No!" The deep voice boomed through the clearing. "Julia is dead, Katerina! You can no longer possess her!"

Kat gripped her sword. "Her body lives, Asteroth."

A strong wind gusted over them, whipping Kat's hair from her face and making her squint. She raised her voice above the whistling of the gale. "Julia was never yours. She has free will, Asteroth, and she never chose to follow you. Julia, come back to us!"

Asteroth's laughter ricocheted around them. "Once again, Katerina believes herself the lawyer of the universe. Perhaps your ability to fabricate an analysis for any given situation is well prized in the physical realm. In my reality, you are little more than amusing!"

"Obviously, I am much more, Asteroth," Kat said through clenched teeth. "Because if I weren't, you wouldn't need to get me out of your way, would you? Somehow, I matter more than you care to share."

A howl tore the air, although Kat couldn't tell if the sound came from Asteroth or from the wind.

"Julia!" she called again.

The little fireball bounced in response.

"Julia, return to your body," Kat ordered, eyes on the vapor. It was changing, taking on a shape of some sort.

The ball of light skittered through the air, stopping to hover over Julia's body. The earth rumbled. The fireball hesitated, quivering.

"Pay no attention to him," Kat said. "I'm your mother, Julia. Do as I say. It's okay to go back into your body now."

"If she does," Asteroth said, "all hell will descend upon you. Do you understand?"

Kat squared her shoulders. The vapor seemed trying to acquire a shape now. The figure of a man wavered before them, made alternately of vapor and granite. She'd never seen Asteroth assume this form before. She wondered how tangible it could become.

"Julia," she said in a strong voice, "do what I told you to do. Return to us. Now."

The fireball dove toward Julia's body, burying itself in the girl's hair. The body began to glow, a soft, strong light radiating from the inside out.

The wind whipped so violently that Kat, Alys, and Gregory had to cling to each other just to keep their balance. Then, as quickly as the wind had come, it vanished, leaving an eerie stillness in its wake. The silence in the clearing was broken only by the dying flames of what had once been Hugh and Isobel.

The mountainous vapor remained, boiling before them in silence.

"Mom?" Julia sat on the ground, one hand pressed against her forehead.

Kat raced to her daughter's side, pulling Julia against her as if she would never again let her go.

An ominous roar sounded in the distance as the sky grew dark.

# 36

"KAT!" STEPHEN REACHED FOR THE ALTAR. HE HAD DROPPED to his knees somehow, although he couldn't remember doing so.

A gentle hand landed on his shoulder. He looked up to see the old man behind him, Claire by his side.

"Do you understand what you've seen?" the man asked.

Stephen felt his mouth move, but no words came out. Understand? Was that even possible? He swallowed hard and tried again. This time, he found words. "That huge black shape . . . that's Asteroth."

The man nodded. "In essence. He has lost the body he borrowed, of course. And, thanks to our Katerina, he has nearly lost this opportunity to reach the child of light."

"Child of light!" Stephen nearly spat the words. "Everyone throws that phrase around like I know what it means. I don't even know which of my children is supposed to be the child of light!"

"No," the man said. "But someday you will. All you need to understand at this moment is that you must protect your wife."

"Protect her?" Dazed, Stephen slowly rose to his feet. He checked the image flickering against the altar. Asteroth loomed above Kat, who held Julia tightly in her arms. Francesca lay motionless at the feet of the priest and the prioress. Protect Kat? He'd never felt so helpless in his life.

"There's nothing I can do," he said. "You, on the other hand, seem capable. Bring them back. Get them out of there."

The man smiled but shook his head. "If we bring them back now, we bring Asteroth back along with them."

Stephen felt Claire's hand steal into his own. He looked down at her. She stared back, green eyes wide in her pale face.

"I'll try to help, Daddy," she said, and her willingness to plow ahead where there was no obvious path strengthened his heart.

He licked suddenly dry lips, then turned back to the man beside him. "You're my angel of light, aren't you?"

The man nodded. "One of many."

Stephen thought for a moment. It was hard to make his mind conjure up anything coherent. Fear and doubt blasted most of his ideas before they even had a chance to crystallize. His own confusion irritated him. Reflexively, he raised the sword in his left hand and cut through the suffocating vines that curled around his head.

"Very good," the old man said. "You remembered your sword."

Stephen blinked, and the sword was gone. He was surrounded by the quiet stillness of the chapel, with the old man and Claire beside him.

"The sword of truth," the man said. "It will cut through the tendrils of evil every time."

"How did I just do that?" Stephen asked.

The man merely smiled.

Stephen lowered his arm. "All right. There won't be any answers. Just do me a favor, okay? Don't turn this into a bad party game. Don't make me guess. Tell me what to do. I'll listen, no questions asked."

The man nodded again. Then, without another word, he placed both hands firmly on Stephen's shoulders and turned him to face the altar.

Kat's eyes widened as the greasy black cloud grew more consistently human in shape. Soot rained down from the rough head materializing nearly twenty feet above her.

"Mom!" Julia gripped her hand so tightly that Kat winced. "What is that?"

Kat shook her head as the outline of broad shoulders appeared.

A low voice twisted through the wind: *Kat-er-in-a.*

She fought back a swell of nausea, then leaned over Francesca's motionless body. "Come on, Aunt Frannie," she said, jostling her. "We need you. Wake up."

"Katerina." Alys dropped to her knees beside her. "She cannot hear you. She is with our Lord, now. Her fight is ended."

"No," Kat said through clenched teeth. "That can't be. She wouldn't leave me here like this. If Aunt Frannie is gone, then evil has won."

Alys sent Gregory a glance. Kat read it easily. They pitied her, believed that her inability to accept Francesca's death stemmed from grief. She hated being misunderstood. She longed to shake them until they recognized how desperately she needed Aunt Frannie to rise from the ground and lead this battle.

She turned back to Asteroth. The imposing figure was defined to the waist, now. Its broad chest rippled with muscles. Massive arms bulged with barely confined strength as the figure flexed its thick, heavy fingers. Facial features shifted constantly, reminding them that this creature was still composed more of vapor than granite. Still, the face was defined enough that all could recognize its sneer.

*Kat-er-in-a.* The syllables bubbled over themselves. They sounded as if drawn from the depths of a well.

"Leave now," Kat told Gregory and Alys in a low voice. "You have done more for us than I can ever thank you for. You deserve better than to share in Asteroth's hatred."

"What will become of you if we leave?" Alys asked.

The vapor swirled into two thickly sculpted thighs. The creature's mouth opened and closed like a huge ventriloquist's dummy with a life of its own.

"I don't know," Kat said. Her hand trailed across Frannie's forehead and down her cheek, coming to rest against her cold fingers.

Alys's hand landed atop hers.

"We stand with you," Gregory said. "Our Lord challenged such evil. How can we not rebuke it in His name?"

Kat closed her eyes. Aunt Frannie wasn't coming back. There'd be no return-to-life miracle where Francesca leapt to her feet and single-handedly vanquished the foe. Somehow, though, all that her aunt had taught her must mean something. What would Aunt Frannie tell her to do?

"Look carefully, Katerina," she heard Frannie say. "Use your spiritual eyes, not your physical ones."

Kat's eyes flew open. "Did anyone hear that?" she asked.

Julia looked up, eyebrows raised. Alys and Gregory once again exchanged glances.

Kat straightened and placed shaky fingertips to her temples. Whether anyone else heard anything was irrelevant: this could be their only hope.

Spiritual eyes. Like she knew how to find them.

But she instantly remembered the light that had surrounded Alys and Gregory. It had been born of love, but its energy, its intensity, went far beyond modern-day sentiments of hearts and flowers. She'd forgotten all about it the minute she'd seen Asteroth begin to manifest before her. Now she saw that to remove herself from the power of that light would be a huge mistake. Perhaps Aunt Frannie had been literal as well as figurative when she'd told her to stay in the light.

Kat opened her eyes and turned toward Alys and Gregory. Sure enough, she could once again see the light surrounding them, that brilliant white aura tinged with pink and gold.

"This light is your homeland," she heard Frannie say, and while she didn't quite know what that meant, she understood enough to know that she needed to stay within this force field of light if she had any hope of beating the darkness that spread like ink before her.

"Extend the light," she heard. This time, the voice did not belong to Aunt Frannie. She forced herself not to analyze it. It was amazing enough that she knew what to do. In her mind, she quickly wrapped Julia in the light, making sure that the edges enveloped her aunt, too.

"All right," she said, startled by the clarity of her own voice, "here's what we do. Imagine us bathed in a column of light. Enclose us within it. Don't let anything interrupt it."

"But . . ." Julia's frightened gaze focused on the behemoth before them. The huge arms were moving now, although nothing had materialized below the knee.

"Smoke and mirrors," Kat said briefly. "Don't trust it. Don't even look at it. Fill your mind with light and nothing else."

Julia hesitated. "But I don't understand how—"

"Just do it, Julia," Kat said. "Do it now!"

"Extend the light," the old man said, and suddenly the column of light Stephen had noticed around the priest and the prioress leapt forward to enfold Kat, Julia, and Francesca as well. Or had Francesca already been lighted? He couldn't remember.

The man smiled. "Your wife hears well," he said. "Her spirit is stronger than she knows. She'll be quite a force to contend with once her mind accepts what her heart knows as truth."

Stephen knew better than to waste time asking questions that started with "how" or "why." He watched as the column of light grew brighter.

"Are they safe in there, or what?" he asked.

"Somewhat," the man said. "It's a curious thing, the light. It has the power to protect, but it can only be maintained through faith. Doubt eats holes in it, holes that darkness can easily penetrate."

"Can they destroy Asteroth this way?"

"They'll probably use all their energy to keep the

light steady. I doubt they'll have any left to destroy him. They're in physical reality, remember. It takes quite a lot of concentration to make spiritual light effective in the physical world."

Stephen tried to process the information as quickly as he received it. "What about Asteroth? Isn't it hard for him to manifest in the physical world?"

"Yes."

"So if they were to attack him—"

"He's like an iceberg, my friend. So much of him is unseen by their eyes. I suspect that the best course of action is to confront him in the spiritual rather than the physical realm. The light is more easily used there."

Stephen gestured wildly toward the altar. "Well, how are they supposed to know that? Do you plan to tell them?"

The man nailed him with a level gaze. "That's not their task," he said.

"Oh!" Claire's gasp made both men turn her way. "Look, Daddy! There's a hole in the light, right near Julia's head!"

"Ah." The man nodded slowly. "Your sister has doubts. Hmm. That will need to be repaired before the demon senses it."

Sure enough, the giant's mammoth head began a slow swivel in Julia's direction. His craggy eyebrows raised in recognition.

"Warn them." Stephen gripped the man's wrist. "Kat heard your voice before, didn't she?"

"Katerina is doing what she must do," the man said. "You can fix this one. Don't look at me like that. It's high time you took your post. Fix it, Stephen."

Stephen opened his mouth to protest, then remembered that he had promised to do as he was told. With a helpless shrug, he closed his eyes and concentrated on the column.

A strange hum sounded in his ears, a dense block of musical notes stacked one atop the other and crowned by a high, clear frequency. It brought to mind pure-aired mountaintops, the crisp, invigorating bite of clean, salty ocean air. The cathedral chapel fell away until he stood in the midst of undefined gray space. His sword once again rested securely in his hand. It glowed with light, shimmering until the gray around him crackled with bright points of energy. Warmth and vitality coursed through him, as if years had slipped from his body.

Stephen lifted the sword and focused on the column of light. He could see it more clearly from this vantage point. The patch near Julia's head looked particularly dark and ominous.

He extended his right hand. Light spilled from his fingertips, dancing in nearly visible particles.

"Wow," he said.

"Yes," the man answered. "It's rather marvelous, isn't it?"

Stephen glanced up. The man didn't look nearly as old as he had in the cathedral. His hair glowed in this unearthly light. His skin, so pale only minutes before, shone with a gleam that seemed to emanate from within.

"Fix the hole fast, Daddy," Claire said.

He stared at his daughter, unable to pinpoint why she, too, seemed different. Her hair was the same riot of tousled curls as always, her eyes that same clear green. The change obviously didn't rest in her appearance. She seemed somehow older here, far more at home in these surroundings than he was.

"She's right," the man said. "There isn't much time, my friend."

Stephen returned his attention to the hole in the force field of light. He raised his hand. Light again poured from his fingers. He imagined it streaming across the open space until it covered the patch of darkness. He wasn't entirely surprised when it actually did that, looping over and over itself until the hole was closed.

"Very good," his companion said. "You are a natural warrior, Stephen. And you need to be. Look."

How could he do otherwise? Those within the force field seemed very close to him, now. He could see the rapid rise and fall of Kat's chest as her breathing quickened. He noted the quick sideways glance the prioress sent the priest.

"Kat!" he called, but his wife did not turn his way.

"She can't hear you," his companion said. "You have entered a reality she doesn't see. This is for the best, my friend, for she could never concentrate on protecting those in her care if she saw you now."

"Where are we?" Stephen demanded, momentarily forgetting his promise to ask no questions.

"That doesn't matter. You have no time to ponder it. Look beyond those you love."

Stephen pulled his gaze away from the column of light to see the murky darkness seeping beyond it. He no longer saw the hulking giant that threatened those in physical form. Instead, the oily vapor he knew to be the essence of Asteroth roiled before him, constantly shifting shape and density.

"My God." Stephen felt his chest constrict.

"Don't study him," his companion said.

"But what exactly am I looking at?" The tip of his sword scraped the ground as the triumphant vigor of youth drained from his body. Disillusionment crept through him. He felt old and defeated, unable to fight an enemy he could neither clearly see nor define.

A strong hand cupped his chin, roughly turning his head from the darkness. He found himself staring into the deep brown eyes of his companion.

"What are you looking at, Stephen? You are looking at pure evil and its fruits. Despair. Hopelessness. Hate. Look a little closer, and you will sink to the depths of pain and torment. Do not study this. Do not even look at it. Asteroth can use your own fears and choices against you. Do not provide the fodder for his fire."

"But how can I fight what I can't see?"

The man shook his head. "I forget how physical a being you truly are, my friend. Remember: you no longer operate in physical reality. Your tactics must reflect that."

Stephen again turned toward Kat. Her eyes were closed. The hint of a smile brushed her lips.

A smile? Stephen squinted. What thoughts could allow her to smile under these circumstances?

It didn't matter. More than anything, he wanted to gather her into his arms, to rock her against his chest and tell her that he loved her enough to believe that everything would be all right.

"I don't know how to do this." His voice trailed away into emptiness.

"You're mistaken, Stephen," a new voice said. "You know exactly what to do, and so do I."

Stephen jerked around to see Francesca before them, sword raised high in her hand.

# 37

"AUNT FRANNIE!" CLAIRE'S JOYOUS SHOUT FILLED STEPHEN'S ears. "I knew you'd come!"

Stephen could not fully interpret the expression that crossed Francesca's face. She'd always loved his daughters, but emotional display had never been her forte. Now her smile spoke of a love deeper than any hug or kiss could convey.

"Of course I came," she said. "I see you've been in good hands, Stephen." She pointed in the direction of his companion.

"You know him?" Stephen managed to ask.

She nodded. "You do, too. You just don't recall. You can say good-bye to him now. He's gotten you here in one piece. What more could we ask?"

Stephen turned to thank the man, but only Claire stood in the odd gray twilight.

"You missed him," she said. "He's gone. He said to tell you good-bye."

"Well, Stephen," Francesca said. "Are you ready to play white knight?"

"But . . ." It was the best he could do. He felt like a ball in a pinball machine, bounced from emotion to idea and back to emotion again without any chance to process all the unfamiliar information thrust his way.

He stared at the woman before him. This was

Francesca, all right, yet not quite Francesca. Her face, smooth and unlined, brimmed with the glow of health and serenity. Her graceful fingers rested around the hilt of a glowing, white-hot sword. She wore something resembling armor, but it sparkled and shimmered so brightly that he couldn't look at it long enough to make out its design.

All this, yet when he looked toward the column of light, he saw Francesca's body lying motionless on the ground.

Francesca followed his gaze. "That body is only a shell, now," she said. "This is me, Stephen. This is the Francesca you've always known."

He shook his head. "You're more than the Francesca I've always known."

She stepped before him and placed a gentle hand on his arm. His skin felt warm and tingly where she touched it.

"I'm simply more than either of us has been able to see," she said. "And, unfortunately, so is Asteroth."

"Don't look at him," Stephen warned as Francesca lifted her head to examine the scene. "He'll suck you in."

"I can look at him. I am purely spirit, now. It's amazing how much easier everything is without the heavy anchor of a body." She narrowed her eyes, considering. "Just don't start liking this state too much, Stephen Carmichael. You have much to do yet. We need to get you and your family back home as quickly as possible."

He wanted to vehemently second the motion, to tell her that all he wanted was to return to the normal, boring humdrum of everyday existence.

A low, dull groan from Asteroth's direction froze the words in his mouth.

"What was that?" he asked, not daring to look.

"He's growing stronger," Francesca said. "He must be drawing energy from someplace."

"It's mostly Julia's fault," Claire said, as if busting her older sister for visiting forbidden chat rooms online. "I know you patched one hole, Daddy, but it looks like another one is starting to form down by her knee. Do you see it?"

Stephen looked carefully. Sure enough, the force field of light seemed thinner at that spot, almost as if it were a piece of pizza dough stretched too far.

"She's got to stop letting that happen," Francesca said, almost to herself. "Asteroth funnels his energy from fear and doubt. This will only make him stronger."

"I don't understand," Stephen said. "He seems strong enough on his own."

"He's particularly strong at this moment because he just devoured Isobel's soul. She gave herself to him of her own free will—the most powerful source of energy darkness can get. But nobody within that column of light is willing to do that. In order to keep his form in physical reality, Asteroth will need to siphon additional energy from negative emotions . . . from fear, doubt, anger, hate . . ."

Stephen raised a hand to his forehead. "I can't digest this now, Frannie. I'm sorry. Just tell me what to do, and let's get it over with. Give Claire some marching orders, too."

"I'm already doing something," Claire said. "I'm talking to Mommy."

He gave what he hoped was an encouraging smile. Why contradict her? It was probably good that she thought she could help. It would keep her focused and unafraid.

But Francesca nodded. "Good, Claire. Tell your mommy that she has to keep the light strong. Let her know that Julia needs strengthening."

Claire closed her eyes. Stephen watched as, once again, a small smile appeared on Kat's face. She wrapped an arm around Julia's shoulders, then leaned to whisper into the girl's ear. Almost immediately, the weakening light by Julia's knee burst into brightness.

"She meant it," Stephen murmured beneath his breath. "She's really talking to Kat."

Francesca raised an eyebrow, apparently surprised that he'd even questioned it.

"Does Kat recognize Claire's voice?" he asked.

"I don't know. I doubt it."

"But, Frannie, how does Claire know to—"

Francesca pierced him with a steely stare. "Stop asking questions, Stephen. Listen closely. We need to talk strategy."

"I'm doing my best, Mom," Julia said through chattering teeth. "But I've never been so scared in my life!"

"I know." Kat brushed a kiss against her daughter's brow. "I'm right there with you, believe me. But we have to stay strong, Julia. Concentrate." She gave her a reassuring squeeze and straightened up. Somehow, it seemed intensely important that Julia think only about light. Kat wasn't completely sure how that would help, but she wasn't about to question any impulses that came her way.

"What must we do now?" Alys asked.

Kat paused before answering, caught by the slight

break in the prioress's voice. Alys, so determined only minutes ago, had gone chalky white. Her left hand trembled. She was afraid. Well, who could blame her?

Kat's eyes flickered across the brilliant column of light. She didn't know how it was made, but that same compelling urge she'd felt only moments ago told her that she needed to keep it bright and whole. No problem. The more instructions, the better. Unfortunately, directives never came until needed, which made it hard to answer Alys's question. Still, the prioress had to derive some comfort from the presence of this glorious light all around them.

"Alys, I'm not really sure what happens next but, so far, this light seems strong enough to protect us."

Alys knitted her brow. "I see no light," she said. She clasped her trembling hands firmly in her lap.

Kat's shoulders slumped. She'd forgotten that her companions might not see the light that so obviously shielded them. But, of course, that would explain Julia's intense fear as well.

"Um . . . ," she started, at a momentary loss for words, "we are surrounded by light—a whole column of it. It's very clear, very pure, and apparently very powerful."

The huge, manlike figure pivoted to face them. His bulging eyes focused on Alys. A twisted grin crossed his face. Kat wondered how much of Asteroth this representation housed. It seemed almost like a puppet, a huge fortress of a disguise sent to distract them.

She didn't like the expression on that ugly face. She'd seen it on opposing counsel dozens of times. Asteroth was planning his next move, and she had the sinking suspicion that it would involve the prioress.

Alys flinched. Her palms flew to cover her ears, as if she'd heard whispers she didn't want to hear.

"Alys?" Gregory peered into her face. "What ails you?"

Alys lifted her chin. "I see no light," she repeated.

Kat had no viable answer to offer. "I know," she said. "But it's here, Alys. Believe me. I can describe it to you, if you'd like."

"You? You are addled by grief!" Alys said, obviously parroting a suggestion just heard. "How are we to know if what you see is really true? Your visions could kill us all!"

Kat's heart flew to her throat as she recognized exactly what Asteroth's next move was. Hadn't she herself experienced his mind-twisting so many years ago? He was the master of illusion, the king of taking one's own fears and hurling them straight back at the intended victim.

"Alys," she pleaded, not even trying to keep the urgency from her voice, "please, you must trust me. If you don't, if you fear, Asteroth will use your thoughts against all of us."

Gregory's head whipped her way. She didn't know how much the prioress could hear, but the priest was certainly listening. His attention bolstered the resolve she needed to steady her voice.

"He will try to confuse you," she continued. "And he gains strength through your confusion. Do you understand?"

Alys's eyes widened slightly. Kat could only imagine the distortions Asteroth had handed her. She did not know Alys well enough to know her personal weaknesses.

"I see no light," Alys said again through clenched teeth. "I know only that if we sit and do nothing, the demon will kill us all. We must fight."

"No." Kat gripped her arm. "That's exactly what we must *not* do. The more fear and anger we provide, the stronger Asteroth will grow. You've been brave for so long, Alys. Please, just stay brave a little longer."

The creature before them opened its mouth in soundless laughter.

Stephen did not have to look at Asteroth to recognize that the demon's next attack was well under way. Darkness gathered like a fog just outside the column of light. The light flickered in front of the prioress, leaving her fully exposed to darkness for seconds at a time. Worse, the force field seemed thin near Kat as well.

"What's happening?" he demanded.

Francesca did not take her eyes from the scene unfolding before them. "Alys is afraid and doubting, obviously."

"Yes, but surely Kat isn't falling, too. Why is the light so weak around her?"

"She's distracted," Francesca said slowly. "She's so busy thinking about how to restore Alys that she isn't maintaining the light. This is bad, Stephen; Asteroth can derive strength from Alys's fears, but it's Katerina he wants."

Stephen extended his sword and aimed for the gap before Alys. It seemed darker and more ominous than the thinning light near Kat. Once again, light from his sword flashed across the darkness in thousands of dancing particles. He gave a sigh of relief, but it was short-lived. The darkness quickly took over again.

Francesca's hand landed on his arm. "It's too far gone for patchwork," she said. "Come on. We'll have to distract him."

"Distract him?" That sounded almost playful, as if they were going to drive Asteroth around the block and deposit him at a surprise party in his honor. *"Distract him?"*

Francesca's eyebrows rose. "You have a better idea?"

Of course he didn't.

"Then follow me," she said, starting toward the mass of dark vapor they knew to be Asteroth.

She stopped mid-stride and turned to face Claire. "Claire, my darling, you must go back. You can't be here."

"I know," Claire said. She walked slowly to Francesca and tilted her head up for a kiss. "Good-bye, Aunt Frannie."

Francesca cradled the child's face in her hands, then kissed her gently on the forehead. "God go with you," she said.

"Daddy, I'll see you soon." Claire slipped through the mist and disappeared before Stephen could ask even one of the myriad questions ringing through his mind.

# 38

Kat drew back, stung by the expression on the prioress's face. Alys looked like a thundercloud collecting enough strength to explode into a wrathful storm.

Gregory gathered Alys into his arms. "Tell me more," he said to Kat. "Quickly."

Kat shook her head. "It's hard to understand. I can see why Alys—"

"There is much in this world that I don't understand," he said shortly.

The prioress shifted against him, turning her head to catch sight of Asteroth. Kat watched as Gregory shielded Alys's eyes with his hand, pulling her close until he'd blocked her view.

"Katerina, tell me what I must know," he repeated.

Kat complied. "I don't know why you see the demon but not the light, but the light is here, protecting us. If we doubt, if we fear, we weaken the light and strengthen Asteroth. It's that simple."

"Ah," Gregory said. "I believe you."

Her eyes widened. "You do?"

He sighed. "Saints and martyrs also tell of visions that only they can see. I do not wish to believe in this monstrosity before us, yet it exists. Tell me what I must do."

Kat studied him for a moment, understanding for

the first time the grace of faith. Gregory could believe without a constant search for proof. How she longed for that kind of peace!

"Gregory." Alys twisted free of his embrace. Her wimple had slid to the back of her head. She reached with a shaky hand to pull it off. Cascades of red-gold hair tumbled about her shoulders, accentuating the glittering gray of her eyes.

As if of its own accord, Gregory's hand streaked through the tumbled waves of hair. He cupped Alys's face in his hands, gaze locked with hers.

"Gregory . . ." Her voice trailed away.

Kat wanted to keep staring at them, to absorb the intensity that flowed between them. She knew that the love she shared with Stephen ran deep and true, but there was something different here, something she longed to catch and keep with her. It seemed to her that her love for Stephen had faded into a backdrop, a comfortable feeling that she knew was always there. Their relationship was never a priority these days, just a state of being that she visited whenever the rest of the world's demands and distractions allowed it.

The current between Alys and Gregory pulsed pure and immediate. Kat wanted it. She wanted to feel the strength and energy of such a love race through her, filling her to the core.

Suddenly, her yearning for Stephen felt almost tangible.

"Did you see that?" Stephen asked. "The light in front of Kat jumped."

Francesca nodded. "The frequency increased. It's brighter."

"Why?"

"I'm not sure. But it happened just in time. Asteroth was about to strike."

Sure enough, the vapor loomed particularly dark and oily near where Kat knelt.

"How can you tell?" Stephen demanded. "I'm trying not to look, but every time I do, all I see is a mass of smoke or something."

Francesca paused. "Do you want to see Asteroth?"

"I'm not supposed to."

"You can, Stephen, if you keep your armor intact and harness your mind. Do you want to see him?"

Stephen took a deep breath. Of course he didn't want to see this ancient demon. He didn't want to be standing here in this netherworld, either, but here he was.

He glanced at Kat, who still held Julia close. He thought of Claire, apparently safe, but far from here.

He had to bring them all home safely.

But he was no superhero. He was just a regular guy, a restaurateur playing games with pretend armor and a stupid sword that nobody on earth could see.

His head jerked up toward the vapor. Those were not his thoughts, not by a long shot. They sounded familiar; he recognized enough of his own wallowing to know that the thoughts were based in reality. But they certainly didn't represent the man he meant to be, the man he knew he could become.

He again studied Kat. She lifted her head, staring toward him almost as if she knew he was there. The determination on her face strengthened him. He gripped the sword in his hand and straightened.

"Yes," he said, eyes narrowing. "I want to see him."

Francesca nodded. "Tell him."

"Tell him?" He hadn't counted on that.

"You fight with the light, Stephen. You speak with authority. Tell him to show himself. He'll be only too happy to meet you one-on-one. But hurry. Time grows short."

"I thought time didn't matter here."

"It doesn't, not as you think. But you want to return to the cathedral, don't you? Time matters there."

He thought fast. It was surely long past 2:15, the time he'd assumed the door of time would open again to allow a reentry from the medieval to the modern world.

Francesca seemed to read his thoughts. "The time coordinates of the fourteenth and twenty-first centuries are not the same. But they will align briefly, and that will be your last opportunity to go home. You must move quickly."

The force field wavered again, mostly around the prioress. Kat seemed oblivious to it, but the vapor began to drift in that direction, clearly focusing on any weakness it could find.

"Sometimes," Francesca said, "the best battle plan requires timing, not weaponry."

Stephen locked his gaze on the vapor and stepped forward.

Kat stared at the behemoth, mesmerized by the immensity of him. He was fully defined, now, right down to his dirty toes. Could he walk? As if in response to her unasked question, the huge man lifted one sandal-clad foot. Kat's fingers flew to her throat. Could he come closer, perhaps thrust a fist through this flimsy wall of light and rip them toward their deaths?

No. She yanked herself away from the thought. The light before her had wavered perceptibly the second she'd given in to fear. This situation was bad enough with Julia so afraid and Alys wavering. She couldn't afford to follow their example.

As if in response to her renewed resolve, the sheet of light in front of her brightened.

She did a quick check. The light near Julia seemed strong enough, though nowhere near as intense as her own portion of the column. Alys's section remained thin, a patchwork of constantly shifting gray, leaving a Swiss-cheese mosaic of holes behind.

"The light is weakest near you," she told Gregory, who still held Alys close.

He nodded, filling Kat with relief that she did not need to waste her energy in explanations. She could already feel Julia's body tense beside her. She followed her daughter's gaze to the mass of evil outside the force field. Julia's jaw had dropped. Kat sensed the thoughts racing through her mind. She knew her daughter envisioned herself crushed lifeless in the fists of the abominable creature towering before them.

"No, Julia." Kat gripped the girl's wrist as the light began to fade. "Look away. Think of home. Think of how good it will be when we're back with Dad and Claire. Just look away!"

But Julia remained hypnotized by the ugliness before her and could not turn her head until Kat did it for her.

"Alys."

Alys looked up into the dark eyes of the man she'd loved for so many years.

"Tell me of the thoughts that haunt you," Gregory said, and as always, the soft honey of his voice poured over her like a soothing balm.

She tried to wrench free of his arms, but it was a halfhearted attempt, one she'd never really expected to complete. "Gregory, can you not see? If we have any hope of victory, any chance to live, we must fight!"

He nestled his cheek against the silk of her hair and gently stroked her arm. "I don't fight," he said. "It is not my way."

"But if it is the only way to escape death—"

"It's not my way," he repeated, and she fell silent.

She had known this of him from the earliest days of their friendship. It had been, in fact, one of the reasons she'd grown to love him. She remembered the loud, raucous banquets in her father's manor hall, where sweaty men bawled out tales of blood and lust between draughts of ale. She remembered one such banquet in particular. She'd sat on a hard wooden bench under the threatening glare of her father, the old man he'd selected as her betrothed beside her with one hand in the trencher they shared and the other grasped firmly around her waist. Even now, the memory of his knobby fingers splayed across her rib cage raised a shudder of revulsion. How he'd rambled on and on about his victories on battlefields and crusades, the noxious fumes from his toothless mouth causing her to gasp for breath whenever she could. How proud he'd been to recount in detail each thrust of his sword, each decapitation or amputation he'd inflicted. She'd paid scant attention, so busy was she squirming away from his clawlike hand as it dropped to her thigh.

And she would never forget when her desperate

glance met the eyes of the priest who stood at the door. She'd known of Gregory's gentle patience even then. She'd met him two summers before, and he often lingered to talk to her when no one else would bother. In her father's eyes she was merely a fourth daughter, useful only as a pawn for power through marriage, and even then an expensive proposition because of the dowry required. Through Father Gregory's eyes, however, she glimpsed within herself something of value and beauty.

How calmly he'd strode across the room, stopping only when he stood directly before her. Her betrothed's soiled hand had slipped away from her body.

"My lady Alys," Father Gregory had said, eyebrow raised.

"Yes." She'd risen hastily, knowing that even her father would not cross this man of the cloth and the Church that had sent him. "Yes, Father Gregory, forgive me. I had forgotten that I'd asked earlier to speak with you."

She would confess the lie later. For now, it was enough to follow this serene man out of the hall. Drunkards parted to let them pass as he led her away from the harsh noise of daily life. At that moment, her young mind had understood clearly that quiet intent said far more than loud boasts and brags.

Now she could see in his eyes that he remembered, too. He knew her heart as well as he knew his own. She loved him more than she could ever say, more than life itself.

She raised a hand to caress his cheek. Her fingers rested on the familiar curve of his jawbone, lingered on his chin. She opened her mouth to speak of her love for him.

The words stuck in her throat as a thought, searing as a fireball, blazed through her head.

*If he loved you, truly loved you, he'd have found a way to marry you and give you the life you so richly deserve.*

She saw herself bedecked in a golden silk gown trimmed with ermine, a contented smile illuminating her face into brilliant radiance. Rings of ruby and emerald dripped from her fingers. Her hair, braided with intertwined ribbon, was looped into lustrous coils on either side of her head. She sat on a plush chair, surrounded by children. A boy of perhaps fourteen stood beside her, his confident grace marking him the obvious heir to the manor house. He had Gregory's dark hair and eyes, but his features were undeniably hers. A younger boy smiled up from the floor, where he sat at her feet. A girl of perhaps twelve flanked Alys's other side. Her hair, dark like Gregory's but glinting red in the shaft of sunlight that lit the room, flowed to her waist. She so favored Alys's dead mother that the prioress could not prevent the anguished moan that escaped her.

Gregory grasped both her hands.

"Alys," he said in a low voice, "do not see it. It is not truth."

*But it should have been,* the relentless voice in her head mocked. She sensed knowing laughter as an image of Gregory entered the scene, the essence of virility as he flung back his cape and surveyed his family with pride.

The Gregory of her vision held out a commanding hand, and as if watching a dream, Alys saw her gold-clad counterpart rise to accept it. She watched as the man pulled her close. With a low chuckle, he drew her lips to his. He kissed her hungrily, as if no amount of her could ever satiate his desire.

*Ah, what you have missed,* the voice said.

Alys drew back. With difficulty, she pulled herself away from the story unfolding in her head. She wanted to stay there, to drink in every moment of the life she had not lived, but something was wrong.

Her eyes focused on the very real man before her. Gregory's face was lined, now. He was not vigorous like the man in the vision, nor had he married her, given her children or a life of wealth. But everything this man was, he had given freely to her. When he held her, when she looked deep into his eyes, she knew that he loved her to the depths of his soul. She did not need frenzied lust and possession. She did not need wealth. She saw very clearly that she'd missed nothing at all in her lifetime.

She tilted her head back and closed her eyes.

"Gregory," she whispered, "kiss me."

He did not question her, merely bent until his lips touched hers.

Alys wrapped her arms around his neck and knew that she would rather die with this man than live without him. Perhaps she could not trust Katerina, but she would trust Gregory forever. And she would trust the God who, against all odds, had granted her a love this sweet and true.

The light surrounding the priest and the prioress blazed to life with bright, clear strength.

"Whoa!" Stephen shielded his eyes with his arm. "How did that happen?"

No response. Surprised, he lowered his sword and

looked around. He'd expected Francesca to be right behind him as he closed in on Asteroth. When had she gone? Was this his cue to leave, too? The column of light appeared intact. No part of it burned more brightly than the section near the priest and the prioress, but there were no holes.

Suddenly, the light in front of Julia collapsed, leaving her totally exposed.

"No!" Stephen and Kat cried in unison as Asteroth turned her way.

# 39

"JULIA!" KAT GASPED AS THE COLUMN OF LIGHT PROTECTING her daughter vanished. "What happened?"

Tears streamed down Julia's cheeks as she stared at the seething hulk before her. "I can't do it, Mom. I'm not like you. I can't pretend that . . . that . . . *thing* isn't out there!"

"Help me, Gregory," Kat pleaded as Asteroth turned toward her daughter. How had they gotten stuck inside this horrible, relentless video game? She only hoped this creature couldn't hurl thunderbolts or shoot laser beams.

"What must I do?" Gregory asked, and Kat remembered that not only couldn't he see the light, he probably had no idea how to maintain it.

There was no time to explain anything now.

"Just take care of Alys," she said. "No fears, no doubts. Stay strong."

Asteroth's heavy hand reached for the sword at his side. Kat had not noticed it before, but now she couldn't tear her eyes away from it. Its blade, chiseled from dark, hard flint, sliced through the air as he raised it high.

"Dear God." A heavy, dark fear threatened to engulf her. She pushed it aside, angered by its very presence. No, anger wouldn't do, either. None of these negative emotions would save Julia, who'd crumpled to the ground in a useless heap.

"A fly." Asteroth sneered. "The merest trifle, a small annoyance, easily destroyed." The tip of the sword circled in the air as he considered. "Shall I slice you in two now or wait another moment?"

Kat closed her eyes and concentrated. Somehow, she had to reerect that shield of light. But she was terrible with light, could never envision it completely. The image of it always faded in and out whenever she tried to use it. Why couldn't it come in a form she could easily understand, one that would stay where she put it? Something like a toothpaste dispenser would come in mighty handy about now.

Her eyes flew open. Why not?

Asteroth's sword began a heavy, downward fall toward Julia's head.

Clenching her teeth, Kat averted her eyes and quickly pictured Julia covered in a thick, sticky paste of glowing light. The paste dripped from the girl's head, encasing her arms and torso. Kat imagined it streaming from a tube. She applied it to her daughter's legs, working until every part of Julia was covered. Then she fell back, exhausted. Lighting Julia hadn't seemed particularly strenuous, but it had taken nearly every ounce of energy she had.

The paste glowed like the armor Julia had never learned to wear. Kat used the little energy she had left to keep it in place. She banished every other thought from her mind and bathed her daughter in a clean, white glow.

Asteroth gave a low, angry growl, but his sword had gained too much momentum to stop. It landed atop

Julia's light-drenched head. She apparently felt little. She simply looked up as if awakened from a nightmare. Dazed, she raised a hand to her head, patting to feel what could have possibly saved her.

The sword shuddered in Asteroth's hand. A loud crack reverberated through the clearing. A series of breaks traveled up the massive arm as it shattered from wrist to shoulder, dropping to the ground with a smash. The sword clattered at the creature's feet.

Startled by what she'd somehow managed to do, Kat gaped at her daughter. Julia stared back through a veil of light.

"Mom, how did you do that?"

A dangerous fatigue washed over Kat, leaving her limp and drained. "I don't know. But Julia, you can see that all is not lost, can't you? Can you tell that you're covered with light?"

Julia studied her hand. "I don't see it," she said. "But I feel different. Safe. Something must have happened, or I'd be dead right now."

Kat saw color return to Julia's face. Her daughter had regained a sense of hope. "Julia, imagine yourself bright like a torch, okay? Please, think of nothing else. You've got to protect yourself. Can you do it?"

The girl swallowed, then squared her shoulders. "Yes. I'll try."

Kat turned back toward Asteroth. A sharp, jagged edge protruded at his shoulder where the destroyed arm had once been. He could probably create another limb, but the lack of an arm did not seem an obstacle to him. His cold stare rested on her, chilling her through and through.

She raised her hands to rub her throbbing temples.

To her right she saw the light surrounding Gregory and Alys. To her left, Julia glowed like a steady flame. Good. They were all safe. Perhaps they could finally maintain their own shields of light.

"Kat-er-in-a," Asteroth said slowly, advancing toward her.

She saw him far too clearly.

With a start, she realized why. Only a thin scrim of light now separated her from this monster. She must have given more of herself than she'd thought to protect Julia. Panic gripped her, threatening to overpower every other emotion she had.

Before she could control her instinctive reaction, the last of the light before her disappeared.

"Yes," Asteroth said. "You are the one I want."

Too late, she realized that she'd been tricked into leaving herself defenseless before him.

The column of light in front of Kat peeled away like skin from a banana. Stephen lunged toward his wife as the greasy cloud of darkness stretched above her, ready to engulf her completely.

A low rumble stopped him in his tracks. "Do something, Kat," he murmured beneath his breath. "Do it *now.*"

He sensed a cacophony of emotion emanating from the core of the vapor. How could something so amorphous project such a barrage of raw sensation? Triumph, conquest, victory—the vapor pulsed with the energy flow of each, a bundle of exposed wires ready to electrocute on contact.

Kat stared up, white and immobile. A dark shadow fell across her face.

"Asteroth!" Stephen's voice rang across the gray distance.

The vapor paused, a barely contained mass of movement.

"Asteroth," Stephen said again, this time with more authority.

Another hesitation, as if Asteroth could not decide whether acknowledgment of this human was worth the effort.

Kat looked confused. Stephen thought she must recognize the pause in the massive flow of darkness but not know what caused it.

He had to buy her time.

"Asteroth," he said, "you owe me an explanation."

He could swear the vapor laughed. A hoarse, rough grumble ricocheted off unseen boundaries, sending an unpleasant vibration through his body. A deep voice echoed all around him.

"I? Owe you?"

Stephen straightened, suddenly assailed by an image of his fifty-year-old self standing in a field, armor dented and helmet on backward. Asteroth, it seemed, planned to answer nonverbally as well as in ringing syllables.

He tore his focus away from the ridiculous picture. "You mean to destroy everything important to me, Asteroth. Surely you owe me something for that."

A dark wall of scorn shot up on all sides, surrounding him. Stephen jabbed at it with his sword. Tiny shards of glass shattered at his feet, then vanished into the illusion they'd always been.

"As if an explanation mattered," Asteroth said.

"It matters to me," Stephen said. "Show yourself. I want to talk to you."

The shadow left Kat's face as the vapor drifted toward him.

"You wish to see me?" Asteroth sounded amused, but there was something else in his voice as well. He was intrigued.

"Yes," Stephen said. "I want to see you."

"There are many aspects of my being," Asteroth said. "I appear in many different guises to many different people. What would you have, sir? Power or nobility? Beauty or intimidation? A picture you long to hold, or a thing so hideous that its visage will remain burned upon your soul for all eternity?"

"How do you decide which to be?"

"I choose the form the situation requires."

Stephen brushed the words away with a wave of his hand. "Choose, then. I'm tired of your games."

"Games?"

Stephen narrowed his eyes and glared into the heart of the vapor. "Manipulations. You want to terrorize us with ugly images and threats of evil, but you can't win. You are nothing, Asteroth. There is no image you can present that will frighten me, nothing that will turn me away from the light. Go ahead and give me the worst you can dish out."

"What if I choose to entice you, instead?" The words wrapped themselves around him, bringing with them a seductive whiff of perfume. "Once, Stephen Carmichael, I could have made you one of my own. You'd have followed me anywhere in exchange for wealth. My offer remains open."

Stephen clenched his jaw. "That door closed long ago. Your offers don't interest me."

Asteroth paused, digesting the words. "Very well,

then. You are immune. I shall show you the truth of who I am."

An eerie silence descended. Stephen forced his gaze to remain on the vapor. In his peripheral vision, he saw Kat rock back on her heels. She drew in a deep, ragged breath. He hoped she'd regain her equilibrium quickly.

The vapor began to lift and part, changing in color from black to slate to ashy gray. Then, from its depths, the outline of a man emerged. He was Stephen's height, with dark hair and green eyes. He wore armor and carried a sword in his left hand.

Stephen gasped as the figure stepped into the clearing. He rubbed his eyes, then looked again.

There was no doubt about it.

He saw himself.

# 40

THE MONSTROUS GIANT HAD TURNED AWAY, BUT KAT DIDN'T know why. Something must have distracted him. She could think of no other reason he'd have given up at the very moment he might have prevailed.

There was no time to ponder this. Who knew how long this unseen distraction would last?

She was exhausted to her core, a bone-weary exhaustion that nailed her to the ground and made her feel as if each limb weighed about five hundred pounds. Still, she knew what must be done. She had to engineer a wall of light so strong and bright that it obliterated all surrounding darkness. Whatever the century, this was still physical reality and, lacking a body, Asteroth could remain present in corporeal form only if fed by darkness. He'd built this hideous man from their own anger and fear. Somehow, she had to cut off every source of negative emotion.

If only she weren't so tired.

"What do you think of me?" Asteroth gave a deep bow.

"Handsome." Stephen winced. Hearing Asteroth's voice resonate from a replica of his own body rattled him.

"Not really. I've presented myself in far worthier forms. But this will do."

Stephen rested on his sword, studying the figure before him. It was an uncanny resemblance, right down to the pale scar on its wrist from the bicycle accident he'd had as a teenager. Still, there was a certain vacancy within the representation, a blankness to the features that reminded him of an empty vessel. Perhaps Asteroth could not replicate a life force he did not possess.

Kat rose to her feet. She looked pale, but Stephen recognized the stubborn set of her jaw. She would strike back as soon as she'd regained enough strength to do so. He just needed to keep Asteroth occupied.

"You don't like resembling me, do you," he said.

"I am spirit. This realm is my home. In this realm, I can choose any form I wish."

"But you don't like this one."

"No. It is lowly. Unworthy."

"Gee," Stephen said. "Thanks a lot."

He watched a smirk cross his own features. "I leave it to the Other to embrace humanity," Asteroth said. "Most of it is not worthy of my attention."

Stephen nodded in agreement. "I want to see you in the form you believe best represents you. Show me your glory, Asteroth."

Particles of energy whirled about him, throwing him backward to the ground with their force. A throne shot up before him, extending into the sky until he could not see its end. He recognized a man ensconced within it, but the immensity of both throne and man was so great that he could barely comprehend them. His fingers scrabbled for his sword as he propped himself up on his elbows to stare.

"My majesty is so much more than you can understand," Asteroth thundered. "I shall lower myself to a size you can absorb."

Immediately, the huge throne shrank back until it sat, large and imposing, atop a marble podium. Hundreds of candles flickered at its base, illuminating the man who sat upon it. He was perhaps eight feet tall, with white-blond hair falling in tangles and braids to his waist. A gold circlet gleamed against his forehead. The rings on his fingers were weighted with gems. His turquoise eyes glittered, and his mouth seemed sculpted into a permanent sneer. He wore a leather loincloth and sandals. The rest of his heavily muscled body glistened with musk oil.

"Behold my majesty," Asteroth said. "I share my perfection with few. You should be honored."

Stephen slowly stood, dazed by the opulence before him. An unearthly light surrounded the throne. It reminded him of nineteenth-century gaslight, so dim and ill defined did it appear.

"Am I not magnificent?" A bejeweled goblet appeared in Asteroth's hand. He drank deeply, then dragged the back of his hand across his mouth. "All this can be yours. Join me. You, too, will grasp perfection."

He took another swig from his goblet. Stephen stared, momentarily mesmerized by the sight.

"The elixir of life," Asteroth said. Beads of liquid sparkled on his upper lip. "*My* life. It could bring you the fulfillment of all your desires. Stephen Carmichael, you have always won. You have never joined a losing team. Why start now? I must win. You know this." He swept an arm back toward Kat, but did not bother to look at her. "This is what remains of their powerful army."

Stephen watched as Kat closed her eyes. A faint force field of light jumped before her, then disappeared, leaving only a film behind.

"Yes," Asteroth continued, "this is what is left. A sprig of a woman barely able to fend for herself. She cannot conquer me."

Stephen licked his lips. "I'm not interested in what you have to offer."

Asteroth leaned back against the purple cushions of his throne. "No? Why not? Is it your outdated love for this woman? For if it is, my friend, you are sadly deluded."

The light in front of Kat jumped again. It was obviously stronger this time, and more of it stayed behind. Kat, too, seemed aware of her increased strength. Her chin lifted as she crossed her arms against her chest. The light increased.

Asteroth's brows lowered. He shifted in his throne as if to turn her way.

"I am not deluded," Stephen said quickly, trying not to look at Kat. "My wife and I are solid. You'll have to do better than weak allusions if you want to get my attention."

"Why? You know very well that Katerina is more loner than wife, more interested in her own desires than in you."

"Weak, Asteroth, very weak."

"Can you deny that she has little time for you or for your affairs? She occupies herself with worldly pursuits. You are an afterthought, nothing more than an intrusion in her life. Why not leave her before she leaves you?"

Stephen shook his head. "This is unimpressive. I expected better from you."

Asteroth drew himself up in his throne and fixed Stephen with a sharp stare. "Imagine her rage when, at the height of her worldly success, she finds herself burdened by the birth of your child."

Stephen blinked. "Excuse me?"

Asteroth lifted his goblet into the air, a silent toast that Stephen had no desire to join. The goblet vanished, plucked from the demon's fingertips by some obliging, unseen force.

"Your wife is with child," Asteroth said, savoring each word. "Surely you knew this."

Stephen rocked back on his heels as if struck. He hazarded a glance toward Kat. The force field of light surrounding her was brighter than before, but he scarcely noticed. He stared at her, amazed. Of course. Why hadn't he paid attention to how sick she'd been lately? Sure, she had a history of migraines. And yes, the life they'd constructed encouraged exhaustion. But these last episodes of illness and fatigue had been different, far more draining and incapacitating than usual. Kat, who never gave in, had been laid low. And he'd been entirely too self-absorbed to think about anything other than how much time at work he lost when he had to pick up the slack at home.

He clapped a hand to his forehead. "Jesus," he groaned. "I am such an idiot."

Asteroth gripped the arms of his mighty throne, a twisted smile on his face.

"Yes," he said softly, misinterpreting the words. "Imagine her rage. And you are the sole cause of it. She will hate you until the day she dies."

Stephen caught a glimpse of the image Asteroth sent. He and Kat were too old to start all over again with an infant. A new baby would bring nothing but chaos to their household. It would flip their ordered days upside down, require more than anyone could expect them to give at this stage of their lives.

Ordered days. Quite a euphemism for the stilted regimen they now followed simply to complete every task and appointment listed on their daily schedule. He and Kat had become swept into a frenzy of constant motion, onto a treadmill that obscured the truth: they were strongest when together, yet had somehow managed to concentrate on everything except each other.

He pushed the image of chaos from his mind and remembered instead that afternoon weeks ago when he and Kat had made love in the quiet shadows of a waning autumn day. How soft the sheets had felt against his skin. How luxurious it had seemed to love his wife in a leisurely fashion, blocking out the noise and demands of the world long enough to remind himself how much a part of him she was. He'd propped himself up on one elbow to study her face. She'd studied him right back, eyes wide, hair streaming across the overstuffed pillows of their bed. Even after fifteen years of marriage she was still something of a mystery, this woman who knew him better than did anyone else on earth. He'd known with certainty then that there was a reason they'd been given to each other.

A spark leapt from the light surrounding Kat. Stephen allowed himself a small smile. She was remarkable, really, brave beyond belief, and in love with him for reasons beyond his comprehension.

He squared his shoulders and turned to face Asteroth. "Thanks," he said. "I needed to hear every word you said."

A muscle in Asteroth's neck twitched. This was clearly not the response he'd expected. "Katerina will not enjoy this news nearly as much as you do."

Stephen shook his head, still dazed by his recent revelations. "Oh, she'll be a little shocked, but she'll get over it. She's not in this alone, after all. You see, I love my wife."

He thought he noticed Asteroth wince at the word "love," but that seemed too theatrical, a cheesy effect, like a movie vampire who shrieked at the first sign of light. Surely it wasn't love that threatened this creature of darkness. There had to be more to it.

But Asteroth's image did look somewhat less solid, as if part of him had been called elsewhere. The candles at the base of his throne flickered.

"Katerina will not want this baby," Asteroth said, his voice nearly a growl. "And she will not want you. If you join me, you will emerge victorious from this abomination."

Abomination? It was a baby, for heaven's sake. Sure, it was life-altering, but it wasn't some insurmountable disaster, the arrival of some creature who—

"Oh, my God." Stephen's eyes widened as he met Asteroth's frigid stare. "Tell me the truth. Is this baby the child of light?"

Asteroth's image wavered again. He was starting to resemble a hologram, semi-transparent and not completely there. Still, Stephen could make out the furrow of his brow, the downward pull of his mouth.

"I don't know." Asteroth clenched his hands into fists. "I command you to tell me, Stephen Carmichael!"

The booming words did not register right away.

"Are you serious?" Stephen finally whispered. "You really don't know? How can that be?"

Asteroth pushed himself up from his throne, rising until he towered above Stephen. Stephen straightened, willing himself to stay firmly planted in his spot. A chill spiral of wind emanated from behind the throne, snuffing half of the candles.

"I know the prophecy," Asteroth said.

"What prophecy?" Stephen demanded. "Where is this prophecy written? What does it say?"

"That is unimportant. You and Katerina were destined to conceive the child of light. I tried years ago to sway you to my side. Had you joined me then, the child could not have been created. I tried to end Katerina's life before she could come to you. That, too, failed. Now, I command you: identify the child of light. Tell me what you know!"

Stephen shook his head, bewildered. "You're supposed to have all this power. If you don't know who the child of light is, how am I supposed to know?"

"You lie!" Asteroth thundered, but Stephen detected an edge of doubt in his voice, a slowly dawning recognition that the words he heard were true.

"I don't lie," Stephen said quietly. "I don't know which of my children is the child of light."

"But I do," a new voice said, and Asteroth grew slightly more transparent as Francesca's warm hand rested on Stephen's shoulder.

# 41

For a second, Kat thought she heard the ground rumble in a mild earthquake. Then she realized that the rumble came not from the earth, but from the huge figure still hulking before them. She stared at the behemoth from behind the curtains of light now shining all around her. As she watched, spiderweb cracks raced through his remaining hand. His fingers crumbled. The entire hand broke away, falling to the ground in a little pile of stones.

"What is this?" Gregory asked in a low voice.

Alys lifted her head from his chest, narrowing her eyes as she glanced toward the creature.

"Don't look too closely," Kat warned. "We're doing so well. Whatever you're thinking, whatever you're doing—it's working. Don't stop."

As if in response, another crack reverberated through the clearing. This time, the creature's ear fell off.

Julia actually laughed as the ear shattered into pieces on the ground. Kat turned just in time to see the light brighten around her daughter.

"I'm sorry, Mom," Julia said. "I know it's not funny, but—"

"No." Kat forced a smile. It almost hurt to start it,

but she had to admit that she felt better once she'd done it. "Laugh all you want, Julia. The light gets stronger when you do."

Alys gasped. "I saw it!" she cried. "A flicker of flame before me . . . I think I saw this light you speak of!"

"Maybe you'll see more soon," Kat said, sincerely hoping that this was true. "Picture it, Alys. The stronger we make our light, the weaker this creature becomes."

"Yes." Gregory squeezed Alys's hand. "Soon there will remain only a pile of rocks where this evil stands, and we will have won."

The smile left Kat's face. She wanted to agree with the priest, she really did. But she knew that Asteroth was essentially spirit. They could perhaps banish him from physical reality, but she doubted that they could make much impact on the spiritual realm where he dwelt. Surely his evil would continue to exist there, even if they managed to obliterate this manifestation.

She saw no point in sharing that information with the others. She looked from Julia to Gregory to Alys. There was something in each of their faces that she hadn't seen before. They were finally confident, certain that they could overcome darkness and win this battle. And, in reaction to this newfound assurance, the intensity of the force field increased until it was so bright that she could barely see through it.

She heard the next minor rockslide rather than saw it, and wondered which part of the monster had fallen away due to lack of an energy source.

Stephen watched as the huge throne wavered, then faded completely away. Asteroth didn't seem to care.

He stood as still as a statue, even when his own image began to waver as well.

"So, Francesca," Asteroth said. Stephen took a step backward as he caught the jagged edge of ice in his voice. "You think yourself impressive indeed. Do you hope to meet me spirit to spirit, force to force?"

Francesca's hand dropped from Stephen's shoulder. "Your energy is draining away, Asteroth. Are you sending it elsewhere?"

Asteroth gave a visible start, then turned toward the force field of light. It danced and glowed, infused with a brilliant life all its own. The dark gaseous vapor outside its border had diminished in both size and density. It hovered beyond the force field as if uncertain of what to do next.

"Hmm," Francesca said. "It appears you're losing your physical energy source."

"Katerina," Asteroth said, almost to himself. "I must have Katerina."

"Good luck," Francesca said. "It doesn't look like you have enough energy to sustain whatever form you've assumed in physical reality."

He turned to her with a snarl, but Stephen caught something else in his expression, something he'd never seen there before: fear.

"Francesca," Asteroth started slowly, "do you mean to remain in the spirit?"

Francesca hesitated, then turned toward Stephen. "You must watch carefully. Very shortly, you will be able to enter the fourteenth century long enough to pull Katerina and Julia out of it."

"He cannot!" Asteroth's form flickered with the intensity of his response. "I will not allow him to interfere!"

Francesca's eyes flashed. "You don't have a choice. What will you do, Asteroth? If you try to maintain a physical manifestation in the fourteenth century, you'll lose spiritual strength. If you pull your energy away from physical reality, you've lost your access to Katerina."

He stared at her. "No, I haven't," he whispered. "You know very well that I haven't. But are you willing to make the sacrifice?"

Stephen touched Francesca's arm. "How will I know when to go?"

"You'll know," she said, gaze still locked with Asteroth's. "The time is coming fast. Stay alert."

"It's very beautiful," Alys said, and Kat knew that she could finally see the light in all its glory.

"Yes," Julia said. "I've never seen anything like it."

The light shot up all around them in fountains of sparkling radiance. It illuminated each of them, bathing them in comfortable warmth.

"I wish I could see beyond it." Kat searched for a weak point that could serve as a peephole.

"Why?" Gregory asked. "You know what awaits on the other side. Why would you want to see that?"

"Well . . ." Kat floundered, at a momentary loss for words. "I just want to know what we're supposed to do next."

A half smile crossed Gregory's face. "I don't think you'll learn that by studying the darkness. Our answers lie in the light."

She wanted to argue. It made no logical sense whatsoever that they should just sit here, convinced that they would know what to do next but not actually doing anything to acquire the necessary information. Still, she knew that he was right. This was the antithesis of a rational legal case where she gathered all available facts and then planned her strategy. This required a blind leap of faith.

"So," Gregory prodded gently, "deep in your soul, what do you think we must do now?"

Kat swallowed. The answer was there, even though it made no intellectual sense. "We're doing it. Let's make this light as strong and bright as we can. Let's make it a veritable wall."

She heard more stones hit the ground as she allowed herself to rest within the vital glow of the light. That was followed by another thud, and then another, as rock after rock apparently joined the pile growing outside the force field.

Asteroth broke the gaze he and Francesca held, turning his eyes from her to Stephen. Stephen flinched but stood his ground. The demon's form appeared more solid than it had a moment ago. Stephen once again noticed the muscled definition of his chest, the fine beads of perspiration on his brow.

"Asteroth, you're leaving the fourteenth century," Francesca said.

He ignored her and turned to Stephen.

"Think, Stephen Carmichael," he said, tone dripping in pools of thick, rich caramel. "You say you don't know which of your children is the child of light. Perhaps you speak truth. Maybe your mind does not know. But think deeper. Your soul knows. Who is the child of light?"

Almost against his will, Stephen considered each of

his children. Julia, who had somehow become a viaduct accessible to energies well beyond the borders of her daily existence. Claire, who had shown an uncanny comprehension for the language and ways of the spirit. And this unborn baby, a child whose birth offered so much possibility and potential.

Francesca's sharp voice cut through his reverie. "What does it matter, Asteroth? The prophecy is fulfilled. You know it is. You've lost your chance to alter the course of the child's birth."

Asteroth glared at her with such raw hatred that Stephen averted his eyes. He stared instead at the vapor outside the force field. It could hardly be considered menacing. It was simply a little ball of darkness bobbing through the air. Little remained of its former intensity or hulking shape.

Asteroth's form was heavy and solid now. Tendrils of dark smoke curled from his body like steam from a hot tar road. He unclenched his right fist, holding his palm open. The tiny gaseous ball dropped into it, leaving a scaly gray mark on his palm. Instantly, the gray scales snaked across his body, covering his skin completely until he stood before them in wretched ugliness. His startling turquoise eyes had grown black and opaque. Blond hair still sprouted from his head; the wooden beads clasped at the end of his braids clicked against his scaly back.

"Asteroth in all his glory," Francesca said. "Now, Stephen. Walk toward Katerina."

A strangled snarl escaped Asteroth's mouth. It sounded more animal than human, as if his vocal cords were in a state of transition.

Stephen took a tentative step toward the force field, then broke into a run. From the corner of his eye he saw Asteroth lunge forward. He instinctively recoiled, but did not break his stride.

Francesca aimed the tip of her sword. A beam of light shot forward, etching a razor-thin line in the ground. Bars of light shot up from it, nearly knocking Asteroth backward with their force. The line of blazing spears continued until it had encircled Asteroth in a cage of glowing flame.

"You have no authority, Francesca!" Asteroth shouted.

"I don't fight in my name," she replied, holding the sword steady.

Asteroth aimed a powerful punch at the barricade. It held fast. "You cannot keep this light strong enough to contain me. It is beyond your strength and ability."

"I can hold you as long as I please," Francesca said, glancing over in time to see Stephen reach the force field. He hesitated.

"Adjust your armor and step inside," Francesca called.

"But—" He waved a helpless arm in Asteroth's direction.

"Never mind him," Francesca said, turning to face her nemesis.

Asteroth paced in his lighted cage. "Very well, Francesca. They must return this way. I can wait."

She said nothing.

Asteroth turned suddenly. "You did not answer my earlier question. Do you plan to remain in the spirit?"

She raised her chin. "I plan to keep you as far away from Katerina as I possibly can."

She checked the force field. Stephen was gone, carried into the fourteenth century with more light than she'd ever known she could send.

# 42

"DAD!" JULIA'S VOICE SHOT THROUGH KAT'S EARS. SHE opened her eyes to see Stephen just within the force field, squinting as his eyes adjusted to the light. He looked so wonderfully familiar that she could only sit and stare as her mind struggled to believe that he was not an illusion.

"Kat." He dropped to his knees beside her, gathering her tightly in his arms and rocking her against his chest as if he'd never let her go. His lips brushed her forehead. No illusion could feel this complete. He had to be real.

Her fingers traced his cheek. "Stephen, how did—"

"No time." He scrambled to his feet, tugging her up beside him. "I've come to take you home, but we need to move quickly. Julie—" He pulled his daughter to his side in a loose hug. "Are you all right?"

She nodded. "Can you see the light, Dad?"

"Yes. I can feel it, too. It's downright hot in here."

"We did that." Julia looked a little smug.

"God did that," Gregory corrected. "We were merely His instruments."

Kat turned pink as she realized she'd momentarily forgotten all about the priest and the prioress. "Father Gregory, Dame Alys, this is my husband, Stephen Carmichael. Stephen, we owe Gregory and Alys the world."

Stephen instantly extended a hand toward the priest. Surprised, Kat realized that the bar for the extraordinary had been lowered for her husband. He didn't seem to find it at all odd that he now spoke to medieval people.

"Thank you, both of you," he said. "Please, forgive our rudeness. There's no time to explain. Kat, Julia, our window to home won't stay open very long. Claire is there waiting for us. We have to go."

Kat hesitated. "What's outside this force field? Last we looked, there was a huge manifestation of Asteroth just waiting to pounce."

Stephen shook his head. "There's nothing out there now but a big pile of rocks."

Alys's jaw dropped. "I want to see it," she said.

"Follow me." Stephen firmly grasped Kat's hand in his own and stepped through the curtain of light. Julia paused briefly, then followed her parents. Gregory and Alys emerged last, surprised to find themselves in recognizable surroundings.

"Look!" Kat pointed at the force field. It broke apart as they left its protective circle, tiny pieces of it raining down upon them like a gentle shower of shimmering confetti. She half expected the sparks to burn as they grazed her skin, but each one brought a sense of peace, the understanding that all could work as it should.

"Ah." A smile crossed Alys's face as the sparkling light fell down upon her. "The air feels different—sweeter, somehow, and scented with roses. I want to feel this way forever."

Gregory took her hand. "You can. As it was created through us once, so it can be again. It is always within our reach."

Kat opened her mouth to ask exactly how he knew this, then shut it. The truth of his words nestled within her heart. Perhaps the curtains of light would never again appear so tangible. That would not mean, however, that this beautiful light did not exist. It would be forever theirs to request and use.

"Is this what you were talking about?" Stephen gestured toward a huge pile of rocks.

"Unbelievable." Kat slipped her hand out of his and approached the rubble. Rocks of all sizes and density lay in a hill before them. They looked scorched.

"This used to be human in form," Kat said, reaching out a tentative finger. Despite its burned appearance, the rock she touched felt like an ice cube.

Stephen's arm encircled her waist. "Not anymore," he said. "That physical image of Asteroth is gone."

Kat turned toward him. "Is *all* of Asteroth gone?"

She could tell that he didn't want to answer. His green eyes flickered away from her, then returned to hold her gaze. He placed a firm hand on each of her shoulders. "Listen to me, Kat. You've been brave for so long. You need to be brave just a little longer. We will meet Asteroth on our way back to the twenty-first century, and he will do everything he can to get to you."

She could not help the shiver that raced through her, even though the words came as no surprise.

"I know," she said.

"Okay. Remember, you are not alone. I'm with you. And Francesca—"

Her heart leapt. "Aunt Frannie! She's—"

Stephen shook his head. "I don't know what she is, Kat. She's in the spirit; I know that much, and that's all. She's doing her best to keep Asteroth at bay, to buy us the time we need to get home. You and Julia must stay strong. Julie, can I count on you to do that?"

Julia swallowed hard. "Yes," she said. "I'll think of the light. I'll remember the force field."

Kat felt Stephen's arm propel her away from the clearing.

"Wait!" she cried, breaking free. She turned back toward Alys and Gregory, who stood as still as statues not far from where the light had once dazzled them all. "I can't ever thank you enough. Please, forgive us for bringing such chaos upon you. I feel as if I should take you with us, as if I—"

Gregory raised a hand to stop her rambling flow of words. "Do you think that God works His plans for you alone? We, too, have surely benefited by His workings here."

Kat stared from Gregory to Alys, once again longing for the logical explanation she already knew could not exist. She had to admit that Alys wore a mantle of serenity that had not existed before. Gregory, too, seemed to have acquired an aura of strength not previously possessed.

"And, think of it," Alys added. "We cannot even know yet how God will use this knowledge revealed to us. We will pray for you, Katerina. Do the same for us."

"Yes . . ." Kat's voice trailed as Stephen took her hand and led her away. She noticed Julia at his side as a sudden wind pushed her hair from her face and filled her ears with noise.

Francesca stood guard outside Asteroth's cage, her sword aimed toward its burning bars. A ribbon of light shot from the sword's tip, reenergizing each bar in turn. She studied the light. This was not the peaceful, caressing light she remembered from her most focused moments of meditation. It was not even the hot, powerful protection she'd experienced while in the spirit. This light was razor-sharp, each particle of energy crackling and jumping like water droplets flung against a hot skillet. This light meant business.

Asteroth, too, seemed to recognize the nature of his entrapment. He'd paced away from the blazing barrier and now stood in the center of its circle, head bowed and fists clenched. Francesca could sense him rifling through strategies in search of his next move. His form flickered, changing beneath her gaze from gray scaly demon to blond giant and back again.

He was weakening. Well, of course. Francesca knew that her own strength came from an endless source of light. Asteroth had estranged himself from that source eons ago. His energy came from his consumption of the wicked and the hapless, from sucking dry those souls who would never commit themselves to the light. He was a parasite, a scavenger who thrived on the destruction of others. He required constant feeding.

How much energy still fueled him?

"You grow weaker," she said.

He grunted.

She wondered if psychology worked as well in the spirit as it often did in the physical. "What is left for you to do, Asteroth? You can't summon your acolytes or I will call the angels of the light to fight beside me. You aren't strong enough to battle them. Shouldn't you leave us while you still can?"

His spine straightened. The upper part of his torso

assumed the form of the regal blond prince. The lower part remained encased in platelike scales.

"Katerina," he said, his tone still more bestial than human.

"But you can't have her! How can you possibly hope to claim her when you are so weakened, trapped behind a barrier of light that you can't possibly destroy?"

Asteroth took a deliberate step forward. The rest of his body regained human form, and to her dismay, Francesca realized that he was stronger than she'd thought.

"You forget," he said, and his voice fell smooth upon her ears, "that the consumption of sweet Isobel has nourished me well. And, Francesca, this 'barrier,' as you call it, will vanish when you do."

"Don't be stupid, Asteroth. What makes you think I'll vanish?"

He smiled. "Because, Francesca, although you meet me in spirit now, your nature is still very human. You will go back. You must go back."

Pounding footsteps saved her the trouble of a reply. Stephen raced toward her, Katerina and Julia close behind him.

"Aunt Frannie!" Katerina catapulted into her. Francesca instinctively wrapped an arm around her niece, holding her so close that she could smell the delicate scent of her hair. A flurry of memories washed over her; this woman she embraced so tightly was all at once the child she'd loved so thoroughly, the teenager she'd worried about nightly, the young adult she'd regularly prayed would find peace.

"Oh, Aunt Frannie, I thought I'd lost you forever. I

thought—" Kat suddenly noticed the sword in her aunt's hand. She pulled back, her gaze following the stream of brilliant light from sword tip to barrier. She staggered backward a step as her eyes met Asteroth's.

Asteroth gave a sweeping bow. "We seem destined to meet again and again and again, Katerina."

Stephen appeared at his wife's side, Julia in tow. "Let's get out of here, Frannie," he said in a low voice.

"Yes, Frannie," Asteroth said, each syllable distinct. "Let's get out of here."

Francesca watched his eyes travel up and down Katerina as he spoke. His tongue protruded from between his lips, misshapen and too large for his mouth.

She kept her sword steady and her eyes trained on him. "Katerina, Stephen, what do you see beyond us, over my shoulder?"

"Space," Stephen said. "Lots of it. It looks like someone went wild with a fog machine."

"Run toward it as fast as you can. Keep running and don't look back."

"And you won't look back either, will you, Francesca?" Asteroth's voice dripped with honey. He stuck his head between two bars of light. He remained in human form, but a small puddle of drool formed just outside the barrier as he stared at Kat.

"Aunt Frannie." Kat grasped her aunt's wrist. "You're coming with us."

"Kat-er-in-a." Asteroth's arm reached through the bar, fingers groping to make contact with his prey.

Francesca stared at him, amazed that evil did not know how disgusting and repulsive it actually was.

"No," she said. "I'm not going with you."

Asteroth's roar, once again bestial, reverberated endlessly about them. "You must return with them. Think well, Francesca. If you remain behind here in the spirit, you will be dead to them!"

She shook her head. "No," she said. "They will simply learn to sense my love for them in a different way. That's all."

"But, Aunt Frannie." Kat's eyes widened, and her hand flew to her throat. Francesca resisted the urge to pull her close again.

"Frannie." Stephen spoke slowly. "If you come with us, the barrier around Asteroth falls, doesn't it?"

She nodded. "Yes."

Kat tried to absorb the situation. "We can run quickly. We can get home before he has the chance to—"

Stephen placed a hand on his wife's shoulder. "Kat. There's a possibility that Asteroth can follow us back into the twenty-first century."

"Yes, Stephen," Francesca said. "The doorway opens only briefly, but it could be enough to allow him access to your time. I'd rather keep him here until I know the opening has closed completely behind you."

"Then I've lost you forever." Kat's voice trailed in the emptiness.

"No, Katerina." A full smile broke across Francesca's face. As if connected by some unseen current, the light from her sword blazed even brighter than before. Julia lifted an arm to shield her eyes. "You could never lose me. I will always be with you. I belong here now, but you don't. Not yet. Go, my darling, before it's too late."

"But . . ." Kat's words trailed as Stephen pulled her arm, guiding her away.

"Stephen." Francesca's voice made him turn to face her. "Take care of her. You know the stakes."

He hesitated briefly, then nodded.

"Okay," he said, gripping Kat's hand in one of his own and Julia's in the other. "Run!"

Francesca watched them race away until, quite suddenly, they were no longer there. She sensed them break into the stillness of the Lady Chapel. She felt Claire's energy join with theirs and knew that her family had made it home.

Her sword trembled as a sense of euphoric well-being coursed through her. She could not prevent her triumphant smile.

"It is done, then," she said beneath her breath.

Slowly, she lowered her sword. The stream of light stopped. The bars of Asteroth's cage diminished, sputtering away like a fountain when the water supply has been shut.

Asteroth's form flickered, growing less solid by the second.

"It is never done, Francesca," he said, and vanished into nothingness before her. Only the echo of his voice remained behind, an unpleasant reminder of more to come. "Never."

# 43

Snow fell softly outside Angel Café, blanketing the sidewalks and dulling the noise of the city to a muffled hum. It was only three o'clock in the afternoon, but to Kat it might as well have been three o'clock in the morning. She had misplaced her sense of time. She was bone-weary and oddly restless all at once, unable to focus on a single thought for more than a few seconds.

She shifted in her chair, propping her chin in her hands as she glanced through the lace curtains that framed the restaurant window. The sky was bright with heavy white clouds. It would probably snow through the night.

"Hey."

Kat looked up as a shadow fell across the table. Stephen stood above her, tie loosened and suit jacket draped across the crook of his arm.

"Is this seat taken?" he asked.

She managed a small smile. "Sit at your own risk. My husband is the jealous type."

Stephen sank down beside her. "He's got every reason to be," he said, wrapping an arm around her shoulders.

"Where are the girls?"

"In my office, listening to the radio. They needed to chill out a little."

She nestled into him, grateful for this quiet moment in the midst of a difficult day.

Francesca's funeral had taken place that morning. How strange to sit in Saint Leo's listening to prayers and farewells for someone who certainly did not seem gone. Later, during lunch at Angel Café, Kat had listened to the reminiscences of friends and relatives. Everyone, it seemed, had a story to tell, a tribute to the kindness and wisdom of Francesca Piretti. But Kat, standing in a bewildered haze with Stephen by her side, had recognized that all of these stories could only hint at the essence of Aunt Frannie, a woman who had always lived more in the spirit than in the physical.

"Are you all right?" Stephen asked now.

She nodded, then swallowed hard. Even the knowledge that Francesca thrived in the spirit hadn't dulled the shock of arriving home from the cathedral to find her aunt's lifeless body lying on the bed in the upstairs guest room.

"Heart failure," the doctor had solemnly proclaimed. "A blessing, really. Her quality of life had been sadly compromised."

Kat had stared at Francesca's body, understanding that its earlier transparency had reflected an energy pull between the spirit and the physical. She'd hugged both her daughters close, taking comfort in the solid feel of their bodies against her own. Julia, too, might have flown away well before her mother could have stood to let her go. At least they'd been spared that sorrow.

A snowflake landed on the windowpane, bringing Kat back to Angel Café. She reached for her coffee cup.

Stephen's hand covered hers before she could even grasp the handle.

"We need a vacation," he said.

"Actually, we probably need to get back to work. It's been a while. Life goes on, doesn't it?" She sensed her own reluctance behind the words. She was preaching a sermon she wasn't quite sure she even believed anymore.

He stroked her cheek, then let his hand fall back down to hers. "A rest, Kat. You need a rest. You're exhausted. You're not feeling well."

She averted her eyes from her husband's face as a pink flush flooded her cheeks. His hand, gently insistent, once again traveled to her face. He lifted her chin until her eyes met his, and she saw that he already knew for certain what she had only begun to suspect these past few days.

"You're pregnant," he said quietly, and the words felt familiar, as if he'd just told her she had brown hair and brown eyes.

"Well," she said, and then fell uncharacteristically silent. There seemed nothing else to say.

"Kat." He was on his knees before her, almost a parody of a Victorian wedding proposal. Her tired mind wondered for a moment if her middle-aged husband could actually get up again, but when she looked into his eyes, she recognized a flash of determination from his younger days, a spark she hadn't even realized she missed.

Stephen cleared his throat. "Kat. I've let a lot slide, lately. I know that. I'm sorry."

"It's okay, Stephen. Living is just like that. We get busy and—"

He shook his head. "It is not okay. We can't even plead ignorance, because both of us know better. We know what's important and what isn't. And if we aren't fundamentally changed after what we've just been through, if we can't remember how fragile and profound our existence in this world is—"

She placed a silencing finger against his lips.

"I know," she said.

"You mean the world to me," Stephen said. "I love you, Katerina Piretti. I'd marry you again in a heartbeat. And I think this baby thing is awe-inspiring."

One side of her mouth turned up in a crooked grin. "Oh, you do, do you? Do you have any idea what this will do to our lives?"

"No." He gathered her up in his arms and held her close. "I have no idea at all. That's the point. We don't need to know anything beyond this moment."

And, as they held each other in the dim dining room, Kat was inclined to believe that he was right. The only way to live was to savor the energy of each moment as it whirled through body, mind, heart, and soul. Each second possessed truth ripe for the asking. All it required was enough faith to actually listen for the answer.

"Jamaica," she said, tightening her arms around him.

"What?"

"Let's go there. I promise I'll rest. We'll talk, Stephen, and catch up a little."

"You got it. I'll get on it first thing tomorrow."

Even their kiss felt different: soft, deep, and filled with renewed promises for the days to come.

# Epilogue

JULIA DROPPED AN EMPTY LAUNDRY BASKET ONTO THE FLOOR outside her sister's bedroom. "Mom wants all your dirty laundry, Claire."

No answer.

"Claire?" Julia poked her head through the doorway.

Claire sat cross-legged on her bed, eyes closed, smile on her face. It was so unusual to see her completely still that Julia entered the room.

"Hey, Claire." She hurried to the bed and gave her little sister a shake. All that weirdness several weeks ago still lingered. Any behavior that did not smack of business as usual worried her.

But Claire's eyes opened readily. Her smile widened. Even better, she started chattering away in her normal mile-a-minute style. Julia couldn't help smiling herself.

Claire bounced on her bed. "Julie, you will not believe how light I got your room just now."

Julia's smile faded. "What do you mean?"

"The light. You know, like the light you saw when you were back in England. Remember?"

"Yeah, Claire, I remember. But you never saw it."

Claire shrugged. "Light is light."

Almost against her will, Julia sank down to the edge of her sister's bed.

"Look, Claire, you might not want to talk about that stuff anymore. People will think you're weird. Besides, we've got a new baby coming. We're all going to be too busy to deal with anything outside reality."

Claire's eyes widened. "This *is* reality. Besides, he'll be okay with it."

"He?"

"The baby. It's a boy. Can't you feel that, Julie?"

Julia slowly stood. "I don't want to talk about it anymore."

"But Julie . . ."

"Your laundry." Julia glanced at the balled-up clothing on her sister's floor, then met Claire's gaze. She obviously had more to say, but Julia was sure that she didn't want to hear it. It was time to move on.

"Come on, Claire," she said. "I'll help you pick this up this mess."

Claire studied her sister for another moment. Then she knelt and began to gather her clothes.

JILL MORROW has enjoyed a broad spectrum of careers, including practicing law and singing with local bands. The author of *Angel Café,* she lives in Baltimore, Maryland. She has just completed her third novel. Visit her Web site at *www.jillmorrow.net.*